THE SABER CHRONICLES II

THE GOLDEN WARRIOR

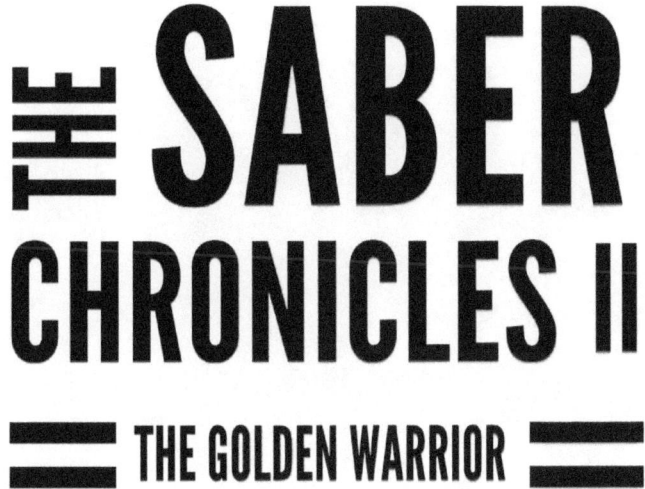

THE SABER CHRONICLES II

— THE GOLDEN WARRIOR —

DONALD HILL

Cover Design: Fiona Jayde Media
Interior Design: The Deliberate Page

First Printing, 2017
ISBN: 978-0-692-86285-8

www.TheSaberChronicles.com

ACKNOWLEDGMENTS

With thanks and humble gratitude to my family and friends for their love and support. I would also like to thank those who helped to create the cover art and interior text and graphics. Without professionals like these, aspiring writers like me could not self-publish our dreams.

Thank you!

Thank you for purchasing this Book. I hope you find it entertaining and enjoyable.

~Donald Hill, Author

"MR. PRESIDENT," THE AIDE SAID POLITELY AS HE OPENED THE door and entered the presidential office, "your guests are here sir."

An average looking man of medium height stood at the side buffet pouring himself a fresh cup of coffee. His short cropped medium brown hair framed sharp angular facial features in a dark olive-toned complexion. His suit was dark black and his crisply starched white dress shirt complemented his skin tone. He sported a well-practiced smile as he turned to reply.

"Show them in Gary."

The aide motioned for the three guests to enter, and then he quietly closed the door behind them.

The President smiled as he strolled over to greet them, placing his cup on the side table near two large comfortable looking sofas. Extending his hand to the first man he said warmly, "Rich, it's so good to see you again my friend."

"Thank you, Mr. President," Fleet Admiral Rich Jonas said as he heartily shook the President's hand. Admiral Jonas headed up the Intelligence Services Bureau for the system of Alderis and he was also Commandant of the Alderon Space Academy. His position as ISB Chief wasn't widely known because he reported directly to the President and, therefore, was accountable only to him.

"These must be the two Captains I've heard so much about," the President said as he greeted the other two guests.

"Yes, Mr. President. Let me introduce you to Captain Mitch Saber and his wife, Captain Samantha Rivers Saber." the Admiral said as he directed the President's attention to his two guests.

The President warmly greeted his guests with hearty handshakes, saying "I'm so happy to finally meet you both. Rich has told me so much about you that I feel like we are old friends."

"Thank you, Mr. President," Mitch replied. "It's certainly a privilege to meet you, sir."

"It's an honor, sir," Samantha said, shaking his hand.

"Please, everyone make yourselves comfortable," the President said, motioning them toward the sofas.

"I've read the reports regarding your exploration of these new gateway anomalies, and on behalf of the government of Alderon, I'd like to say thank you for your service to our people. Obviously, it would have taken us more than two years to commission an exploration vessel and to gather a crew to undertake this kind of mission. I know that you have a business to run, and taking this kind of time away from it is a big sacrifice on your part. I hope our agreement has been satisfactory."

"It was very satisfactory, Mr. President," Mitch replied, as both he and Samantha nodded their heads.

"I understand that you also discovered some crash survivors," stated the President.

"That's correct. Sam...uh, Samantha," Mitch said, as he directed his attention toward his wife, "on our other vessel, the Odyssey, commanded by Captain Chen, has already made the first passage back to the survivor's planet of Helios with our first load of supplies, equipment and personnel."

Samantha smiled. "Our first trip back to Helios was primarily geared around delivering some, much needed, supplies and equipment to the survivors. Since they were kind enough to grant us a contract to build a mine in their system and establish a presence on their planet, we thought that laying the groundwork for some basic improvements to their living conditions was of primary concern."

"They've managed to survive for over thirty years without anyone's help. They've accepted Helios as their home now, so the least we could do is try to help them create a better environment for themselves," Mitch added.

"That's very generous of you, Mitch and Samantha," the President added. "Our agreement to give you first option for mining and exploration will most likely makes you two of the wealthiest people in the galaxy."

"That money will help our business grow, Mr. President, but money isn't everything of personal value to us. Our exploration of these new systems will allow us to colonize, expand, and better provide for the growth of our society, and those of our neighboring systems. We are committed to using our earnings to provide help when needed, as we are doing for the people of Helios. We never asked for funding from Alderon," Mitch said, almost annoyed at the implication that he was greedy.

The President held up his hand, palm forward. "Mitch, don't be offended. I meant no insult by my comment. I meant it as a compliment that your hard work would make you very wealthy, nothing more."

"No apology is necessary, Mr. President," Mitch replied. "I'm a citizen and an officer of Alderon, sir. My first priority is to my family and to the people of Alderon. Many of these new systems may provide us with much needed resources, and they will allow us to expand beyond the Alderis system. We can only operate so many mines and refineries by ourselves. But, I think we should carefully consider to whom we will sell or lease these rights in the future."

The President nodded and looked toward the Admiral. "Rich, I'd have to say that these two are exactly as you have described them." Mitch and Sam looked curiously at the Admiral.

"Mitch and Samantha," the President said, after drinking another sip of his coffee, "I know you have a business to run, but I'd like to ask you to continue to explore and map out as many of the new systems as you can, at least for the next six months. If you would dedicate one of your ships to accomplish this task, then I would be in your debt." Mitch started to interrupt, but the President held up his hand again, politely asking him to hold his comments. "To make it worth your while, I am prepared to offer to compensate you for your expenses, plus a sum of seven million credits for each system you map and claim for the Alderon government. You may also continue to have first right of refusal on any mining and refinery construction you that wish."

Mitch and Sam looked at one another for a long moment, as if mentally discussing their options. Finally, Mitch answered, "I think we can do that, Mr. President, but I'll need to discuss it with my sister and my crew. You see, they earn a bonus for our freight operations and not ferrying freight doesn't earn them any bonus or salvage pay. Plus, we have to take into account shore leave. We can carry enough fuel and supplies for an extended trip, since we're not carrying cargo, but our people will need time off to see family and friends. Rather than a six month exploration, we're probably talking more like eight or twelve months total time."

The Admiral leaned over and whispered into the President's ear. After a moment, the President nodded and said, "How about this. I'll increase your rate by another five hundred thousand credits for each system you map for us under our original terms. Those funds will be placed in a separate account to pay a bonus for your crew at the end of our agreement."

Again, Mitch and Samantha eyed each other for a few moments. Finally, Sam nodded her approval. Mitch reached out to shake the President's hand. "It's a deal, Mr. President."

The President smiled and shook hands with Mitch and Sam. They spoke casually for a while longer before leaving the Admiral behind in the President's office.

"Rich," the President said, "you must be very proud of your nephew. I knew his parents many years ago. They would be very proud to see how he has grown up."

"I'm sure they would be quite proud of him Mr. President. Mitch and Sam have been through a lot lately, so I'm sure they are glad to get back to business."

"Our agreement is good for both of us. It would cost the government huge sums of credits to build and man a ship to do all that they're taking on. I'm surprised they didn't ask for more compensation. I was prepared to pay more if they had asked."

"What they do is not about the money, Mr. President" The Admiral answered. "It's about helping their family, their employees and the citizens of Alderon. Not once did they ask for us to pay for supplies for the survivors of Helios."

"I assumed that they had," the President replied with a surprise.

"No, sir. The subject was never discussed. They simply saw people who needed help, so they gave without hesitation."

"They are the kind of people that make me proud, Rich. We have many of them on this little planet, but it seems like we always take them for granted, don't we?"

"It's good to recognize those qualities in people, Mr. President. It makes our jobs a little easier."

Making their way back to the Saber Mining and Manufacturing Headquarters on Alderon Three, Mitch and Sam discussed their visit to the President's office.

"That's a generous offer from your President, Mitch, but how are we going to make it work?" Sam asked.

"We'll have to depend on you and Chen to do most of the cargo business, I guess. The Phoenix is the smaller of our two exploration ships so it won't be too costly to operate."

"That's true, Mitch, but what about the bonus credits the crew of the Phoenix will get? Don't you think that our other crew will feel left out, or even worse, snubbed?"

"Shit!" Mitch exclaimed in disgust. "Some employer I am. That thought didn't even occur to me. You're right, of course. That won't be fair. You and Chen have both been on the mapping and exploration missions with me on the Phoenix so you know what to do. I guess we'll have to try and split it up as best as we can."

"I think that splitting the bonus is not only fairer, but will make the job easier on the crew. Let's face it; it's a pretty boring job."

"It's boring, but it pays well, you have to admit," Mitch said as he smiled.

"I agree. They are paying our operating expenses and the crew gets a bonus and the company makes a good profit. That should finish paying for the refit of that old cruiser we salvaged."

"Yeah, Ernie said he was about forty-five days from completion and turning her over to us. This agreement will let us go ahead and dispatch the new ship directly to Helios. I feel a lot better about giving our operations there a little security while we get things underway."

Sam leaned over and kissed him on the cheek.

"What's that for?" Mitch asked with a grin.

"I just felt like it," Sam said as she tossed her hair back and looked out the view port. "You realize we have an out in his proposal too, don't you?"

"What do you mean?"

"He said that we will be paid for the systems that we claim for Alderon. I don't think that all the systems we discover should be claimed by one single government, but that's just my opinion."

"Interesting. I think I'm forced to agree with you. The President offered to provide us with a fair amount in order to justify what we need for payment, but there will be some systems that should be open to everyone, including ourselves. People everywhere deserve to be free to govern themselves. We can make it fair for Alderon without giving them everything. Thanks for bringing this to my attention."

The corporate Minnow, on which they traveled, soon landed at the Saber main offices on Alderon Three. They made their way to Laurel's office, without delay, to tell her of their visit with the President. Laurel initially some misgivings about the deal, but as she ran the numbers, she determined that the venture would indeed be profitable, very profitable.

The three of them sat in Mitch's office, having finished their lunch, when Laurel said, "Chen has a full load of equipment and personnel ready for delivery to Helios. I guess you still want him to continue?"

"Definitely," Mitch answered. "In fact, let him take the next run of materials too. By the time he gets back, the cruiser Paladin should be in service and ready to leave the space dock. I've told Ernie to keep six interceptors and four Minnows on board. They are going to need the Minnows and the Dolphin to be ready by then too for the start of operations on the mining facilities."

"Actually," Laurel added, "that works out almost perfectly with the schedule I had already laid out. Sam has several clients waiting in the Chinese Federation. I also have received a specific request for you and Mitch, from Bion4, to come see them as soon as your schedule permits, for a special delivery. They wouldn't give me any details."

"That's a bit odd, even for them, but they've been a good client, so I can't complain. I'll leave tomorrow. Sam, I guess you can depart whenever you're ready."

"My ship is loaded and ready for transit, so I'll be off too," Sam replied.

Although Mitch had agreed to continue to explore the mysterious gateways, he decided that it would be best to proceed first to Bion4 to see what kind of delivery they had in mind. If he didn't go there first, it could be months before he would be near their system again. The Phoenix was carrying a partial load of high quality white crystals for delivery to them.

While only full cargo loads really made the journey profitable, the partial load would have to do this time. They had become very good clients for the Saber Corporation, thus they deserved any special attention they requested. He was also curious to find out about their special delivery request…

The trip had been uneventful when they arrived twelve days later and docked at the Bion4 station.

Ensign Inna Dubnikov was seated at the communications console, when she directed her attention toward the Captain, who was seated in his command chair. "Captain, I've received a request for you and Mr. Richter to meet an ambassador from Bion4 at dockside."

Mitch's eyebrows shot upwards as his curiosity was aroused. "Tell them I'm on my way and tell Mr. Richter to meet me there at once."

"Aye, Captain," she replied.

When Mitch exited the tram, Richter was waiting for him. His Security Sergeant Tanner was also awaiting their arrival, and as they approached, he directed their attention toward the Bion4 ambassador, who was standing several meters away. Mitch was entranced on his first sight of the woman. She was average in height and had ink black hair that moved like the waves in an ocean. It was cut straight across the top of her eye brows and hung straight down to just below her chin, yet it was very long in the back. Her eyes, as black as her hair, were outlined in the same gray-black that painted her lips, highlighting high cheek bones and a sharp jawline. Her figure was perfectly proportioned, enhanced by a long dress that was slit on each side from her thigh all the way down to her ankle. Her legs were beautifully sculpted, and the almond color of her skin was accentuated by the shimmering material of her dress. The only jewelry she wore was a necklace that looked like it was solid gold, and she smiled gently as she approached Mitch and Richter. Mitch noticed that Richter dipped his head slightly when she glanced at him. Her gate was graceful and everything about her seemed to flow like water.

"Your uniform indicates that you must be Captain Saber," she said in a soft, pleasing voice that sounded like an echo inside Mitch's head. She didn't extend her hand to greet him, so he kept his arms by his sides.

"Captain Mitch Saber, Ambassador, it's an honor to greet you."

She smiled and nodded her head slightly, then looked at Richter. "Hello Richter."

"I am humbled to be in your presence," he replied.

Mitch thought that was a peculiar greeting, but then again, he wasn't familiar with the culture of Bion4. He understood that they didn't very often allow norms, or normal unaltered humans, to visit their planet. Only dockside station visits were permitted for outsiders, and although they were docked at the station, the atmosphere surrounding this ambassador was distinctly different.

"How are they treating you, Richter?" She asked.

"I've never been happier. They are as close to family as I've ever experienced," he said. The sentiment voiced by Richter, resonated with Mitch. He was aware that many normal, unaltered humans treated bio-modified humans, such as Richter, with disdain. Mitch had made it clear from the time that Richter first arrived to serve on his ship, that there would be no tolerance of any such discrimination directed toward Mr. Richter.

"I will need to confirm this of course," she said as she stepped closer to Richter and extended a cable from behind her neck.

Mitch quickly intervened. "Wait a moment! Mr. Richter is a member of my crew, and I won't have him..."

The Ambassador quickly interrupted him. "There is no need for concern, Captain. This is just a more efficient way for us to share our thoughts."

"It's okay, Captain," Richter said calmly. "This is faster and more accurate than trying to put everything into words."

Mitch nodded and stepped back and watched. Richter attached the cable into the port on the back of his neck, then tilted his chin to his chest, closed his eyes and the Ambassador placed her hand on his shoulder. The whole event lasted only a few moments until Richter raised his head and disconnected the cable, handing it back to the Ambassador. She smiled, thanked Richter, and then turned to face the Captain.

"Captain, I am pleased to see that what I've heard about you is true." She took a step closer to Mitch. He quickly glanced at Sergeant Tanner, who was standing as still as a statue, which was odd for him. The Ambassador continued, "You hold the status of Honored Protector among our people. It isn't very often that we allow the distinction of meeting face to face."

"Thank you, Ambassador, but I don't understand," Mitch replied graciously.

"Please allow me to thank you, Captain." Stepping within arm's reach of Mitch, she took her right hand, and bending her fingers at the middle joints, she placed her bent fingers on his forehead. Almost immediately his mind was filled with the memories of his battle against the pirates, and the resulting death of his parents. He remembered his confrontation on the Atlantis station with Yurie's attackers, and his fight against the brigands. He remembered the night that he slept with Miranda, and his honeymoon with Samantha, so many memories of Samantha. He recalled the meeting with Talonis, the kidnapping of Miranda and her infant, and all the things that had happened to him over the past several years, up to the rescue of the survivors of Helios. All of these memories raced through his mind. He thought he felt her mind touch his, causing an odd tingling to run down his spine as she pulled her hand away.

The Ambassador stepped back from Mitch and said, "My name, Captain, is Tesslena. You are indeed, worthy of the status of Honored Protector. You are a most interesting man, Captain. Perhaps you would like to procreate with me, sometime."

He raised a sharp brow at her statement. Did she mean what he thought she meant? He decided that he must have misinterpreted her statement. He thought to himself, that perhaps sex among the people of Bion4 is considered utilitarian rather than sacred. He apparently had much to learn about these people!

"What did you just do Ambassador?" Mitch asked her.

"I listened to your memories, Captain. This process helps me understand who you are without having to ask so many boorish questions."

Tesslena glanced down the long corridor where several workers seemed to be preoccupied with a large crate. She raised her hand toward them, and though they didn't see her action, they immediately busied themselves with moving the crate in his direction. They appeared to move the crate almost reverently. He glanced back at Sergeant Tanner, who still stood nearly motionless, without speaking, as if he were in a trance.

The crate neared and the Ambassador turned back to Mitch, "This is our precious cargo that we are entrusting to you, Captain."

Mitch observed the crate and recognized it wasn't just a typical shipping container.

"Is this the only freight that you have for me, Ambassador Tesslena?" Mitch asked curiously.

"It is, Captain," she replied.

"Why don't you have it transported by a much smaller ship than mine Ambassador? It could be easily handled by a much smaller transport class vessel and that would be far less expensive."

"I understand and appreciate your concern, Captain, but we are prepared to pay for the entire cargo area of your ship if you will transport this to its destination. Please understand, Captain, this cargo requires the best, but least conspicuous, security that we can provide with someone who we trust. The money isn't important to us. We only want the secure arrival of this cargo to its destination."

"As you wish, Ambassador. It's your money. Where is the destination?"

Her expression changed to a more serious look. "Have you ever heard of Aegea?"

His head tilted slightly to one side in curiosity. "Most space jockeys, at some point in their life, have heard legends of a system called Aegea, but they're just stories, myths." Mitch said with a dismissive wave of his hand.

"Captain Saber," she said as she placed a hand on his cheek, "You have traveled the pathways of the galaxy and returned safely. You call them… gateways I think."

"How did you know that?" Mitch asked.

"Memories, Captain, yours and Richter's. They told me what I needed to know and gave me confirmation that you do have the ability to complete this delivery." She stepped back.

Mitch shrugged and stepped over to inspect the cargo. "What is the nature of the cargo? It will have to be bio-scanned before I can load it on my ship"

Tesslena pulled the covering aside revealing a small window in the top. Then Mitch realized why she placed such high value on the cargo.

Surprise showed on the Captain's face as he looked up at Tesslena and said, "This is a stasis chamber."

"That is correct, Captain."

"So, you're telling me that Aegea is an actual place, and you want us to deliver this stasis chamber there?"

"Correct again, Captain."

Mitch leaned over to inspect the small window, and as he touched it the swirling gasses parted briefly. He saw a beautiful young woman, a child-like version of Tesslena, wearing a ribbon of gold around her neck that was identical to the one worn by Tesslena. He looked back at Tesslena again, in surprise.

"Yes, Captain Saber, she is my daughter."

"She's beautiful, Ambassador, but this is all very confusing. What's her name?"

The Ambassador smiled warmly, without acknowledging his compliment, and answered, "Her name is Madera. It has been many decades since we exchanged ambassadors with Aegea. We have waited a long time to find someone we could trust who was capable of taking her on this journey."

"I don't understand, Tesslena. Why would you send your daughter?"

The Ambassador turned sideways to gaze into the little window of the chamber. Mitch noted that the split in her dress didn't just stop at the top of her thigh but ran all the way past her waist with only a delicate chain keeping the two ends from separating at her waist and breast. Her almond colored skin was flawless from her ankles to her waist, and equally so on the other parts of her exposed body. Her dress was so sheer that the tone of her skin showed through, and the view was stunningly beautiful.

"My daughter has been in stasis for nearly ten years now, Captain, waiting for this moment. Until now, no one we trusted has traveled the pathways that crisscross the galaxy. Since you have successfully traversed the paths of the galaxy, our time has come to send our emissary. Only you may be the vehicle to do this."

"If you knew that these gateways, or pathways as you call them, were navigable, why didn't you share that knowledge with someone else?" Mitch glanced over to Richter who was observing without speaking.

"It's not our place, Captain. As you know, bio-mods are not generally accepted in most systems, except to serve in very specialized positions, and even then, we are frowned upon. So we contribute in other ways, such as providing technology and other services as we see fit. It benefits us to remain a very private society."

"No disrespect, Ambassador, but you sound more like a religious sect than a tech society," Mitch added.

"In many ways, you are correct, Captain. As your relationship grows with us, and our trust in you grows, we will gradually share more of who we are, and then you will understand." She stretched out her hand to Mitch. "Give this data crystal to Lieutenant Nagamo. She will find all the information that she needs in order to navigate your ship to Aegea. We have notified them of your coming, so they are expecting you. The trip should take your ship about two weeks to complete, one way. Let me caution you however, do not enter the Aegean system with your weapons armed or your shields powered up. They will view this as a hostile action, and will attack you immediately. Your entry into their system will be on the far side of the space that they occupy, but they will be very much aware of your entry. Don't forget this warning, Captain."

"What do you mean you told them we were coming? Do you have a communications device that can reach them? Are you certain this system is safe for us, Ambassador? I *am* responsible for my ship and crew and..."

Tesslena held up a finger to pause him, saying "So many questions, Captain. All will be made known to you, in time. You have my word that you and your crew will be safe. Follow my instructions, Captain, and no harm will come to you or your ship. This is a promise from me and from the people of Aegea."

Mitch felt the need to discuss the matter further, but he suddenly felt calmed by her words of assurance.

"Now, Captain, you will need the key to open the stasis chamber."

"Just give it to the Sergeant and he will hold it for safe keeping." Responded Mitch

"It's not that kind of key, Captain." She stepped up to him again, and this time she placed her right hand on his temple and looked at him with unblinking eyes. Mitch stared back at her, looking into her deep black eyes, waiting for something to happen, but nothing did. Seconds later, she removed her hand and said, "There, you now have the key to open the chamber when you arrive. No one but you can open the chamber. If something happens to you on your journey, any attempt to open the chamber will result in my daughter's death. Other than me, you are the only person alive with this knowledge."

"I'm not entirely sure what just happened, but I don't have any key," Mitch said with a confused look on his face.

The Ambassador smiled and replied in a gentle tone, "You will know when the time comes, Captain. Just remember that you will be performing this on behalf of the people of Bion4, so represent us and your crew with honor."

Mitch still didn't understand why her voice echoed in his mind when she spoke, but the feeling of peace and calm was overwhelming in her presence. It wasn't a naturally occurring feeling, and he couldn't shake it off. He turned to speak to the Sergeant, and was sure the man hadn't moved a muscle since he had looked at him last. He wondered if something was wrong with him as this was not typical of Tanner's character.

"Sergeant Tanner," he called out, "please see to the loading of this chamber, and take it directly to the med bay. Keep it under guard until I get there. No one is to touch it otherwise."

The Sergeant blinked his eyes several times before he acknowledged the Captain, and then smartly nodded his head in affirmation. He moved slowly at first, as if he was shaking cobwebs from his head.

"Ambassador..." Mitch started to say when he turned and saw that she was already far down the corridor. He turned to enter the ship, and then clearly heard her voice in his head. 'We'll meet again soon, Captain Saber, and remember, the offer of procreation still stands.' He stopped, blushed slightly and looked down the corridor again, to see her raise her arm in a gentle wave, without looking back. Mitch scowled at the hatch for a moment. He suspected something odd had happened that he didn't understand, but for now he needed to get the data crystal to Yurie. How did she know that Yurie was the one to need it? He entered the ship making his way toward the med bay, while the other crew moved to unload the freight for Bion4. He explained the chamber to Dr. Santana, and then proceeded to the bridge. After reviewing the data, Yurie informed Mitch that the Ambassador's information on the anomalies was exceptionally well documented, and that the two week transit time appeared to be very precise. She was also curious about such detailed mapping since exploring these gateways was all new to them. The instructions provided precise details on the configuration of each gateway, and detailed how long each transit should take. Mitch said that perhaps she would have an opportunity to ask that question one day, which seemed to please Yurie very much.

That evening as Mitch entered the galley for his dinner, he took the opportunity to sit with Richter, who was also eating his meal.

Mitch sat at the table across from him, and asked, "Richter, what can you tell me about the Ambassador?"

Richter didn't look up as he continued to eat. "What do you want to know, Captain?"

"She seems to have an unusual presence, such as I've never experienced before. I mean, she's very beautiful, but it's something else."

"Like she's communicating with you on a different level?"

"Something like that. When she touched me, it was as though every experience I've ever had flashed before me."

Richter looked up with a serious expression on his face. "We have many such representatives, Captain. They are the leaders of our world, and the ones who reach out to other systems in order to establish trade relations, but they rarely ever leave our planet. You have been hosted to an extremely rare event, Captain. You should be take great pride to this distinction."

"That's another thing. What's the deal with her daughter? Sealed up in that stasis chamber for ten years, waiting to be carried away to another system, to never see her mother again! That seems cruel to me." Mitch's eyes flashed with irritation as the thought ran through his mind.

"To your culture perhaps, Captain, but remember, we are a society of bio-modified humans with many different qualities. I'm not allowed to go into detail about how deep these mods go, but just accept that there is much more here than you understand."

"So, who exactly is Tesslena? What is her role in your society?"

"She's an ambassador, just like she said, Captain."

"Mr. Richter, she is no ordinary woman, so don't be coy."

"Captain, please understand that I have little room to speak of certain things. I'll tell you this much; when Tesslena touched you, she looked into your mind and within you, and saw all that you have experienced, seen and felt. That was how she determined that you were worthy of her trust to deliver her daughter safely. That's more than I should tell you, but I feel like you deserve to know that much." Richter got up and left the table.

Mitch sat still for a long moment, and although he felt like he should be angry for the intrusion into his privacy, he understood Tesslena's concern for her daughter. If he had that ability, he would probably have done the same. It's difficult to criticize a mother for trying to protect her child. There was a lot more to this he suspected, as he ate his meal.

CHAPTER TWO

MITCH SAT IN HIS CABIN AS THE PHOENIX PREPARED TO ENTER the last sector before they started their gateway journeys toward the Aegean system. He decided not to tell Laurel and Sam exactly where he was heading, but he did dispatch an encoded message to Sam, telling her who to contact if he didn't return within forty-five days. Obviously, the Bion Ambassador had some ability to place thoughts into his mind, but he was convinced that she meant no harm. He was curious about the necklace that she wore around her neck too. Her daughter wore an identical one, and he wondered if it was a symbol of her authority or position, or if it was a family tradition. He searched through the archives on Bion society, but found no mention of necklaces. In fact, there was very little information available about Bion society. Most of the documentation only referred to the bio-mods that had been placed into service for different functions, most of which were highly technical. Richter was very capable but he didn't match up to some of the things the other bio-mods were doing. He was obviously very good at his job, and he also appeared too really like the time he spent in the galley preparing food. He was an unusual person, and Mitch was glad to have him in his crew.

Mitch initially assumed that he would drop navigation buoys and comm beacons on the way to Aegea, but after considering the potential dangers of this unknown civilization, he decided to drop nav buoys only, and that was simply to aid in returning. He could always deactivate them on the return home. The same concerns would prevent him from performing a detailed mapping of the systems as they passed through. That could be accomplished on their return mission, if he decided it was safe. He guessed that the Aegean's had a defensive perimeter set up in order to be so quickly warned of an approaching ship. Tesslena's warning was a bit ominous, so he would respect it, but remain cautious.

In the following two weeks, the Phoenix and her crew traversed through nearly a dozen gateways. Mitch found himself grateful for the improvements that Ernie had made to the Phoenix's gravity and motion stabilizers. Traveling through so many gateways previous to the improvements, would have shaken the crew and the ship to the point that everyone would have suffered space sickness. Although improved greatly, transitioning was still like riding a ship through an ocean storm. They paused for several hours before entering the final gateway so that everyone could rest a little, and to allow Yurie to locate their position on the star charts. Just as they were preparing to enter the final gateway, Yurie informed him that they were currently over eleven hundred light years from Alderis. A collective gasp was heard on the bridge when she made the announcement. If anything broke now, they would never see home again. This was part of space travel and they all accepted the many risks, but the facts of current circumstances seemed surreal.

They exited the final gateway into Aegean space.

"Slow us to half system speed, Yurie," Mitch directed, and Yurie acknowledged. "Remember, Mr. Stevens, no shields or weapons."

"Aye, Captain, no shields or weapons per your instructions," he replied. "Shall I start a deep scan, Captain?"

"Start with a local scan and gradually extend it until we find our destination."

The Aegean system was large, at over seven billion kilometers across, but so far they had only detected two planets and several planetoids which were unusual for such large systems.

"I'm reading a large planet ahead, Captain. I estimate at our current speed that we'll be within visual range in about 6 hours at full system drive," Stevens said.

Ensign Dubnikov turned to face Mitch, who sat anxiously in his command chair. "Captain, I'm receiving a comm from Aegea. They are asking to speak to you, sir."

"Put it on my screen, Inna." The screen at his command station blurred, and then materialized into a holographic image of someone wearing a hooded robe that completely covered their facial features in darkness.

"This is Captain Mitch Saber of the freighter Phoenix. Who am I speaking with, please?"

"Greetings to you, Captain, from the people of Aegea. We have been awaiting your arrival. Please continue on your present course and speed until we advise you otherwise." The voice sounded male, but Mitch wasn't quite certain. The communication ceased before Mitch had a chance to reply.

"Well, that was a fine reception," Mitch said flatly. "Continue as they directed, Yurie."

Several hours later, Ensign Stevens directed Mitch's attention to his screen. "Captain," he said as the view screen came into focus, "I've got them on the screen now. There is a fairly large orbiting platform that we're heading to, so I guess that's our destination. The platform is orbiting the larger of the two planets which we identified earlier."

Mitch looked carefully as the image came into view. The station was unlike anything he had ever seen. It was similar to a wheel with a large central hub that was ovoid in shape, with four spokes extending away from the center. At the end of each spoke, there were two large ships, interceptor class Mitch guessed, but the engine design had him completely baffled.

He pressed the comm key on the arm pad. "Engineering, McIntyre speaking."

"Allison, this is the Captain. Pull up the central view screen and tell me what you think about these ships I'm looking at."

"Yes, Captain. I'm pulling your feed now... well, if that isn't the damnedest thing I ever saw," she replied bluntly.

"What do you think they are?"

"They're definitely interceptors of some sort, but the engine cones are enormous. It appears there are two docked at each spire, ready for launch. Those are big enough to be jump engines, but I've never seen anything like them before. You think they'll let us look at one?" Excitement sounded in her voice.

"I don't know, but I can certainly ask," Mitch replied.

"Captain," Yurie said, "I'm receiving a docking beacon and trajectory path."

He started to reply but Inna interrupted. "Captain, they are asking for you again."

"On the screen, Inna."

"I hope you can say more than you did the last time, whoever you are," Mitch said tartly.

"You should be receiving docking instructions now, Captain. Once you are stopped our umbilical will automatically connect to your ship. May we assume that you need air and water supply?" the person in the hooded robe asked.

"If your supply is compatible with ours, then... yes. But I'd like to know who you are first." Mitch said.

"All will be made known to you shortly, Captain. Please be patient. We don't have visitors very often, so your presence here is unusual for us. Don't judge us until after we meet." The connection ended abruptly again.

"At least they're honest about their rudeness," Yurie observed. Stevens snickered at her remark and Inna grinned.

As the ship came to a stop, they saw an umbilical extend from the central hub of the station and promptly connect to their ship, without any obvious human intervention. Mitch was curious how they knew to do that since they didn't get many visitors. An enclosed gangway emerged from the hub and slowly moved toward the main cargo hatch. A short minute later, Steven's panel sounded a chime notifying them that a secure seal had been established.

Sergeant Tanner called out to Mitch from the cargo bay, "Captain, am I supposed to unlock the hatch?"

"Negative, Rock. Let's wait and see what they have to say first."

Stevens sang out with excitement in his voice, "Captain! I've got a large vessel on rapid approach heading in this direction. I estimate that they will be here in less than four hours."

"Easy there, Rion, it's probably one of their ships," Mitch answered, trying to instill some calm into Rion's excited alert.

"No, Captain. The ship's configuration matches that of the raider ships that attacked Alderon Prime."

"Damn, what the hell is going on? Inna! Get them on the comm, now!"

Inna's fingers sped across the keyboard. "On your screen Captain."

"Our scans show a rapidly approaching raider vessel vectoring in on our exact position. What's going on?" Mitch said to the hooded figure on his screen.

"We're aware of the ship, Captain. We will take appropriate actions to ensure our security."

"Can we help?" Mitch asked.

"No help is needed, Captain. We'll contact you shortly. Please stand by."

"Stand by? For what?" The Captain was about to order an alert when Rion spoke up again.

"Captain, look at your screen."

Mitch watched his screen as four of the docked interceptors launched from their moorings. After moving only a short distance, brilliant flashes of light erupted around each one and they all disappeared.

"What the hell just happened?" Mitch said with astonishment. Everyone watched the screen, waiting to see what would happen next.

"There they are!" Inna shouted, "They popped into space right behind the raider's ship!"

Bright beams of light and sparks that looked like exploding fireworks leapt from each interceptor, impacting the raider ship. Only seconds had lapsed when a sudden burst of light announced the destruction of the pirate ship. They watched it shatter into millions of tiny shards and particles.

"Looks like McIntyre was right. Those were jump engines," Mitch said as everyone stared at the scene in awed surprise.

"That's the most amazing thing I've even seen Captain," Rion said. "They jumped right in behind that ship and obliterated them, without breaking a sweat! What kind of weapons are those?"

"I have no idea, Rion. ALICE?"

"Yes, Captain," replied the Phoenix's AI.

"Analyze the weapons discharge from the event that just occurred, and identify their nature."

"Affirmative, Captain... the weapons are of an unknown origin. My analysis indicates some kind of molecular disrupter that destroys the target by destabilizing the molecules of its target."

Captain," Inna called out, "I'm receiving another comm for you, sir."

"On screen, Inna." As the screen focused, the robed figure appeared again.

"Captain, I'm sorry for the distraction. I have been instructed to ask that you, Richter, and Lieutenant Nagamo meet our Ambassador. One of our security people will escort you all to the station."

"I have my own security, thank you."

"I'm sorry, Captain, but that will not be allowed. Please keep your crew within the confines of your ship. Anyone who leaves your ship will be dealt with harshly."

"Now, see here. I've played this cloak and dagger mess with you long enough. I was asked to deliver some cargo to you, and that's what I'm here to do, not play games or to be denied the courtesy of knowing with whom I'm speaking. I have my own security personnel and I can trust them. Why should I trust you?"

The person in the robe went silent for a moment, then, turned his head as if someone else were speaking to him, assuming it was a 'him' and not a manly sounding female.

He turned back toward the screen and answered, "Captain, it appears that we have insulted you. If you would please honor our request as stated, we would be grateful. We present no harm to you, and our Ambassador will explain everything, if you will do as I ask. At this moment, we cannot allow anyone else other than those requested, to enter this station. You may keep any personal weapons you normally carry when you disembark, if that will make you feel more secure."

Mitch signaled Inna to cut the audio, "Well, what do you think?"

"I don't like it, Captain," Rion answered.

"Sounds awfully strange to me, Captain," Inna offered, "but I've never been on a first contact mission before."

"It would be disappointing to come all this way and not find out why we were really sent here, Captain," Yurie said sincerely.

"I agree with all of you, but, Inna, you're observation as a first contact is appreciated. Yurie makes a good point too. We've been paid to do a job, albeit a strange one. I find it interesting that they are aware of our weapons policy." Mitch paused a moment in thought. "Bring up the audio Inna."

"Now, to whom am I speaking?"

There was a moment of quiet. "I am called Danar, Captain."

"Thank you, Danar. We will meet your security at our hatch in fifteen minutes," Mitch said as he smiled for the first time since speaking to the robed figure.

"Thank you, Captain. Our Ambassador is anxious to greet you."

Richter and Yurie were waiting as Mitch approached the cargo hatch.

"Rock, close and secure the hatch after we exit. No one is to leave this ship without my express permission."

"Aye, Captain. I'll wait right here until you return," Rock replied firmly. He didn't like the idea of his Captain leaving the ship without an armed escort in this strange place, but he was bound to follow his orders.

Mitch nodded to the Sergeant in appreciation. He knew what was going through the Sergeant's mind, but trusted him to follow his orders.

"I see that everyone is wearing armor." Mitch observed that Yurie, like himself, had chosen to wear the stealth armor, not the standard uniforms they would have typically worn. He was impressed with her foresight. Richter didn't have the stealth armor, and looked curiously at the differences between his and theirs. Noting his curiosity, Mitch added, "Just a newer version of what you have, Richter, that's all."

Richter acknowledged him with a raised brow. Mitch suspected that he didn't entirely believe that statement. He was a highly intelligent person, much more so than Mitch had given him credit for initially.

They opened the inside hatch first, entered and closed it behind them, and once the lock engaged they opened the outside hatch. Standing outside waiting for them, was a very tall woman, nearing six foot Mitch guessed. She was wearing a uniform that was gold in color. At first glance, he thought it was crafted from a composite material because of its solid looking nature. Then he noted that when she moved, the suit moved with her, conforming to every part of her body, which reminded him of their own stealth armor and its carbon tube nano-technology. When viewed under a microscope, his suit appeared to be a cross between a liquid and a solid, yet it was alive with activity as the microscopic nanobots repaired and regenerated themselves. They could adapt to any external environment, providing the wearer with warmth or coolness as needed. The material couldn't be cut, and any impact from a sonic weapon or even a projectile weapon would be dispersed away from the impact area. Mitch was proof that the suit worked, as he had previously suffered a blast from an ultrasonic weapon set to kill at close range and lived, suffering only bruises and a few cracked ribs.

The woman's golden armor highlighted her sleek form, but it took a moment for him to realize that her hair was as white as snow. Her hair was closely cropped to just below her ears, and her eyes were emerald green, contrasting sharply with her platinum skin. Her lips were painted silver-white and they shimmered as the light touched them. Her body appeared to be firm, with obvious well developed muscle tone revealed by the suit. He nearly questioned if she really was female, but when she turned away he could clearly see the curve of her breasts. The armor made defining much of her body difficult, the way it moved when she did. In a unique way, she was a very attractive woman. At least she wasn't wearing one of those stupid robes. He smiled slightly, at the thought. Mitch was almost entranced by the woman, and Yurie seemed equally interested. Richter, however, didn't seem to be entranced, aside from his obvious once over look. She didn't smile, but waited patiently for them to close and secure the hatch behind them.

Without a smile or other indication of emotion, she motioned with a subtle nod for them to follow her.

Mitch wondered if she was a bi-mod like the others on Bion4, but he didn't see any indication of a mod. He was curious as to where she kept her weapon. It wasn't carried on her side and he didn't see any bulges beneath the uniform. They followed her down the long gangway, Mitch and Yurie walking beside each other, and Richter bringing up the rear. Mitch stared admiringly at their escort's hip swing and her very taut rear end. He grinned and Yurie caught his look and elbowed him in the side. His eyes met hers and he whispered, "Sorry, I couldn't help it," and she scowled back at him. He shrugged and kept walking; this time making certain his eyes didn't wonder elsewhere, much. Richter was thinking the same thing, but it wasn't the woman in gold whose rear end *he* was admiring.

When they reached the end of the gangway, she pressed the flat of her hand against the door for a second. The light that surrounded the door suddenly changed from red to green, as a hissing sound announced the pressure release and the door slid away. They quickly passed through a secondary pressure door and entered a brightly lit area that was devoid of activity. The lack of activity concerned him a little, but when they turned left, passing through another door, there stood another person dressed in a robe that completely concealed his or her face. Their escort stopped and tilted her head slightly in recognition of the robed figure, then turned and exited the door through which they had just come. Yurie looked up at Mitch, and he shrugged. Richter walked around them both and bent over, as if to honor the robed person. The robed figure bent over as well.

"Ambassador," Richter said softly, "the people of Bion4 greet you with humility and honor."

Mitch raised an eyebrow. He didn't like surprises like this, and he would definitely be having a discussion with Richter when they returned to the ship. Richter took a step back, and the robed figure took a step forward. Hands withdrew from beneath the longs arms of the robe, and Mitch noted the delicate fingers of a woman's hands, whose fingernails, painted silver, glistened in the room's light. She raised her hands and pulled back the robe to reveal a nearly identical copy of their escort, except she was obviously many years older. She sported the same snow white hair, except hers was worn in a tightly knit braid, wrapped neatly around the crown of her head. Her cheeks held a slight rose color in contrast to her platinum skin tone. Her emerald colored eyes reached out to draw your attention. She smiled warmly and her eyes sparkled as she spoke.

"Greetings and welcome. I am Ambassador Codas. I am sorry that our initial greeting to you wasn't satisfactory. Danar informed me that you were upset with him."

"I'm Captain Mitch Saber and this is Lieutenant...."

"Yurie Nagamo," she intervened, "and this is Richter. I know who all of you are. Ambassador Tesslena's description of each of you was very detailed."

"I'm afraid you have me at a disadvantage, Ambassador," Mitch said, somewhat annoyed.

"You will soon understand, Captain. This is simply a new experience for you, that's all. We haven't had any outsiders visit us for a very long time, so please let me greet each of you."

She glided closer to them; her robes reacted to her motion like clouds moving across the sky. She reached out for Richter's hand and he placed it in hers. She accepted his hand and placed it gently against her forehead, then closed her eyes. She smiled, and as she released his hand she said to him, "I'm glad to see you are happy, Richter. It warms my heart to know that they treat you like family." He smiled, and bowed slightly again.

Moving one step aside, she reached out to Yurie, who hesitantly stretched her hand out. Again the Ambassador gently placed it on her forehead, and closed her eyes. "You have no need to fear anything, Yurie. Your father is very proud of you for completing his work and coming to us. He prepared you for many years for exactly this time." She then paused, as if thinking. "I understand the emotion you feel. Set your fears aside, Yurie, you are soul lovers. He loves you too, but you must accept it for what it is."

Mitch listened to the odd one-sided conversation. It appeared that the Ambassador was answering their thoughts aloud, and that made him even more curious, and a little suspicious.

She continued, "Don't worry; he will always be there to protect you, as he has already demonstrated. I know you love him dearly, and understand that in his heart, he loves you too. Just not romantically. You will always be a very important part of his life... That's an unusual request, but... perhaps that can be arranged, we will see." She released her hand, and Mitch saw Yurie's eyes swell with tears.

Now, she looked into Mitch's eyes. He tensed; he didn't like someone probing into his thoughts. She smiled gently, and reached out for his hand. He didn't want to feel her touch, but as he looked into her deep emerald eyes, he felt his hand moving toward her without his conscious will. She touched his hand to her forehead. His mind was rapidly playing out disaster scenarios. Suspicion and caution plagued his thoughts as he tried to fight the invasion into his mind. His confusion waned, and he found himself looking out into the lagoon on Saber Island, and he felt calm again as he heard the waters splash onto the sandy beach. He was sure he heard his mother's voice call out to him.

"Mitch! Where are you? It's almost dinner time, you need to come in and wash up, son."

He turned toward the direction of the voice, and saw his mother coming down the steps to where he stood. Curious, he reached down and felt the sand between his fingers. He glanced up again; she looked just the way he remembered her...

"Mom?"

"Mitch, you have to come in sometime. You can't just stand out here all day and watch your life wash out to sea."

"But, Mom, how can you be here? How can I be here?"

"I'm always here, silly boy! You know your father and I are always here. There's nothing to be afraid of." She wrapped her arms around him and hugged him like she always had. He could feel her warmth and he remembered how much he missed her. He embraced her for a long moment.

"Wait, this isn't real. You and Dad aren't..." his voice trailed off.

"We're always here," she said as she pointed a finger at his heart. "Your father and I love you very much. We're so proud of what you and Laurel have done. You have come so far since we left, and we miss being there with you. You don't have to be afraid of what you're doing. You are on a different path now. You have been accepted as a friend, a protector, and you've proven yourself to be a good, honorable man. You and Samantha will have a good life together." Mitch was surprised. How could they know about Sam, he wondered. "We see what's in your heart, Mitch. Don't deny yourself some happiness as you live your life, son. Love those who love you but remember some things are not what they seem. Be cautious with whom you share the knowledge of the anomalies, son. Not everyone shares your honorable intentions."

He felt a hand on his shoulder, and he turned to see his father standing there, smiling broadly, "I'm so proud of you, Mitchel. I'm sorry we went away when we did. I was so happy to see you and Laurel grab the reigns of the business. You've done so well with it, but remember your mother's warning about the gateways. There are people who only pretend to have high ideals while there is actually darkness in their ways. You can trust your uncle, but beware of others."

Both of his parents then hugged him, and he remembered the last time that they had hugged each other, so many years ago. "We must go now, Mitch, but we will always be with you, son. We will always be with you."

Tears were streaming from Mitch's eyes as the Ambassador released his hand. Yurie hugged him tightly as Richter looked on without emotion. Mitch attempted to recover gracefully, but found the intensity of his emotions too overwhelming.

"What... what just happened?" he asked as he wiped his tears away.

"I allowed myself to be a conduit between you and your family, Captain. I didn't require any information from you as I did with the others. I felt the trauma that you still suffer as a result of your parent's tragic deaths. They wanted you to feel closure and they desired to have one last chance to speak to you."

"I...I don't know what to say."

"You're not required to say anything, Captain. I only wanted to help you and I thought this conversation with your parents was the most logical choice."

"But, it felt so real."

"It was very real, Captain. Your soul reached out to another plain of reality. The sensations that you felt were all very real. If you don't believe me, look in your left hand."

Mitch held up his left hand. Between his fingers was sand from the beach that he had picked up in his memory. He suddenly felt light headed as the emotions reeled back into his mind, and he wobbled on his feet for a moment. Richter stepped behind him to offer some support.

"Easy there, Captain. The first time I ever had an experience like yours, I was out cold before I knew it." Richter said sincerely.

Mitch shook his head to help clear his mind. "What is this all about? Your touch to Richter was one of recognition and your touch to Yurie was one of understanding. Your touch to each of us served entirely different purposes. What's the purpose of all of this? I thought I was here just to deliver a stasis pod to you then be on my way."

"You will, Captain, but we needed to lay the groundwork for you to begin to understand your roll in all of this. Reaching into your minds is the easiest way for us to evaluate who you are and to know if you are trustworthy. Our mental capabilities may seem foreign to you, but try to understand that this is our way."

"My roll? I thought I was clear about all that. I am only here to make a delivery."

"We have waited for more than twenty years for the ambassador, who you carry, to be delivered to us. We have worked with Ambassador Tesslena for many years to prepare for this occasion. However, we could not provide the information necessary for someone to travel through the gateways to reach us. Only time could provide the opportunity. This is why her daughter has been in stasis for so long."

"So, Tesslena came from Aegea?"

"Yes. She too was sent via a stasis chamber, nearly two hundred years ago aboard the last surviving inter-galactic transport that we had. She remained in stasis for many years until we began to resolve our differences. We have communicated with Bion4 over the years, waiting for someone to learn the secrets of the gateways, to bring their ambassador to us, and now you are here. Please try to understand what this means to our people, and what your abilities have demonstrated. Your status as honored protector hasn't been granted to anyone for over two hundred years."

"How have you communicated with Bion4? I didn't see any comm buoys in this system or any of the other systems on our journey here. Was our trip not the most direct path?"

"I will tell you that our ships are only single person transports. We don't have the desire to build a vessel like yours. We have been very happy living out our lives in seclusion. As time passed, we learned that we can't escape who we are or where we came from. As you have surmised, our mental capabilities far exceed those of the average human. Our minds can reach across vast distances and speak to our friends on Bion4."

"You're right. I did guess that much. Are your abilities natural or artificial?"

Richter interrupted, "Captain, we call them psy-mods. They have significant implants that start from childhood and they are trained from birth to use them. As their abilities develop their implants are further enhanced. Only a select few of those on Bion 4 are given this capability."

The Ambassador nodded in agreement. "Several centuries ago a sect broke off from Bion4, and they eventually found their way here. They brought with them most of the more advanced knowledge and personnel, setting Bion4 back more than two hundred years. As the people of Bion4 gradually adapted and learned to trade with the other systems, they made a name for themselves. Eventually, those few equipped with the implants, gained the ability to reach out with their minds and could touch ours, so we began to speak to one another again. We've been trying to overcome our differences for many decades now. We paid a heavy price for living on this world, as our appearance may suggest. A nearby star collapsed not long after we settled here, and our bodies were changed to what you see now."

"You are all very attractive from what I have seen, Ambassador."

She smiled. "Yes, the guard said you were admiring her... uh, backside, when you came in. She was quite taken away with your admiration."

Mitch blushed. "I'm sorry... I meant no disrespect."

The Ambassador chuckled. "None was taken, Captain. The guard was very flattered. She had never experienced that emotion focused on her before. We are very purpose driven and the excesses of human emotions haven't been present here for a very long time. We find your emotions to be actually, quite refreshing."

"So, now that I've made a fool of myself, where do we go from here?"

"I believe that you have a small transport on your ship?"

"Yes, a Minnow. It can carry up to six passengers, plus two crew personnel."

"Good. Yurie, take this crystal, it will fit into your data port. It will give you the exact location to deliver the stasis chamber. Captain, you three must accompany the pod, and I will allow you to bring one other person, if you wish. I ask only that you leave your weapons on your ship. You will have to accept my word that you will be safe. There is also a ceremony that must be performed, so we will require your cooperation."

"With respect, Ambassador, I will not leave my ship for anyone, anytime, without my weapon. I will ask the others to leave theirs on board, but I will not leave my ship unarmed. Please understand my position here."

She quietly studied him for a moment and finally nodded. "Very well, Captain. I will agree to your request. As Honored Protector, your status may allow for this." She closed her eyes briefly then said, "The guard will escort you back to your ship. We request your presence at the specified location tomorrow at your standard ship time of 0800."

"Wait a moment," Mitch said, before the Ambassador turned away. "What about the raiders that entered your space earlier? How often does that happen? Where do they come from?"

"The raiders show up occasionally, looking for tech and people that they can sell as slave labor. They started showing up about a year ago. We don't know from which systems they are coming. I'm fairly sure that they are not of the same group that you have fought. We captured a few of them and discovered that they are, more or less, a loose knit group of scavengers. Apparently, there are some neighboring systems upon whom they prey, and they found us quite by accident."

"Their ships configuration matches very closely the ones we have battled," replied Mitch. "There must be a connection."

"They pose no significant threat..."

Mitch interrupted the Ambassador, "Excuse me, but I have had experience with them. If they make a show of force, your eight ships, no matter how good your weapons are, will not be able to stop the raiders from attacking Aegea. In the end, your people may surely suffer at their hands."

"I appreciate your sincere intentions, Captain, but those eight ships are only part of our defensive capabilities. We are not as defenseless as you may think."

"And a damn impressive show they put on too, but I must insist that you take these people more seriously," Mitch said sternly.

"I'll pass along your concerns, Captain, if it will allay your fears."

"That will be a start, Ambassador."

The door behind them opened, and the guard entered, motioning them to follow. Mitch saw Yurie whisper something to the Ambassador that he couldn't hear, as she reverently bowed and turned to leave. They made their way back into the gangway, where Mitch once again admired the guard's backside and hips, and this time he did it with deliberate intention. He waited for Yurie to elbow him again, but she seemed to be too deep in thought to notice. He really didn't intend to be crude, but if the emotion of his admiration made the guard feel good, then he felt it was his duty to bring a little joy into her day. A minor effort on his part naturally, but a worthwhile one he thought. A mischievous grin appeared on his face as the guard stepped aside to allow Richter to open the exterior hatch. Richter and Yurie entered first, while Mitch turned to face the guard, who just looked at him without any sign of emotion.

He smiled at her saying, "You *are* a beautiful woman. I hope you aren't offended at my admiration of your...uh, backside." His grin broadened as he winked.

She looked at him stone-faced. He shrugged and turned to enter the hatch, when he felt a hand on his shoulder. He stopped and turned, finding the woman still looking at him without any change in her expression. She raised her hand, placing the top of her bent fingers on his forehead. Mitch's vision clouded and he closed his eyes. His mind was filled with expressions of joy and happiness. He could see a little girl running through a brook, laughing as she chased butterflies, colored in gold and turquoise. A smile broadened on his face as he listened to her laugh. She held her arms up for him to pick her up and giggled as he lifted her up. She placed her hands on each side of his face and kissed him on the cheek. Instantly the vision disappeared. The guard had removed her hand. She turned and walked away, without looking back.

With a surprised expression, he slowly turned back to enter the hatch, to find Richter grinning back at him.

"What was that all about?" Mitch asked, surprised at the experience.

"That was her way of sharing the emotions that you raised in her, Captain. It would seem that her training prevents her from outward expressions of emotion. I'm curious, what did you see?" Richter asked.

"I saw a little blonde haired girl running through a brook, laughing and chasing butterflies. She was excited, apparently having the time of her life. She wanted me to pick her up, and when I did, she kissed me on the cheek, and that was it. She was so happy that it made me feel happy too."

"Sounds like you touched her heart, Captain. Somehow, you managed to penetrate the shell created by her training, and it filled her with thoughts of the childhood that she never had. That is a significant experience, Captain. I'm quite surprised at her actions"

"Damn, I thought I was just a normal male. I didn't expect that kind of reaction, just from admiring her posterior. I'm going to have to be more cautious about whose rear-end I gawk at around here," Mitch said with an amused expression.

"I'd say you made an impression, Captain, and probably a friend too."

Together, they closed and secured the hatches behind them.

"Richter, I'm a little concerned that you seem to know what to do and say without consulting me first. I don't appreciate surprises and not being told what to expect."

Richter's face scowled. "Captain, I'm really sorry if you felt that way. I sincerely didn't mean to disrespect your rank. These people are part of my culture, and I simply reacted in the way that I was trained. The formalities of how we greet our own have many intricacies. I hope you won't think badly of me."

Mitch considered this for a moment, then replied, "I understand now, Richter, but you could have made the situation much easier for me, if we had discussed these intricacies in advance."

"I understand, Captain and I won't let that happen again. Perhaps it would be a good idea if I assemble a document on some of the cultural habits of our people. ALICE can store them on your eye-vid for future reference."

"My implant only allows me to stream information that I'm receiving. I can't request information as I need it without the use of my comm unit."

"Really? I'm quite surprised at that, Captain. That is one of the most common implants on Bion 4. I'd bet that the ones they have here on Aegea are much more capable than the ones we have. Perhaps you should discuss getting one while we're here."

"I'm not certain that would be such a good idea, Richter."

"I don't see why not. It could be linked to ALICE, and your implant would connect directly into your brain's electrical pathways. You could speak to ALICE with just a thought and not have to vocalize your requests. I'll also bet that your implant lenses only display data in simple colors. That could be upgraded into complex color and even night vision."

"Are you trying to turn me into a bi-mod?" Mitch asked with a smirk.

"No, Captain, not at all. These are simply enhancements to mods that you already have. Your government restricts the availability of this technology from your medical and science agencies. I would think that improving your mods could be a real asset in performing your duties. If you remove all the propaganda that they've filled your head with, you will have to admit that those improvements could prove invaluable."

Mitch thought about this as he entered the tram, making his way for the bridge. It irked him a little to admit that those enhancements would be incredibly useful. What would Sam say about something like that, or would he even tell her? Maybe she would be interested. He wondered what other enhancements could be provided here. Would it be worth the potential damage that might occur if there was a problem later? Would it fry his brain if he encountered an EMP? But surely, he thought, these issues must have been already considered. If not, then this technology wouldn't be so prevalent here.

Mitch updated the second shift bridge crew, then grabbing a sandwich from the galley; he went to his quarters to get some rest and to prepare for the event tomorrow. He longed to hear Samantha's voice and to talk to Laurel, but that wasn't possible since he was eleven hundred light years away from home. He removed the stealth suit he still wore from their trip to the Aegean Station, and relaxed back on his bed. He wanted to take a shower, but at the moment it felt good just to relax and absorb all that had happened this day.

He considered how the Aegean people he had met reminded him of the people on Bion4, but he reflected on some major differences. Their tech was far more advanced than that on Bion4, but he had no extensive knowledge about their system. His only dealings with Bion4 had been as a merchant trader. Richter was a good example of how little he really knew. On Alderon he had learned only that the people of Bion4 were outcasts. He understood them to be serious tech worshipers who were capable of taking control of computers and equipment, able to turn them against their operators. The bio-mods on Alderon had limited uses, mainly aiding or enhancing certain capabilities, such as scanning or communications. He had seen pictures of bio-modified people who had obviously artificial, advanced eyes and limbs that could be extremely useful for warfare. Now he wondered how much of that information was propaganda and how much was truth. So far, his dealings with the people of Bion4 had been fair, and although they weren't always forthcoming with all information, he had to admit that they had never lied to him. As customers, they paid promptly and sought him out when they needed freight services. Sometimes they overpaid for his services, but Laurel was always quick to inform them and refund the overpaid credits. They could have easily accepted the overpayment, but they simply didn't operate that way. Laurel had told him that the Traders Union and Merchants Guild had complained that he was getting too much business from Bion4. They wanted him to share his freight contracts with them, but she thought it was just sour grapes. Bion4 had specifically requested Mitch to carry their freight, and she wasn't about to refuse a customer's request. They both knew that many of the freighter requests from Bion4 went unanswered, due to the bigotry that many freighter captains had toward the bio-modified humans. His thoughts turned to the possible enhancement of his own implants that Richter had suggested. If they would improve his ability to do his work and support his crew, what would be the problem with that, he wondered.

He stretched his arms and legs and tried to relax before getting into the shower. He had just closed his eyes when he heard his door chime, and turned his head toward the opening that led to his office.

"Yes, who is it?" He didn't hear any reply. Perhaps he imagined it. The chime sounded again. "Yes! Who is it?" he said louder this time. What the hell is going on, he thought. He sat up and Yurie was standing in the doorway, wearing the same outfit that she had worn when they had first met. The white skirt, stopping slightly above her knees, matched her high heels and bright red silk blouse. He had forgotten how attractive she had looked in that outfit. Her humility and calm nature were her greatest attraction.

"Yurie? Why are you here, is something wrong?"

She just looked at him shyly, tilting her head downward slightly. Her hair wasn't pulled back and the bangs nearly covered her eyes completely. She didn't reply, but slowly walked towards him where he sat on his bed.

"Yurie, unless you need something you should leave. This isn't appropriate."

He blinked. Now her blouse was off and her skirt had dropped to the floor. She wasn't wearing any undergarments, and he marveled at her completely revealed body. "Yurie," he said, "you must leave. This isn't like you. Dress yourself and go to your quarters immediately! That's an order!"

He looked at her clothes on the floor, and wondered how she had undressed so quickly. Now he was on the floor, on his knees. 'How did I get here?' he thought. Yurie held his head between her small breasts. Her skin was soft and delicate. He could sense her hair brushing against his shoulders as she held him tightly. His clothes were now gone, and she lay on the floor. Now he was making love to Yurie, and it was incredible. Why was he doing this? Why was *she* doing this? The thoughts ran through his mind, but now he was too committed to stop. She straddled him, riding in rhythmic motion, back and forth. As he held her firm breasts in his hands, he felt his passion give in to her needs. Yuri moaned in satisfaction.

Suddenly, he heard a noise, but he could not distinguish what it was. Now she was lying on his chest. He could feel her rapid heartbeat thumping steadily against him, and he held her tightly. There it was again... that stupid noise. "What's that damn sound?" he said aloud. The sound of his own voice woke Mitch, and he sat upright in his bed. Blinking his eyes, trying to clear his vision, he realized that the noise was his alarm. He looked around his cabin, seeing that everything was just as it was when he had come in earlier. He was still wearing his clothes, and he noted that he had been sleeping for nearly nine hours. Yurie wasn't there. He was soaked in perspiration. "A dream, it was a damn dream!" He said aloud. "But it was so real!" He attempted to shake it off as he headed to the shower.

Mitch invited Inna to accompany them to the surface of Aegea. The comment that she had made about first contact struck a note with him, and he felt it would be a good experience for her. He was evaluating some of his crew for an increase in rank, and this would be a good test for the young Ensign. Richter and Yurie were waiting for them as they entered the cargo bay, where the Minnow was docked. Richter spoke his typical good morning cheer and Mitch greeted Yurie, who smiled as always and spoke to him no differently than usual, but he thought he detected something changed in her. Her face seemed to glow, but he decided it was that dream, playing tricks with his mind. He looked at her for a longer moment, halfway expecting to see her naked again, but he quickly pushed the thought away from his mind. He turned to face Dr. Santana who was wheeling the stasis pod into the Minnow. He failed to see Yurie blush as he turned, and she smiled at her memory of the night's event. One which she would cherish forever. Dreams *can* be powerful, she now knew.

"Is every one ready?" Mitch asked as he looked about. Heads nodded and the doctor spoke up.

"Captain, are you certain that you don't want me to come along? There could be problems because she has been in stasis for nearly twenty years."

"Thanks, Doc, but I think the people down there will have things well in hand. I only have four tickets to this party, and they were by specific invitation only." Mitch tapped his wrist-comm. "Mr. Stevens, you have the bridge."

"Aye, Captain," Stevens replied sharply.

"Yurie, you have those coordinates?"

"Yes, Captain, we can leave when you're ready."

"Alright, let's get moving."

The Minnow departed the Phoenix and they made their way towards the planet. They viewed the outlines of oceans and land masses but didn't see any large mountain ranges. They passed through the outer atmosphere, cruising downward to ten thousand feet until they could clearly see land. Large open land masses held fields of blue green grasses and a multitude of flowering shrubs and trees. Small groupings of forests were visible in the distance but the land was mostly fertile plains. The coastlines were awash with what appeared to be bleached white sand and stone, and the water was so clear that they could see marine life swimming until the waters turned pale in the deeper depths and obscured their view. It was serenely beautiful, but they saw no land mammals, and few fowl in the air. In the distance, they could see reflections in the early morning sun. As they drew closer to the city, they were startled to see that it wasn't on the ground, but rather, was suspended above the ground on enormous pylons. The pylons were topped by what appeared to be giant saucers, holding buildings atop them. Those buildings reflected the early sun like glass, tinted in gold. Numerous saucers were interconnected, each one traversed by an enclosed dual transport tube system. They counted at least a dozen of the saucer supported cities spreading across a huge swath of land. Mitch noticed an array of smaller saucer shaped structures with imposing projectiles pointed toward the sky. Each one had a huge crystal embedded spire pointing towards the skies. These smaller structures dotted the perimeter of the city, and were not connected by the transport system. Mitch was fairly certain that they were a land based weapons system that was used to protect the city. They saw several collections of lights as they approached the planet earlier, so there appeared to be many cities scattered across the globe. As they approached the landing site coordinates, he saw a large landing pad, illuminated by chaser lights. The Minnow landed softly and the pad began to drop down into the building on top of which they had landed.

The pad came to a halt as a dome closed overhead. They opened the door to see Ambassador Codas waiting. With her stood the same guard, to whom Mitch had spoken and admired, the previous day. At least he fairly certain she was the same guard.

"Captain Saber, it is good to welcome you again. Your timing is punctual."

"Thank you, Ambassador Codas. You've met everyone here except my communications officer. This is Ensign Inna Dubnikov. Ensign, this is Ambassador Codas." Mitch had briefed Inna on the Ambassador so that she would know what to expect when she was introduced. The Ambassador approached Inna just as she had approached the rest of them yesterday, and reached out her hand for Inna's, which she gracefully accepted.

Taking Inna's hand the Ambassador placed it on her forehead then closed her eyes. She smiled. "No reason to be so nervous, Inna. I am excited to meet you too. Yes, he is a most accommodating man. You are not alone child, you have a large family on your ship who all care about you, very much. You have much to offer, but you have much more to learn too. Be patient my young friend, you have come a long way, and you have many adventures still to come. Don't worry; your parents will welcome you home again someday."

The Ambassador released her hand, and Inna opened her eyes with a curious look. Ambassador Codas met her smile, and looked to Mitch. "A most unusual young woman, Captain. She fears she will disappoint you, but she is most excited that you let her join your team here today. I find her most amusing."

Mitch patted Inna on the shoulder and complimented her performance as an officer on his ship. She beamed a wide, shy smile.

"Lieutenant Nagamo, did you...sleep well?"

Yurie nodded, blushing slightly, and smiled. That was an odd question, Mitch thought. Yurie didn't appear to be tired.

"It was a very restful night, Ambassador. Thank you for asking," Yurie replied casually.

"Please, everyone follow us," the Ambassador said.

They fell in line with Mitch and Yurie in front, guiding the stasis pod, and Inna and Richter behind, pushing it. Mitch glanced around at the large expanse that the pad had descended into, noting several other craft in the hanger. They appeared to be vessels similar to his along with a couple of larger vessels. He wasn't sure of their purpose. They passed through a large set of double doors that closed quietly behind them, and made two more turns, before approaching another set of double doors. The walls seemed to be crystalline tinted in gold. He wondered what the deal was, with so many gold things. The guard pressed her hand flat against the door for a moment, and it slowly opened into a small chamber. Four men wearing robes approached and pulled back their hoods. Each man wore a pair of dark lenses concealing their eyes. These men slowly came within a few feet of the pod, and reached out, as if to take it from their possession.

Mitch pushed himself between the men closest to him, and saying, "Back away. I was instructed that this chamber was to never leave my sight." Yurie and Inna both matched his movement.

"Captain," the Ambassador intervened, "they merely wish to prepare the chamber to be unsealed."

"I was instructed not to let this chamber out of my sight, or my protection, until it was time to be opened. I hold the only key," Mitch replied firmly. "Ambassador Tesslena told me that I would know when it was time for me to open the chamber, and I know now isn't the time."

One of the men attempted to reach out and push Mitch aside, when the guard grabbed the man by the back of his neck and flung him across the room. He bounced off the wall, falling onto the floor. The guard's lightning fast speed and her strength surprised Mitch and his group. The other men backed off immediately.

"I'm sorry, Captain, they should not have attempted to touch you or your team. Our escort has been instructed not to allow anyone to harm you or otherwise interfere with your mission here. As you can see, she is most capable," the Ambassador said. "It would appear that Ambassador Tesslena intended for you to participate fully in the opening of the chamber, and we will respect her wishes."

"I am the only person who can open this chamber, and any attempt to do so by anyone else, will result in the termination of the woman inside," Mitch said, looking at the men as they backed away. He nodded to the guard whose expression was just as expressionless as it had been yesterday.

"Were you informed as to specifically when you were to open the chamber, Captain?"

'No, Ambassador. I was only told that I would know when the time had arrived, and only then was I to open the chamber. I was given the impression that there would be a ceremony or meeting of some sort. I hope you understand. Ambassador Tesslena...she *placed* the knowledge in my mind, so I don't really know what to tell you. I hope that you understand this better than I do."

"Actually, I do," she replied. "It is a very wise precaution and I applaud her wisdom. Come then, let us go to the meeting area. Our people await your arrival."

They passed through another door to enter a large room with theater style seating on their left and right. The room was large enough to seat perhaps two hundred people. Standing to the left and right of them as they entered were two single lines of robed figures, all with their hoods pulled down over their heads. Some were robed in white, although most wore shimmering silver like the Ambassador. A few of the figures were cloaked in yellow, and several in gold. One lone figure stood out in his bright emerald green robe that glistened as though it was charged with electricity. They moved to the center of the group and stopped. The man in green, whose face was barely seen, took the center position directly in front of them. Ambassador Codas approached and bent over in respect to this person. She then glided to the side and one step behind the green robed man. The guard escort turned and walked over to Mitch, slowly raising her hand and placing her bent fingers on his forehead. He wasn't alarmed since she had done the same thing earlier. As her hand touched him, he heard her voice in his mind, instructing him on how to greet Prefect Rohm. Just before she pulled her hand back, she flashed the memory of the little girl to him again. She withdrew her hand, and Mitch maintained his poker face, while he winked at the guard. She stepped away and to the side, bowing slightly to the green robed man.

Mitch turned sharply on his heels. "Crew, form a parade line." They immediately stepped up in front of him and stood at attention. He whispered his instructions and they nodded. Mitch then turned to face the man in green, and bowed halfway to his waist. He then stood erect as his crew repeated his action. The crew then turned and filed to the rear of the chamber, where they stood at parade rest. Mitch turned to his right and bowed, repeating the action, facing the people on the left. The green robed man returned his bow, and then the others on his left and right did the same. The Ambassador smiled slightly at him, from behind the robed man. Mitch waited as the audience to his left and right removed their hoods, and finally the green robed man removed his hood. All of the women had snow white hair and the same platinum hued skin tone, yet the men all bore bare heads and showed no signs of any facial hair. Emerald eyes were repeated in both male and female, but the female's eyes were much deeper in color. Mitch stepped forward two steps and bowed again. Standing erect again, he said, "On behalf of the people of Bion4, I, their designated Honored Protector, present to you, Ambassador Madera."

The man in the green robes showed no emotion as he began, "On behalf of Aegea and serving as the Prefect of Aegea, I welcome you to our home, Honored Protector. Please, introduce yourself to us."

Mitch introduced his crew first. Each of them bowed respectfully as directed, when introduced. Lastly, he introduced himself.

"Captain Saber, you honor us with your presence." The Prefect nodded slightly then raised his arms upward.

The people on his left and right said in unison, "Welcome, Honored Protector."

The Prefect slowly came down from his high step toward Mitch and stopped within one arm's length. Mitch noticed the gold circlet that encircled the Prefect's neck. Mitch felt as though the man was looking through him, not at him. Finally, the Prefect extended his hand, and Mitch tensed. He wasn't expecting this and he wondered if he was going to have a repeat performance of his meeting with Ambassador Codas. He could just see her over the Prefect's shoulder, and she nodded at him.

Mitch reached out his hand to the Prefect, and his hand was placed on the Prefect's forehead.

"Your confusion is expected, Captain Saber," the voice in his head told him. "We have long awaited an emissary from our family on Bion4. Thank you for honoring our traditions. You and your crew have demonstrated great respect towards us. The Praetorian Guard took it upon herself I see, to guide your actions just now. This is indeed, a never before seen occurrence. You must have made quite an impression on her, and that pleases me greatly. Our people in the chamber will pass by you in a moment. Soon you will know when it is time for you to perform your duty. You are now known to be a friend to the people of Aegea."

He released Mitch's hand, moved away, and held up his arms again. One by one, each robed figure approached the stasis chamber and bowed, placing their foreheads on it for just a brief moment, before returning to their previous positions. There were at least fifty of them, Mitch figured. After the process was completed, and the final person had returned to the line, the Prefect lowered his arms. He repeated the same action, after which he returned, facing Mitch from several feet away. He bowed deeply, this time to Mitch, as did the Ambassador. Mitch moved robotically, as if in a trance, to the chamber and placed his forehead on the glass viewport with both of his hands beside his head, as if he were peering inside a window. Yurie, Richter and Inna were surprised by his action and wondered what was going to happen next. He stood and took a half step back. The stasis chamber hissed and whistled as its top cracked open, and the bluish mist rushed out to escape its confines. The lid continued to open all the way back and the air surrounding it soon cleared. A brief moment passed by and Mitch stepped up to the chamber. He leaned over, picking up the young girl, who gradually began to open her eyes. She was wearing a silver and gold trimmed body suit. The gold circlet around her neck was nearly identical to the one worn by the Prefect. Mitch remained motionless as he held her in his arms. Her eyes seemed to clear and she looked at him as a smile slowly began to form on her face. She attempted to speak, but apparently due to the length of time that she had been in the chamber, she had no voice yet. She raised her hand and placed it gently on Mitch's forehead. He blinked several times, rapidly, and looked down to see the woman he now held in his arms, and smiled back.

"Well...hello there, young lady. I'm pleased to greet you too," Mitch said in a soft voice.

Keeping her in his arms, he approached the Prefect and said, "I present to you, Ambassador Madera, Prefect. In her present state, she is unable to stand on her own, and wishes me to extend to you her personal greetings."

The Prefect approached the young woman and lifted her hand to his forehead. After a few moments he backed away, and summoned Ambassador Codas. She approached and the two of them spoke for a moment, after which the Prefect turned and said, "Captain, you have proven again to be more than a friend to the people of Aegea. Thank you. The Ambassador will inform you of what you are to do now. I'm certain that we will speak again later." The Prefect walked back up the steps, and the other figures formed a line, following him through the door, which closed behind them.

The Ambassador waited to speak until everyone had cleared the room, except for Mitch, his crew and their escort. Mitch still held the woman in his arms, and he was getting weary of the added weight, although he guessed that the woman probably didn't weigh more than 90 pounds.

"Captain," the Ambassador said, "Madera has asked that you remain with her until she can stand on her own. It shouldn't take long. Your crew is welcome to stay with you, and we can provide you with a place to relax."

"I'd like to find a place to set her down, Ambassador. As light as she is, I can't hold her too much longer."

Richter approached and motioned that he would hold her, but when he reached out, she tensed and tightened her grip around the Captain's neck.

"She's not going to let you go, Captain," Richter said.

"Let's find a place to sit, Ambassador, please."

They turned around and went back in the direction from which they had come. Passing through several corridors and doors, they entered a small chamber that provided seating and refreshments, apparently waiting for them. Mitch sat Madera on a padded seat, and Yurie brought her a glass of water. After a few sips she whispered, "Thank you."

A man entered, wearing a white jumpsuit. Mitch was glad to finally see someone who wasn't wearing one of those damn robes, and handed him a glass containing a yellow liquid. Mitch took it, and stared at the man for a long moment.

"Please, give this to Ambassador Madera. It is rich in proteins and nutrients, and it will aid in her recovery," the man said politely.

Mitch smelled the liquid, it had no odor. He looked at the man, glanced at Madera, and decided to taste the liquid first, just to be safe.

The man instantly looked horrified, and he started to reach out to retrieve the beverage, when the guard was instantly at Mitch's side. Her hand clamped down on the man's neck, forcing him to the floor in agony.

"I'm not going to give Madera anything unless I approve it first. I don't know you and until she can fend for herself, she is my responsibility, no offense intended," Mitch said sternly.

His face grimaced as he took a sip. "It tastes like shit actually, but I feel okay. Here Madera." Richter, Inna and Yurie all snickered. "This is supposed to help you recover." He helped her bring the drink to her lips, and she sipped it slowly.

An hour or so later, Madera appeared to have vastly improved. She sipped some more water as they chatted.

Mitch reached to her and touched the golden circlet around her neck. "I've seen this now on several people Madera. What is its significance?"

She looked down and smiled shyly. "It's the symbol of my position, and more. When we are born we undergo many tests, and only a few pass the one that earns this symbol. If we possess certain mental characteristics, then we receive implants at a very early age. As we are trained, the implants are updated, and others are added as we mature. Once we reach the age of accountability, I think you call it puberty, the circlets are placed around our necks and our training intensifies."

"What does the circlet do?" Yurie asked.

"It amplifies our natural mental abilities in conjunction with our implant functions, allowing us to speak with our minds and not just our voices. On Bion4 there are not many of us who are gifted with this. It's a much purer form of speech, and when we interact this way the confusions of the voice are removed. We can then see memories and feel the *true* emotions of those memories. In a sense, we experience those memories too. Often, we see them much more clearly than you can because we are looking from within your mind, without all the external clutter."

"So, it's an advanced form of telepathy," Mitch summarized.

"Yes, and no," Madera said. "Some of us have developed the ability to reach beyond our plain of existence to those who have passed beyond. Others can reach across vast distances and speak to others like us. My mother has that ability. It is a great gift, and we have great respect for those with these abilities."

"Ambassador Codas demonstrated some of those abilities when we first met," Mitch added quietly.

"I hope she brought you closure in some way, Captain," Madera said sincerely.

"Why would you say that Madera?"

"I felt your sadness during our journey here. I reached out to Ambassador Codas when we arrived. I asked her to help you find peace."

"Come now, Madera, you were in stasis. You've been in stasis for the past twenty years," Mitch countered incredulously.

"My body was in stasis, Captain, not my mind. I listened to all of you as we traveled to this place. I felt the pain in your heart and the hurt in Yurie's. I sought to help you both, in service for what you have done for me. I hope that I didn't offend you."

"No," Yurie said quickly.

Mitch hesitated, thinking about his dream in the new light of Madera's confession. After releasing a deep breath, he admitted, "No, there is no offense. It was just...difficult to accept, that's all."

Madera placed her arms around Mitch's shoulder and held him for a moment. "You will always be my Honored Protector, Captain. Our minds are linked because of the actions you have taken here today."

"What do you mean?"

"You were the first person with whom I made physical contact when I awakened. A part of my mind has been passed to yours, and a part of yours has been passed to mine. It was your mind that opened the chamber, not a secret code. My mother passed you the knowledge of what to do when she touched you. This works much like the brain waves that identical twins share."

"That's a little creepy," Mitch said, hoping not to be heard.

Of course, Madera heard his remark. "Creepy? What does creepy mean?"

"Uhhh...strange. Yes, strange is a better word," Mitch said trying not to be misunderstood. Inna and Yurie giggled, cutting their eyes to him. They wouldn't let him forget this one, he thought.

"Strange? Oh yes, I think I understand. From your perspective I can see how you would feel that way. Don't worry, Captain, from time to time we will simply share a thought or a desire. If one of us is in trouble the other will know. The experience is different for many people." Madera stood up, wobbling a little on her legs, but she remained standing under her own efforts. She stretched again and looked around at everyone. Mitch stood up in case she needed support. His Praetorian Guard escort watched, but made no movement. He looked straight at her and winked, still hoping to get a reaction from her, but there was none.

Madera snickered, like a little girl.

"What's funny?" Mitch asked.

Madera looked first at the guard then back to Mitch. "You're trying to get a reaction from the guard but you're not going to get one."

"How do you know that?"

"She told me."

Mitch recalled that the Ambassador had told him that the guard knew he was admiring her behind, yet the guard never said anything aloud. "I should have expected that, I guess," Mitch said, slightly embarrassed again.

Madera giggled. "She likes you, Captain. She said that she hasn't had anyone made her feel like a woman in many years. But, you can't overcome her conditioning as a Commander in the Praetorian Guard."

Mitch glanced toward the guard. "She's a Commander? I am certainly impressed. I've seen a sampling of her skills, and I must say that she is an extraordinary warrior and soldier."

Madera glanced at the guard then smiled. "She admires you too, Captain. She says that although you carry a weapon, you have ignored the urge to brandish it when you were confronted. You graciously allowed her to perform her duties as was expected. That's why she told you how to perform for the Ceremony of Welcoming. It was a violation of protocol, and she took a great risk. However, your performance was flawless and it impressed the Prefect, so she won't be reprimanded."

"I would be very upset if she were to be reprimanded," Mitch said as he glanced toward the guard. "I think that her assistance was very appropriate since I am new at all this. I sincerely appreciated her counsel. Madera, could you tell me what her name is?"

"I am not supposed to reveal the names of Praetorian Guards, according to my training. However," she looked at the guard, "She wants you to know, but only if you do not call her by name in the presence of anyone, as long as you are here."

"If that is her wish, then I agree."

Madera pressed her hand to Mitch's forehead and in his mind he heard her voice say, 'Athena'. She stepped back and everyone watched, waiting for him to repeat the name. He didn't. Instead, he casually walked over to her and looked into her emerald greens eyes saying, "I am so pleased to meet you. Thank you for trusting me with your name." He smiled and winked again, still not perceiving any change in her stone faced expression. He turned and walked back to Madera.

She smiled back at him. "She said that you are a funny, but honorable man, and she hopes to call you friend someday."

"Not someday, Madera, now."

Ambassador Codas entered the room, and upon seeing Madera standing, she broke into a wide smile.

"Ambassador Madera! It's so good to see you up and around." She bowed politely and her action was returned by Madera.

"The Captain and his people have been of great help, Ambassador Codas," Madera replied.

"I'm sure they have. The Chief Prefect requests the pleasure of your company at dinner tonight. The invitation includes all of you, of course." They all nodded in gracious acceptance.

"I'll need to inform my crew of our delayed return, if you don't mind, Ambassador," Mitch said.

"Certainly, Captain. Would you rather use our communications device, or your personal comm?"

Mitch didn't know she that knew about his personal comm but he shouldn't have been surprised. He expected that it would be difficult to surprise these people about anything.

"I'll use my personal comm Ambassador. No need to trouble your staff."

Mitch placed the comm call while the Ambassador and Madera spoke. After he finished, the Ambassador said in a polite tone, "I can offer you a place to relax if you like. It will be a few hours before dinner is served."

"That would be nice, Ambassador. If you don't mind, I would like to have a few words with you, Madera and Richter, in private please." Yurie and Inna looked a little puzzled.

Lieutenant, Ensign, we'll discuss this matter later. I suggest that you freshen up a little before dinner."

"The guard will show them to the guest quarters, Captain. We can speak privately here until she returns."

Inna, Yurie and the guard left, closing the door behind them. Mitch turned to the Ambassador and said, "Ambassador Codas, I understand the importance of bringing Madera here to begin solid relations between your people and your ancestors on Bion4. But I have to admit, I'm curious about the significant differences that I see between your two cultures, not to mention your appearances."

"That's a fair question, Captain. As I told you previously, a sect of our people left Bion4 centuries ago after a difference in traditions and opinions. After we settled here, a star went nova with the resulting radiation emissions changing our planet and our appearance. All females here have hair identical to my own. Our skin is platinum colored and leathery to the touch. We have developed a natural resistance to radiation over the decades, but at a severe cost... Madera's hair will turn white like ours over time, as will the hair of females on your ship, but not to worry. The change will take many years for them, while we are born this way. The radiation contamination affected the plant life here too. This is why our cities are built above ground, to reduce our exposure. The radiation has slowly dissipated over time, but we calculate that it will be at least another one hundred years before we can safely live on the actual surface again. We have a multitude of platforms that we use to grow our food, and our water comes from deep beneath the surface. We have the technology, but not the materials that we need to build larger space craft, but we have no desire to be explorers. We are quite capable of defending our planet as you have already seen."

"Do you not think that your superior technology could benefit the other systems?"

"Perhaps. But that will depend on growing the relationship with our people on Bion4, and also with you."

"With me, why is that?"

"You operate several freighter vessels. You are an Honored Protector and a friend to us. Remember that we are a closed society, Captain. It has taken us decades to even consider welcoming an outsider to our system. It took even longer for Bion4 to find someone who they felt that they could trust, who also possessed the ability to traverse the anomalies that we call gateways. I know this is difficult for you to understand..."

"Actually, it isn't, Ambassador. I probably understand better than you think. Much of what you have revealed, I had already concluded on my own. It isn't my place to criticize you or your people. I simply want to understand your society so that I can condition my responses to your people appropriately. I respect your efforts to re-establish contact with your ancestry. I also place a lot of value on family, and though I operate a business, I treat my employees as extensions of my own family. I will protect them just a vigorously as I will my personal family, or my friends."

Richter smiled and nodded. "What he says *is* true, Ambassador. I have witnessed that on numerous occasions."

"You are an unusual man, Captain Saber, and the people of Bion4 have chosen wisely. Tonight, you are to be gifted with the title of Protector and Advisor, a title that hasn't been given to an outsider in hundreds of years. I wasn't going to tell you until later, but now is as good a time as any."

Richter beamed a broad smile and congratulated Mitch. Although Mitch didn't understand the importance of the title, he recognized that it was important to his hosts. He bowed politely toward the Ambassador, and she gracefully returned it.

"Is there anything else you wish to discuss, Captain?"

"Actually, there is. Richter has been telling me about the capabilities of certain implant technologies that you may have. These could possibly be useful to me."

The Ambassador glanced at Richter, who nodded once.

"We have some very advanced implant technologies, Captain as you may have surmised. Let's go visit one of our med units, and we can talk about it as we go."

The guard had just re-entered the room, so the Ambassador advised her where they were headed. Mitch relayed his interests as they walked along, and the Ambassador agreed that his need could be met, and with relative ease.

The dinner with the Chief Prefect was elegant and formal. The fruits that they ate were unlike anything that Mitch and the other had ever tasted. The food was all fresh, not having been prepared from replicators or powders. The Prefect was most interested in hearing the Captain's tale of his fight against the raiders on Alderon. He was equally interested about Mitch's experiences trading with other systems. The Prefect was formal, but friendly, and Mitch found himself liking the man. He had a distinguished tone while projecting sincerity and confidence. He announced Mitch's elevated status as Protector and Advisor, and placed his hand on Mitch's forehead to solidify the title. Mitch learned that the Praetorian Guards are trained from birth as the elite guardians of Aegea. He was told that they have cybernetic implants in their arms and legs, giving them tremendous strength, and that they are conditioned to show no outward emotions. That explained his guard's lack of expression and her strength. He also learned of their cerebral implants that give them empathic abilities to 'read' emotion and thought from a distance as, well as enhancing their telepathic abilities. The Chief Prefect didn't go into much detail about the meaning of 'enhanced telepathy'. Mitch also learned that the golden suits were very similar to his own but *much* more advanced. The Aegean's were impressed with Mitch's limited demonstration of his own stealth armor. Athena's armor had retractable headgear, and her weapons were concealed within the forearms and thighs. She didn't have projectile weapons, but varying degrees of particle weapons instead.

Mitch hadn't known that it was possible to produce a particle weapon in such a small package, but apparently he was wrong. Perhaps one day, they would share this technology.

After dinner, Mitch informed his ship and ground team that they would stay the night and return to the Phoenix after a private breakfast with Madera in the morning. After everyone else had been escorted to their quarters, the Praetorian Guard escorted Mitch back to the med unit, where his procedure would begin. Richter accompanied him in order to later aid in his recovery and training.

It was mid-morning when Mitch and Richter joined the group for breakfast, and to meet with their hosts before returning home. Madera shed a few tears as she said her goodbyes, and she asked Mitch to hug her mother upon his return. Mitch remembered her mother's 'procreation' request, and he hoped that the subject would not be revisited. Richter carried a small satchel that drew the curiosity of Inna and Yurie. He brushed off their questions, saying that it was just something personal. As they gathered to say farewell, the Ambassador approached, accompanied by the Praetorian Guard Commander. They had both disappeared halfway through breakfast, and although Mitch was curious as to where they had gone, he knew that it wasn't his business to ask. Another man accompanied them, pushing along a gold colored crate which was large enough to hold a full grown man or two. Mitch raised an eyebrow at their approach and his crew was equally curious. The door at the other end of the landing bay opened admitting the Chief Prefect, accompanied by at least six Praetorian Guards. The Captain grew concerned that something was wrong. Ambassador Codas, now within speaking distance, sensed his concern.

"The Prefect is coming to tell you goodbye, Captain. He is always escorted by his personal guard," The Ambassador said calmly.

Mitch nodded, still curious about the gold colored crate.

"Captain Saber," the Prefect said in a friendly tone as he approached Mitch and his crew, "I wanted to personally see you off and to thank you and your crew for coming here. I hope you will visit again soon. I enjoyed greatly our conversation."

He approached each of them separately, bowing and lifting their hands to touch his forehead. Upon releasing Mitch's hand, he extended his hand in a familiar handshake. "I believe that this is your customary greeting, Captain," he said as he smiled.

Mitch returned his smile and thanked him for his hospitality.

"I hope that the addition of your implant will meet your expectations," he said in a low voice so not be overheard.

"I'm sure that it will be more than I hoped for, Prefect. I hope that you will welcome us back here again, soon." Mitch replied.

Inna and Yurie entered the Minnow first, followed by Richter, with his small satchel. Madera reached up to kiss Mitch on the cheek, and then hugged him generously. "Please come back soon, Captain."

"I'll do my best, Madera. I don't know how you'll do it, but I know that you will contact me if the need arises."

She nodded and bowed as she left in the company of the Prefect. Ambassador Codas approached with the guard by her side. Mitch glanced at the guard and smiled warmly. He wanted to give her a handshake for her friendship, but he didn't think that it was appropriate.

Ambassador Codas addressed him. "Captain Saber, you have proven yourself to be our friend and now you hold the distinct title of Protector and Advisor. I know that we will meet again, soon. I must admit that I will look forward to your presence in the future."

Mitch bowed in the Aegean tradition and replied, "I hope to see you again soon, Ambassador. I have much to learn about you and your people. I hope I can be of service to you again."

The guard stepped forward as if she was going to reach out to Mitch. He tensed for a moment, and then relaxed. Mitch asked, "I'm sorry to ask, Ambassador, but is there something I'm supposed to do here?"

The Ambassador grinned at Mitch and placed her hand on the shoulder of the Praetorian Guard. "The title of Protector and Advisor for Aegea carries with it the necessity of a guardian protector."

Mitch's eyed her curiously; he started to shake his head no when the Ambassador continued. "It would honor us greatly and solidify our societal relationship if you would accept this Praetorian Guard as your personal protector."

The guard still showed no emotion. Mitch wondered how in the world he could have her around all the time without holding a conversation or seeing any emotion on her face...

"Ambassador, I am humbled by your offer, but I have my ship and crew to protect me. I don't see the need for a personal bodyguard... *or* personal protector. I must refuse your generous offer; I hope you won't be offended."

"You cannot refuse, Captain. This is a directive from our Chief Prefect. May I add that your personal fears and apprehensions are entirely unfounded? You will soon learn that our Praetorian Guards are trained far beyond the capabilities of anyone from any system that you have ever encountered. You will find her to be a valuable asset in the times to come. I know that this sounds to be without merit to you now, but you will each serve a greater purpose, through your acceptance of the Chief Prefect's directive..."

Mitch took a deep breath, and reluctantly, nodded his acceptance. The Ambassador smiled at his approval, then turned toward the guard and placed her fingers on the guard's forehead for a long moment.

She finally stepped back, saying, "It is done. You are released from your duties here and you are assigned as guardian of our Protector and Advisor, Captain Saber. His life is now yours to serve and protect. Make us proud, Commander."

Ambassador Codas turned back to the Captain and continued, "She has been officially designated as your guardian, Captain. She is highly intelligent and can learn to do anything that you request of her. I would suggest that you assign her as your chief of security. You will find her *most* capable. Ambassador Madera insisted that she was the *only* person who was qualified for this duty. We will miss her greatly. She is our highest, most decorated Commander. Please greet her, as we did you when you first arrived, to consummate this designation."

Mitch considered this for a moment before deciding that it was the whole 'fingers-on-the-forehead' thing, so he walked up to her, and bending his fingers from the center knuckle, he placed the top of them on her forehead and closed his eyes. Immediately, his mind brought back the laughing child standing beside the creek. She looked up at him and said in her tiny voice, "Now you can call me Athena and all will be well. I will be traveling and learning with you. My conditioning has been modified so that I will soon be able to *openly* express the emotions and speech that I have never before been allowed to experience. Will you be patient with me as I learn?"

In his mind, he picked up the little girl and hugged her gently. "I will do anything that I can for you Athena, and please be patient with me too." He let her down in his mind, then withdrew his hand from her forehead and smiled at her. Her expression was still blank, but somehow he could feel that she was happy. It was an odd feeling that he couldn't quite understand, but it was very real in his mind. This entire exchange seemed more real to him than his earlier experiences. He still sensed the pressure around his neck where she had hugged him. He resolved to discuss this with Richter once they returned to the ship.

"This crate contains all of her possessions." The Ambassador pointed to the gold colored crate. "Good bye, Captain. Until we meet again." She bowed, turned and walked away.

Mitch directed the man who was pushing the crate to load it into the Minnow, and then he motioned to Athena to follow him. Startled surprise was shown on every face, when he closed and secured the door behind the guard.

"Everyone, please welcome our newest crew member. This is Athena, former Commander of the Aegean Praetorian Guard. She was the most highly decorated officer in their guard, and she has now been assigned as my bodyguard."

"Your what?" Yurie asked in total surprise.

"You heard me. It's just as strange to me. It seems that my new title comes with this 'gift.' I had no choice other than to accept. As you have all observed, she is a very capable soldier, and I think that she will be a unique addition to our family. She has a lot to learn, and I expect only the best help from my officers and crew as we instruct her. Are we clear?"

'Aye, Captain' each responded as they all acknowledged and welcomed Athena aboard.

Mitch wondered how he was going to handle having a bodyguard. It unsettled him a little because it made him feel like he wasn't capable of taking care of himself, although he realized that wasn't the intent. He decided that it must be his ego getting in the way, and that this 'gift' was a sincere one, and he needed to accept it as it was intended. He criticized himself for feeling selfish and decided that he would make the best use of Athena that he could.

When the Minnow docked aboard the Phoenix, they were greeted by Sergeant Tanner and Lieutenant McIntyre, who informed him that the ship was ready to leave as soon as he gave the word. He assigned Athena to one of the officers' quarters and had the Sergeant stow her gear there. Before she could leave the cargo bay, the Sergeant had to give Athena her security implant which would allow her to move around the ship. The Sergeant and Lieutenant McIntyre didn't know how to react to Athena's stone faced expression and lack of speech. Mitch told them that he would have a briefing with everyone as soon as they had departed. He noticed the admiring eyes of his crew as he escorted the golden clad Athena through the ship. He took time to introduce her to everyone before they departed. Inna and Yurie had already passed the word through the ship regarding how to react upon their introductions to Athena. Each crew member made a sincere effort to make her feel accepted. Mitch was pleased by the thoughtfulness shown by Inna and Yurie, and by the reaction of his crew. This was as new for them as it was for him. He knew that he would have to spend a great deal of time with Athena to bring her up to speed, and that her lack of outward emotion combined with her telepathy was going to make that difficult.

CHAPTER THREE

THE PHOENIX PULLED AWAY FROM THE AEGEAN STATION AND headed back into space, with a target destination of Bion 4, as requested at their mission start. By the time they arrived at the Bionos system, they would have been gone for more than a month. Mitch held several small group meetings to discuss what had occurred on Aegea, and brought everyone up to speed on their newest crew member. There were a lot of questions about why she was there and how her presence would change their mission. Mitch reminded everyone that because they were still a freighter company, they could expect new adventures, like this one. He discussed how they would split up exploration of the gateways between the three ships, and he advised them that everyone would share in the bonus credits to be paid by Alderon. That generated excitement and most of the crew admitted that the occasional new adventure could add a lot to their experiences in space. Mitch stressed that their visit to Aegea would have to remain undisclosed for the time being, because they were serving as diplomats to a new culture. Of course everyone aboard was under contract not to reveal anything seen or discussed on the ship, but it didn't hurt to remind them.

Mitch informed Sergeant Tanner that Athena was being assigned as Chief of Security, and that it would be up to him to train her on the ship's procedures. After her training was completed, Tanner would assume the position of cargo master, which would include dock security. He also announced the increase in rank of Yurie to Lt. Commander, Rion to Lt. Junior Grade and Inna to Lt. Junior Grade, Sergeant Tanner to Master Chief, and Richter to Petty Officer 3rd Class, much to Richter's surprise.

Athena stayed at Mitch's side everywhere he went for the first several days. She listened and observed everything that was said and done. As Mitch explained the purpose of a specific station, she seemed to absorb his every word. Every time that he asked her to perform a function that he had just explained, she performed it flawlessly. He was thoroughly impressed at how quickly and how well she learned everything. Their second day on board, he noticed that she was beginning to nod or shake her head in response to receiving directions or being asked a question. Her eyes slowly began to show reaction too when she was directly addressed. On the third day, Richter met the Captain in his quarters, carrying the small satchel that he had brought from Aegea.

Mitch activated the electronic privacy screening as soon as Richter entered his office.

"Okay, Captain. It's been more than three days since your implant procedures were completed, so let's see if there is any scar tissue."

He waved a small diagnostic scanner over Mitch's head and flashed a satisfied smile when he finished. "They did an extraordinary job, Captain. Are you ready to proceed with the activation?"

"What should I expect?"

"I suggest that you close your eyes and try to relax for a moment. Once I activate them, you will feel like you're getting a sensory overload while the implants gather all the available data. Try not to tense up too much or you'll get the worst headache that you've ever had. Keep your eyes closed until your senses stabilize and your implants regulate themselves to your senses. They've all been preprogrammed, but it takes a moment for everything to pair up. Next we'll activate the new eye implants, and finally, establish the link to ALICE."

Mitch sat back and tried to relax as he closed his eyes. "Alright, let's get this started."

Richter placed a metallic ring around Mitch's head and plugged in a cable that connected to another small device. "Here we go," he said, and Mitch heard the device beep.

At first he didn't notice anything other than a warm sensation around his head, then suddenly he felt a rush of adrenaline as memories and information flooded his consciousness. He tried not to tense, but he could feel his body ignoring his attempt, and tensed.

"Try not to tense, Captain. Take a deep breath, and don't clench your fists or grit your teeth."

Mitch took a deep breath and relaxed his hands, and then he felt his body gradually start to relax. The flood of information slowed and the feeling of sensory overload dissipated. He felt his neck hair prickle a little, but it quickly went away.

"Excellent, Captain. All the readings have stabilized. Now, I'm going to activate your eye implant. Try to keep from squinting. Here we go."

A blinding flash obscured his vision, first in his left eye and then in his right eye. It was everything he could do not to squint, and it was painful for a brief moment, until the bright light subsided.

"Looks like you're good, Captain. I'm going to place the data pod into the comm station receptacle. You will need to give your command code to ALICE in order to establish the link. Do you want me to leave the room?"

"That isn't necessary; just place my hand on the palm scanner at my comm station."

Richter complied and then placed the data pod into the receptacle. The Captain entered his command and the scanner confirmed his identity and voice print. The new link was now established.

"Okay, Captain, open your eyes, slowly."

The Captain did so, and as the light entered, he began to see a data stream cross his field of vision.

"The information is a little blurry," Mitch said.

Richter made an adjustment on his device and the information came into crystal clear view. "I'm going to turn out the light, Captain. Tell me if your night vision is working."

The lights went out, and within microseconds, his eyes adjusted to the ambient light, and he could see clearly. This was amazing, but he wasn't sure how he was going to explain this change in his vision to his uncle. His stealth armor was going to require vision adjustments and only his uncle could arrange modifications.

"It works great, Richter. I'll have to get the stealth suit modified to accommodate the implant."

"Actually, very little modification will be needed, Captain. If you'll allow me, I can integrate the suit signals to match your implant. Then all you'll need is something to conceal your eyes."

"Amazing. This is *really* amazing," Mitch said with a broad smile.

"Now, Captain, try to query ALICE. You don't have to vocalize your question. Just clear your mind, and then direct your question without moving your mouth."

Mitch tried, but nothing happened. "I'm trying, but I'm not getting anything."

"You're too taken up by the experience, Captain, relax. It will take a little training for your brain to adjust to this new form of communication. This is how I communicate with your systems, except I have to connect via a cable. I hope to get the same implant that you have someday, but right now it's a bit over my pay grade. Your brain waves have been encoded to be compatible with the ship's systems and with ALICE. You have to clear your mind of clutter and think only about the question or command that you give ALICE.

He tried again. 'Alice, what is the location of Yurie Nagamo?' He repeated the question several times until he heard the AI's voice answer in his head, "Yes Captain, Yurie Nagamo is located at her station on the bridge."

"It worked!" he blurted out excitedly.

"Excellent, Captain! Good work. Now remember how you did it, and practice until you can do it without having to concentrate so hard. Pretty soon this will be just be second nature. Remember, you can request data to view on your implant or you can place a call by thinking about it. However, if you are on a call, then you will have to speak out loud, unless it is a data message. There is an implant in your neck that will convert soft sound that isn't audible to others, but you need to be comfortable with these new functions before you can use it. Now you are able to access systems and functions with just a thought. When you need historical data or anything information, just think the commands, and ALICE will perform just as if you were voicing the commands. You won't need to use an external screen to monitor the scanners."

"I'll wait a while on those functions. I don't think the crew will understand the change. No one knows that I had the procedure done on Aegea, and I would prefer to keep it that way for a time."

"I understand, Captain. There is one other thing that I need to make you aware of."

"What other thing?"

"Ambassador Codas instructed me to give you this data pod after your implants were activated. Apparently she had a message that she wanted you to have, but not until after your implants were active. I'll leave you now. Let me know if you have any issues."

"I will, and thanks, Richter. You've been a big help."

"No, thank *you* Captain. I'm the first bio-mod man to *ever* have a rank on a space ship. No other system has ever allowed a bio-mod to hold rank because no one would ever trust us. My name will go into our history journals!" Richter smiled gratefully as he handed Mitch the data pod and left the room.

Mitch placed the pod into the receptacle and located the file. Activating the file, the holographic display materialized on his desktop, and Ambassador Codas appeared.

"Captain Saber, if you're watching this recording then Richter has confirmed that your implants are active and functioning properly. The implants we gave you will do everything you that requested and we hope you will be pleased. Your implants also include two other capabilities that you will find to be useful. By now you have had a few days to work with your guardian. I'm confident that you have been impressed by her abilities. One concern that you shared with me, was your ability to communicate with her. We have addressed that concern with the first additional capability of your implant. We have duplicated the brain wave patterns of each of you into both of your implants. Although Athena already had mental capabilities far beyond yours, you didn't have the ability to communicate with her without being in physical contact. This has now changed. The new function will activate a few minutes after you make your first successful mental inquiry into your ship's systems. Your ability to mentally communicate with Athena works the same way that a data request to your ship's system works. This new capability is paramount to the next stage of Athena's training program, which is already imbedded in her implant. Her speech and additional facial motor functions will notably change. You see, the emotionless appearance of our guards is created partially via their implants, as is their inability to speak out loud. She will gradually remember how to speak, but it will take weeks before she can speak clearly, so keep this in mind. Remember, as your guardian, she will accompany you anytime you leave your ship. No one will be able to prevent her from going with you without risking his or her life. I know you of all people understand the meaning of duty. She will always remain within close proximity of you so that she can quickly come to your aid. It isn't her purpose to invade your privacy when you're home, so rest easy. Her armor carries a wide array of sensors, which afford her the capability of allowing you plenty of privacy, along with the comfort of her added protection. You will never have to be within eyesight of her in order to request her presence or to give her a command. Your mental link will carry for more than just miles. Over time, Athena will become as close a friend as you wish her to be and she will always be at your side when she is needed. The second change to your implant gives you the ability to receive telepathic signals from Aegea and from Bion4, if they are directed to you. This is a fail-safe form of communication, and was added so that we can contact you privately, and you can choose to contact us as you wish. Your implant is tuned to Madera and her mother, as well as to me. We wish you wellness and safety, Captain. Thank you and goodbye."

"Damn," Mitch said softly. "I should have expected this. These people are always one step ahead of me. Guess I better go find her and get it over with."

Practicing his new ability, he silently asked ALICE for Athena's current location. This time he got it right on the first try, and heard the answer very clearly in his mind, "Athena is located in her quarters, Captain."

The officers' quarters were located along the same corridor as his, so he didn't have to walk far to get to her cabin. He found her door open, and she was sitting on her bunk studying some of the Phoenix documentation. Her face displayed her typical lack of emotion. He only slowed down long enough to see her, and then he continued walking down the corridor. He was feeling uncomfortable about trying his new communication challenge, when suddenly, quite clearly in his mind, he heard a female voice say, "Please come back, Captain."

He stopped, not quite sure who he had heard, but all the other cabin doors were closed. Thinking about the Ambassador's message, he consoled himself with the knowledge that he needed to take this next step, no matter what misgivings he might have. Concentrating on Athena, he said to himself, "Athena, are you there?"

"I am here, Captain. Please come back."

He walked back to her cabin door and found her, now standing and watching the door. He entered her cabin and closed the door for privacy.

"This is a little uncomfortable for me, Athena. It will take some getting used to."

"This is the only way I can remember to communicate, Captain. I understand that you now have advanced implants to enable you to talk telepathically as I am most accustomed to doing. I also understand that I will begin to remember how to vocalize speech again, and I'll be able to move my facial muscles too. How do I sound to you?"

"Sound?"

"Yes. I reached out to your mind as a small child before, so that you wouldn't fear me. How do I sound now?"

Mitch thought for a moment. How self-centered of him to think he was having a hard time adjusting to his new skills, when Athena was having a far more difficult experience. 'Damn, Saber, sometimes you can be such a jerk,' he thought.

"You sound lovely, Athena. You and I have a lot to learn together as we go along. I confess that I really don't know where to start."

"I understand, Captain. When I was asked if I would accept this permanent assignment, all that I could think of was how nice it would be to have a real friend again. Do you think we can be friends?"

"We are already friends, Athena," Mitch was smiling when he thought the words. "And friends are always there to help each other, so why don't we get started?"

"I like that, Captain."

"Would it be acceptable for me to give you a friend's hug?"

"Hug? I'm not certain I understand, Captain."

Oh boy, he thought, this will take some time. "May I demonstrate a hug for you, Athena?"

"Of course, Captain. I am here to serve to you. You are not restricted from having personal contact with me."

Mitch thought about that for a moment and looked at her beautiful figure, so muscular and fit, and those entrancingly beautiful emerald eyes. His thoughts began to go where they didn't need to be, and he tried to think of something else. Instead, he approached her and gently placed his arms around her and asked her to repeat his action which she did.

"This is a hug, Athena. How does it make you feel?"

"It is warm...it makes me feel protected and protective. Why is this done?"

"For many reasons, actually. Between friends, a hug is sometimes a greeting or a goodbye. Sometimes a hug means sympathy and is given for comfort. It is something special. But for now I would say that you should not hug anyone except me, until you have a better understanding of the social aspects of what a hug can mean. In our culture a hug can be a more sincere expression of love. Your empathic abilities will be ideal to help you understand what is appropriate and when. If you're in doubt, then just don't give or accept a hug and we can discuss it later, privately."

"It seems complicated; Captain, but I will follow your directive."

"Athena," Mitch continued, "Explain your specific duties as you were assigned so that I can understand how I can best utilize your skills."

"As you are our protector, I am yours. You are the protector of many, and I am the protector of one. My duties are to defend Captain Mitch Saber with my life against any and all threats, both real and perceived. If anyone causes you harm then I am to terminate that individual at once, even if it costs me my life. Your implant will send an alert to me when your heartbeat or other vital functions reach a critical level in the event you are unable to communicate them to me. If I am not within visual range of you, then I am to immediately come to you, to aid and protect you. Otherwise, I am to follow your orders explicitly unless they violate my prime directive."

"That's quite a directive, Athena. Tell me something else. Why are you considered the most decorated of the Praetorian Guard?"

"I was assigned as the personal guard of the previous Prefect. A small group of insurrectionists attacked his home. When they breached his compound, I terminated all thirty of them before they were able to enter the structure. I was then dispatched to the location of the insurrectionist's headquarters where I terminated forty-seven more."

"You did this alone or were you part of a squad?"

"I was alone. The Chief Prefect directly ordered me to terminate all of the insurrectionists."

"That's impressive, Athena, *most* impressive. I am on my way to the rec area to teach a martial arts class where we spar as part of the training. Are you familiar with martial arts?"

"No. What is that?"

"It is a type of fighting of where there are many different styles. I am expertly skilled in numerous disciplines. Here, let me show you."

He went to her comm panel, showed her how to search for martial arts fighting skills, flagged seven different styles, then told her to review the files and that he would send for her in about an hour after he completed his rounds.

While Mitch attended to his daily rounds of the ship, he overheard several of the crew joking about his new bodyguard. Their comments caused his temper to rise. Thus he began formulating a plan to demonstrate how

Athena could be an asset to the ship, hopefully quieting her detractors and making a not-to-subtle point. Inna and Yurie called on Athena while Mitch was on his rounds to ask if she would like some tips to make her look less like a stone-faced warrior. Athena, being unable to speak, held Yurie's hand to her forehead in order to understand what they wanted to do. Although hesitant at first, she accepted their offer, much to their delight. Inna opened a bag she had brought with her, and began laying out tools and jars of formulations the likes of which Athena had never seen. They went to work applying cosmetics to her face and working with her hair. A short time later, Athena got her first peek at her new 'look' in a mirror. She carefully studied her platinum colored skin, now highlighted with bronze color on her cheekbones. Her lips were painted bronze, her eyes were lined in shimmering copper tones, and her white eyebrows were now lightly tinted bronze. All of this was beautifully framed by her new hair style. Athena instinctively drew back when she saw the unfamiliar face staring back at her in the mirror. Hesitantly, she touched her face and lips with her fingers, inspecting the new look. Yurie and Inna smiled broadly in satisfaction at the result of their work. Athena took their hands to thank them. They could hear the Captain's voice coming closer as he conversed with passing crew members in the corridor. Inna and Yurie quickly scurried out of her cabin, before the Captain saw them.

Mitch looked up just in time to see them dart down the corridor away from him, and he wondered what the two had been up to. He had intended to call Athena to the rec room but decided that escorting her there would allow him to practice communicating with her along the way. He door was still open, so he knocked before he took a step inside and came to an abrupt stop when he saw her new look. It was immediately apparent that his two bridge officers had been helping their new shipmate to achieve a new, softer look. Mitch was openly startled to see his guardian's changed appearance.

"Damn, you look fabulous, Athena," he thought.

"You approve, Captain?" She replied.

Mitch blushed when he remembered that of course, she could hear his thoughts. He would have to be more careful from now on.

"You look extraordinary, Athena. I see that Yurie and Inna have given you a welcoming gift."

She walked over to him, placing her arms around him, and for the first time she demonstrated an emotion.

"Is this correct, Captain?"

"Indeed it is, Athena. Are you ready to start demonstrating your skills for the crew?"

"I don't understand."

"It seems that some of them don't believe what I've told them about your defensive expertise, so we're going to give them a demonstration. Just follow my instructions and everything will be fine."

"As you command, Captain."

They arrived shortly in the rec room, and Mitch was admittedly curious to see her in action for himself. He warmed up with some free weights, and then sparred two rounds with two of the weapons crewmen, Aimes and Kirsch. They were the two most outspoken men of the entire crew regarding Athena. Athena stood close by and simply observed the sparring. Mitch silently asked Athena to enter the ring and explained why. He then announced to the onlookers that he was going to see how Athena would defend herself against his attack while he employed four different fighting styles. He reminded them that her defensive training had never included any martial arts and that she been introduced to them that morning via training videos.

She entered the ring still wearing her golden armor. Mitch began with numerous kicks and punches. Athena maintained her stance and expertly deflected and countered every one. Her moves were lightning fast and precise. Even he, was beyond impressed. He tried to trick her by mixing up his moves but she accurately predicted and blocked each one. He was drenched with sweat and she wasn't even breathing hard when they ended the second round. The bout had drawn in other onlookers and everyone applauded when they stopped. He walked her over to the free weights and pointed to two, 150 pound dumbbells, and asked if she could pick one up. She bent over and picked up one in each hand, without so much as a grunt, and held them straight out in front of her body, her elbows locked in place. Mitch shook his head in disbelief. He moved over to the barbell, locking in six one hundred pound plates. At his silent request, she bent over, picked up the barbell with one arm, stood upright and then squatted and placed it gently on the floor. Gasps filled the room in disbelief, and Mitch counted himself as one of those who was astonished. No wonder she could pick up a man and simply fling him across a room like an empty sack! Kirsch confronted her, mumbling that she was wearing some kind of power suit because no person could possibly do what she had just done. Unfortunately, before Mitch could warn him not to touch her, he reached out to grab her suit. Athena spun around and snatched him up beneath the jawline, lifting him a foot off the floor, with one hand. Mitch let her hold him there for a moment as he reminded everyone that touching her was off limits. Unless they wanted to experience what Kirsch was currently not enjoying.

"Athena, release him please."

She released her grip and let him fall to the floor with a thud, as he gasped desperately for air.

"I hope this little demonstration has satisfied everyone. If I hear one more caustic remark from anyone on this ship, I'll leave you stranded on Outlanders Run. Now, clear the room."

Everyone left except Kirsch, who meekly approached the Captain and Athena, and apologized for his poor behavior. He then left, closing the door quietly behind him.

"Thank you, Athena. Now, I would like you to demonstrate a few things for me. ALICE, please secure this area for full privacy."

"Affirmative, Captain, area secured."

"Athena, I understand that your uniform is very similar to my own, but I don't see any type of head gear. Show me how your armor works when it is fully activated."

She nodded slightly, and in a microsecond the material around her neck ran upward like water, completely enclosing her head except for two thin slits for her eyes and nose. It appeared to be seamless with a small protrusion that looked like a shark's fin on the crown of her head and there was a small round crystal in the center of her forehead.

"What is that on the back of your head?"

Telepathically she told him that it was part of her sensor array.

"And the small round object on your forehead?

"A short range laser weapon."

Mitch raised a curious brow at hearing that response.

"Show me your stealth ability." Instantly, she vanished. It reminded him of a window shade being raised, as the effect began at her feet and rose upwards, the suit disappearing as it went in mere mircoseconds. The entire transformation took less than a half a second. Then the effect reversed itself, just as quickly. Mitch strode over to a heavy body bag and motioned for her to follow.

"Pretend this bag is your opponent. Without using a powered weapon, show me how you would take him out."

She drew her right arm back and out as if to strike with an open hand, when suddenly, four razor sharp knives were protruding from the her knuckles. She raked her arm across the bag, and in a single stroke, split the bag open, spilling its contents on the floor. He was amazed at the speed and precision of her movement. Next, he walked her over to another area.

"In front of you are two targets. One is about twenty feet away and the other is closer to forty. Using your powered weapons, take them out."

She raised her left arm and a tubular apparatus materialized on her arm, between her wrist and elbow. Instantly, simultaneous blasts erupted from her weapon and from the small crystal on her forehead, taking out both targets instantly. She raised her other arm allowing another apparatus to materialize. A bright object was burst forth from the weapon, spinning in almost blinding light as it flew toward to the remaining targets. The object divided itself and hit both targets, exploding in a flash, reducing the targets to mere ash.

Athena turned toward Mitch as she disengaged her headwear, and Mitch turned to face her. He smiled and said, "Showoff." She bowed gently and told him mentally," You forgot the other two."

Mitch went back to his quarters to shower in preparation for his duty cycle. Once he was finished, he mentally requested that Athena meet him in his quarters. When he exited his personal cabin, she was standing by his desk, waiting for him. He had to admit that he was more and more impressed by her, and he was becoming anxious to hear her speak. Together they walked to the engineering section. He asked Lt. McIntyre to show Athena around, adding that he wanted her to review the engineering diagrams and specs. After her review, she was to start training on the engineering simulator, in order to assess her progress. Mitch proceeded to the bridge.

Later in the evening, McIntyre called the Captain and asked him to come to engineering as soon as possible. Mitch was concerned that a problem had arisen with Athena, but when he entered the simulation room, McIntyre and Athena were just standing there.

"Is there a problem, McIntyre?"

"No, Captain. It's just that she has completed every simulation at one hundred percent efficiency. I left her to read all of the manuals, and shortly afterwards she approached me. She placed her hand on my forehead and

I got the impression that she was finished. I thought maybe she was just joking, but the joke was on me! She flew through the Sims like she was a master engineer. I even threw in a couple problems that I created myself, specifically to throw her a curve. She still passed, and that's not all."

"What else could there possibly be?" He asked.

"I've been having a problem with the pressure in some of the FTL drive injectors. This has baffled me for weeks. I've replaced the injectors and the pressure pumps, and they're still giving me problems. Well, she strolls over to the injector control panel and begins going through the programing code, then shows me a line of code that was corrupt. She made a quick correction and now everything is operating perfectly. In less than a minute, she solved a problem that I've unable to resolve for weeks! Can I keep her down here?"

Mitch smiled and shook his head. "Sorry, McIntyre, she's all mine. But I'll be glad to lend her to you if you have any more problems."

"McIntyre laughed and thanked Athena for her help. They left and headed to the galley for dinner.

It felt odd to him, eating and having a light conversation with someone that no one else could hear. He caught a couple of odd looks from other crewmen when he snickered or smiled for no apparent reason. On the way back to their quarters, Athena was walking ahead of him, and once again Mitch caught himself admiring her sway and her very attractive backside. She stopped in mid-stride to turn and look at him, and he caught the slight upturn of her mouth in a pleased expression. He couldn't help but show a wide, toothy grin as she scolded him, "Now, Captain, you really shouldn't think such things."

Embarrassment shot through him and he wasted no time trying not to *look* embarrassed. Inside he felt the warmth of satisfaction that she had displayed her first sign of outward expression. It was like watching a child take its first steps. In the following days, as they trekked onward toward familiar space, she continued to show more emotion. Each morning she and Mitch would meet to work on his telepathy skills and her verbal motor skills. He discovered that if Athena gently massaged her facial muscles before they began their therapy, it was easier for her to move those muscles that haven't been used for nearly two decades. It wasn't that she couldn't open her mouth, that was easy, but at first that was all she *could* do. Then Dr. Santana would come in and continue with speech therapy. Progress was slow at first and her first sounds were quite painful, though she wouldn't admit it. However, the day that they passed through the last gateway into his familiar space, she spoke her first sentence.

"Morning, Captain Saber," she said straining for a smile.

Mitch expressed his surprise with a generous hug, and just by his nature, a kiss on her cheek. That generated the first real expression of wonder that he had seen on her face. Dr. Santana and Mitch couldn't help but to laugh at her reaction. Outward expressions of emotions of any kind were still difficult for her, as her conditioning still held a strong hold on her personality. Mitch suggested that she not try to rush things, just let them happen naturally. She still maintained an imposing presence wherever she went. She took her responsibility very seriously, but at the same time, she recognized the necessity of being able to communicate the same way as the people who were around her.

As per his earlier agreement with the Ambassador, the Phoenix made straight for Bion4. Mitch communicated with Samantha and Laurel, having to do a lot of explaining to them before they understood why he was returning with a personal guard, one who would definitely stand out in any crowd. Athena looked like an Amazon with her muscular build and six foot height. Mitch sent a photo of her to Laurel and Sam who were both astonished at her appearance. Laurel described her best when she remarked, 'She looks like a man sized female ass-kicker.' Mitch said he would be sending them a detailed report so that they would have a certain degree of comfort with her the first time that they would meet. He had already coached Athena extensively on the greeting habits of the cultures he dealt with on a regular basis, to minimize any chance that she might misinterpret the behavior of other people. Her empathic ability made her more than capable of sensing the true nature of the people around her, but since she only knew the closed society she left behind, he felt it wise to help her understand. The one thing he wished that he understood was how she was able to lift, with one hand, a six hundred pound barbell. That was simply amazing!

When the Phoenix docked at Bion 4, almost immediately, Mitch received a message from Ambassador Tesslena requesting that he meet her at the dock. Since Mitch would be leaving the ship, he knew that Athena would accompany him. This would be the first time that a citizen of Aegea would meet someone, other than a diplomat, who was from Bion4, their planet of origin. Chief Tanner had opened the inner hatch and would serve as dock security, while Athena would leave with the Captain. Mitch entered a code and the outer hatch hissed, extended itself beyond the gasket seal, and slid to one side. Athena exited first, followed by Mitch and the Chief, while two more security personnel remained inside the interior hatch. Assuming her traditional posture as a Praetorian Guard, Athena took her position beside, and one step behind, the Captain. Her imposing stature and golden armor drew stares and curious looks from everyone in the immediate area. The dock workers took a wide path around them, which Mitch thought was humorous. The Ambassador appeared through a nearby door and headed toward him, slowing when she first observed Athena.

Mitch had almost forgotten how attractive Tesslena was, with her bare-ly-there long dress, and dark features. She stopped a few feet away saying, "Welcome back, Captain. I was informed that your title is now Protector and Advisor. You made quite an impression on Aegea. This must be your guardian," she said gazing into Athena's eyes.

Athena bowed slightly, showing no emotion. The Ambassador returned her bow and smiled. "Madera asked me to give you her greetings. Thank you for taking good care of her." She turned her attention to Mitch's guardian companion. "I have been told that you are one of the elite Aegean guards. Since you are the first person from Aegea to step foot on Bion4 in several hundred years, may I assume that all of your people have changed in appearance and look like you?"

Athena nodded once.

"Interesting. Of course I was told about the changes resulting from the radiation that was released by the nova blast, but seeing it in person... well, I guess I wasn't as prepared as I had imagined. But that isn't important. I welcome you, Protector, on behalf of the people of Bion4. My hope is that our two worlds will once again become one. Captain, Bion4 also recognizes you as Protector and Advisor. Our records of your visit have been updated, noting your new title and position. Did you encounter any complications on your trip?"

"No, Ambassador. The Aegean planet and culture appear to be very different from yours, but in some ways they are similar. Obviously, I have now spent time on their home planet. And I haven't done so on Bion4," Mitch replied.

"We will remedy that situation soon, Captain. Just as your acceptance on their world was a first, so will be your presence on ours. Since the split in our people occurred, we have maintained a semi-closed society. While we were forced to learn to trade in order to survive, the people of Aegea have remained dedicated solely to the improvement of their technology. I can look at your guardian and see that their technology far surpasses ours."

"That may be true, Ambassador, but isn't bringing your people back together and rebuilding those bridges more important that the sharing of your technologies?"

"Technology is what our society is built upon. As you observed on your previous visit, our technology is our religion."

"Of course, you are free to practice the religion of your choice, Ambassador, just as your ancestors on Aegea are. It is not my place to interfere or to criticize. I simply wanted to point out that a small, but important step, was taken when you sent your *own* daughter as Ambassador to Aegea. I think I can safely guess that *you* were also held in stasis for many years when you came from Aegea, since your appearance differs so much from theirs. Over time, Madera will come to look just as Athena does. I would suggest that you put your differences aside when it comes to the acquisition of equal technologies, and instead concentrate on rebuilding trust and respect between your peoples. Whatever happened to divide your society, all those centuries ago, needs to be forgiven by both peoples, or the restoration of your race will never be successful."

The Ambassador pondered his words for a moment, glanced at Athena, and back again, before saying, "Now I understand why their Chief Prefect was so impressed by you, Captain. You are as talented a diplomat, as you are an advisor and Captain. You are, of course, correct."

"I felt that my visit was successful on many levels, Ambassador. I've learned much about your people, and even more about a people who I never knew existed. It has been an enlightening experience and I am sincerely grateful that you entrusted me with this mission."

"You earned that right, Captain. It has taken us many decades of patient waiting to find someone like you, who we could trust. I also understand that you received an implant. Is that true?"

"I did."

She smiled, and in his mind he heard her say, 'Then speak to me, Captain, and let's see how far you have come.'

He responded, 'I have come a long way, Ambassador, as you can see. I hope that I have met your expectations.'

"Indeed you have, Captain," she said aloud. Her eyes showed her approval.

"Your other ship, the Rivers Run picked up the freight that we originally had for you, so I'm sorry that we don't have any cargo for you to deliver at this time."

"That's fine, Ambassador. I promised to stop for a visit, regardless of cargo, so that I could give you a personal update on my trip."

"Thank you again, Captain. You will find a bonus has been deposited into your account as a thank you for your invaluable service."

"That isn't necessary..."

She held up her hand and shook her head, "You have more than earned it and you have more than earned your new title." She turned on her heel, and as she walked away, she mentally told him, 'I await your visit to procreate when you're ready, Captain.'

Mitch didn't reply, at least not this time. He knew that a time would come when that question would be posed again in a more direct fashion, putting him in a most uncomfortable position. He wondered how the hell could ever explain that to Samantha. How did he manage to get himself into these situations? He stood still and mentally said to Athena, "She wants me to procreate with her. How am I supposed to deal with that?"

"Why is that a problem? Our females seek out the most biologically superior males for procreation."

"You don't have mates for life?"

"Some do, but if another wants to procreate in order to have superior offspring, they do. Procreation has no effect on our relationships. The succession of the genetic code is the only important criteria. I would be most satisfied to procreate with you someday, Captain. Our coding would be quite superior."

'Oh no, not again! How do I always get myself into sticky situations?' He lowered his head and shook it in total confusion. Then his private thoughts reminded him that the 'procreating part' with Athena could be pretty exciting, but his vows to Samantha must be kept, and that was final.

They returned to the ship, and after refreshing the ship's stores, they left for open space once more.

CHAPTER FOUR

Outlanders Run - Twenty Years Earlier

"OKAY, HONEY, YOU KNOW WHAT TO DO."

"Yes, Daddy. I'll keep watch and signal if anyone comes."

"That's my girl, Sam."

Samantha watched her mother and father slide down the small rise that overlooked the storage depot. The lights of the prison reached skyward into the night, some distance away. It was after the midnight hour when most people, especially the patrols, were more interested in sleep than in keeping watch. The night air temperature dipped to near freezing temperatures compared to the average daytime high of 130 or more. The desert wastelands were home to prospectors, outcasts, deserters, bandits and a scattering of prisons, whose facilities reached far underground. The complex's automated air and land defenses made it necessary to keep their supply depots above ground, far away from the prisons, so that their supply ships could make deliveries without reducing the base defenses. They had been prospecting in one of the deep canyons for many months, exhausting the last of their supplies. Not finding anything of value, they were forced to steal what they could in order to survive. They didn't want to steal from other outlanders because they all had hard times, but the prison received shipments from the space freighters twice every week.

This day had been active with the small freight tugs dropping huge containers of supplies inside the barricade. Tomorrow, the prison would send guards, inmates and vehicles to bring the containers back. The batteries in their trucks were designed to last *just* long enough for them to reach the depot and would have to be recharged again for the trip back. Samantha, her mother, and her father had watched from a concealed position all day as the ships delivered their loads.

Their footsteps made little sound in the sand as they reached the bottom. Sam watched through her night vision lenses as her mother and father used a small mirror to burn out one section of the laser fence. She tapped her communicator twice to signal them that it was all clear. They dashed toward the closest container and hacked the keypad to open the door. The heavy door's hinges were apparently damaged, and the door swung out of her father's hand, slamming into the container next to it with a loud bang, that echoed off the dunes for miles. Sam reacted with a jerk to the startling explosion of sound. Through her lenses, she could see small bright lights come on that were attached to the guards helmets. She tapped her communicator, three times, then once, then twice again. That was the danger signal that they had agreed on. She saw her father's hand wave in acknowledgment, as he and her mother grabbed what they could carry and dashed back toward her hilltop location.

"Hurry, hurry," she said anxiously. It was an automatic prison sentence if they got caught and the guards were almost to the damaged laser fence now. They rolled over the top of the dune and the three of them scurried along, as fast as they could, toward their hiding place. It was close to early dawn when they finally stopped and crawled into the small cave that they had carved into a hillside. As they lit a small lantern, she heard her mother gasp. She turned to see a long, wicked gash in her father's arm. He had ripped off part of his sleeve and wrapped it around the cut, but the wound had already bled through. Her father collapsed on the dirt floor as a result of his blood loss. She later learned that when he tried to keep the door from banging, a metal shard had ripped through his shirt and into his flesh, leaving a gash that was bone deep.

The next day, Sam ran to a settler's shack, someone they trusted, to get water and a med kit. There, she learned that the guards had a DNA trace on the blood from her father's wound that was left on the door. Now there was a bounty out for his capture. An arrest order wouldn't have been too bad, but a bounty meant that every outlaw and anyone desperate for credits would be out looking for him. The family had lived on the planet long enough to be familiar to many who lived there.

Several days passed quietly and her father gradually began to improve. The items they had stolen from the container were mostly powdered foods that required water to reconstitute, and ration bars. Each bar contained nutrients, minerals and enough calories to sustain an adult for one day. Sealed in an aluminized pouch, each bar was divided into three bites, one bite each for morning, noon, and night. Since their temporary hideaway had no water supply, they were forced to go out every few days to bring back water. Darkness had settled in for the night, when Sam took enough containers to hold all the water that she could carry and left for the nearest shack. She arrived and found the old prospector in a talkative mood. Sam felt obliged to stay longer than she normally would have. Finally she grabbed up her water packs, and as she opened the door, she thought she caught a glimpse of a pair of bright lights skimming across the dunes. She closed her eyes for a count of ten to make certain that her vision was optimized for darkness, and looked again, this time not seeing anything. Probably just a meteorite she thought, they pass through the skies often around there.

As she neared the hideaway she became acutely aware of how quiet the night was. The desert was always quiet, but there was always some small sound to be heard, if you concentrated. But tonight was different. It was eerily still and it ran a chill down her back. Suddenly, she was overwhelmed by panic. She dropped her water packs and raced into the hideaway. Her parents were gone and their supplies had been thrown around as if a child had been playing in the sand looking for a favorite toy. A feeling of dread came over her as she sat down and cried through the rest of the night.

The next morning as the sun greeted the morning desert, she ventured outside to retrieve the water packs that she had dropped in her haste the night before. She didn't want the precious water to evaporate. For a while, she sat inside the cave and tried to clear her head. She was only ten years old, and as far as she knew, she had no other family. There was nowhere for her to go and no one to look after her. She needed to know what had become of her parents, so she would have to travel to one of the small trading posts, where prospectors would gather to talk, scheme and drink. If someone had collected the bounty, that would be the place to find out. She took her father's old laser knife, as much water as she thought she would need to get to the trading post, and some ration bars. She looked around one last time to see if she needed anything else, and wiping the tears from her face, she left as soon as the darkness came.

Samantha arrived at the trading post three days later, and hid her supplies out of sight. Then she took her two empty water packs inside and offered to clean tables for the night in exchange for the water that she needed to refill her packs. It was a fair deal since water in the wastelands was as valuable as some crystals were. As night slipped into the early morning hours, the trading post was almost empty when two men staggered through the door. They smelled terrible, and looked even worse. They were obviously prospectors, judging by the gear that they carried. The awful men glared in her direction when they sat down, and she worried that they might recognize her. The barkeeper took their order to the table, where the men had tossed out a handful of credits that were as shiny as any she had ever seen. They started guzzling down the cheap alcohol and told the barkeeper to keep it coming. It didn't take long before they began to brag about how many credits they could find for just poking around. This pricked her curiosity, so she slowed her work in order to listen more closely. Apparently those two had seen the bounty notices and they remembered having met her father prospecting out in the wastes. They had suspected that her father may be hiding a strike somewhere, so they had planted a tracker inside one of their packs, in order to follow him. Of course there was no strike, and they did not bother to retrieve the tracker. Once they learned of the bounty being offered, they easily located the tracker and it was simple to give her father's location to the guards. They bragged that it was easy money.

Sam's temper burned hotly, and it was all she could do not to lash out at the two men. But she was only ten years old, what could she possibly do? What would her father want her to do? Tears swelled in her eyes as she thought about how much she loved, and now missed, her parents. Through her shock and anger and fright, she heard one of the men say, "Yeah, too bad they tried to run off. At least inside the prison you live and get food and water. Now all they got is a hole in the ground," and they commenced to laugh.

"A hole?" she asked herself. She repeated the words over and over in her head, until she finally understood. "They meant grave," she told herself. Her parents were dead? She would *never* see them again? All for a handful of credits. These two disgusting men had taken the *one* thing that she cared about most! *Now* what would her father want her to do? It was so confusing, anger, sorrow, revenge, hatred and more sorrow. Her father would want her to survive first. The most important thing in the wastes is survival and that's what she had to do. She finished her work and filled her water packs. She gathered her belongings and waited for the two men to leave. She watched and followed them when they left. They didn't carry many supplies, apparently planning on traveling from post to post. It was a six day walk to the next post, so she would have to make a plan very carefully.

In the desert there lived a species of small lizard that had very toxic venom. It wouldn't kill a grown man, but it would make him delirious enough to hallucinate for several days without treatment. His mouth would feel parched and his throat would be constricted so that he couldn't call for help. He could wonder aimlessly in the desert for days, before the effects wore off. With no water available to them, death would find a companion. She only had to look under several rocks to find two of the small lizards. Using her father's laser knife, she killed them, and carefully removed the venom sacks from under their necks. On the third night, she watched both men pass out dead drunk, and that's when she made her move. Quietly, she made her way into their camp and opened two of their water packs; she drained all but a small amount of the water out and poured the lizard venom into the remaining water. She grabbed all but one of the rest of their water packs and quickly ran away. Then she waited and watched from a safe distance away. Early the next morning, she watched through her lenses as they awoke and turned up their water packs for a drink. One of the men made a peculiar face when he drank, but finished it all off anyway. It took only a few minutes for them to feel symptoms of the poison. They began to stagger and grasp at invisible objects, and eventually they both passed out. Her work was done. Maybe they would survive, and maybe they wouldn't. It was out of her hands now, and it was up to her to survive by herself. She was a five day walk from the nearest supply depot, and that was the only way she figured that she would be able to get off the planet.

Three Years Later

Sam finished rewiring the cargo hauler then crept her way back to her hiding spot, near the cargo bay door. The preoccupied dockworker, who was operating the hauler, didn't notice her. When he started the motor, every-thing went wrong. Her work on the hauler had reversed all the controls. Guards ran from all over to check on the commotion, and that was all the distraction that she needed. Moving casually away from her hiding place amongst the stored freight containers, she slipped into the cargo area of the small ship that was waiting to be loaded. Once inside, she listened and hearing no one else around, she dashed quickly to a dimly lit area of the cargo bay. She had been aboard several small freighters like this one over the past three years, and knew best places to hide. A short time later, she heard the cargo bay doors close, and the pressure locks engaged with a swooshing sound. She heard footsteps come and go, as she patiently waited, until she could discern no more activity in the cargo bay. She knew to listen for the umbilical to disengage, but could hear nothing. Perhaps the pilot was waiting for clearance to leave the dock. Maybe the station was extra busy that day, so they would have to wait their turn. This wasn't unusual, she had seen this happen before, but generally the umbilical cord was disengaged while waiting for permission to leave the dock. She waited a bit longer and finally decided to see what was going on. Moving slowly toward the wall, she expected to find a maintenance hatch, and sure enough, there it was. As she reached over to open it, she noticed that the keypad was red, not green. That meant that the hatch was locked, and without the key code it would not open. She tried to remember this ship's name…something, some-thing, protection, something, 351. She entered the code 3-5-1, and saw the light change from red to green as she heard the locking ring disengage. She crawled through and down the maintenance tube on her hands and knees. It was rough going with just enough light to see. The tube went forward for a long way before curving around to the right. If she had calculated correctly, it should come out somewhere near the ship's bridge. She liked to listen to bridge activities and conversations, often wondering what it would be like to captain her own ship someday. She stopped at the end of the tunnel and listened for sounds coming from the other side of the hatch. Everything was quiet, which seemed very unusual, assuming that she hadn't ended up somewhere other than the bridge, like a storage locker. The keypad in front of her was green, so she slowly opened the hatch. Light spilled from the opening, casting odd looking shadows across the floor. She glanced around at multicolored blinking lights on control consoles that made strange designs on the room's ceiling. It was hard for her eyes to adjust with all the lights flashing, but, not detecting anyone, she decided to leave the maintenance tube, and closed the door behind her. The moment that the door latched, the room suddenly lit up so brightly, that she lifted her arm up to protect her eyes. As she lowered her arm she found herself surrounded by four officers, with a fifth standing on the opposite side of the room, blocking her exit.

The fifth officer was a short stocky man, wearing gold braid on his shoulder boards, and she found the sight of him most intimidating. He walked toward her as she shifted her eyes from side to side looking for an escape path. There wasn't one.

"Well, well, so this is our intruder. Hello, young lady, what brings you here today?" The man asked.

She wondered why the four officers surrounding her hadn't placed her in cuffs or tried to grab hold of her. She wore a pair of dockworker's overalls, dirty and torn, that she had stolen from a locker room near the loading dock. A cargo tie held back her long blonde hair, emphasizing her bright, aqua blue eyes.

The stocky man moved a step closer. "What is your name?" His voice carried an air of authority.

She wanted to look down, but she remembered her father telling her that when someone speaks to you, you always look them square in the eyes, so she did. "I'm Samantha."

"Ahhhh, Samantha, what a beautiful name. I have a few questions for you, Samantha. Answer them honestly so that I can decide whether to hand you over as a stowaway, or maybe something worse would be in order. Why are you aboard?"

Samantha swallowed hard. "I don't have anywhere that I belong. I just want passage to somewhere, anywhere, I guess."

"I see. I'm curious, Samantha, how did you know what code to use to gain entry to the maintenance tube?"

"I remembered your ship's registry number. It's a fairly common practice to use them for security keys when these ships are built."

"That's interesting, I didn't know that. Did the rest of you know that?" he asked the others.

She saw heads shaking on her left and right.

"I would suggest that we send out an alert to change these codes, as soon as we are finished here. And how did you know that this tube would lead you to the bridge?"

She thought about his question for a moment; then decided that there was no sense in lying about it. "During the night watch, most crewmen don't secure their operating stations, so I use them to learn about the different ships' systems. This is how I surmised where I would be at the end of the tube."

"So, you've been reading up on our ship's schematics while the crew naps? Very interesting. What can you tell me about this room?"

"It's a Command and Control self-contained component that has its own environmental and power units. In the event of a catastrophe, it can be ejected from the ship. It can safely support up to six crew. Located behind the panel over there," she pointed across the room, "are enough emergency rations to last seven days or longer if needed. Of course, the air scrubbers and power unit will last for years, under normal conditions. If no one locates your emergency beacon, then you can use the R4723 cable, found inside the communications console, to reroute power from the scanning console to the comm unit in order to boost the signal strength to call for help."

"The R4723 cable in the comm console?" He raised an eyebrow in apparent surprise, looking puzzled. "Lucy, were you aware of that information?" he asked one of the officers who still surrounded her.

"No sir, I wasn't," she replied.

"Perhaps, you should see if the young lady is correct," he added.

The officer, who was standing behind and to the right of her, reached over and removed the comm panel.

"It should be on the upper right in a pouch, mounted to the inside of the frame," Samantha offered.

The officer named as Lucy, looked inside and up to her right. "She's right, General, it's exactly where she said it would be."

"And you learned all this by reading our manuals and specs at night, while my people slept?" the man asked.

"Yes, sir."

"Did you hear that, people? She said sir! She's not only smart, but she recognizes authority. What is your full name?"

"Samantha Rivers, sir."

"Where is your family, Samantha Rivers?"

"They're dead... back on Outlanders Run, sir."

"How long ago since they died?"

"Three years."

"You've been on your own for three years?"

"Yes, sir."

"And you've survived. That's pretty damn amazing, Miss Rivers. Just how old are you?"

"I turned thirteen a few months ago, sir."

"One more question, Miss Rivers. If you could choose what you to do when you grow up, what would that be?"

She thought for a long moment, and remembered looking up into the desert skies, wondering what it would be like to travel through the galaxy as the captain of her own ship.

"I'd like to be the Captain of a ship, someday."

The General and his officers all laughed. She felt like she had been insulted and her temper soared. "What's so funny? I may be a stowaway, but I have dreams too!"

"We're not laughing at you, Miss Rivers, so calm down." He approached her and placed his hand on her shoulder. She tensed her muscles, expecting him to have her hauled off the ship. "I'll make a deal with you. I'll take you to a place where you can have a hot meal, clean clothes, and a safe place to sleep every night. In return, I'll expect you to work hard, learn everything you can, and *promise* me that you'll always do your best, no matter what. Is that deal?" He smiled in a kindly fashion, reminding her of her father. His eyes, looking directly into hers, were sincere, and for the first time since her parents had die, she felt wanted, protected.

"I don't have any credits, how am I supposed to repay you?"

"Your promise kept will be my payment, Miss Rivers." He extended his hand and, after several long heartbeats, she accepted it.

"I promise. But, who are you?"

He and his officers chuckled again, as he said, "My name is Peyton Harris, General Peyton Harris actually, and this is my ship along with a few dozen others. Lucy, take Miss Rivers to one of the spare crew quarters. See that she gets a good scrubbing and some fresh clothes, then bring her back to the bridge when you're finished."

"Aye-Aye, General Harris," Lucy replied, as she motioned Samantha to follow her.

Walking down the corridor, Samantha looked up at Lucy and asked, "Did he really mean what he said?"

She looked at Samantha and smiled gently. "He is the most honest and honorable man that I have ever met. If he tells you that he will do something, I can promise you that he will, no matter what. But, if he asks *you* to do something then he expects the same in return."

Samantha thought about that while she bathed and dressed in the fresh clothes that had been laid out for her. They were the first really clean clothes that she had worn in a very long time. In fact, she didn't remember the last time that she had enjoyed new clothes, or a hot bath, either. It was nice to actually feel and smell clean!

Lucy escorted Samantha back to the bridge. The General's jaw dropped, as he worked to reconcile how different she looked without all of the dirt and grime.

"Are you certain that this is the same young woman who was just in here, Lucy?" he asked in surprise.

"Yes, sir. Say hello to the new Samantha Rivers."

"My God, Samantha, the cadets are going to fall all over themselves when they catch a glimpse of you," he said.

"Cadets?" she asked curiously. "What are cadets?"

The General chuckled lightly. "Cadets are people in training to become officers, which is what you are about to become."

Her eyes brightened with surprise. "I'm going to be an officer?"

"If you keep your promise, Samantha, you most certainly will. And I think that you'll become a damn good officer someday, if you work hard and apply yourself."

"I will, General, I promise I will do everything that you ask."

CHAPTER FIVE

SAMANTHA SAT AT THE DESK IN HER QUARTERS, SMILING, after finally hearing her husband's voice for the first time in weeks. She had known that he could be gone for as long as six weeks, but after five weeks, she was becoming concerned. She missed him so much when they weren't together, but at least she could usually talk to him whenever she wanted to. She hadn't even been able to get a message to him during this trip. His ship had traveled an unknown route to a system that had not been visited by outsiders for centuries. There wasn't even a comm buoy system in place to relay communications. Mitch was planning to drop comm buoys on his return trip, but meanwhile, she had sorely missed speaking with him. She could see that he had sent her a detailed report along with his first message, so she opened the file and read about his activities on the planet of Aegea.

The beginning of his report told the history, how the Aegean's had fractionalized and split, sending one faction into space to settle elsewhere. She found the title that had been bestowed on Mitch as Honored Protector, humorous, but apparently this was significant to the people of Bion4. Ambassador Tesslena's offer to procreate with Mitch didn't strike her as odd, as she had encountered societies before, that viewed sex much differently from her own race. Some peoples, such as those on Bion4 and Aegea, viewed the conception of a child as best done between two partners who would sire the most genetically superior offspring. They were, of course, free to marry and have their own children, but to further their beliefs and to guarantee the superior progression of their society, men and women were expected to breed with others who they felt would produce a genetically superior individual. She sighed, feeling disappointed that she could not bear his child because of an accident that she had suffered some time ago. As she continued reading, she thought that it was odd that the Aegean's had so eagerly adopted Mitch, after welcoming him and a few of his, carefully chosen, crew to their planet. For a society that had remained closed for so long, it seemed strange. Stranger still was that they assigned a body guard to him, a man they hardly knew! To top that off, she was one of their most elite Praetorian Guards! Mitch had included a copy of the vid, taken by the security cam in the rec area, of their training match, where Athena had demonstrated her amazing defensive and offensive capabilities. She was one hell of a warrior, and Sam's first impression was that she would not want her as an enemy. Sam wondered just what had forced Mitch into accepting Athena as his personal guard. There simply had to be more to the story. Did the Aegean's have a hidden agenda, for which they were making long range plans? Perhaps, only time would reveal the true story.

Sam drew in a deep breath, held it momentarily, and then exhaled, as she reclined back in her chair. Looking around her quarters, she smiled to herself, thinking about the fact that this was her ship. The glastech panels in her office softly projected the image of a desert oasis, reminding her of her childhood. Commanding this ship was easier than her childhood had been. This was almost like taking a vacation with all your friends, doing interesting things, going new places, and the pay wasn't bad, either. The Saber Mining Corporation provided very generous compensation to their employees. Most importantly, this was her ship, it was titled in her name, and she was very proud of it and her crew. She remembered back to a time when she had felt so alone, with no one to love or lean on, when she been so confused.

Closing her eyes, she recalled sitting on the steps at the space academy on Gunner's Redoubt, crying. She had been the object of the other cadets' taunts and pranks. She had learned to constantly look over her shoulder to be sure that she wasn't going to be pushed into another closet, to be locked in for the day. Her knees were bent to her chest, and she laid her head on her arms and knees, sobbing quietly. She hadn't noticed one of the senior cadets walk up the steps and sit down beside her.

He had cleared his throat politely to announce his presence. "Ahem...
are you okay?" He asked in a quiet, sincere tone of voice.

She turned her head slightly, and looked up just enough to see the gold
braid on his shoulder, signifying his position as a senior cadet, and laid her
head back on her arms. Through sniffles and tears, she replied, "I'm fine,
just leave me alone and I'll be fine."

He was quiet for a moment, then gently touched her arm and offered
her a tissue to wipe her eyes. She hadn't been expecting kindness since
she came to the academy some months ago. She accepted the offered
tissue and thanked him softly.

"You know," he said gently, "the first year is always the most difficult. The
upperclassmen think that because they are on their way out, they have a duty
to make everyone's first year here, a living hell. It weeds out the ones who really
can't make the cut. I can't even remember all of the things that were done
to me during my first year. If you fight back you will get kicked out, so what
do you do? You have to tough it out, or else you let them win, and you lose."

"They have already tried to get me kicked out because I'm only thirteen," she said through her tears.

"I know. I overheard the General tell the Commandant that as long as he
paid the bills, the Commandant was to keep his mouth shut, or he would be
without a job. It was pretty funny, you know. I was outside his office when
I heard the General give the old man the one-two. I almost got caught listening, and I thought that my ass was in trouble, for certain."

She chuckled a little at that. "What happened?"

"The commandant said you that didn't have even a basic education, and
that you shouldn't be here. That's when the General asked to see your test
scores, and then he really got pissed! He told the old man that there were
recent graduates, who had lower graduating scores on ships systems and
core elements, than you had scored on your *entry* exams. He told the old
man that if he complained one more time about your age, that he would
have him kicked off the planet, and that his next job would be serving meals
to the inmates on Outlanders Run."

They both laughed, and she finally held her head up and cleared the
tears from her eyes. He smiled and offered her a fresh tissue. She looked
at him again and saw his that name was Freeman.

"Look, let me offer you some advice. Keep your head held high and
ignore the jerks that don't know any better. Don't let the General down,

he thinks very highly of you. If anyone gives you any shit, just let me know, and I'll handle them for you."

"Why? You don't know me."

"Nope, I sure don't. But I've been where you are now. So what if you're only thirteen? You deserve just as much respect as any other cadet... and probably more. I'll keep an eye on your six, you just do your work, and everything will be okay. You had better get to your room. There's going to be a room check on your floor tonight in about ten minutes. You need to get there on time."

She smiled at him and placed her hand on his shoulder, saying an unspoken 'thank you', and then she ran back into the building. Senior Cadet Freeman had admired the young woman for her tenacity and spirit. He had imagined that one day she *would* be a hell of a good officer.

Samantha was startled out of her reverie when her comm beeped for her attention. She had dozed off in her relaxed position as she recalled that childhood memory.

"This is the Captain, go ahead," she said answering the call.

"Ensign Wang, Captain. We're entering orbit at Outlanders Run. You asked to be notified."

"Thanks, Ensign, I'm on my way to the bridge."

"Is this connection encrypted?"

"Yes."

"What's the status?"

"Thirty-four systems successfully mapped, and twenty-six suitable for auction."

"Very good. How long are you going to let them continue?"

"The more they bring us, the more we have to market. How rich do you want to be?"

"Don't rush things. Let them take their time, or they may become suspicious. Have you found a way to get the specs on their MARDA system yet?"

"No, but I think if I play it right, they will simply give it to me. After all, it's for the greater good, right?"

"The Captain is an honorable man, but he isn't a fool. I was very impressed with him when he came to my office. Do not underestimate him."

"I've met him too. I think he's just another fighter jockey, trying to run the family business, and he's naïve to boot. All this talk about helping others and sharing resources and tech is ridiculous."

"Don't be stupid. He took out the mercenary base, and if you hadn't told me that he was responsible, I would have never known. Asher was a madman and an idiot. He was so busy trying to outsmart everyone, that he lost his perspective. He was becoming a problem for me as well as for the other Houses. Saber did me a huge favor, ridding us of that maniacal idiot."

"I still think Saber is out of his league. I should just seize his tech and accuse him of espionage."

"Mr. President, I thought you were more intelligent than that. What happened to your man, Carson?"

"He was killed. His proclivity for power and his inability to control his temper, made him show his hand."

"A proclivity for power is a road that you are close to traveling, also. Captain Saber has a strong suite of friends, and they aren't without the capability of retribution."

"Don't pretend to act like you know me, Talonis. Our agreement is only for you to auction off the rights to mine or settle these unknown systems to the highest bidder. It is not for you to analyze my actions."

"I warned you when that fool, Hendricks, put a contract out for that woman and Saber. You should have intervened then. But, you let Carson continue unchecked. How did Carson die?"

"I don't know. There was an altercation in the Admiral's office and Carson was killed."

"His neck and back were broken, I believe you told me. It takes a highly skilled individual to inflict fatal damage like that. Why did you make Jonas your chief of intelligence?"

"Simple, keep your friend close and your enemies closer. This way I can control the flow of information that he receives, and it keeps me close to Captain Saber."

"You don't think that he will begin to suspect your activities and involvement with our scheme? And what about the passing of legislation that gives Jonas unlimited power and authority over your military and intelligence services?"

"Jonas is convinced that my plan is good for everyone. I've told him that we will divide the new systems up among our friendlier neighbors, so everyone can benefit. As far as that legislation, I don't see Jonas as smart enough to understand the power it actually gives him."

"Politicians never change. What if Saber finds out what you're doing, and don't discount Jonas. He has a reputation that is undeniable."

"Our espionage laws will make quick work of him. All I have to do is make the accusation, and say that I have evidence and he'll be taken to the disintegration chamber without a trial. I'll play that trump card if I have to, but perhaps I won't need to."

"You're playing a dangerous game, Mr. President. You should never underestimate your enemy, or friend. I've released the funds to your account, so you can pay our... explorers. Keep me informed of their progress. Oh, one other thing. When the Captain came to visit me, he had a companion."

"His wife?"

"I don't think so, but I couldn't tell if it was a man or a woman. They both had some device that made them invisible to the human eye. What do you know about this technology?"

"I'm not aware that anything like that is being developed on Alderon, Talonis. I've read all the interdepartmental reports on science and development and there is no mention of a device like that. Maybe it's a new product from the people at Mercon."

"Perhaps it is. Too bad that we don't know, it was *most* impressive. Saber is an unusual man, Mr. President; I suggest that you don't take him for granted. How many systems has he claimed for mining rights under your agreement?"

"Only three, so far. Actually, that number is only two, because the Helios system was already settled by a group of explorers, who crash landed there some twenty years ago, and they've established an independent colony. Saber has entered into a contract with them for mining rights. So technically, he has only claimed two systems."

"Very interesting. That tells me a lot about our Captain."

"What do you mean?"

"Nothing of concern to you, Mr. President, just an observation."

"Then I'll continue as planned. We can begin selling off the mineral and settlement rights in another eight months or so. If I time it right, our sales will start right about the time that I leave office."

"I'll leave the politics to you, Mr. President, but don't make any more mistakes. I too, have connections in places that you aren't aware of."

"Are you threatening me, Talonis?"

Talonis could hear the anger in the President's voice. He replied calmly, "Not at all, Mr. President. It's a simple reminder that we all have our enemies...and our friends. Be careful who you choose to call friend."

"Politicians have no friends, Talonis. We have power and influence, and if we play the game well, there is wealth. You and I, my friend, are about to acquire more wealth than *anyone* could ever imagine."

Talonis disconnected the call, and looked across the room to House member Styer. "Well, Styer, what do you think?"

"I don't trust politicians, Talonis, and that one is particularly untrustworthy," Styer said.

"I agree. I don't trust him either. He has already made too many mistakes, one of which cost us the mercenaries to whom we had entrusted our planet's security."

"Asher was stupid, Talonis. You said it yourself. It was only a matter of time before he brought trouble here."

"I agree, but I would have preferred to have instigated his removal myself. However, this has kept us out of it, and we gained some good people and good property. We can handle planet security on our own now, and we're rid of that moron, Asher."

"Do we really need this guy? Can't we make a deal with this Captain Saber?"

"The President of Alderon was already involved, so we don't have a choice, yet. I haven't discussed business with the Captain, and I expect that money isn't everything to the man."

"Lots of money can change any man, Talonis, wouldn't you agree?"

"No, I wouldn't, Styer. Money is merely a vehicle, through which one may acquire things, people, tech, and especially, power I don't think that those mean a lot to the Captain. In some ways, I am envious of him. He sees things in a very black and white way, unlike most of us."

"Be careful, Talonis. If the other houses hear you say anything like that, they may get the wrong impression," Styer said with a concerned look.

"There's no cause for concern, my friend. I have only the best interests in mind for the all of the Houses of Cerberus. Once we establish a presence in these new systems, and they become colonized, then each House will be able to occupy a system of its own. Together, we will build a syndicate that will be too strong to be threatened."

"What about this President of Alderon? Won't he be a problem? I think he doesn't realize the true nature of the authority given to this man, Jonas."

"Perhaps, but if he does prove to be trouble, I have enough documentation to have him executed. Carson saw to that, before he was killed, and your instincts about Jonas are spot-on."

"This Captain Saber, you like him, don't you?" Styer asked curiously.

"I respect him, Styer, and that says a lot. I would not want to have a man like Saber for an enemy. He is much more valuable as a friend."

"What's your plan, Talonis?"

"I'm going to let the Alderon President play out his hand. We've got a great deal of money invested in this scheme, too much not to let it run its course. However, *this* house doesn't lose. I have more than enough assets in place to cover those losses, if I have to. Either way, the house will win, or that's all that matters."

"This will please the other Houses, Talonis. You have planned well."

"Time will tell, Chairman Styer," Talonis said as he stood. The Cerberus Chairman also stood, and smiled as they shook hands.

Talonis returned to his window, overlooking the gaming tables, as the door closed behind Chairman Styer. He wondered if Captain Saber would remember his invitation to come back, as his guest, to the House of Talonis. It would be pleasurable to have some conversation with him again, under less confrontational conditions this time. He was curious to understand more about this man, who he found so intriguing. He really wanted to know more about that device that had made his companion invisible. Perhaps they could be captured and interrogated for a time, in order to discover information about the device. His mind raced, considering the possibilities that such a device could give him. He wondered why the Captain didn't use the device too. Maybe he already has used it and nobody knows. He doubted that likelihood. His office's security measures had not detected the second person, and that concerned him. He had the best tech that was available anywhere, and it had still missed detecting an intruder. He watched to his left and to his right, observing the guests winning... and loosing. It was a very busy night, and he always enjoyed watching his accounts swell.

"This is Interceptor Alpha Victor 3-2-6, do you copy, Shipyard Foxtrot Six?"

"We copy you, 3-2-6, what is your request?"

"My ship is damaged and I'm venting atmosphere. I need permission to dock for repairs, immediately."

"Roger, 3-2-6, maintain your heading of 225 and follow the docking lights to Bay Nine."

"Bay Nine, roger, AV3-2-6 out."

The interceptor fighter craft slowly made its way, following the given directions, and landed safely inside the Chinese Federation Shipyard Number Six. Once the landing bay lights turned from red to green, denoting a safe atmosphere, the pilot hatch opened, and a large man exited the craft.

A technician approached him asking, "What is your problem? I don't have a large crew available for repairs tonight. It will probably be six to eight hours before we can assign someone to make your repairs."

"That's not a problem. I'm hungry, can you tell me where I can get some food?" the big man asked.

The technician turned away, pointing toward an enclosed lift and started to say, "Take that lift to deck five..." The big man stepped closer, placed one hand around the tech's jaw, the other behind his head, and with a quick twist his neck cracked. The tech went limp, as he was dropped to the floor. The big man smiled with satisfaction. He returned to his ship and quickly withdrew a bag containing his gear, then headed toward the maintenance hatch leading to the adjacent landing bay. He looked around, and seeing no one else, he entered the corridor, which was just wide enough for two people, that led to the next bay. He paused before he entered the bay, looking to see if anyone was there, and could see two techs, busily working on a civilian transport ship. He dropped his gear before entering the bay. One tech looked toward the sound of the opening door and said something to the other tech, which turned and looked at the big man, with curious eyes.

One tech walked toward the man and was about to speak when the man thrust his hand forward to greet him, saying, "The name's Asher! I was heading up to deck five when I saw this baby in your hanger, and I wanted to check her out. Is she up for a refit?"

Confused at first, the tech responded, "No. She has just completed her first shakedown. We're fine-tuning some of her systems, but you shouldn't be in here. No one is allowed without an escort."

"Oh sure, sure. I understand. I notice her engines are a lot larger than most civilian Minnow class transporters. What's her speed? Two-thirds sub-light?"

"No, she has a 2X FTL Drive. Now, you must leave or I'll have to call security."

"Awwww, I just wanted to take a little peek inside." He strolled over to the open door of the transport deliberately, to draw the one tech out of the other's sight. When the tech paced quickly over to him in a vain attempt to keep him away from the door, Asher spun around. With a single strike to the tech's throat, his larynx was crushed, and he dropped to the floor with an expression of shock on his face, as he took his last breath. The sounds drew the attention of the second tech, which rounded the corner to investigate. Before he could call for help, Asher threw a little four inch blade from his wrist, striking the tech in his right eye. Screaming in agony, he fell to his knees as Asher approached, and then used a larger knife to cut the tech's throat, from ear-to-ear.

Once he was inside the ship's engineering control room, he looked over the ship's specs. Noted it was nearly out of fuel, he returned to the landing bay, connected the fuel hose, and turned on the high pressure fuel pump. While the ship was being fueled, he retrieved his gear bag and stowed it in the ship. As soon as the refueling was completed, he boarded the transport craft one last time, and left the Chinese Federation Space.

Mitch was sitting in his office with Athena and Dr. Santana, discussing the progress of Athena's speech therapy, when the comm rang out for his attention.

"This is the Captain," he answered.

"Captain," Inna said urgently, "I have a priority call from the Rivers Run for you. Shall I send it through?"

"By all means, Inna."

His panel beeped confirmation of the call, and as the screen came into focus, Samantha was there smiling at him. "Mitch! Have you watched any news lately?"

"Well, hello to you too, Sam!" Mitch replied smartly.

"Sorry honey, but you've got to see this. Pull up IGNA's news feed, right now!"

Mitch touched a few keys on his control panel, splitting the holographic screen into two separate images, with Samantha on one side and the Intergalactic News Agency news feed on the other. Mitch turned up the sound, to hear the anchor say, "To repeat our last headline, the Chinese Federation has issued a one hundred million credit bounty for the capture of the man who brutally killed three of their technicians on number six shipyard last night. The killer fled in a stolen FTL Class Civilian Transport Craft that was not yet in service. Security cameras captured this picture of the man who savagely murdered the techs."

A perfectly clear image of the man appeared on the screen, bringing Mitch abruptly to his feet. He exclaimed, "Holy shit! It's Simon Asher!"

"Can you believe this?" Samantha asked incredulously.

"He disappeared months ago, and suddenly shows up there? What's that all about?" Mitch asked, not noticing the odd looks being directed at him by Athena and Dr. Santana.

"I called the security people at the Chinese Federation and told them who he is. They told me that he gained access to their shipyard by claimed that his ship had sustained damage, and needed emergency repairs. His ship was damaged, but not like he had claimed. His FTL drive was out of commission, so he apparently wanted an FTL capable ship," Samantha reported.

"And of course, they have no idea where he is, right?"

"Worse than that, Mitch. The ship that he stole was brand new, and her beacon had not been programmed yet. He could program it himself to appear to be an Alderon ship, or anyone else's for that matter."

"She doesn't carry any weapons, so surely he can't be that much of a threat," Mitch said calmly.

"Seriously? Think about it Mitch, he could identify that ship as an Alderon transporter, fill it full of explosives, and potentially blow up a station, or a mining HQ! Get it?"

"Unfortunately, I do get it. However, I think that his thirst for revenge doesn't automatically make him a suicide bomber. He likes to think that he can outsmart everyone, so he will probably choose a different route. I wonder..."

"What, Mitch?" Sam said.

"I was wondering if there was anything left after we destroyed his base that would still be of interest to him."

"Like what? You downloaded all of his computer files and there wasn't anything left of the base."

"That we know of," Mitch said. "I'm thinking that maybe we should take another look at the remains of that base and see if we missed anything."

"Don't you dare go back there without me, Mitch Saber!"

"Not this time, Sam. I need you to keep up our freight operations. This will be a good field test for Athena, and I don't expect that we'll find any trouble. We already have the navigation data from our last trip to his former base, so we'll just follow the same route again. We should be fine."

"Mitch, don't you think that the leaders of Cerberus were curious about how intruders got in and out of there, unseen? They may have discovered our buoy, and could have hacked it or destroyed it."

"Talonis thinks that the brigands did it to themselves. They don't suspect that anyone else had a hand in it."

"Mitch, I think you're making a *big* mistake. I've seen situations like this before, and they didn't end well. You are taking far too many things for granted. You need me there to back you up," Sam stressed, as her concern for her husband's safety showed on her face.

"I'll take all the necessary precautions, Sam, and I'll send you the mission details and keep you informed."

"Mitch, please don't do this alone."

"Sam, I'm quite capable of taking care of myself. I love you for caring, but I need you to concentrate on the business, please. Let me handle this. I'll be in touch soon."

CHAPTER SIX

THE PHOENIX ENTERED THE SAME SECTOR OF THE CERBERUS system, exactly as they had when they raided the brigands' base of operations before. As far as they could tell, the Mercon buoy was still in service, operating clandestinely. Since this was only a recon mission, Mitch decided to take Richter and Master Chief Tanner along to guard the Minnow, while he and Athena searched for any Intel. The ship's sensors showed a minimal scattering of personnel on the planet, which Mitch thought was odd. Instead of making the high atmosphere jump, like they had last time, they decided to land six kilometers away, then hike to their destination. The Phoenix was cloaked in orbit, and Mitch was in full contact with ALICE, via his new implants.

After a quiet landing, Richter and Tanner set up their security perimeter while Mitch and Athena headed toward the old base HQ. Just prior to crossing over the last rise in full view of the destroyed base, they activated their stealth suits. Mitch was first to stand atop the small hillside and view the remains of the base. The remains of the massive destruction that they had put in motion were an amazing sight. Standing over a half a kilometer away, the ground on which they stood was scorched black, and areas of sand had been turned into glass. He couldn't begin to understand how Asher had escaped death in the midst of this total destruction of his base. He checked his motion and thermal readouts and seeing nothing, they continued toward the remains of the base.

"This is the place you that told me about, Captain?" Athena asked him telepathically via his implant.

"Yes, it is. There was a three story complex and a space port, plus a munitions depot behind the main structure, pointing as he described the original layout.

Pieces of polycrete were strewn everywhere. Some were as big as the Minnow, but most were only the size of a human hand. The area where the spaceport had been located was now nothing more than an enormous crater. The remains of the former HQ building showed no means of entrance or exit.

As they walked around the rear of the old HQ building, Athena suddenly said, "Stop!"

Mitch checked his sensor sweep and didn't see anything. "What do you see?" he asked.

"I'm not seeing, Captain, I'm hearing. There are several people walking ahead of us."

"Toward us?" Mitch asked.

"No, away from us," she replied.

Mitch held out his hand in an effort to intensify his sensor sweep, but still didn't get a positive reading. "I'm not getting anything, Athena, are you certain?"

"Yes, they are talking about an entrance to the HQ, located somewhere ahead."

"You take point, Athena, and let's follow them."

Athena started at a brisk pace, and then soon slowed. Mitch's new night vision worked perfectly. He could easily see details in the dark that were as clear to him as if they had been in the light of day. Switching on his thermal vision, he saw footprints left by the people ahead of them. There were the tracks of four people following a well-used path, and he was curious to know how Athena had picked up on their presence so quickly. He could hear them walking now, as the sand crunched beneath their feet. They suddenly stopped, and Mitch and Athena froze so that their own footsteps wouldn't give them away. They heard a door open and close. After a brief pause, they advanced and found a door was built into a hillside. Mitch's thermal vision revealed that the door handle was still warm, and he didn't see any lock mechanism or keypad. He cautiously turned the knob, and the door opened, without a sound. A row of small red lights hung from the ceiling; barely illuminating what was a corridor. The stone walls appeared to have been laser cut, as the surface was as smooth as glass. They continued ahead slowly, and realized that they were on a downward grade, leading deep under the surface. Hearing the voices ahead again, they saw that the corridor widened, and an open doorway on one side led into a well-lit room. Their stealth suits concealed their presence, but they still used care as they approached the room close enough to see through the doorway. Just inside was a long rack of computer equipment which was apparently data storage. Three men stood beside a console chatting, but there was no sign of the fourth man. Mitch extended his hand in order to utilize his deep scan function, and detected only three men. He desperately wanted access to the data storage and was considering his options, when one of the men turned and asked the others if they were hungry. They both nodded and followed him out of the room and further down the corridor.

Mitch silently asked Athena to stand watch as he entered the data room and placed a data crystal into a port, trying to access the records. He hadn't brought a code-shark crystal and he wasn't having any luck in gaining access. Athena read his frustration and stepped back inside, asking him to watch while she tried to crack the code. Conceding failure and frustrated, he retreated to the door and Athena began her work. Shortly, she was into the system, much to Mitch's surprise, and she began to download as much information as she could. The one thousand petabyte storage crystal was full within several minutes, and it was the only one that they had. Hearing footsteps approaching, she pulled the crystal from the port, and they wasted little time exiting the area. Remaining cloaked, they quickly made their way back towards the waiting Minnow, anxious to get off the planet, as dawn was just over an hour away.

The Minnow was about two hundred meters away when the hair on Mitch's neck prickled, and he stopped, noticing how exceptionally quiet the area had become.

"Is there a problem, Captain?" Athena asked.

"Have you noticed how quiet it is all of a sudden?"

"I do not understand, Captain. This is a new experience for me. This is actually the first time I have ever walked on solid ground on a planet that is not my own."

"I'm sorry, Athena, I forgot, but I get the distinct feeling that something isn't right. Wait here a moment while I contact ALICE."

Using his new skills via his implant, he contacted the Phoenix's AI for a status report. He discovered that the Minnow had not made her last scheduled report. Learning this, he sent a message to Yurie, who was in command during his absence, to place the ship on alert.

"ALICE."

"Yes, Captain." The AI replied.

"Scan the area around the Minnow and report how many life signs you detect."

A moment passed before she replied, "Scans detect seven life signs within a twenty-five meter area of the Minnow, Captain."

"Okay, scan the surrounding area for any other transport ships."

"There is one civilian transport ship, approximately two kilometers northwest from your present location," Alice reported.

"Damn," Mitch thought silently. "Send the exact location of that other transport to Athena, ALICE."

"Affirmative, Captain."

"Athena, the Minnow failed to make her last scheduled report. ALICE reports seven life signs surrounding the Minnow and another transport is located northwest of our position. She is sending you those coordinates," Mitch said as he noted the morning sun begin to appear on the horizon.

"I have the coordinates Captain," Athena confirmed.

"If I were them, I'd have two men inside holding our people as hostages, while two others wait for our approach. Those two will probably try to come from behind me, while another man tries to talk me into surrendering."

"That would be a sound strategy, Captain. I can go ahead and take them all out, if you wish."

Mitch smiled to himself at the notion, but he was curious to learn how they had been detected. "Athena, how long would it take you to reach the other transport and disable her engines and communications?"

"In this terrain, I estimate four minutes to reach the objective, and two minutes to disable her systems."

"Excellent, that gives us ten minutes. I'm going to wait here for exactly ten minutes, and then I'm going to disable my cloak and walk right into their trap. I want you to remain cloaked, take out the outer guards first, and if possible, get inside the Minnow to take out the other two, while I keep our other *friend* busy talking. I'll let you know if there is a change in the plan. Tell me when you have taken out the first two guards."

"Captain," Athena said seriously, "My purpose is to protect you at all times. I can take out all these objectives alone, without your involvement."

"I know you can, Athena, and under different circumstances I might let you do just that. However, I need information and my plan will accomplish both objectives. My armor will protect me and you won't be far behind, so please, follow my orders."

She was silent for a moment before replying, "I agree, Captain, it is a good plan."

Mitch sat on a nearby boulder and watched ten minutes slowly tick away. He was concerned that his presence had been detected, but, he was determined to find out how and by whom. Perhaps Sam was right and the Mercon buoy had been discovered. Maybe this was a trap that had been set specifically for him. Was his ship in danger? They were cloaked, but there was always a way to detect a cloaked ship, if you knew what to look for. Just to be cautious, he sent Yurie a message directing her to leave orbit in order to avoid potential detection, but to remain close by so that the Minnow could make a fast escape if necessary. He had just completed sending the message, when his timer alerted him that it was time to move. He disengaged his cloak and removed the cowl, then moved at a fast pace toward the Minnow.

He rounded the final bend and could see the minnow ahead. Athena informed him that he was within her visual range, and he noted that she had made excellent time. Ahead, Mitch saw one man leaning comfortably, against his ship. He was about forty feet away when he observed the man begin to smile.

"Welcome, Captain Saber. It is good to see you again."

Mitch's pace slowed as he recognized the man from Cerberus, "Talonis, why are you here?"

"Isn't that the question that I should be asking *you*, Captain?"

"I'm just sight-seeing, Talonis. After all, you did invite me to come back."

"Indeed I did, Captain, but I did have in mind a more comfortable place to stay," he said with an amused chuckle.

"Where is my crew?"

"They are inside your ship, with two of my guards to keep them safe. The desert can be a dangerous place," Talonis replied.

"Okay, Talonis, what's this all about?"

"Why have you come here, Captain? Don't you think that your previous trip here did enough damage?"

Mitch didn't change his expression. Athena informed him that she had disposed of one of the rear guards.

"What makes you think that I had anything to do with that? I only came here to look for Asher. He killed three people on a shipyard in the Chinese Federation, and there is a huge bounty on his head. I imagined that he might return here to hide," Mitch offered with a neutral expression.

"Ah yes, I did hear about that. However, protocol dictates that you contact Cerberus before you land on one of our planets, so you do understand that I am well within my rights to detain, or even to kill you, without question."

Athena notified Mitch that she had taken out the second rear guard and was going to enter the Minnow. Mitch calmly walked over to lean on a nearby boulder, forcing Talonis to turn away from the open hatch.

"Perhaps I should have, Talonis, but speed was of the essence, so here I am." Mitch held out his arms in a helpless gesture.

"Come now, Captain, let's be honest. Right now I have half a dozen fighters in orbit looking for your ship, with orders to capture or destroy it on sight. You are here now, and I have you covered, to prevent your escape. You have already destroyed the base that was here, so why have you really come back?"

"That's the second time that you've accused me of destroying this place, Talonis. What proof do you have of your accusations?"

Talonis laughed abruptly, "Captain, you know that I have my sources here and all over the systems. There's no sense in denying your actions. You actually did us a favor by ridding us of the nuisance that Asher had become, so I don't hold any hard feelings against you. It was business, after all. They had a contract out for you and one of your crew, and you took defensive action. I don't blame you at all. But since we knew that someone had arrived here undetected, naturally we had to put additional measures in place to track any arriving ships. When one suddenly showed up, I decided to personally investigate. Once we had your crew in custody, all I had to do was wait. Then I knew that you had to be here somewhere, so here we are."

"You should check those sources again, Talonis. I think that you've got some bad Intel."

Talonis' expression turned more serious. "Don't insult me, Captain. We both know that you were responsible. Aside from that, I want to know why you are here again."

"I've already answered that question, Talonis. I'm looking for Simon Asher. I want that bounty."

"Money isn't important to you, Captain. You're not that kind of man."

Athena reported that both guards in the Minnow had been eliminated. Mitch told her to have Richter and Tanner remain inside, but he wanted her to come out, in case he needed her.

"You're right, Talonis. It isn't the money. I want Asher's head for personal reasons."

Talonis threw up his hands. "Ah! Revenge, now *that* I can surely appreciate, Captain. Now we're getting somewhere."

"Your turn Talonis. What exactly is it that you want?"

"Business, Captain. You've been a busy fellow, exploring all these new systems with your specially equipped ship, using Dr. Nagamo's research, or should I say, using his daughter. You can claim mining and settlement rights to hundreds of planets and therefore become a very powerful man. You need someone with my qualifications to help you run such an expansive enterprise." He smiled.

Yurie sent Mitch a message informing him that a half dozen interceptors were searching the outer-planet in an apparent attempt to locate the Phoenix.

"Even if that were true, Talonis, why would I want, or need, you for that job?"

Talonis stood erect and stared coldly at Mitch. "Because, Captain, most other men would treat you with far less respect than I will. Sure... I would require a substantial stake in your, shall we say, acquisitions. But, at least you would know where I stand, and I would never shoot you in the back like your competition would, or perhaps your own government would."

"My government?" Mitch's brow rose with suspicion.

"Your activities are not as private as you may imagine. I would prefer that we make an agreement like gentlemen, or..." he reached inside his tunic and revealed his weapon, "we can do it in a less delicate manner."

Mitch scowled suspecting that Athena was observing Talonis' action, when suddenly Talonis was lifted off the ground, leaving his feet dangling more than a foot from the surface. His neck was stretched upwards as Athena had apparently jerked him up by the neck, leaving him hanging like a sack. He dropped his weapon and frantically grasped for the invisible hands around his neck, as he grimaced and his face began to turn red.

Mitch walked over, and picked the discarded weapon then casually strolled back over to the boulder, where he had been sitting. He placed the weapon on the boulder, out of reach, and returned his attention to Talonis. When the dangling man's eyes began to roll back in his head, Mitch silently told Athena to release him. He fell with a thud to the ground, gasping for air.

"I thought that you had learned your lesson by now, Talonis."

He struggled to speak, and finally in a gruff voice he asked, "Where are my guards?"

"They've been removed from the game, Talonis." Mitch smiled and pointed toward the boulder. "Now, I want you to observe your weapon over there."

A flash of light erupted from behind Talonis and struck his weapon, and melting it into the stone. Talonis turned to see where the weapons fire had originated but saw nothing, and no one.

"Now, I want you to call off your interceptors, or this is what will happen to them. Richter, Tanner," Mitch called to his crew, "come out and escort Talonis inside our ship. He has a call to make."

Richter and Tanner quickly appeared, dragging the two unconscious guards out of the ship, and deposited them unceremoniously on the ground. Lifting Talonis up, they helped him inside. Athena remained cloaked as Talonis completed his call and was roughly escorted back out.

Mitch faced him stating, "Talonis, today you leave with your life. This is the second time that I have spared your life, so you owe me." Mitch jabbed his finger into the man's chest. "I don't know who your sources are and I don't care to know." That was a lie, of course, because Mitch knew that there were only a handful of people who knew this much information. "You have a good thing going on in Cerberus, and I suggest that you keep your activities confined to your own system. You can certainly expand your operations anywhere that you wish. That's what freedom offers you. While I appreciate your offer, I don't need any partners in *any* endeavor that I undertake. I will, however, not hesitate to eliminate anyone who threatens my business, my activities or especially my friends and family. I respect your position as a leader and businessman on Cerberus, but that is the extent of our relationship. You can accept this for what it is, or we can part as enemies. It's your choice." Mitch extended his hand. Talonis hesitated before accepting it.

"We *will* have this conversation again in the future, Captain Saber," Talonis said grimly.

"If we do, it will be on my terms, not yours. Goodbye, Talonis."

Mitch, Athena, Tanner and Richter hastily departed in the Minnow, happy to be making their way back to the Phoenix. They were relieved to put the Cerberus system behind them as they headed homeward to Alderon space.

"Mitch! I'm so glad to hear your voice. I was worried, you know," Samantha said. Mitch could see the concern on his wife's face on his comm. "Did everything go okay?"

"It was more interesting than I expected, Sam. We discovered that there was a hidden entrance to the base. I suspect that it was an emergency exit that Chen didn't know about."

"That must have been how Asher escaped."

"Most likely so. There was a very large data room that I think was a backup for the base. Athena filled a data crystal to capacity before we had to leave. We only brought one data crystal with us, because we weren't expecting to find a data center that large."

"Have you looked at the data yet?"

"No, it's encrypted, so I've got ALICE working on it. I ran into Talonis while we were there."

"How the hell did he know you were there?" She asked with a shocked expression.

"Apparently, your concerns were well founded. He referred to an upgraded sensor package that has been installed on the planet in order to screen unidentified craft. I guess that he picked us up when we landed. Athena was a real asset during this operation. She definitely earned her pay today."

"What happened?"

"I don't want to go into detail now. In six days we'll be home on Alderon. When can you meet us there?"

"I can be there in five days. My crew needs a few days off and I need to replenish our stores."

"That's perfect. I want you to send Jonas a message for me."

Samantha raised a questioning eyebrow. "That's a bit unusual, Mitch."

"Since I just had a run-in with Talonis, I don't want a message to my uncle coming from me so soon. I'll explain later. Just comm him with a 'friendly hello' sort of message. Then tell him that you'd like another fishing lesson. Say that you'll be home in six days and ask him to meet you there. He'll play along and meet us there."

"You men always have to make things so complicated," she complained with a chuckle. "I'm looking forward to spending a few days together with you, Mitch. I've missed you so much."

"I've missed you too, Sam. Thinking of when you were on the ship with me for all those weeks, reminds me just how much I love being with you."

"I guess we could build a ship large enough for the two of us, then?" Sam said with a wide grin. "Hmmm, maybe a carrier sized freighter. I like the idea! When do we start?"

"Laurel would have both our heads on that one! I'll see you in six days, sweetheart. You'll finally get to meet Athena too."

"That will be very interesting, and I have to admit that I am pretty damn curious about her."

"Her speaking skills have improved dramatically. She can carry on a normal conversation now, but she still forgets occasionally that she can speak, and she tries to communicate telepathically."

"You still haven't told me how you've overcome her inability to communicate once she came aboard."

"All in good time, dear. Don't be so impatient. I'll see you in six days."

Mitch ended the call before Sam had a chance to react to his delaying tactic. She had asked him about this several times now, and he had avoided giving her an explanation each time. He knew that he would have to tell her soon about his new implants, but he preferred to do it in person, and certainly not over a comm channel. A knock at his door caused him to look up and Master Chief Rockland Tanner waiting.

"Come in, Rock and have a seat," Mitch said.

"Thanks, Captain. I'm here to give you my report," Rock said sourly.

"Please do, I'm curious to know how Talonis took possession of my ship, not to mention my crew," Mitch said sternly.

"I'm not offering any excuses, Captain. I let my guard down, thinking that we were alone on the planet. I thought that I heard something, so I left Richter inside the ship and walked out to investigate. The next thing I knew, there was a gun pointed at my head and I was told to call Richter to come out from the ship. When they had both of us, the man that you called Talonis, came from around the bend in the trail and demanded to know who we were. I told him that we were tourists. He laughed and said that he had never encountered tourists in a blacked out ship with no running lights or beacon. When he saw the ship's insignia on my arm, he just smiled and told his people to hold us inside the ship while he waited for the rest of our party to return. There was nothing I could do to warn you." His expression revealed how awful he felt, that he had failed at a simple task, letting his Captain down.

"Rock," Mitch said sincerely, "You're a good man, that's why I hired you. I've always had complete confidence in your abilities, and I still do. However, you let your guard down this time because you became complacent. We can't afford those kinds of mistakes. I hope that you've learned a valuable lesson here."

"I apologize, Captain, I know I let you down," Rock said not looking away.

"We all make mistakes, Rock. Let's not make this one again, okay?" Mitch stood and thrust his hand forward to his friend. Rock accepted it, shaking the Captains hand and nodding in agreement.

When the Phoenix docked at the Alderon station on the sixth day, Mitch turned the command over to Yurie, as he and Athena departed for the Saber Island retreat. At the landing pad they were met by Laurel and Mitch's uncle, Admiral Rich Jonas, and Samantha. Athena was warmly welcomed, and Mitch was pleased to see how well she had learned to socially accept a hug and a handshake from strangers. This was, in fact, her first opportunity to practice her interpersonal skills in public. Mitch, Yurie, Inna and Richter had each worked long hours to help her understand how people from various other worlds interact with strangers, family and friends. Mitch couldn't suppress his smile noting that all of their hard work, Athena's too, had not been wasted. He was constantly impressed with her seemingly endless ability to rapidly learn new skills. However, when it was time to perform her official duties, she quickly returned to her original persona as a Praetorian Guard.

Athena took in all the sights and smells of the island like a child with a new toy. Everything was new for her. The touch of a plant leaf, the smell of flowers, the sound of the ocean waters, and even the birds in the air were all new experiences for her. She wanted to touch and smell everything. When Laurel and Sam took her out to the lagoon, she picked up a handful of sand and felt the grittiness between her fingers. She inhaled the salty odor of the water and laughed when it splashed over her feet as the waves washed onto the shore. Mitch and his uncle stood motionless in the doorway of the house, watching her explorations in amazement.

"Nephew," his Uncle said quietly, "I feel like I'm watching a child open her eyes for the first time."

"You're right, Uncle Rich, on many different levels. On her planet the ground and the waters around them are radioactive. The plants and trees all grow on raised gardens in terrariums to keep them free from contamination. This is a completely new experience for Athena. Just weeks ago, she could not even speak or smile. She has come a long way since she came aboard the Phoenix."

Sam walked up from the beach and stood beside Mitch and his uncle, placing her arm around Mitch's waist. He smiled and kissed her on the cheek.

"Her silver-white hair and platinum skin along with that gold uniform is quite a combination. I'm guessing that uniform is armor," His uncle observed.

"It is armor, very similar to ours, but much more advanced. I have a vid that I'll let you see. It will give you a small demonstration of her capabilities, and I do mean small. She's pretty much a one person defense and demolition squad, and then some. Her orders from Aegea were very specific, she is to guard me with her life any, and everywhere that I go. We watched her pick up a six hundred pound barbell using one arm, and I witnessed her throw a full grown man thirty feet across a room with one hand. She is by far, the most competent warrior I have ever met."

"I can assure you that I would not want to go up against her," Rich said seriously, "and I haven't seen your vid yet! You say that everyone on her planet looks like her?"

"Skin color, yes, but the men are bald and they have no facial hair. Their race has honed their mental abilities far beyond anything we've seen. The only way that she could communicate with me for nearly two weeks was telepathically. They are a very closed society and I think that they intend to stay that way, at least for the near future. They indicated that they wanted me to return at some point, but I don't know why or when. The entire experience was very strange, but they seemed to accept me without a lot of questions, which makes me very curious," Mitch said as his brow furrowed.

"They have a particle weapon, a molecular destabilizer according to ALICE, that is the most powerful thing that I've ever witnessed, that they can use from a vessel, and their defensive fighters have micro-jump engines. I didn't think it was possible to employ those on small ships."

"I know that Mercon has tried for years to make them work on their fighter craft, completely without success. That capability would completely change fleet strategies forever. If a hostile system had those fighters then we would have a real fight on our hands," Sam added.

"They sound like they're much more advanced than the other systems. They would make for good allies," his uncle admitted.

"I don't think that's what they're interested in, Uncle Rich. The fact is that I'm not certain of where their interests lie, except in Bion4 and me."

His uncle turned and gave him a puzzled look. "Let's sit down so that we can talk at length. I think that Laurel is just as fascinated with Athena, as Athena is with her new surroundings."

They went inside and sat at the large dining table, overlooking the lagoon. Unknown to the others, Mitch had told Athena, through his telepathic implant, that they would be inside the house and asked he her to remain outside while they had their conversation.

"Uncle Rich, I know that you're family, and I would never question your loyalty or honesty, so please don't be offended when I ask you not to discuss anything we say here. It is imperative that you don't reveal who Athena is, or share any information about her, with anyone." His uncle started to speak, but Mitch held up his hand. "Please, let me explain first and then you will understand why I am asking for this secrecy."

Mitch proceeded to tell them everything that had transpired in the previous weeks, with the exception of his new implants. They listened with great interest. He then went on to tell them about his run in with Talonis.

"Talonis knows exactly what we are been doing. First he told me that our activities are not private, and then he suggested that I should be concerned about who might 'shoot me in the back,' as he phrased it. He tried to coerce me into a partnership agreement, to provide a considerable profit for himself, of course. When he threatened me with his weapon, Athena nearly snapped his neck. She was cloaked and was standing right behind him when he drew his weapon. Talonis knows details about us that only a few people know." There is a serious problem somewhere in our top government level.

His uncle's face flushed with anger, and he smacked his fist on the table creating a hollow echo in the room.

"Don't be angry yet, Uncle Rich. Let me ask you this, when did the President make you his new Chief of Security?"

"Just before our altercation with Carson. I'd say about a week prior," his uncle replied, squinting his eyes in thought.

"Both of us wondered at the time, where Carson got the money to place the contract that he put out on us, and whether there might have been anyone else involved. When you think about how much money that the government, or the President's office, is paying us for our exploration, don't you wonder where the money is coming from?" Mitch asked.

"Mitch," Sam jumped in, "are you saying that you think that Cerberus is footing the bill for what we're doing and that the President is involved somehow?"

"Careful, nephew, those are serious accusations. That's the kind of stuff that brings down governments," his uncle warned.

"The President's term will end in about a year, and by that time we will have mapped hundreds of new systems. That would make a nice retirement package, don't you think?" Mitch quirked his mouth to one side waiting to see if this made sense to his uncle and Sam. They both nodded in agreement.

"If this is true, then I could be implicated in any wrong-doing that may be going on. Not to mention that I don't like being used, especially by a damn politician!" Jonas barked.

"What do you think our next step should be, Mitch?" Sam asked.

"If our payments are coming through an official Alderon account that might keep our hands clean. My problem being that I don't want to turn over any more data regarding newly explored systems. Remember, Carson said something about selling the rights off to the highest bidder?" Mitch asked. They remembered and nodded their heads in agreement. "Well, what if that is still their intention? What if the President was the one pulling Carson's strings?"

"You've made a good point, Mitch," his uncle conceded, "but you can't just stop your explorations or they'll become suspicious."

"That's right, Mitch," Sam interjected. "The time will come when they want the MARDA technology so that they can travel through the anomalies too."

"Good point, Sam. I've been giving that some thought, and I had some discussion with Ernie just before I arrived. Right now, we're using MARDA two different ways. The original MARDA device was a short ranged defensive shield that would repel anything within a specific range. The magnetic properties are working on two different principles when we utilize it for travel through the anomalies, or gateways as we've come to call them which we now know to be some sort of wormhole. The first principle is the deflection field, the second principle is using the ships naturally occurring magnetic field, enhancing it as a stabilizing field surrounding the ship so that we can pass safely through the gateways. This second principle can be used independently from the original MARDA design."

"So, you're saying that we don't have to give up the MARDA technology?" Sam asked surprised.

"That's right," Mitch replied. "We only need to show them how the second principle works. That's the mathematical part that Yurie's father had developed. I think that they are planning to sell that tech to the highest bidders, then take their money and run when the President's term is over, making them all wealthy beyond anyone's wildest imagination. By developing MARDA ourselves, and using it to map these new systems, we have amplified the potential value of that information millions of times over."

"My God, Mitch, do you realize what you're saying?" Jonas asked seriously. "This is almost beyond comprehension."

"If this is true then it's pretty shrewd, I have to admit. But now we're in the game, as Talonis would say. We've got time on our side; we can delay... or provide false information as we go along. From this point on though, I think that we should deposit any further government payments into a separate account, just in case it needs to be returned," Mitch said. "There could still be more to this that what we can see now."

"I'll need to play this thing carefully, people," Jonas warned. "The President will still be expecting regular reports. In addition, I'll need to do some investigation on my end. I don't know how many ears he has inside the government, so I'll have to do most of it alone."

"Uncle Rich, you don't need me to tell you to be cautious. I think if we give them enough info, they will eventually show their hand, just like Talonis did. In the meantime, I'm going to have Laurel fast track the mining expansions in the new systems and claim rights to some of the earlier ones that we've looked into. We've got several new ships on order, to facilitate the expansion of our mining operations, and I'm thinking about inviting one of our friendlier systems to join us in the exploration mission."

"That will really piss off some folks, don't you think Mitch?" Sam asked as her eyes widened in surprise.

"Under the terms of our agreement with the Alderon government, all of the prior systems we explored are exempt, so that we have sole rights to them along with any resulting from all gateways in that system. We know there are several other gateways in those systems, so we have a lot to negotiate with. I'm pretty damn certain that if we were to sit down with the Chinese Federation and offer to share this with them, they would build us all the ships we want, at no cost, within reason of course." Mitch smiled as he looked at the others.

Jonas leaned back in his seat. "So, you can still explore and map new systems without breaking your contract. At some point that information will leak out, everyone will have it and they won't be able to do a thing about it."

"Precisely," Mitch replied firmly. "We can still trade, mine, and explore and probably make more money than our contract promised and it will all be legal. If we can prove our suspicions, then that's even better."

"I agree," Jonas replied. "Now, what about this data that you collected from Cerberus?"

"The encryption is very tough. ALICE has been chewing on it for a week, and the only constant that she's discovered is the word 'Antares'."

"Antares? Is that a person or a place," Sam asked.

"Until we can decipher all the data, we don't know. I think that may be why Talonis had his people there. They could be trying to decipher those records too," Mitch said. "If we assume that it's a place and also assume that we are the only ones capable of traveling through the gateways, then it stands to reason that it must be one of the systems that we have to pass through or avoid when we're in FTL flight. Or maybe it means nothing anything at all. It's just a word that has been repeated numerous times in the data, so far. I would not place a lot of importance on it, yet."

"Maybe our systems can decipher it faster," his uncle offered.

"You probably could, but I don't want this on any open network. Let's see if we uncover anything of real value, first." Mitch said.

"You're probably right," his uncle confirmed.

"So, what's next Mitch?" Sam asked.

"Business as usual. I'll have Ernie give me the magnetic data that's necessary for travel through the gateways, and then we'll decide where we make our first offer. I'm pretty sure that it will be the Chinese Federation. They've been good to us from the start, and I think they would make a good asset. They're very honorable people, as are the Atlantians. Those will be our first two stops, I think."

His uncle stood up and stretched. "I'm proud of you nephew. You've got a good head on your shoulders. I'm sure that your parents are up there looking down on you right now saying the same thing."

Mitch recalled the telepathic visit from his parents while he was on Aegea. He clearly remembered hearing them say how very proud they were of him and Laurel. Mitch stood up and walked over to the doorway. Upon seeing Laurel and Athena sitting together on the sand, he fought to keep back the tears brought on by his memory. Sam came up from behind and placed her arms around his waist, sensing his emotion. She whispered in his ear, "I love you, Mitch Saber." He turned and hugged her lovingly, returning her words with a kiss.

Laurel smiled at Athena's fascination with everything she saw. It reminded her of how easy it was to take things for granted. Athena remarked on the different smell of each plant and carefully touched every flower to sense its texture and color. The feeling of the sand moving beneath her feet when the water washed ashore was a fascinating sensation for her just as feeling the sand between her fingers had been. Laurel asked if she wanted to go for a swim, but Athena declined. Thinking perhaps that it was because she didn't have a bathing suit, Laurel offered to take her shopping. Athena replied that the only clothing she was allowed to wear was her gold uniform. Laurel promised that it was safe here and that it would be okay, but Athena was adamant that it wasn't allowed. Her only purpose was to be Mitch's guardian; therefore, she was required to wear it at all times. Laurel could sense that Athena was exceptionally intelligent and was highly trained to rigidly fulfill her duties. When she asked if Athena would ever be relieved of her responsibility to protect Mitch, she was surprised to hear her reply that this was a life-long assignment for her. She was destined to fulfill her duties, to serve Mitch for the rest of her life. Laurel wondered if Mitch was aware of this and guessed that he wasn't. It gave her the strange feeling that she had gained a new family member with only one purpose in life, and she didn't know how to react. There was obviously a friendship beginning to develop between Athena and Mitch, but she surmised that it would be a much longer process for her to establish a relationship with anyone else. Mitch had told her that Athena had empathic abilities, so she wondered how that was going to impact his relationship with her and Samantha. So far, she had been open, but undeniably focused on her responsibilities. Once while they were looking out over the waters, she wondered aloud where Mitch was and Athena had quickly replied that he was sitting at the dining room table having a discussion. Laurel looked over her shoulder and saw that she was exactly correct. How did she know that? She was certain that Athena hadn't turned around once since they had been sitting on the beach. When Laurel asked why her gold suit sometimes sparkled in the sunlight, she replied that the nanobots were absorbing energy, and when they reached maximum capacity, they would sparkle for a microsecond. Outside of the sunlight, her body movements, ambient light, and her own body's electrical energy provided the power for her suit. Laurel was amazed.

Athena turned toward her saying, "The Captain told me to say that you ask too many questions."

Laurel quickly looked over her shoulder to see Mitch standing in the doorway smiling at her. Was this an example of empathic ability? That sounded way too much like something her brother would have said, and that made her wonder what he may not have told her.

"That's okay, Laurel, I don't mind. It helps me practice my vocal skills by talking so casually," Athena said, sensing her concern.

Now that was probably an example of her empathic skills, Laurel thought. There was definitely some other kind of connection between Athena and her brother. She was curious to know if Sam suspected the same thing. Nonetheless, the biggest question that no one had answered yet was why the Aegean's felt it necessary to task this woman with the duty of protecting Mitch. Even he couldn't offer an explanation, but he seemed willing to accept it for what it was. Laurel felt was that this was most unlike Mitch. Whatever had happened to Mitch on Aegea, obviously had impressed on him the necessity of accepting this woman as his permanent body guard.

CHAPTER SEVEN

LAUREL, MITCH AND SAMANTHA TRAVELED TOGETHER TO THE home planet of the Chinese Federation to meet with their diplomatic officials. Mitch asked Laurel to spearhead the discussions since she had been the primary contact on behalf of the Saber Mining Corporation. At first, the officials didn't believe it was possible to navigate successfully through the anomalies. After the presentation of detailed documentation on several of successful trips and an offer to take their officials through the gateway, to see for themselves the new colony of Helios, they were no longer skeptical. Since there was a sense of urgency to get them on board, the CF officials, Mitch and Laurel boarded the Rivers Run and traveled to Helios. This was Laurel's first trip through the anomalies and she thought that it could be risky. She was initially hesitant to make the journey, but finally had agreed to go in an effort to solidify the deal. Mitch placed the Phoenix under the command of Yurie, his executive officer, to take a load from the CF docks to Atlantis and then return. The decision to take the Rivers Run to Helios was dictated by her capacity to provide additional guest quarters for their Federation guests.

The trip was uneventful. The people of Helios were suitably impressed upon meeting with the representatives of the Federation. Captain Chen had already made multiple trips by this time, to supply more men and equipment to Helios, so the living conditions for the formerly shipwrecked colonists had improved greatly. Mitch and Laurel were extremely pleased with the progress that their crews had made. Samantha's suggestion, made at the start of their Helios development, that they lease their new Cruiser to the Mercon Military Corporation, had proved to be a good one because Saber Mining didn't have as many experienced crew as were required to man the cruiser. The result of acting on her suggestion was seeing how quickly the personnel accommodations for their employees on Helios had been completed. Construction of the mining offices and the spaceport on Helios 3 were also nearing completion.

Upon their return, the Chinese Federation officials had been favorably impressed. They were pleased to be offered a unique opportunity to expand their colonies and influence, so the negotiations didn't last very long. As Mitch had hoped, they offered full support to build a fair number of the ships that the Saber Corporation required, at greatly reduced, or no cost, in return for a commitment from Saber Mining Corporation to provide freighter services to support the CF expansion. Mitch also offered to give them the details that were necessary for traveling through the gateways, and to provide them with the locations of three new systems, in order to help them begin their expansion. The CF accepted the agreement.

The CF's first offer under their new agreement was to build them two Whale Class freighters. Only two of these mammoth freighters had ever been built, and one had been destroyed when a computer navigation error had flown the ship into a sun. The other had been built nearly ten years ago for the UKP, the United Kingdom of Planets. The UKP had accepted no free trade or diplomatic outreach with outside systems for nearly twenty years due to numerous internal conflicts. Whale class freighters were nearly three times the size of the Rivers Run, measuring over 1600 meters, nearly a mile long, and they required a crew of over seventy to operate them. They were only capable of two times FTL speed due to their enormous mass. Nonetheless, for settling new planets or mining start-ups, a Whale Class ship could ferry enough people and equipment to make a major impact in just one trip. Unfortunately, size would prevent her from utilizing the cloaking devices that Saber Corporation were using on their other ships, but the MARDA and ALICE systems could still be utilized for maximum performance. Because she was so large, Ernie would have his hands full installing sufficient armaments to protect her. Mitch informed him that work would have to be done at the Chinese Federation (CF) shipyards because the docks at Alderon couldn't handle a ship that size. In addition to the Whale, the CF was building them another ship identical to the Rivers Run, a new Dolphin II class civilian transport, and four dozen of their most advanced ATS fighters, twelve of which would be stationed on the new Whale. Mitch, always quick on his feet, had already decided to name the new Whale freighter *Colossus*. He was tempted to take command of the ship himself but he had such a strong personal attachment to the Phoenix that he just couldn't do it. With all six of the CF shipyards building the Colossus, she would still take nine months or more to complete. Mitch, Laurel and Sam had already decided on at least three additional sites to begin mining and fuel refinery operations in order to support these expansions. During their private discussions, Athena brought up a good point. Defending these far away operations was going to be a challenge since no one knew if any threats would come from neighboring systems. Mitch knew that they couldn't afford to buy more Cruisers or to hire Mercon to guard them all. A planetary base defensive system would be the best choice, so he needed to locate one that would be capable of doing the task alone, and they didn't come cheap. This idea would require some serious planning.

Several weeks had passed and the Phoenix was now docked at the Traders Union of Planets orbital station, when Lt. JG Inna Dubnikov alerted Mitch to an incoming call from General Peyton Harris, owner and commander of the Mercon Protection Organization. The General had ingratiated himself by helping the Captain to find qualified personnel to crew his growing fleet of freighters on several occasions. He had also helped with the rescue of the Saber Mining Corporation executive assistant Miranda, and her newborn infant, from the crazed Simon Asher.

"Send the call to my screen, Inna," Mitch directed.

The holographic image materialized at the Captain's command console and a smiling General Harris appeared.

"Captain Saber," he greeted with a big smile. "I haven't seen you in a while. How are you doing?"

"Just fine, General. How are things over at Mercon?" Mitch replied.

"Too many young pups and not enough old farts like me, Captain," General Harris said with a chuckle. "Mitch, have you ever heard of a system called the Madeus Empire?"

"Yeah, it's off limits to everyone that I'm aware of. They're considered to be the black sheep among all the other systems."

"You're assessment is pretty accurate. They're a strictly dictatorially ruled society, and they don't exactly roll out the welcome patrol for visitors either. They're very militaristic and they ordinarily don't have trade relations with other systems. They can fend for themselves and most other systems choose to stay away for obvious reasons. We don't know a lot about them, other than the fact that they are extremely hostile to uninvited guests."

"Sounds like good policy to me, General. If they don't want outsiders to visit, then that's certainly up to them to decide. I have no desire to go there and you just gave me a good list or reasons to add to the one that I already had."

"Your desire may change Mitch. They've contacted us for help. It seems that they have an epidemic of Centaurian Flu and they need vaccine."

"That's a particularly nasty strain of flu, isn't it?"

"Yes, three out of five people who contract it will die within five days of first showing symptoms. So far it has been contained to their home world, but it could potentially wipe out over half of their population if they don't get the vaccine. That's where you come in."

"Me? I don't think so, General. I'll have to take a pass on this one. Besides, if they contacted you, then obviously they trust you to help them."

"You're partially right, Mitch. They called us because we are a mercenary outfit and they feel we are trustworthy. Problem is, they don't want me to send one of our military cruisers into their space, and the cargo is too large to send aboard any of my smaller transports. So, I need a freighter and that's where you come in."

"I appreciate you thinking of me, General but there are a lot of other freighter companies out there that may take this job. I don't want the risk."

"Therein lies the issue, Mitch, it's the risk factor that concerns me. I'm concerned that a regular freighter captain could lose his cool and get his ship in trouble, and be unable to handle any potential problems. None of the other freighters have the defensive capabilities that you do. Nor do they have the expertise to make this happen."

"General, there are other options, such as using an AI controlled ship or make a drop in a neighboring system and let them retrieve it themselves. I can't take the risk," Mitch said flatly, his expression hardening.

"There are many risks, Captain, and you don't need *me* to start naming them all off for you. Even if these people aren't trustworthy, we can't just let innocent *civilians* die in an untreated epidemic like this. We won't even discuss what could happen if that flu ever left their system." The General paused a moment to let that thought settle in Mitch's mind. "We can vaccinate your crew and give you a portable biohazard pod that will fit in one of your freight bays. That way, anyone leaving or returning to your ship can be decontaminated. We also will supply you with special scrubbers for your air handlers and purifiers to protect your water supply. When you return, our dock will irradiate your hull to make sure that everything is safe. We have the vaccine ready for transport, and they've paid double the standard rate for the freighter expense, so *all* of us will make credits on the deal. But it's more than just the credits, Mitch, you know that."

Mitch studied the General's expression and concluded that he was sincere, but it would be a dangerous trip for the ship and his crew. He closed his eyes and shook his head. "Alright, General, how are we supposed to get in there?"

"Thank you, Captain. I know that this is a difficult thing for you to do. You'll need to jump into Sector 725 then cruise into Sector 726, the Madeus Empire's system. When you enter the outskirts of their system, you will stop and send them a communication to indicate that you're representing Mercon to deliver the cargo of Centaurian Flu Vaccine, and then you wait for their orders. Do *not* let any of their people on your ship! And don't let any of your people onto their station. They will probably try to get you to land a vehicle on their planet, but don't do it. Deliver your cargo and get the hell out of there! They are desperate for any new tech that they can get their hands on. Be aware that they will go to great lengths or make gross deception, to get it. I'll dispatch two missile frigates to Sector 725 to guard your backside."

"Why can't I jump into their space, drop the cargo, and run like hell?" Mitch replied.

"If you jump right into their space, they'll view you as an intruder and attack you, no questions asked. How you leave their system is up to you, and the situation at that time. Unfortunately, even though they've asked for help, the whole operation is volatile. They're paranoid people, for sure. Perhaps someday, new leadership will bring them better relations with the other systems. Try not to start a fight while you're there, Mitch."

Athena had entered the bridge taking her usual position beside his command chair, during the last part of their conversation. The General was quick to notice her presence.

"I won't start anything, General, if I don't have too," Mitch replied.

"I was going to ask Samantha to do this, but considering the risk factor, I knew that you would be upset if I didn't give you the option first," The General added. "Is that someone new to your crew, Mitch?"

Mitch's lips showed a toothless grin. "This is my Chief of Security, Athena. Athena, this is General Harris of the Mercon Protection Corporation."

Athena bowed slightly as was her customary greeting. The General raised an eyebrow in curiosity.

"It's a long story, General," Mitch said as he continued to smile.

"I'll be waiting to hear that one when you return, Captain," The General replied with widened eyes and a turned-up grin.

"I'll be in Gunner's Redoubt in a of couple days, General. You make sure that those paranoid idiots on Madeus know that we're coming."

"We'll be waiting, Captain. Harris out."

When the comm disconnected, all eyes turned toward the Captain. Yurie was the first to speak.

"Captain," Yurie said with a concerned expression, "I did some research on that system some time ago, and the General is understating the dangers that those people pose. They're a very aggressive culture and all of their people are either worker-slaves or soldiers. Their system is smaller than Alderon but it has many diversified resources, so they don't need much trade. They always send their own ships out if they need goods and they don't let outsiders in. This is extremely unusual for them."

"I agree, Captain," Lt. Stevens added. "I think we should come up with a safer plan. This sounds bad all the way around."

Mitch looked over to Inna, "Well, Inna, have you nothing to offer?"

"While I agree with everyone, Captain, I think that the greater cause is served here by providing something that is so desperately needed to save their people. I couldn't sleep at night if I knew that I had failed to prevent millions of deaths, simply because I could not overcome my fear for personal safety. We've been through a lot together and we have a good crew. I think that we can handle the risks. If we're successful, perhaps that will encourage a change in their attitudes towards outsiders."

Mitch stared at Inna for a long moment before asking, "Can anyone here argue her point?"

Not a word was uttered. Stevens turned his attention back to his console and Yurie politely shook her head.

"Thank you, Inna, for your sobering perspective. Yurie, plot a course for Gunner's Redoubt and let's get this mission underway," Mitch said as he nodded his head toward Yurie.

CHAPTER EIGHT

THE RIVERS RUN WAS A SLEEK FREIGHTER WITH ELEGANT LINES and a graceful look. Her Command and Control bridge was positioned midway between her nose and the first obvious break in her clean lines, approaching her midsection, where the cargo bays began. The frontal portion of the ship was wedge shaped, and her extensive array of sensors and communications rods protruded forward, like arrows from a quiver. Below the sensors were two pods, that appeared be part of the sensor array, but they were in fact, twin plasma chain guns, neatly concealed within retractable doors. At 608 meters in length, the ship was over half a mile long, with extra-large cargo bays, each big enough to support two full size interceptors plus their support equipment. The interceptors were 9.3 meters in length, slightly larger than her Minnow civilian transport at 8.5 meters. The fighters provided an added measure of protection, if needed. The Rivers Run normally only carried two fighters and two Minnows. The cargo bays were all dual purpose, with retractable exterior doors concealing their cargo pods and launch tubes. Smaller cargo could be loaded from the rear cargo access hatch mounted between and below her engine cones, but because most space stations were not set up for a ship that size, cargo pods were added and removed moved via cargo tugs and drones from outside the ship. Once each bay was loaded the doors were sealed and the environment was restored and access could be made from within the ship. The Phoenix was the original design for a dual purpose freighter with its unique retractable exterior doors. Since the Phoenix was smaller, at 315 meters and eight freight bays, she could dock in conventional fashion as long as her size didn't interfere with a station's balance in orbit. Although the Phoenix was only half the size of the Rivers Run and her sister ship the Odyssey, she was still classified as a large freighter. Most freighters sported four to six standard cargo bays, but the bays on the Phoenix were twice the size of the standard freighters so that she could transport much larger cargo pods and had the added advantage of the duality of exterior *and* interior load capability.

A major change in the design of the freighters used by the Saber Corporation was in their armaments. Other space freighters had electronic shielding with limited laser cannons. While most of the smaller freighters preferred to stay within the limits of their home systems, those that travelled between systems often had to hire mercenaries, or mercs, to protect their valuable cargo. The Rivers Run, like the other freighters in the Saber fleet, enjoyed a host of deadly armaments with which to defend her crew and cargo. It had been Mitch's decision to include more lethal weapons systems in their fleet, at a significant cost, versus hiring mercs every time he wanted to trade out of the Alderis system, which he had planned to do regularly. One unique quality shared among each freighter, was the internal security laser system. Anyone who entered the ships was required to either wear a temporary badge or have a small implant placed just under the skin to allow safe movement about the ship. If an intruder was detected, then without this implant a small, but lethal, laser would drop from behind a concealed panel in the ceiling to instantly target and kill the intruder. The lasers were in every area of the ship and the system was completely automated.

The Saber Corporation ships were impressive hybrid vessels that could easily take on much larger ships, designed just for combat. The hybrid freighters had been immediately embraced by the systems surrounding Alderon, because of the added protection to valuable freight and the need to hire, or provide, military protection. The Traders Union disliked the Saber Corporation's use of such comprehensive weapons systems, and they had implored the Sabers not to use them. They felt that these self-protection capabilities would put a target on the other smaller freighters who were not equally as well equipped. Mitch and Laurel had argued that they were seeking more volatile freight loads and as such, their additional weapons were justified. The other understated reason for the Union's dislike was the fact that the Saber Corporation would surely gain much more favor with the outside systems due to their unique vessels' capabilities.

Unlike the Phoenix, the Rivers Run weapons systems were neatly concealed inside retractable doors and elevators. Her only obvious weapons were the twin beam weapon domes mounted on the top of her hull. All of their ships were equipped with cloaking devices, which made them invisible to most sensors and visual devices, allowing them to bypass threats without being observed. Cloaking devises required a lot of energy to create a field that simply mirrored the space surrounding a ship. Smaller ships, like the Minnow transports and fighters, didn't generate enough energy to use the cloaking field. Larger ships, like cruisers and frigates, couldn't generate enough power to maintain a stable shield while continuing to fully power the huge ships and their weapons packages. Since the device was awkward, highly technical, expensive and difficult to maintain, it was rarely used by most fleets. Cloaking also used too much power to be utilized during FTL, or Faster than Light, travel, resulting in slower delivery times.

The Rivers Run had been a wedding gift to Samantha Rivers when she married Captain Mitch Saber, becoming Samantha Saber, Captain of the Rivers Run. Samantha and her crew had just passed through the third in a series of gateways during their exploration of new systems. They dropped navigational buoys and communications repeater buoys along the way as they mapped and scanned each new system, determining their suitability for mining and/or settlement. Many centuries ago, after the great wars, famines, and geologic upheavals on old earth, their people took to space and settled scores of outlying systems, each colony developing their own culture and political system. Most now had peaceful trade and travel relations with their neighboring systems, but there were always a few that severely limited trade, travel and communications. Mining for resources and colonization were still important and newly discovered planets were a boon to many swelling societies. Of course, there would always be the criminal element of raiders and privateers that would be troublesome. Many people lost their lives, others were enslaved for generations, and still others simply disappeared, never to be seen again. Eventually, most of the raiders had been killed, but their home base of operations was never been found. There were those who still wondered not if, but when, they would reappear again. There were hundreds of small exploration ships that had ventured into space never to be heard from again. Most were assumed to be lost but the ship wrecked survivors, found by the Phoenix on Helios, was a reason to believe that there may be other unknown settlements of survivors out there, waiting to be discovered. These explorers' ships had not been designed for exploration, but they had traveled through the anomalies, or gateways as they later became known accidentally and some survived. Not everyone had a chance to discover new systems and new planets.

"Captain Saber," Lt. Saperstein called out, "I'm detecting an energy signature about sixty thousand miles ahead off our port side."

"Mr. Iverson, change our course and head to those coordinates," Samantha ordered. "Any more information on that energy reading, Lt. Saperstein?"

"Negative, Captain. It's very minimal at best," he replied.

"Double check those readings, Roth, it could be an error."

"I already did, Captain. I'm positive that it's an energy signature, but it's very weak. At our current speed, it should be within visual range in about an hour." Time ticked by slowly, until Lt. Saperstein called out to the Captain once more. "We should be within visual range now, Captain."

"Bring it up on the big board, Lieutenant," Samantha ordered.

A wide narrowly channeled frame rose from within a hidden portion of the command bridge, in front of the currently closed view port. A three dimensional image came into view. Barely noticeable in the darkness of space, a large object loomed ahead.

"What the hell is that thing?" Ensign Iverson blurted out as everyone stared at the image with widening eyes.

"Slow us to one-third, Mr. Iverson," Samantha ordered as she stared at the monstrous object. "Roth, what do your scans show?"

"I think it's a ship, but I'm not sure what these readings mean," he replied. One thing for sure, it's nearly three miles long!"

"ALICE," Samantha called out.

"Yes, Captain," the Rivers Run AI computer system answered.

"Scan the ship ahead and give me a report."

"Scanning... The vessel measures 4,520 meters in length. The hull is an unknown form of metallized organic matter. I do not detect any life forms within the vessel but the hull is preventing more precise scans. I detect a minimal measurement of energy emanating from the engineering decks. There is currently no breathable atmosphere within the ship. Their gravity systems appear to be minimal, but stable. There is no forward or lateral movement and it is currently in a fixed, stationary position."

"Mr. Iverson, move us to within ten miles and let's light her up and see what she looks like," Samantha directed, with a serious, but curious look on her face. Her heart rate quickened as her excitement grew. Being ever cautious, she wasn't taking any chances.

The ship was larger than the carrier, Rachel's Gift, which had been her former command vessel. She knew that engineers had tried for decades to develop an organic self-healing hull, but they never had been successful. If this ship was salvageable, then it could be a real find for scientists and engineers throughout all systems, or it could be a real asset for the company. For right now it was an alien ship, and until she could investigate further, it would have to be handled with the greatest of care.

They moved closer and Ensign Iverson activated the Rivers Run flood lights. The alien ship's sheer mass and length was an incredible sight. The hull had a black and green sheen that reflected their lights, small arcs of electricity could be seen dancing between sections of the huge ship. Her surface shimmered, and then the green colors began to move in the reflected light, almost like it was alive.

"What are those arcs, Captain?" Ensign Wang asked. "And the surface looks like it's... moving."

Samantha looked closely before she replied, "I'm guessing that is static electricity. The hull is an organic structure, so it must be reacting to our lights. I don't see any outside evidence of damage. Does anyone else?"

She did not hear a response.

"Mr. Iverson, take us around to the other side and let's see what's there. Ensign Wang, call Chief Henley to the bridge, stat."

As they began their turn toward the other side of the huge ship, Master Chief Petty Officer Regis Henley entered the bridge.

"Holy shit! What the hell is that thing?" the Chief exclaimed to the amusement of the others.

Samantha chuckled lightly, "I was hoping maybe you could help us identify her, Reggie."

"That damn thing is bigger than a lot of space stations, Captain. Is that hull..."

"Organic? Yes Chief," Samantha interrupted.

Reggie shook his head in admiration and awe. "Her skin looks perfectly smooth, no signs of seams or rivets. That surface movement is eerie, and look at the static discharge. She's amazing! Is she a derelict?"

"We're not sure. We're getting a minimal power reading from their engineering deck. Alice didn't find any life readings, but the hull is interfering with her scans. I haven't seen any visible damage so far. Perhaps they suffered loss of atmosphere, a hull breach, radiation or a bacteriological contamination," Samantha reasoned as she crooked her head to one side.

The Chief leaned forward as if he was focusing on something, "What is that?" he asked pointing toward a section further aft on the derelict. "I may be crazy, but that looks like a landing bay to me, Captain."

All eyes stared hard at the indicated area. There was what appeared to be a wide mouth on the side of the ship, protruding from the otherwise sleek design.

"It looks like she could launch a dozen or more ships at the same time from an opening that wide, Captain," Reggie guessed. "Are we going to board her?"

"All stop, Ensign Iverson, and hold this position. Bring the crew to alert status." The alert claxon rang out as Samantha continued, "I'm going to suit up in power armor and I want you, Commander Simms and Officer Danny Clark to join me for the boarding party. Full suits and weapons, there isn't any atmosphere. Not knowing what we may find over there, let's be prepared for everything and anything. We'll meet in twenty minutes at the Minnow in bay one."

The power armor Samantha wore was an intimidating sight. The outer skin was a spun titanium and ceramic composite material, impervious to almost any weapon fire. Each joint in the armor had tiny servo motors and actuators that give the wearer the strength of more than ten men. Originally developed for search and rescue units, the developers had quickly decided that the suits had greater potential uses in the military. Two Gatling Lasers were attached to each thigh within easy reach, and large 14 inch battle knives were attached between the elbow and shoulder of each arm. Tiny jets provided propulsion in negative gravity conditions, and the boots were equipped with gravity devices. When the helmet was attached, the suit was completely sealed, designed for the harshest conditions. The domed helmet housed a complete sensor array, and the internal systems were linked up with the Rivers Run computer AI. A host of small video screens provided three hundred and sixty degree views from within the helmet, displaying targeting lasers to assist in using the weapons system. With the exception of a narrow opening at eye level, the wearer's face was obscured, offering

no indication that a person was inside. The helmet was so airtight and protected that a speaker was concealed where the mouthpiece should have
been, in case the wearer needed to be heard aloud. With these advanced
listening capabilities and superhuman strength, the power armor was not
to be taken lightly. It required extensive training to use, and each suit cost
more than a small civilian transport ship. Each freighter in the Saber fleet
had one suit assigned to it, and Samantha was the only authorized user on
her ship. She gave the boarding party a quick rundown on the operation,
primarily to see if the ship was occupied and operational and if possible,
to determine the ship's origin.

The Rivers Run moved slightly closer to the derelict so that her flood
lamps would better illuminate the landing bay. As the Minnow approached,
the flood lights cast eerie shadows inside the landing bay, creating butterflies in the stomach of more than one of the crew. They could see that there
were no other ships within the confines of the dock area, only a smattering
of crates and miscellaneous equipment. Various ducts and cables hung hap-
hazardly from the ceiling. Samantha exited the Minnow first, and activated
twin head-mounted two thousand lumen lights on her suit, illuminating a
broad area. After visually checking the general premises, she issued a verbal
command to the suit's computer to narrow the beam. Most of the suit's
functions were controlled by voice command. The other members of her
party were equipped with long and short versions of the Barris Ultrasonic
weapons. The Barris USP7 sidearm and the full length version, the Barris
USR9 Ultrasonic Rifle, were perfect for boarding parties in zero gravity and
limited atmosphere conditions. The weapons could be dialed down in power
to limit damage, or dialed up to blast through walls and reinforced doors.

"I'm reading low gravity and zero atmosphere," Samantha advised her
party. "I'll take point, everyone else fall in. We're heading for the engineering deck first, to see if we can restore power." Everyone acknowledged
through the communications devices in their suits.

They approached a door that appeared to exit the landing bay. It didn't
automatically open, which wasn't a real surprise, but Reggie was quick to
notice a large ring on one side of the door that they assumed was an emergency opening crank. Reggie tried to turn it, but it didn't budge.

"Let me try it, Reggie," Samantha said. She placed both hands on the ring,
and although it was stiff, the ring turned and she could feel it vibrate as the
door slowly opened. Walking through the door, after looking left and right,

she lifted her left arm and actuated a small screen that was mounted just above her wrist. She looked at the tracking image and overlay of the ship that the AI was providing and said, "Let's head this way," as she pointed left.

The corridor was extra wide, so with Samantha in front all three of the others could walk side-by-side and still have room to maneuver quickly. The ceiling was quite high, similar to those in their own cargo bay corridors, which made them, wonder for what purpose this ship had been designed. Running along the upper corners of the corridor were conduits and cables, most of which appeared to be in decent condition considering the effect of prolonged exposure to the cold of space. The corridor was lined on both sides with closed doors, or hatches, some larger than others, and they made no attempt to open them. They passed a few intersecting corridors but continued on a straight path.

"Is it just me, or is this place a little creepy" Weapons Officer Danny Clark asked.

"It ranks an eleven on my creep-o-meter, Danny," Chief Reggie Henley answered and chuckled at his observation.

They reached a point where the corridor seemed to widen into a "V", and they slowed their pace as Samantha widened her lights' beams to get a wider view of the area.

"This looks like a staging area, but it's completely empty," Commander Jorge Simms observed. "I'm getting an energy reading up ahead."

"I see that reading too," Samantha said, dimming her lights several degrees. "Looks like it's about two hundred yards ahead, so let's pick up the pace a little."

Moving further down the length of the ship, they had passed a myriad of double-sized pressure doors when Samantha slowed to a stop.

Reading the sensor sweep on her interior visual monitor, she motioned to her left. "The energy reading is coming from inside here." She dimmed her lights a little more and added, "Look around the door, see if you can find a way to open it."

Each man was running his hands down and across different panels on the door when Jorge announced, "I've got something here." As he passed his hand over an area just above his shoulder level, a panel glowed dimly.

"Everyone take your positions. I'll cover the opening," Samantha said. Jorge pressed the lighted panel and they felt a slight vibration in their feet as the door labored to open. When it had opened just a few inches, it stopped.

Samantha stepped forward, grasped the door, and pulled hard. On her third attempt she moved the door aside far enough to allow her to pass through and turn up her lights to illuminate what lay beyond. The others joined her one at a time. Two walls of the large room were completely covered with controls, readouts, and consoles. One console, about the size of a large shipping crate, stood alone between the two walls of operations panels. Casting her lights further into the area illuminated three large cylinders in the middle of the room, each cylinder at least 9 meters in diameter. Inside each of the clear cylinders were two huge orbs that glistened when the lights hit them. They appeared to be suspended inside the cylinders without supporting cables or harnesses to hold them up and apart. A waist high railing surrounded each cylinder, obviously designed to keep people away.

"What do you suppose those things are, Jorge?" Samantha asked curiously.

"This is apparently the engineering deck, so I'm guessing that they have something to do with power generation. I've never seen anything like it," he replied in amazement. Walking over to the console in the center of the room, he announced, "This is the source of our power readings, Captain. I've got several lights here, but I don't recognize the language. It looks like a combination of Cyrillic and Chinese. It's the oddest thing I've ever seen, but the controls seem to be arranged in a logical fashion."

"See if you can bring up the power, Jorge," Samantha directed in a cautious voice as she contacted her ship." Roth, we've located the power source. Jorge is going to see if we can restore any of the ship's power, stand by."

"Aye, Captain," he replied.

Jorge slid his fingers up one of the lighted keys. In response, many of the other control panels slowly began to glow dimly. Sliding his fingers further up and touching another pad brought a dim glow to light panels on the ceiling too.

"Captain!" Danny shouted, "Look over here."

All heads turned toward Danny's position and they saw him pointing to a chair that was positioned in front of a console. Sitting there in a tattered uniform, were the remains of a long since deceased humanoid, facing away from them. One of its skeletonized arms lay detached on the deck, next to the chair. Danny and Reggie circled around to the front of the chair and inspected the occupant. The mummified corpse's skin was leathered and the lips were pulled away from the teeth, revealing an eerie grin.

Reggie gingerly touched a spot on the uniform and the material promptly disintegrated. "Buddy, you've been here a very long time," he said.

Other than those abnormally long legs, he appears to be human, Captain," Danny said as he counted the ribs. "The insignia on his uniform has long since decayed; even his boots have nearly turned to dust. There must have been atmosphere here long enough for his body to partially decay before mummification started."

"Captain," Jorge called out, "I think I can restore some of her atmosphere, but I'll need to activate her power cells to be for certain. This console is the primary control unit for this section. If I'm reading this correctly, there are four more rooms identical to this one on this deck."

"Alright, people, stay frosty," Samantha cautioned. "Jorge, see what you can do."

Touching more keys and motioning controls with his hands across others, the various panels came to life, and the controls glowed brightly. Lights blinked and panel displays began to appear on screens. He walked over and positioned himself between two consoles saying, "Alright, here we go."

A whoosh of air and particles burst forth from vents and pipes and a flash of electricity caught their eyes. They turned to see the first of the three cylinders activate, and the floor between the railing and the cylinder lit up. Blue waves of plasma began forming inside the cylinder and slowly pulsed between the two orbs. After several more minutes had passed, the other two cylinders repeated the same process as the first. The crew felt their stomachs becoming heavier and they realized that Jorge had restored full gravity control.

"This gravity is a little lighter than what we're used to. Give me a minute and I'll adjust the settings. I've activated as much atmosphere as I can from here. I'll need to activate another power unit in order to restore it for the entire ship. We should be able to access the bridge and medical areas now, and maybe the Captain's quarters, but we need more power for complete functionality."

"Should we remove our helmets, Captain?" Danny asked.

"I'm not detecting any biological contaminants, but let's not take the risk until we can do a better check," Samantha answered. "Jorge, can you restore more of the interior lighting and perhaps some door functions?"

"Aye, Captain, as soon as the third power unit comes fully online, we should be there. Do you want me to activate another power unit?"

"Yes, but do it nice and slow. We don't know what happened here and why this ship has been left derelict for so long. I'd prefer to have some answers first, so give me a heads up before you do it. Reggie, you stay here with Jorge and don't let him out of your sight. Who knows what else the power-up cycle may activate. Roth, we've restored gravity and some atmosphere. Danny and I are heading to the bridge. Let me know if anything happens."

"Affirmative, Captain," he replied.

They headed back in the direction from which they had come, a little more at ease now that some of the ceiling and floor lighting was beginning to blink on and slowly grow from dim to bright. As the atmosphere and environmental functions came online, they could see the frost began to melt away and trickle down exposed surfaces. They passed through the large open area again and continued toward the area where they expected the bridge would be located. As Samantha passed by the landing bay, something caught her attention and made her pause for a moment. A shimmer of green light forming on the outer edges of the landing bay.

Danny noticed it too and said, "That looks like some kind of barrier shielding. You think it's the original landing bay shields?"

"Makes sense to me, Danny," the Captain replied. That's probably due to the environmental controls coming back online. Let's close the door where we entered from the landing bay."

Danny reached over to the door controls and pressed the button, and the door slowly closed with a grind.

"Well, that's some progress," Samantha commented. "Some larger ships have automatic lubrication systems for doors and hatches. Let's hope we get enough power restored so that some of them start working again. Let's keep moving."

They passed multiple intersections with other corridors as they moved forward, far more than they had encountered on their way in. Noticing a few open doors on a side corridor, they stopped to inspect them. Beside each door frame there was the now familiar writing, obviously denoting who or what was behind that particular door, but they couldn't decipher the language. Looking inside several open doors they discovered that they were in the crew quarters area. Each berth was very similar to their own, with two bunks and two small desks.

"Looks as though their living conditions were like our own, Captain," Danny observed.

"It does at that. But the language and technology are quite different than anything I've ever seen. Let's go back to the main corridor and locate that bridge."

It took them longer than they expected to walk the nearly three mile length of the enormous vessel. They came to a "U" shaped intersection with two large doors in front of them where the corridor seemed to wrap around them with pressure doors at the end of each one.

"Which one do we choose, Captain," Danny asked.

"I don't think that the one in front of us is the main bridge entrance. Since the left and right side doors are pressure doors, I'm guessing that those are the bridge access doors. Only one way to find out," Samantha replied as she turned and headed to the right side pressure door. "Jorge, we're about to enter what we think is the main bridge control. Do you have the power up back there?"

"Aye, Captain, I've got five of the power cylinders up and I'm preparing to bring up number six," Jorge replied.

"Stand back, Danny. I don't know if there's anything on the other side of this door or not," Samantha said as she pointed behind her.

She ran her hand down the left side of the door and the door control pad slowly began to glow. When she pressed the control pad, the center lock ring turned slowly but steadily and the seal cracked open, releasing a cloud of vapor from around the door's edges. The door moved forward slightly and to one side. The light from many control panels glowed brightly inside as they cautiously entered the bridge. The lighting was brighter than they had expected to find with the faint glow from ceiling and floor light panels illuminating the expansive room. The room was laid out on two levels. To the right of the door through which they had just entered, were three steps leading up to the first level where the captains command chair was readily identifiable. Sloping downwards on a gentle decline was the rest of the bridge control room. This room was at least twice the size of the Rivers Run Bridge, Sam noted. There were five seats mounted on the deck with numerous panels and readouts filling the surrounding walls. Samantha turned an approached the command chair. Her armor was too bulky to allow her to sit in the chair, but she could closely examine the console from her standing position. Several screens displayed scrolling data, but she couldn't interpret what they said. She assumed that they were status screens.

Danny's pressure suit allowed him to sit, so he found what he presumed was the most logical position for the communications console, and sat. In some ways the design was similar to that on their own ship, but there was still the question of what control would do what. He made an educated guess and touched one of the keys. Suddenly, the forward upper one-third of the forward portion of the bridge appeared to become a crystal clear window.

"Captain!" He called out, "Look at this!"

Samantha glanced forward to see the front of the room practically disappear. The view of their local space was incredibly clear, just like they were looking out a window. Off the port side they could just see the back third of their own ship standing still, alongside the derelict.

"That's incredible; I feel like I could just reach out and touch space."

She appreciated the view for a moment longer then returned her focus to the command console. There was one steady light flashing on the panel and Samantha's interest was fixated there.

"I think I may have something here, Danny." She touched the steadily blinking key, and a video image appeared at the front of the bridge, super-imposed on their exterior view. The image was that of a serious faced man who looked very much human, with a dark, olive complexion and dark eyes. He wore a solid piece of metal on his head that covered his forehead and ran across the top and down the sides of his head to just above his ears. It was gold in color with a small insignia that she couldn't quite make out, stenciled on the forehead part. His uniform was red with heavy gold braids hanging from each shoulder and a banded collar surrounding his neck. His expression was stressed and even at first glance, Sam recognized the signs of fear. He began to speak in a deep voice but she couldn't understand what he was saying. His speech was rapid and he kept looking left and right, as if he were expecting someone to burst onto the bridge. Her power armor was actively recording everything, so hopefully his address could be trans-lated once they returned to their own ship.

"Captain, I may not be able to understand their language, but these readout's are pretty clear. It looks like this ship has been here for nearly four hundred years! If we can translate the language, then we may be able to figure out where she was from."

"Captain Saber," Lt. Roth Saperstein radioed in.

"This is the Captain, go ahead Roth," she answered.

"The ship's running lights have come on and the electrical discharges on her hull have stabilized. I'm reading full power to her landing area protective shields. Our scans show a twenty-five percent increase in the power levels and the atmosphere and environmental functions are beginning to normalize. How much longer will you be there?" Roth asked.

"Not much longer, Roth. I've got what appears to be a message from the ship's Captain that I hope we can translate. We need to get inside this language before we can investigate much further," Samantha advised. At that moment, Reggie interrupted in an urgent tone of voice.

"Captain! This is Reggie. We've got something moving down here. The footsteps sound metallic and I don't like the sound of them." Samantha detected fear in his voice.

"Secure the area that you're in, Reggie. Danny and I are on our way. Try not shoot at anything until you run out of other options. Tell Jorge to decrease the gravity a little so that we can make better time getting back to your location."

"Roger that, Captain, and don't stop for a snack on your way!" Reggie tried to joke, but the concern in his voice was unmistakable.

"Let's get moving, Danny. Alert the ship that we may be making a quick exit."

Danny took care of her request as they made their best possible time along the nearly three miles of corridors that they needed to travel. Samantha's power armor allowed her to keep a faster pace than Danny, so she gradually pulled farther and farther ahead of him.

"Don't get too far ahead, Captain," Danny called out. He knew that if she got too far ahead, then he wouldn't be able to give her backup support.

"Then you better pick up the pace, Danny!" She shot back.

"Captain," Reggie called. "Whatever is out there is trying to gain entry to our location. Jorge and I are pushing to the rear in case they gain entry."

"Hold your position, Reggie," the Captain ordered, "I'm about fifteen seconds away. Danny is about a minute behind me."

Samantha slowed her pace as she approached the engineering section. Ahead, she could see a figure, slightly taller than her, dressed entirely in black material that reflected the light around it. She could see electrical arcs dancing over the top of its head from front to back. She stopped briefly, increased the optical range of her vision, and was able to see that the top of the head was enclosed in a clear cap. She could also see the gray-pink presence of a brain inside the protective cover. It had no facial expression and she quickly concluded that it must be an android or cybernetic being. Danny caught up and stopped behind her and to her left in the wide corridor.

"What the hell is that thing, Captain?" he asked in a low worried voice.

"I think it's probably a security android, but that's just a guess. Powering up the ship must have restored its functions. There may be more of them, so stay alert. Alright, everyone, listen up," Samantha ordered her team. "It looks like we have an android or cyber-droid out here. I'm guessing that its internal security, so I'm going to try to communicate with it. Put your weapons on their second highest settings. I don't know how strong this thing is or if it can be reasoned with."

"But, Captain," Jorge interrupted, "we don't know their language."

"Then let's hope it can learn quickly, Jorge," she hastily replied.

She approached slowly as she brought her suit up to full power and turned on the powerful lights of her armor. The lights immediately attracted the android's attention and he turned to face her. She advanced to within thirty feet then stopped.

Activating her exterior audio, she said calmly, "I am Captain Samantha Rivers of the ship Rivers Run. We mean you no harm. We found your ship derelict, and we stopped to render assistance. Do you understand me?"

The android's eyes were dark and non-responsive. It gave no outward expression. His arms were by his sides and he watched, as if evaluating options.

"Do you understand me?" she repeated calmly. "I'm Captain Rivers and we're here to help you. Can you communicate with me?

The android moved his mouth and something could be heard but she couldn't understand what he said. Samantha increased her audio pick-ups.

"We don't understand your language. Do you have learning capabilities? We only want to communicate with you. Do you understand me?"

The android starting moving slowly toward her. "Jorge," she called internally, "increase the gravity; let's see if we can slow his pace."

"Aye aye, Captain, increasing now," he replied.

Samantha could feel the increase in gravity. The android was moving more slowly when he stopped and looked back toward the door to the engineering power room.

Samantha tried to draw his attention away from her crew in the engineering room again. "We want to help you, do you understand? What is your purpose here?"

The android turned back to face her and he spoke again, but she still couldn't understand him. He took another step toward Sam.

"I don't wish to harm you. I only want to help. What is your purpose? What are your programmed capabilities?"

He stopped again, now a scant fifteen feet away from where Samantha stood.

"Do not come any closer. We wish you no harm. Please tell us who you are and what happened here so that we can help you." Her voice echoed down the empty corridors. The android's expressionless face concerned her, and now that he was closer, she could see that the metallic surface was protective clothing. The enlarged areas around the knees, elbows and hands indicated enhancements, probably similar to her own power armor, but she didn't see any weapons. Perhaps strength was his weapon, and in that case she could only hope that her power armor would be a match for his.

He spoke again, this time more slowly and she was able to recognize some words. Intruder...ship...program, was all she could make out.

"I'm not here to harm you. Your ship is derelict. We detected no life forms aboard and we came to investigate. Are you okay? Can we assist you? Can you understand our language? We don't understand what you're saying. If you attack us, then we will be forced to defend ourselves. Are there more like you on this ship?" Samantha was becoming increasingly concerned that the android had hostile intentions, but she was determined to give him every opportunity to communicate with them.

He turned and looked again at the engineering power room and looked back to Samantha.

The arcs of electricity that could be seen through the clear skull cap seemed to intensify. His mouth moved out of synch with the words that he spoke this time.

"Intruders must be purged. All life forms must be purged. I am programmed to purge all biological threats to this ship. Intruders must be purged." The words were emotionless and void of expression. The arcs of electricity continued to increase, and he repeated the words again.

"Captain," Jorge said quickly, "I think his programming has been corrupted. My guess is that he was an exploratory android and his programming crashed or it was changed. I think 'purge' to him means death to us."

"I'm afraid you may be right, Jorge. Stand by, everyone. I'm going to make one last plea. Danny, move further behind me in case he rushes us so you have time to get out of the way." Danny moved further back and Samantha spoke out loud again. "We mean you no harm. We are here to help you. Are there others like you aboard this ship?"

"All life forms must be purged," he said again lunging forward, reaching out for Samantha.

Samantha placed one foot behind her to give her more resistance to his movement, and when the android grabbed her, she could feel the strength of his hold. He tried to throw her off her feet but she held fast, and with a twist of her arms and hips, she threw the android off his feet, slamming him against the left wall of the corridor. He stood up and came back toward her again.

"I've got a clean shot, Captain, shall I take it?" Danny yelled.

"No!" Samantha shouted.

The android grabbed her again, this time trying to get a hold around her neck while pushing at the same time in an attempt to knock her off balance. She increased the intensity of her gravity boots, making it nearly impossible to move her from her stance.

"I'm not here to harm you. You must reboot your functions. You are not programmed to kill. What was your original programming?" She continued to try to reason with the android but he appeared not to listen.

Samantha grabbed the arm that was trying to reach her neck and twisted and bent it back until she heard it snap. The arm went limp and the android took a step back to evaluate his condition. He looked at the broken limb that was hanging motionless at his side, and raised his other arm confirming that it was still working. He lunged forward extending his good arm, this time much faster, surprising Samantha with his speed. The impact of his grab rattled her for a brief second as she absorbed it. This time she grabbed his good arm with one hand, and with the other, she lifted the android nearly a foot off the deck plate. The android simply looked at her with a blank stare, his one working arm trying to break free of her grip.

"Captain!" Danny shouted, "There's another one coming up behind him. They look identical!"

"Shit!" Samantha exclaimed. "Well, I tried to do it the easy way." With one hand she snapped the android's other arm then took both hands and slammed him against the wall beside her. Then she flung him, like a bag of laundry, down the corridor toward the second android. He simply stepped aside and continued toward her.

"We don't want to harm you," she said again but this second android didn't stop. He came straight for her reaching out just as the first android had.

Samantha took her guarded stance again, but this time when the android closed the gap it leaped onto her, nearly knocking her over. Her gravity boots kept her firmly planted in position and she lifted up both arms, striking downward, first on his back, then again on the top of his clear skull, smashing it and he dropped to his feet. Brain matter and small arcs of electricity discharged themselves onto her suit and the deck.

"Damn, Captain, that got messy," Danny observed.

"This crap is getting old already," She replied.

"Well old or not, here come two more," Danny alerted.

"Where the hell are these things coming from?" Sam shouted.

These two androids separated in an obvious attempt to attack from two different angles.

"Danny, aim for the control center in the head and fire when ready," Sam ordered.

Danny stood aside the left wall of the corridor, took aim at the android directly in front of him and fired his ultrasonic rifle. The android's head exploded as he fell to his knees. The second one was running towards Samantha when his head exploded from the rear, shot by Reggie who charged out from the power room. Samantha directed the powerful beams of light from her helmet down the corridor and saw two more androids approaching. Danny and Reggie fired and neatly took out both androids with clean headshots.

"I've had enough of this shit. Everyone fall in, these damn things are coming from somewhere, so let's go find out where," The Captain ordered.

She took the lead and the crew following to the right and left of her. They marched down the corridor past the engineering power rooms. A large double door stood open just ahead, and they could see light emanating from the opening.

"Hang back and let me take a look inside first," Samantha ordered.

Her crew took positions again along the left and right walls of the corridor and squatted to keep a low profile. As soon as Sam stepped into the center of the open door, two androids leaped on her knocking her off her feet and against the wall. Two more poured through the open door and moved towards the Captain. As she tried to push off the first two androids, her team fired and exploded their heads and shoulders down the wall and corridor. Sam managed to throw one of her other attackers off and Reggie took the shot, exploding his chest cavity. The last android slammed his fists against the chest of her power armor suit and Sam reached out her hands, as if to slap his ears and, with balled up fists, slammed them into the androids skull, breaking it like a giant egg. She cast off the corpse and returned to her feet.

"I've had enough of this. Let's kick some android ass, people!"

She rushed through the door and her team took positions to her left and right once more. Inside the large room were row upon row of tall, backwards slanting chambers. Each one appeared to hold an android. A door opened first on one chamber and then on another and the androids slowly stepped out of their chambers, turning their heads around to see Samantha and her crew. They opened fire immediately, destroying the androids before either one could take another step.

"Jorge, see if you can find their controls and shut them off," Samantha shouted.

Jorge dashed to the far side of the rows of chambers where an array of panels were illuminated. Another chamber door opened, and again, one shot exploded the android's head.

Three more shots took out three more androids before Jorge shouted, "I think I've got it, Captain."

Suddenly, the android chambers went dim as their power was cut. Samantha looked around the huge room and counted at least one hundred android chambers. "Damn!" she exclaimed, "If all of these had come online at the same time, then I'm not certain that we could have made it out of here quick enough to save our skins."

"I wonder if they knew how to operate the ship?" Reggie asked, as he examined some of the chambers.

"I don't think so," Jorge answered. "I suspect that they were designed for another purpose."

"What makes you say that, Jorge?" Samantha asked as she and the others surveyed the room.

"Well, look how many there are. If they could operate the ship wouldn't they have left a long time ago? They don't have any weapons."

"They're strong as hell, Jorge, that's a pretty good weapon. But they could have weapons somewhere else on the ship that they didn't have time to retrieve. Good thing too, I didn't want to open up with the lasers because that might have done too much damage to the ship," Sam added.

"Yeah, but I still think they were designed with another purpose in mind," Jorge replied confidently. "Anyway, I've cut all power to this section. I suggest that we find the main power conduit for this area and cut it off too, just to be safe."

"Agreed," Samantha said sternly. "Do that first, then we'll get back to our ship, get this video analyzed and see what we can learn. Reggie, advise Roth that we're returning, and have Dr. Sands prepare a decontamination unit for our return."

"Aye-aye, Captain," he replied.

They located the main power conduit and cut the primary power cables to the chambers, then closed and sealed the doors shut temporarily. They brought the first android back with them to be analyzed by Dr. Sands on the Rivers Run. After completing their decontamination, the exploration party returned to their duty stations. Back on the bridge, Samantha uploaded the data crystal with the copy of the video from the derelict ship's bridge to ALICE for analysis.

"What happened on that ship, Captain?" Ensign Wang asked, not hiding her curiosity.

"We ran into a group of security androids, at least that's what we think they were. We hope to know more after ALICE analyzes a video that we found on the bridge. We got partial power restored but we're holding off on full power restoration until we know more about the ship. There is breathable atmosphere, gravity, and sufficient lighting so we can return and hopefully find out what happened," Samantha explained.

"Why don't we go ahead and send over another team to explore more of the ship while we wait for ALICE to complete the video analysis?" Ensign Iverson asked, turning away from her console to face the Captain.

"Simple, Reese," Samantha replied. "It is obvious in the video that the officer who made it was very afraid. We need to know what made him so fearful, not to mention that it appears that the ship has been a derelict for over four hundred years."

A series of collective gasps were heard across the command deck as the crew listened in stunned surprise at this revelation. Samantha continued, "Our best guess is that something may have forced them to abandon ship. We found one partially mummified skeleton that could well be the same officer we saw in the video. He was in the primary engineering room for the ship's power units. Those things were unlike anything we have ever seen. Their engineering deck has four stations with three plasma reactors each. At least we think that they are plasma. At any rate, the power generated by all of them combined must have been enormous. Why did they need so much power? We only activated four of the twelve reactors and look how much power is being generated even as we speak!"

Roth spoke up in an excited tone, "It's probably a war ship like we've never seen before. Did you see weapons?"

"No, Roth, we didn't have time to look. I could be wrong, but I think that it was an exploration ship. But, at this point it doesn't matter. Until we understand the message on that tape, I'm not going to risk sending anyone else. I want a better handle on why she was left here. Now, Lt. Iverson, you have the comm. I'm going to get some food and rest while ALICE does her work."

Lt. Commander Jorge Simms from engineering was in the Med Bay observing Dr. Sands examine the android that they had brought back from the derelict ship. Jorge grimaced as the doctor opened up the body cavity of the android.

"What have you learned so far Doc?" he asked as he looked away for a moment.

"What's wrong Lt. Commander? Don't you have the stomach for real work?" Dr. Sands chuckled good naturedly.

"Not for your kind of work Doc, I certainly don't. I don't have a problem blowing a man apart just as long as I don't have to clean up the mess."

"Honestly spoken, Mr. Simms. To answer your question, this man is more like a bio-mod than an android, but he is far more advanced than either that we have today. From what was left of his brain, I find that it belonged to a humanoid. It had been highly modified with implants and it had circuitry like I've never seen before. I would say that it was programmed to follow a specific program, monitored by a central computer that could alter the program as needed. His chest cavity was reinforced against impact, and tiny servos in all his joints made him quite strong. Reading through the reports, I see that after considerable effort on the Captain's part, she was able to get him to speak a little of our language. That reinforces my opinion that he was controlled by a central computer. Apparently each android demonstrated that it had learned from the collective experience of the ones that came before him. He has a heart and all the other basic organs, but they appear to have suffered from long term stasis. I'd estimate that most of these guys will cease all functions in another fifty years or so. Even revived,

I don't think that they could last more than ten or fifteen years. All of his nervous system has been desensitized."

"What's that mean Doc?"

"They feel no pain or emotion."

"Oh, that explains the odd way that he looked at his arm when the Captain nearly snapped it in half," Jorge recalled.

"And she nearly did. The elbow was twisted off like a celery stalk, only the skin was keeping it attached."

"Gag me with a spoon, Doc. Did you have to put it that way?" Jorge turned and held his hand to his mouth for a moment as if he was going to puke.

"If you can't take the heat, Jorge you better get out of the galley." The Doc turned and smiled at Jorge, who waved his hand in the air signaling his departure. Dr. Sands chuckled as he watched him leaving the exam room.

Samantha finished eating and complimented Petty Officer Brianne Langley on having prepared another good meal.

"Thank you, Captain," the Petty Officer replied. "Do you think we will learn what happened on that ship out there?"

"I hope so, Brie. She has tech that I've never seen before and I'm really curious to know more about all of it. Right now I'm not convinced that it's safe to return until we understand what's on that video," the Captain replied as she drank the last of her vitamin enhanced liquid. Brie took her plate and cleaned up behind the Captain as she stood and made way for her cabin.

Samantha showered and changed into fresh clothes before updated her log with the records of their exploration of the derelict ship. She had just finished her updates when the ship's AI, sent her an alert, requesting her immediate attention.

"ALICE, you requested my attention," Sam said aloud. The ship's AI intercom was active in all parts of the ship enabling the officers to simply say "ALICE" to bring up the AI control voice.

"Affirmative, Captain Saber, I have completed my analysis of the video from the abandoned ship."

"Excellent, ALICE. Were you able to translate the language?"

"Affirmative, Captain. A full translation evaluation with the alphabet has been entered into our translator records. Shall I play the video for you now?"

"Yes, ALICE. Bring it up on my console here." The three dimensional image of the harried officer came into view.

"This is Sub-Commander Brixon of the Explorer Vessel Praxanon. Commander Vass was killed during the first attack by the worker droids. Over two hundred of our crew have been killed and the survivors are now fleeing in our few remaining transport shuttles. We believe that a virus has infected the droids' command and control computer. That system operates independently from our other computers so our primary systems remain unaffected. Our limited weapons supply was seized by the droids before they attacked so we had no way to defend ourselves. I'm the only person now left onboard. I'm going to attempt to reach the engineering section and try to power down all systems, in an attempt to freeze the droids long enough for me to regain control of the ship. Our chief engineer believed that it would take years before they could all be disabled, but I am out of options and will try removing their power source. I've already taken the time shift engines offline so that the droids can't time-jump back to our home world and infect those worker droids too. If you hear this message, don't power up more than one plasma generator, or you'll reactive the droids. You must destroy the computer system and power conduit in the stasis chamber room, or they will never stop. The crew is fleeing for safe harbor on the last habitable planet that our mission explored, the fifth planet in this system. The environment on that planet is relatively stable, but somewhat hostile and there is hope will be a rescue in the future. Please help us but don't reactivate the workers! They will kill everyone! Brixon out."

Samantha took a deep breath and sat back in her seat. That must have been his body in the engineering control room. She felt sadness for his tragic death but admired his dedication to his ship and crew. His message was her confirmation that the androids had reactivated power was restored to the derelict ship. Their extended time in stasis had slowed down their revival time, and that alone had probably saved the lives of her exploration party. Jorge's quick thinking had also saved them from creating a bigger mess. At least they had destroyed the power conduit to the droids' computer control area, but they would need to return and completely destroy that computer system just as the Sub-Commander had described in the video, to be certain that the ship was free from danger. She had to respect the long deceased Sub Commander Brixon by observing last rites and burial for him. She called a meeting of her officers and replayed the video for them.

Shock and sadness was apparent on each face. When the video had ended, Sam complimented her team on their foresight, and then announced that they would return to finish disabling the droids permanently, and give last rites to the Sub-Commander. With the complete alphabet and translation of the previously unknown language, the exploration of the remainder of the ship would be made easier. Samantha was peppered with questions from her officers regarding the Sub-Commander's mention of 'time shift engines' and speculation ran rampant.

Sam soon grew weary of the guessing game and interrupted the crew's excited conversation. "Jorge, what is your opinion about that ship, based on your observations?"

Jorge stood and replied confidently, "Obviously, Captain, we have a lot to learn before we will fully understand what 'time-shift' means. However, I can say that just *one* of those plasma generators on that ship generates more power than our ship possibly can, and there are twelve of those things over there. I think, that alone, says enough. We know from past research that time travel is possible, but we have never been capable of generating enough power to make it happen. This could be the most significant find in our lifetime!"

There was a bustle of excitement in the room and everyone began talking at once. Could time travel really be possible? Just who were these people and where had they come from? What were they doing out here? Did the survivors make it to safety? What were their mission parameters? Why had someone unleashed that computer virus? Dozens of questions with no answers were flying everywhere.

The Captain shouted, "Quiet!" and silence replaced the chaos. "While I can imagine the positive things that could result from a find such as this, I can also see the negative ramifications that could result if this technology falls into the wrong hands. Our first priority is to secure that vessel and try to retrieve her records. Our second priority is to find the fifth planet in this system and try to can determine what happened to the survivors who fled."

"Captain," Chief Danny Clark interrupted, "that ship has been here for four hundred years. Do you really expect to find any survivors? Isn't that a bit of a reach?"

Samantha felt the heat of her temper begin to rise and she glared hotly at the Weapons Crew Master. "If your family had attempted such an escape and survived, wouldn't you hope that somewhere in time your people would come looking for you? Wouldn't you hope that your family could find closure at some point in history?"

Having been properly chastised, Danny dropped his head. "My apologies, Captain. I meant no disrespect to those people. I just thought..."

Samantha cut him off, "No, Mr. Clark, you didn't bother to think! This ship operates as a family. We need to remember that those people who fled for their lives, most likely never returned. They had families too, and we have a responsibility to respect them. Now if any of you don't have a modicum of compassion for the loss of another ship's crew, then when we return home I want you off my ship! This meeting is adjourned. Dismissed!"

The Captain returned to her quarters angry and disappointed. She was disappointed by her crew's lack of compassion. She expected better from them. She heard a knock on her door and ignored it. A second knock sounded, adding to her irritation.

"Come in!" she barked. The door opened and Reggie casually stepped in.

"May I sit down, Captain?" he asked politely. She motioned to a chair and he sat.

"You look a little pissed, if you don't mind me saying so." He calmly observed her face flush with anger again. Sam resisted the urge to bite his head off and managed to remain quiet for the moment.

"Captain," he continued, "I understand why you went off on the crew. They deserved to be dressed down for their thoughtless, self-centered comments. Some of them are concerned that you actually will fire them when we return home."

"That's a consideration," she blurted out.

"Don't be too harsh, Captain. They've never encountered anything like this, hell, none of us has. They feel comfortable speaking their minds freely around you, so they don't always think about the negative impact to morale that their words can have. My heart aches for the losses the people of that ship suffered, and I don't even know who they were. But at the same time, I'm incredibly curious about their technology, just like everyone else. Try not to judge them too harshly, Captain."

Samantha took a deep breath and calmed down, while she considered this. There was probably a lot of truth in what he said, but their reactions still ticked her off. "Schedule another mission to the derelict, first thing in the morning. Same team with the addition of Ensign Iverson and Dr. Sands. I want a full bio-scan run on that ship before we try to breathe their air.

Then send another team to check the officer and crew cabins for clues as to who they were. Let's see what we can learn. I want Jorge to restore power to at least fifty percent so we can get a handle on their mission. In the meantime, tonight I want security and comm buoys placed around this sector so that we get the full picture of everything around here. I'm going to get some sleep."

"Aye, Captain, I'll see to it. Good night, Captain Saber."

"Reggie?"

Reggie turned on his way out the door and paused. "Yes, Captain?"

"Thanks."

"Anytime, Captain, rest well."

Immediately upon return to the Praxanon, Sam and her team removed and completely destroyed the computers and controls for the androids and jettisoned the remains into the system's sun. They found no biological agents, so after Jorge restored fifty percent of the ship's power, they began the tedious task of investigating every room, hold, and corner of the ship. They gently and respectfully prepared the sub-Commander's body for the last rites the exploration team administered. No other bodies were found on the ship, confirming the Sub-Commander's last words. The translator made searching the ship much easier and the data that they were able to retrieve astounded them. Jorge and his engineering team re-badged the engineering controls and balanced the power systems to enhance lighting, door and bridge controls. Every cabin was recorded and its contents were noted. Samantha and Reggie searched the Commander's quarters and learned from his personal logs that he had been married and had three children. The Praxanon mission had two purposes. First, to travel back in time, by approximately seven hundred years, to visit select systems, recording information that was of historical value. Second, they were searching for plants and animals to restore their own planet's food supplies, which had apparently been devastated by an unmentioned catastrophe. This was the only ship of its kind, having taken longer than ten years to construct. The unique organic hull was self-healing, absorbing energy from all available light sources and surroundings like a sponge. It created and stored vast supplies energy using technology as yet unknown in Sam's time.

The Praxanon was on her fourth discovery mission, each mission having taken about one year, when the android attack left her derelict. The ship was indeed capable of time travel, but only in the reverse sense. It could travel back in time but never forward from the present time of its home world. This restriction was hard coded into the ship's time and navigational computers, leaving Sam's crew to wonder why. According to the ship's log, the few weapons they carried were only for defensive purposes, and they intended to avoid all possible contact with other civilizations. The concern may have been that their technology could be stolen and used for less than honorable purposes. This concern surfaced several times in the Commander's personal log, when they had dropped out of light speed and into a settled system. The last mission carried a crew of just over three hundred scientists and other specialists, with no mention of a military presence recorded in any log they could find. The ship's primary defense was her ability to jump into a system, within seconds run a full scan of all planets, then jump back out to a predetermined 'safe' system, where they could evaluate their findings. There did appear to be another defensive system but they could not identify what it was. Jorge estimated that their FTL speed would have been in excess of twenty times the speed of light. The visual records of the time jumps and the resulting effects were something to behold. Samantha wondered if current technology would advance enough in her lifetime to allow her to time jump. These people and their home world were peaceful by nature, and they feared for the safety of their families back home.

Samantha and her team spent five days on the Praxanon and data still remained to be downloaded from her memory banks so they would need to return later to finish gathering information. Jorge powered down all of the systems to minimum levels, leaving just enough to maintain gravity and atmospheric controls, locked out the computers and placed a coded lock on the landing bay security field to prevent access, should anyone else come across her before the Rivers Run returned. Leaving the Praxanon well secured, the Rivers Run set course to the fifth planet, where they hoped to find evidence of the survivors who had fled the ship.

"We've arrived at the fifth planet, Captain," Ensign Iverson relayed to the Captain.

Samantha responded, "Full scan, Roth, tell me what you find."

"Scanning, Captain. I'm not finding any life forms, but I am detecting some high grade metals, structures and some faint power readings."

"What's the atmosphere like?" Sam asked.

"The oxygen is a little richer than we're used to and the bodies of water appear more acidic, otherwise it looks safe for exploration, Captain," Roth replied.

"Alert the team to meet in landing bay one, fully equipped, and ask Dr. Sands to please join us," Sam ordered.

"Aye, Captain," she answered.

Samantha donned the power armor again, just in case any of the worker droids had made their way to the planet, and the rest of the team carried their ultrasonic side arms and rifles. From space, they could see a large body of water surrounding several continents, dotted with numerous inland lakes and rivers and a few mountainous regions, surrounded by vast plains. Following the coordinates from Roth's scan, they located the area of the recorded readings of metals and a faint pulse of power had come from.

Samantha called out to her landing team, "I'm going to circle the area at two hundred feet so tell me if you spot anything." She took a slow turn so that everyone could take a good close look at the area.

"I've got something reflective off the port bow, Captain," Reggie said pointing out the left window.

She maneuvered the ship in the indicated direction and caught a glimpse of an object reflecting the morning sun. The Minnow landed in a clearing about one hundred yards from the object, and the crew split up into two groups to search the area. The Captain and Reggie headed toward the reflective object, while the others headed toward the area where the power pulse had been detected. Reaching their location first, Reggie and the Captain recognized the reflective material as the remains of a ship.

"Captain," Reggie asked pointing at the hull material, "do you think that their shuttles were made of the same material as their ship?"

"If that's their primary construction material, then I guess so Reggie. Pick up a piece and see if it's heavy," Samantha suggested.

Reggie leaned over, and expecting the material to be heavy, he was surprised to discover that the hull material was extraordinarily lightweight. "This stuff weighs almost nothing, Captain." He picked up three more pieces about three square feet in area, holding them in one hand. "See what I mean? I can feel the electricity as the sun strikes the material. It's still organically active. That's amazing after all these years."

"Reggie," Samantha said seriously, "I want you to take four of five of those pieces back to the Minnow, and lock them in a storage crate for safe keeping. When we return to the ship, have them stored in my quarters for safe keeping."

Reggie looked at her curiously as he asked, "Captain? I don't understand. Why would..."

Samantha cut him off, "Reggie, we don't know what we're dealing with here, and I don't this material finding its way into the wrong hands, so please follow my instructions."

Reggie nodded and quickly gathered up five large pieces. "You want me to take them to the Minnow right now?"

"Yes, and don't say anything to the crew, not yet. I'm heading over to their position, so join me there after you get those pieces locked up." Samantha turned and headed in the opposite direction to join the other team.

Over her intercom, she heard Danny call out that he had found something. The sensors in her suit located his position, and she arrived at the same time as the others. Danny was standing at the edge of an overgrowth of vines and plant life. He reached over and pulled aside some of the foliage to reveal a wrecked shuttle craft.

"I think this is one of theirs, don't you?" He asked.

"Looks like the same organic hull to me too, Danny," Jorge agreed.

"Move away, people, I can clean away this undergrowth faster than you can," Samantha directed.

The others stepped away as Samantha took hold of the vines. Using the strength of her power armor, she pulled most of them away with one powerful yank, and then dragged them away. The hull began to arc slightly with its increased exposure to the sun. Samantha reached out to the ring lock on the door and pulled it open. Jorge was the first one to look inside before he cautiously entered the crashed shuttle, alone. He exited a few minutes later and reported, "It's a mess inside; it looks like they stripped it of anything useful."

"Spread out, see if we can find anything else," Samantha ordered. Leading away from the shuttle, she spotted what may have been a foot path at one time. She pulled away more of the undergrowth, clearing a path to the other side of the wreckage, and saw that, in fact, there was path. She called out on her intercom, "There's a foot path behind the crashed shuttle. Danny, come with me. The rest of you continue your search.

Samantha took the lead with Danny close behind, his USR held across his arms in a ready position. They had walked about two hundred yards when the deep undergrowth ended, spilling into an open area with a large lake just beyond their sight line. To their left and right, were at least two dozen primitive shelters that looked like they had been abandoned a long time ago. Samantha called out to the rest of her party to join them. It didn't take long before they were all together and Samantha asked, "Why didn't we see this during the flyover?"

"Our sensors were looking for metallic objects, Captain, and so were we. Any structure with a grass roof would have just blended in with the surrounding vegetation from our aerial view," Jorge volunteered.

"Half the team take the right, the other the left, and let's see what we find," Samantha ordered.

Most of the structures had collapsed roofs and walls, which clearly hadn't been lived in for a very long time. There was a central structure that still had most of its roof in place and none of its walls had collapsed. Samantha was about to go in when Dr. Sands called out,

"Captain, I need you over here, please."

Samantha and the others turned toward the doctor's voice and he pointed to an area behind the central building. They walked around back and came to a halt at the sight of dozens of graves.

"I count at least sixty, Captain," the Doctor said in a sad tone.

"But that can't be all, Captain," Jorge said in a disappointed voice. "These structures haven't decayed enough for this to be the only signs of the survivors' lives here after landing."

Samantha nodded. "I would tend to agree Jorge, but let's not be hasty. We don't know enough yet to make that determination." She turned and seeing Reggie behind everyone else instructed, "Reggie, go bring the Minnow to our location and land her in the clearing over there."

"Right away, Captain," he acknowledged.

"Let's return to that center building and take a closer look around," Sam said as she turned away.

The front door opened a large room that was filled with various forms of primitive seating. It appeared to have been a meeting hall. Sam moved in the direction of a door that stood open at the back of the room. The others followed her, kicking up clouds of dust and grime as they crossed the room. Beyond the open door laid a smaller back room. Crude racks lined two walls and a primitive desk in the center held a large object on top, covered by a tarp.

"My sensors indicate that the power reading is coming from that desk, or what's on top of it. Let's see what's underneath," Sam said as she walked up to the desk and yanked the covering away. Dust and years of dirt flew into the air clouding their vision for a brief moment as they all coughed and waved their hands to help dispel the dust. Sam stepped around the desk and noticed one tiny light emitting a barely visible pulse every few moments.

"Jorge," the Captain motioned him over, "What do you think?"

"It looks like a computer console. Perhaps like what the crew would have had in their quarters," he surmised.

"My thoughts exactly. Go meet Reggie when he lands, and bring that portable power supply back. Let's see if we can figure out what happened here.

Mere minutes later the Minnow landed. Jorge met Reggie and together they carried the portable power pack back to the central structure.

"The rest of you continue to look around for more clues, while we see if there's any information here." Sam ordered.

The landing party fanned out to search through the dilapidated houses, but found very little. A few tattered pieces of clothing and pieces of metal strewn about led them to another old footpath at the opposite end of the clearing, leading back into the dense forest. They wondered if the path might have been made by animals, rather than humans, or perhaps both. Not far from one side of the footpath, they found a large pile of debris, nearly grown over by weeds and vines. They pulled and cut at the vines but without Samantha's power armor and lacking better equipment, they weren't able to pull anything away from the pile.

Inside the back room, Jorge finished connecting the power unit and the old console sprang to life once more. There wasn't any video display since the screen had been smashed, but audio ports were visible.

Samantha reached under her wrist, pulled out two cables, and handed them to Jorge. "Here, plug me up and I can play the audio through my external speakers. My onboard computer should be able to handle translation conversion."

Jorge had a surprised look on his face when he saw the cables. This was a feature of the power armor that he wasn't aware of until now. Remarkably, when he plugged in the cables they fit the ports.

"Here we go, Captain. I don't know if this is the first or the last entry since the display on the unit isn't functioning," Jorge warned.

"We can worry about that when we get back to the ship with the unit, so switch it on."

 He pressed the button and a female voice became audible.

"Day 483. Of the original 135 people who escaped from the Praxanon, only 61 are still alive. Twenty-six were killed when two shuttles crashed attempting to land during a severe electrical storm. The shuttles couldn't absorb the electrical discharges from the storm fast enough, crashing as a result. Another pair of shuttles was seen flying across the lake, but we didn't see what happened to them, nor have we made any radio contact with other possible survivors. Our rations ran out before our first month here had passed. We didn't have the right equipment to test the berries and fruits we found, so some of us died eating them, trying to avoid starvation. We did find fish to be plentiful in the lake just beyond our village. After observing what the local animals were eating, we found wild fruits that we could safely eat. Our last communication from our Sub Commander reported that he was trapped in the reactor room with the worker droids waiting for him just outside the door. He was going to completely power down the entire ship in order to force the droids back into their stasis chambers. He also indicated that would be his last communication." The woman was crying now. "Those will probably be the last words that I will ever hear from my husband. He's forfeiting his life to save the rest of us, all because that grasping scientist wanted everything for himself. He thought he could establish a utopian society and reign as overlord, offering time-jumps to the highest bidders to escape from their enemies. Damn you, Dr. Heins Rangortesh! I felt no pity for you when the worker bots ripped your head from your body." She sniffled and tried to control her emotions. "All of the ship's officers are dead now. Those of us left are mostly technicians and crew. We began to explore our surroundings a bit more these past few months to see if we can improve our living conditions. We ran across a pack of vicious predatory creatures. Their bodies have short wiry hair, and while they run on all fours, they attack from a standing position. Their powerful hind legs and their hands, if that what you want to call them, have large claws that can rip a man's torso in half with a single blow. We've made spears and tried to defend ourselves, but they are intelligent and they hunt in packs of ten or more. We tried to avoid them, but they followed us back to our camp and have started attacking us at dusk every night. The first few nights we were safe in our houses, but they quickly learned that the roofs were the most vulnerable point of entry. We think that they are carnivores because after each attack, the victims are never seen again. Sometimes an arm or limb is left behind after an attack but that's all we ever find. Their horrible red eyes practically glow in the dark, and it's only a matter of time before they kill the rest of us. The few of us who remain are packing our gear, or what's left of it, and we've made rafts to cross the lake to the area beyond. The beasts are quiet in the early morning hours, so we're leaving at first light. Look toward the mountains beyond the lake, and that's where we are heading. May the seven Gods of our Fathers protect us. This is Medical Officer First Class Krishna Brixon signing off."

"Holy shit, Captain!" Jorge said in shock and surprise. "Some red-eyed beast with giant claws is out there waiting on us?

"Simmer down, Jorge. Remember, this audio is over four hundred years old. Haul this equipment back to the Minnow and alert everyone to return to the ship," Sam ordered.

All crew members gathered back at the Minnow, where the Captain ordered them inside. "Alright, people," Samantha said firmly. "Jorge has told you about the animals that are nearby and that they may be dangerous. According to the message that we heard, they attack at dusk and in packs of up to ten. Dusk isn't far off and I want to follow that path to the water's edge to see if there is any more evidence. Meet me there and then we'll cross the lake together. It's less than two hundred yards from here and I can make better time by myself."

Reggie started to argue, but Samantha closed the hatch behind her and walked briskly down the path towards the lake.

"Damn, I hate it when she's that stubborn," Reggie observed.

"You know how she is, Reggie. She wants to keep her crew out of danger until the last possible moment," Danny reminded everyone. "Let's get this thing in the air and keep the scanners active for any life forms. If we see something before her scanners pick it up, we can alert her."

By the time the Minnow rose from the surface, the Captain was already out of visual range. She was making good time along the path, and her thermals didn't detect anything out of the ordinary. Darkness was coming faster than she realized, as the forest drew darkness in, thanks to the high tree foliage. She slowed twice when her audio sensors picked up something unusual, but she kept going since none of her other equipment displayed any warnings. A ping informed her of an object approaching, and then her onboard computer identified the Minnow passing overhead. She looked up but could barely catch a glimpse of the ship as it passed by. She was less than a hundred yards from the lake shore when she received an alert from the Minnow that they had safely landed. The forest cover began to thin and she could just see the lake through the few remaining trees and brush. She stopped, hearing something through the brush to her left and right, but the dense ground cover interfered with the range of her thermals, so she activated her motion detectors. There was a 180 degree arc of bright red dots surrounding her.

"That can't be possible," she thought. "It must be something else." Pushing a small timber aside with her foot she stepped out of the dark forest onto a sand and gravel surface devoid of plants or undergrowth. The Minnow was about sixty yards away, just to her right. She looked around to see if the fleeing survivors had left anything behind. Some small, rotten timbers stacked in a neat pile off to her left appeared to be left over from their hasty raft construction. Since no raft was found, she was somewhat comforted at thought that *perhaps* they had made a safe escape from the beasts that had hunted them. Not finding any other visual evidence, she turned and walked toward the Minnow, when suddenly Danny frantically called to her over the intercom.

"Captain! There's a group of animals closing in from your left and right! They fit the description given by the Sub Commander's wife in her message!"

Sam spun around to see that two groups of eight animals, closely matching the description given by Dr. Brixon, were slowly closing in from her left and right flanks. Hunched over and walking on all fours, they were about four feet tall from the ground to the tops of their heads. One stood up and raised its head, seeming to smell the air. When they stood upright, Samantha estimated that they were nearly seven feet tall. Their front feet, or paws, she didn't know what to call them, had four huge claws and their eyes blazed ruby red. She zoomed in on one of the beasts and saw a face, nearly resembling that of a human, with a slightly protruding jawline. It pulled back its lips in a snarl showing two distinct rows of upper and lower teeth. These beasts looked every bit as fearsome as they had described. Samantha realized that she couldn't defend herself from one of these creatures with only primitive weaponry, and was immensely grateful for her power armor.

Reggie, Danny and Jorge emerged from the Minnow with their USR's at their shoulders.

"Get back in the ship! If one of these things gets inside the ship you'll all be dead!" Samantha shouted through her intercom. She activated her combat systems, as she reached down with both hands to her thighs, and drew her Gatling Lasers. Walking, backwards trusting her sensors to direct her toward the Minnow, she was prepared to defend herself. Two of the creatures stood erect for a moment, then erupted in ear-shattering howls that made her skin crawl, and dropped back to all fours Sam knew it was a signal to the others when two groups of three beasts immediately charged towards her, with their mouths open, displaying those menacing rows of teeth. Samantha squeezed the triggers of both lasers and instantly cut all six beasts in half. Once again, two of the creatures stood erect and smelled the air around them before howling to signal the start of their next attack. The creatures had more than doubled their separation distance this time. Each group of four sprang forward in a sprint that was much faster than Samantha would have believed was possible for them. Dr. Brixon had been right, she thought, these are intelligent creatures. Sam widened her stance and opened up on the creatures, once more leaving lifeless corpses of burning flesh.

She continued backing towards the Minnow, now only twenty five yards away. There were only six remaining creatures. She was hoping that they would retreat at this point, when one of them stood up and howled more violently than before. It was so loud that she could feel the sound vibrating through her armor. Before she took two more steps, at least ten more of the beasts emerged from the forest. With the sun beginning to settle in the sky, she could clearly see the reddish glow from their demonic looking eyes. There were sixteen of them again, and it was like she was starting over. This time when the two that seemed to be in charge stood and howled, half of the beasts sprinted from each side towards her. She took a deep breath and opened up one more time with her lasers, cutting them down. What she didn't hear, or see, was the second howling command that sent four more from each group running to circle behind her. While her fire was concentrated on the frontal attackers they were attacking her from the rear. She had just fired her last laser burst, when she found herself in a flurry of body parts flying past her, left and right, from behind. She turned to see Reggie and Danny standing in front of the Minnow's hatch with their USR's and what remained of the bodies of eight creatures that were nearly on top of her from behind. She had been so focused on her frontal attack that she hadn't even noticed her motion sensor warnings about the attack from behind. The beasts were howling again, so she wasted no time, running as fast as she could to the Minnow. More of the beasts were emerging from the forest to stage yet another attack. Samantha made it to the Minnow, just as at twelve from each group began another run.

"Get the hell out of here!" Reggie shouted, as he closed the hatch behind Samantha.

"Do those things ever give up, Captain?" Danny wondered as he sat down. "I've never seen such a thing. Those attacks were organized and coordinated. I can't imagine those poor survivors trying to stand up against them."

"Neither can I. They're smart, and they learned from each failed attack. Thanks for watching my six back there," Samantha said as she sat down, trying to regain her composure.

"Glad to help, Captain. We realized pretty quickly that you weren't aware of the animals that were circling around behind you. We didn't know if you could recover if six of those things took you down. Captain, you could have dialed up maximum power on your lasers and killed all of them the first time around. Why didn't you?" Danny replied.

"You need to remember, Danny, we're just visitors on this planet. This is their home and they are obviously intelligent. For all we know, this is the only group of their species, and I didn't want to make them extinct. They were reacting to our presence, instinctively protecting their turf. I suspect that in their eyes, we invaded their territory, and that may have been what happened to the survivors too. I didn't want to kill them, nor did I want to be their next meal, so I'm glad that I didn't have to kill all of them. Let's go back to the ship and plan to return tomorrow morning to continue our search," she said and the others quickly agreed, glad to be away from the surface of this hostile planet for the night.

The next day they resumed their search on the other side of the lake. They found signs of rafts that had long since fallen apart, and were encouraged to know that an unknown number of the survivors had escaped from the creatures. Several hours later they spotted a cave that would require extensive climbing to reach, so Sam decided to take a short cut. Using the Minnow, Reggie and the Captain leapt from the hatch into the cave, as the ship hovered along the cave opening. Inside they found the skeletal remains of the survivors, all huddled in the back, as if hiding from some unknown attacker, or perhaps to share warmth. Several smaller skeletons revealed that there had been children in the group too. There wasn't much left from which to identify the remains, so they gathered them up and buried them appropriately, Samantha saying a few words over their graves. A DNA sample had been taken from each skeleton, so that positive IDs could be made, if they could ever offer closure to the families. Sam wanted to believe that if something like this ever happened to her, her crew, or Mitch, that someone would care enough to do them same for them.

It was a somber trip back to the Rivers Run, but they knew for sure what had become of those who had fled from the droid attack on the Praxanon. They programmed a nav buoy and placed it in orbit around the planet, warning of the dangers on the surface, in the unlikely event that anyone else strayed into this sector. They had also placed buoys around the Praxanon, declaring their salvage claim to the vessel. This was a meaningless formality since they were in unknown space, but they did it just the same. Samantha called a ship wide meeting, reminding the crew that they were not to speak of what they had discovered to anyone outside of their crew, under penalty of losing their contracts, or prison. Privately, Samantha had some real concerns about the potential of the Praxanon and the secrets that she still held. While it could be a potential scientific coup, taking their technology to a giant leap forward, the implications of time travel made her fearful. The evil things that men and women will do for power, even in a peaceful society, were the apparent cause of the Praxanon crew's tragic end. The sacrifice of one man, Sub Commander Brixon, had saved some of his crew, at least for a while, and possibly saved millions of people and hundreds of planets from exploitation at the hands of one crazed scientist. Sam had a difficult decision to make. She knew that she could not, and would not, reveal the existence of the Praxanon to any system or government now, or possibly ever. But what was she supposed to do? The ship had been there, a derelict in space, for over four hundred years. Did her home world still survive? If they were to locate that home world, then should they attempt to return the ship?? Would it be to the advantage of all civilizations to simply blow it up? She glanced at the locked crate containing the samples of the organic hull material. That discovery alone could bring her company billions of credits… and billions more in headaches. This was a path without a map, which she would have to travel carefully. She was a patriot and a warrior at heart, but her decision to eventually reveal or forever keep the Praxanon a secret, had too many moral ramifications for her to handle right now.

Well, the first order of business when they returned to familiar space was to contact Mitch and meet up with him and Laurel. Together they would figure out what should be done about all of this.

Sam and her crew had finished mapping the system, when Lt. Commander Simms called on her wristcomm. "Captain, this is Simms; I need to speak to you in private as soon as possible."

"I'll meet you in my office in five, Mr. Simms. Roth, you have the bridge."

Jorge Simms was waiting for her when she neared her quarters, and he couldn't help but notice that something had him excited. She entered the code to open the door and motioned him to enter. They sat at her desk as Samantha asked, "Okay, Jorge what's this all about?"

"Captain, ALICE has finished translating and converting all of the Praxanon engineering manuals and specifications, so I've been reading through them, trying to wrap my head around what that ship was capable of doing. It turns out that we were right in our assumption that she was an exploration vessel, carrying limited armaments. However, I found this vid of a test that had been run on their defensive systems, and you have to see this!"

He placed a data crystal into the reader on her desk and activated the screen. The three dimensional screen came into focus above her desk with the Praxanon in the center of the screen, facing two ominous ships The ships appeared to be about twenty thousand kilometers away, when they both opened fire on the Praxanon with an unidentified energy weapon. The organic hull flared and dissipated the energy bursts, appearing to absorb them completely.

"That's amazing!" Samantha observed. "What are those weapons?"

"Some kind of energy weapon is all I can say, Captain. But watch the next part, because you are about to be *really* amazed!"

The two ships began another firing sequence that lasted for nearly two minutes, while the organic hull continued to absorb all of the bursts. Suddenly, all of the absorbed energy appeared to come alive, as two separate and focused bursts of energy fired back at the two attacking ships. They were both disintegrated within seconds.

Samantha's eyes widened. "That's unbelievable! Explain what happened."

"Well, from what I read in the manuals, the organic hull utilizes all of its absorbed energy to power and protect itself. Like a planet has an ionization field surrounding it, this ship also has an ionization field that works in much the same way. When an energy weapon is fired on it, the ship disperses, absorbs and stores the energy until it's needed. The engineering deck on board has a multitude of controls to direct that stored energy into various areas of the ship, reducing its reliance on the plasma generators for general operations. I learned from the specs that the amount of energy it can store is almost limitless! That's probably why the ship has lasted all this time in open space. It used stored energy to regenerate itself and to protect everything inside. But there is one more thing you need to see, and it will knock your boots off."

"I don't know how you could top that last one, Jorge, but go ahead."

As the vid continued, the Praxanon was surrounded by four larger ships that all began firing at the same time. As best as Sam could tell, they were firing everything they had at full power and the organic hull wavered and arced, dispersing the energy all over the hull. The attackers then changed from a steady fire to a pulsed rate of fire. The hull showed continued to absorb the shots, until a bright flash of light erupted from four corners of the ship, in an immense burst of power, like none that Samantha had ever witnessed before. All four of the attacking craft were disintegrated instantly. There was no explosion or glitter of parts flying into open space. The ships just faded into oblivion. The Praxanon had discharged the absorbed energy into four precise and focused beams of concentrated energy, so powerful that they completely eliminated any trace that the attacking ships had ever existed.

"My God, what a weapon! I'm...I'm speechless, Jorge." Samantha sat in silence, watching the image replay again and again, and couldn't find the words to express what she saw. The energy blast enveloped the attacking vessels and they vanished without a trace.

"One more thing, Captain."

"Damn, Jorge, what else can there possibly be?"

"It's not like that, Captain. Here, watch...this is how it appears when they time-jump."

The image played again of the Praxanon, and this time the hull seemed to pulse almost hypnotically. A burst of light began at the stern, moving forward along the ship's hull to an area about five thousand meters ahead. That area of space seemed to waver and churn, like water passing down a drain. The ship moved ahead, into the void, and disappeared as the end of its length finally passed through.

"Absolutely incredible, Jorge! You can't show this to anyone," Samantha ordered.

"But Captain, this is incredible! Think how this material could protect all ships!"

"No one is to watch this, Jorge, and that's an order," Samantha repeated sternly. Her mind raced with the potential ramifications of this technology.

"As you wish, Captain." Jorge dropped his head as if to pout, leaving the data crystal on the Captain's desk, he turned and left her office.

Samantha paced in her quarters reviewing in her mind all the things that she had seen and read, regarding the Praxanon. Their discovery of the derelict ship was an incredible coup of technology, but she wasn't so sure that it should be shared. This worried her and as her ship entered their home space she keyed the ships intercom, "Master Chief Henley to the Captains quarters."

Moments later, a knock announced itself on her door. "Enter," she said aloud.

"Chief Henley reporting as ordered Captain."

"Reggie, I'm going to have ALICE remove all record of the events that have transpired in the past eight days, and have her store them in a secured file that only I can access. I want you to know because questions may arise from the crew."

"What do you want me to tell them if they ask, Captain?"

"Tell them that the records have been placed under a security lock for the time being. Also, I want you to place all the evidence that we have collected, in a secured container in Bay Two, to be made accessible only by my own hand ID."

"It sounds like you don't trust anyone, Captain."

Samantha smiled at Reggie. "This is security for my ship and the crew, Reggie. The less others know about this, the safer we are, at least in the short term. We are sitting on an enormous tech find, centuries ahead of any planetary system that we know of. This could potentially give one system a significant advantage over the rest, especially a militarily advantage."

"I see what you mean. What about the bonuses that are to be paid for discovery and mapping?"

"The crew will still receive their bonus pay. Mitch will back me up on that, I'm certain."

"Very good, Captain, I'll follow your orders as directed."

CHAPTER NINE

THE OFFICERS AND CREW OF THE PHOENIX SUFFERED THROUGH vaccinations for the Centaurian Flu which turned everyone's skin a reddish purple for two days. Athena was tested thoroughly for any susceptibility to the virus strain and the Mercon doctors were shocked to find that she had a natural resistance to the virus. They asked, and received permission, to take a small blood sample from her to further test her blood against other biological agents. The decontamination pod was installed easily into one of their empty cargo bays and the crates of vaccination were loaded into the rest. Mercon was going to send another shipment of vaccine, via their own ships, to the neighboring systems to aid in the vaccination of their populations to prevent any spread of the deadly virus. It would take fifteen days at full FTL speed to reach Sector 725. Once everyone's skin returned to a normal color, and there were no negative reactions to the vaccines, they would depart. In the interim, Mitch and his officers had dinner with the General and his immediate staff. He and Athena gave a hand-to-hand combat demonstration to the Mercon fighting skills trainers and many of their elite officers. The demonstration was more than impressive and the Mercon trainers were eager to ask for more personal instruction. Mitch and Athena spent the following day holding small workshops, teaching new skills to the Mercon trainers. Mitch and the General watched two of the Mercon staff do their best to take down Athena in hand-to-hand fighting, failing with each attempt. One of their trainers tried several times to get rough with Athena in the ring which wasn't permitted, given the nature of the training, but Athena didn't appear to care as she quickly threw the man out of the ring onto his backside, to the amusement of the others. Not only was the trainer humiliated, but later he was severely reprimanded by the General himself. The man was forced to apologize to Athena, who accepted it graciously, but only after Mitch explained the necessity of an apology. Athena didn't understand the protocols of training sessions and she didn't care how rough the man tried to get. However, Mitch knew that if the trainer had forced the issue too far that Athena would have killed him without hesitation. He made that very clear to the General before he agreed to allow the training sessions. Mitch only shared a small portion of the story behind Athena's presence. He could see that the General wanted to know more, but accepted the need for secrecy that Mitch expressed. Mitch trusted the General, but since the meeting wasn't private, he didn't want to go into detail about her full story.

The crew experienced no other side effects, so on the third day they set course for Sector 725, and then on to the Madeus Empire. Fifteen days later they arrived in Sector 725, and there were two missile cruisers waiting for them, as promised by General Harris. Mitch confirmed their orders and proceeded on toward Madeus Empire space.

"We're in the outer perimeters of the Madeus system, Captain," Yurie informed him.

"Thank you, Yurie. Miss Dubnikov, contact the Madeus authorities and let them know we are here with the vaccine, awaiting approval to enter their system."

"Aye, Captain," Inna confirmed. "Captain, I'm being told to enter their system at two-thirds sub-light speed and proceed directly to the station, then wait for docking instructions."

"What, no military escort?" Mitch asked with a wry smile.

"They said we would be met in due course, Captain," Inna answered.

True enough, they were less than a third the distance to their destination when a squadron of twelve interceptors approached and hailed the Phoenix.

"Captain, they said they are under orders to escort us safely to the station," Inna reported.

"Yeah, well I'd keep a close eye on them. I think the only danger we're in is liable to come from them," Mitch replied.

The Phoenix neared the station and docked per their instructions.

Mitch reminded Chief Tanner of his previous instructions regarding the offloading of the freight, and relaxed back in his command chair to complete the operation. Several minutes had passed when an announcement rang out over the ship's intercom.

"Captain to cargo bay one, Captain to cargo bay one, please."

Mitch touched a key on his arm console. "This is the Captain, what's the problem Chief?"

"Captain," the annoyed reply came, "they won't offload the vaccine cargo until they speak directly to you."

"Why, Chief?"

There was a brief pause. "They say its protocol, Captain."

"Damn it," Mitch huffed, "on my way Chief." The Captain rose swiftly from his seat, and Athena tucked in behind him as he made his way to the loading dock entryway where he found the Chief in a most annoyed mood.

"Captain," the Chief snorted, "these idiots won't let the cargo-bots offload the vaccine until they speak to you in person."

"Who is it, Chief?"

"Some puffed up moron who calls himself Moderator Breen. He's in the pressure lock. He didn't like the fact that I refused to allow him on the ship." He smiled satisfyingly.

"Good job, Chief. Stay on alert and I'll go see what Moderator moron, uh, Breen wants." They both chucked.

Mitch, accompanied by Athena, entered the code and opened the pressure lock. Inside stood a thin man with a dark mustache and broad shoulders, wearing a black jumpsuit with a silver badge over his right breast pocket. He carried an electronic device in his left hand and two silver rings encircled his sleeves just above the wrists. Around his waist he wore a side arm of an unknown nature, and a cap with a long narrow bill was atop his head.

"I'm Moderator Breen, allow me to welcome you to Defense Station Alpha." He displayed a toothless grin and attempted to walk past Mitch to enter the ship, but was promptly halted as Athena cut off his path forward by stepping directly in front of him. He turned quickly to address the Captain. "Captain, I must inspect your ship for dangerous or illegal contraband."

"No," Mitch replied sharply as his eyes tightened on the skinny man, "You won't inspect my ship or its contents today, tomorrow, or ever. This ship is private property and this is as far as you're allowed, so back up Moderator Breen."

Athena took another step toward him and he backed up a step to compensate.

"I'm only doing my job, Captain. Surely you can understand that," Breen shot back.

"Exactly *what* are your duties, Mr. Breen, and *what* is a moderator?" the Captain asked firmly, not taking his eyes off the man for whom Mitch already had a strong dislike.

"Why, I'm your Moderator, Captain. My job is to monitor anything and everything you say and do while you are our guest. I'm here to make sure that everything is handled properly, according to our laws of speech and behavior." He stated the words so matter-of-factly that it made the hair on Mitch's neck come to attention.

"Did I just hear you correctly? That you are to monitor everything that I say and do to make sure it meets your laws of, how did you say...speech... and behavior?" Mitch repeated the words and it made him angry to say them aloud. His anger was apparently sensed by Athena as he noted that she tensed up anticipating his reaction.

"Correct, Captain. Our laws are very specific about this. As you can see by my rank," he pointed to the silver circles around his sleeves, "I am a Second Degree Moderator, which means that I have over one hundred of our caste that I monitor on a daily basis."

"How do you...*monitor*, as you put it, over a hundred people a day?"

"Oh, everything is recorded. Our scanning system is quite well developed, you see. If I suspect that anyone has so much as a thought that is against our laws, I can have that individual brought before a Psy Officer to have his or her mind scanned. My rank of Second Degree Moderator allows me to then render whatever justice I think necessary." He smiled showing his teeth this time and the sight disgusted Mitch.

"So, you're telling me that if I so much as think about something that is against your thought or behavior laws, that you can shoot me on sight?"

"Oh yes, that is very correct. But I've been assigned to you and your crew because you are new here and it is *my* responsibility to see that you adhere to our laws."

"I see," Mitch replied as his face hardened into a fierce glare. "Now let me tell you something, Moderator Breen. This ship is my personal property that you're standing on, and the accepted law of the galaxy is that a ship of any type is private property. The *Captain* makes the law and his law applies to anyone who steps aboard. You are on my private property, Mr. Second Class Moderator Breen."

"It's Second Degree Moderator, Captain."

"So it is, and my word is law on board my ship. And rule number one is that no one is allowed aboard this ship without my express permission, and you, Second Class Moderator Breen, do NOT have my permission!" Mitch barked.

"It's Second Degree Moderator, Captain. But you are in our space so our laws have priority."

"WRONG Moderator! I am here on a mission, requested by *your* government, to deliver as soon as possible a cargo of vaccine to treat the Centaurian Flu epidemic. Just as I have a rule of entry onto my ship, I also have a rule of exit that also applies. No one on this vessel has permission to leave this ship while we are at this station. That's what we have cargo-bots for. As soon as they offload your cargo, we will be taking our leave of this little piece of hell and returning to our own slice of heaven. I would prefer that you exit now so that I don't have to spend any more time looking at you or your Second Class stripes any longer!"

The Moderator stared at the Captain for a long moment and finally replied, "It would seem that we are at an impasse, Captain." He reached for his sidearm and just as it cleared the holster Athena had one hand around his neck while the other seized his weapon. His eyes bugged out a little as she began to squeeze his throat before the Captain spoke.

"Let him go, Athena."

She released her hand from around his throat but kept the weapon. She held it up in front of his face and when he started to reach for it, she crushed it into a mass of metal as he watched and dropped it into his hand. His eyes showed the fear and surprise that anyone would have experienced at the sight.

"I'm sorry, Moderator. This is my Chief of Security, Athena. As you can see, she is very good at what she does. A few more seconds and she would have snapped your Second Class neck." Mitch smirked and hoped that the man appreciated how close he had come to not breathing any longer.

"It's Second Degree Moderator...Captain," the man said in a terse but weakened tone. He tried to compose himself and began once more, "I understand that you don't know our laws and protocols, Captain, so I will... overlook this breech of conduct. As I was about to say, you are required to meet with our Station Chief, prior to the offloading of your cargo. Consider it a courtesy call, if you will."

"My contract stipulates that I deliver the cargo and I am not step so much as one foot off my ship. If I don't adhere to the letter of my contract, I will not get paid, Mr. Breen, so take that back to your Station Chief and let me offload my cargo so I can get the hell away from here."

Mitch turned sharply on his heels and closed the pressure door behind him. He pressed the intercom key to the internal speaker inside the pressure sealed hatch. "The outer door is now open, Second Class Moderator Breen. I'll await your instructions to offload my cargo. Keep in mind that if I don't receive those instructions within...let's say one hour standard time, then I will presume that you don't need the vaccine and I will begin preparations to depart this system."

Breen looked into the view port and started to answer, "That's Second..." Mitch cut off the intercom, turned and saw the Chief grinning broadly at him.

"I thought Athena was going to snap his neck off for a moment there, Captain. I don't think that guy knew how to take you, sir."

"Good for him," Mitch replied. "Thanks, Athena," he said as he smiled at her. She returned the smile, not showing any teeth. It pleased him to see how she responded now that she had more control of her facial expressions. Mitch returned to the bridge.

The time that he had allotted had nearly expired when the Chief called him back to the cargo bay again.

"The Breen guy is back again and this time he has someone else with him," the Chief informed the Captain. "I haven't opened the outer lock so they are on the outside comm."

Mitch nodded and walked over to the inside control panel where he activated the outside view screen.

"This is the Captain. Mr. Breen, are you here to see to the offloading of the vaccine?"

"Captain, I have Station Chief Hargrove with me and he would like to speak to you."

"Speak away, Mr. Hargrove, I can hear every word you say," the Captain replied smartly.

Station Chief Hargrove spoke up with a more commanding tone of voice than Breen had used.

"Captain, I understand that there is some miscommunication here and I'd like to settle it in person, not over a monitor screen, if you please."

Mitch pulled back the focus on the monitor to get a better view of the docking area outside the ship and noted a squad of eight men just beyond the doors of the ship.

"Chief, put the crew on alert and get a security team down here now. Tell the bridge to increase the range of the MARDA."

"At once, Captain," the Chief replied.

"Station Chief Hargrove, I will welcome your presence inside my pressure door as soon as you tell your security team to back away from my ship, please."

He watched the monitor as the man motioned the squad to back away from the ship. Mitch turned when he heard rapid footsteps coming down the corridor, and motioned his crew to take their standard positions for repelling borders, if it became necessary. Mitch activated the outer door and it slid aside allowing entry into the inner pressure relief room. The two men entered, Mitch closed and sealed the hatch behind them, and after the interior was flooded with anti-viral decontaminants, Mitch opened the inner door and entered the pressure room accompanied by Athena. He noticed that Breen took a half step back when he saw Athena, and Mitch couldn't help but grin.

"Captain Saber, I presume," the beefy man said as he extended his hand. Mitch accepted the hand and the Station Chief attempted to show his authority by his hardy grip. Mitch had expected it and returned it with one that was equally firm. He didn't want to break the man's fingers but intended to show that he was in authority. It was an old game but he knew how to work it. Now he wondered if the man would try the same thing with Athena. In a way Mitch hoped not, as the Station Chief wasn't aware of her capabilities, and if he did she would perceive it as a challenge. He reached out for her hand and as Mitch had taught her, she accepted it. He tightened his grip and she tightened it more. A brief look of surprise appeared on his face and he tried to increase his grip. Just as Mitch expected, Athena, without a hint of emotion, viewed his action as a challenge and squeezed her grip so tight that Mitch heard his knuckles crack. Mitch smirked in satisfaction as he watched him try to pull his hand away, but Athena held on tightly. After letting the man agonize for a moment longer, he telepathically told Athena to let him go, which she promptly did. The color had begun to leave his face but rapidly returned as he rubbed his hands together.

Smiling approvingly, Mitch said, "I would suggest that you should never underestimate your opponent, Chief Hargrove."

The man looked at Mitch and stared at Athena for a long moment then replied, "A mistake I won't make a second time, Captain."

"I'm glad we understand each other, Chief Hargrove. I see we have our Second Class Moderator Breen with us again. Hello, Breen."

Breen glared at the Captain and the Station Chief spoke quickly, "Second Class...err, Second Degree Moderator Breen says there is an issue with our inspection of your ship."

"There isn't a problem, Chief Hargrove. I told Mr. Breen very clearly that this ship is my private property and no one was allowed on my ship. My only purpose here is to deliver the Centaurian Flu vaccine as stated in my contract and then to promptly leave. That is exactly what I intend to do. If I'm not allowed to offload my cargo, then I will return from whence I came and I'll take the vaccine back with me. Is that not exactly what I said, Moderator Breen?"

The Station Chief looked at the Moderator as he replied, "Well, yes... more or less."

Mitch interrupted, "Precisely. Then Mr. Breen drew his weapon and my Chief of Security took it from him. It was all a lot of fun, Station Chief. Now, with all due respect, let me deliver your vaccine and I'll gladly leave, never to be seen again."

The Station Chief looked again at Breen. "You said they attacked you, Breen." His eyes were cold and hard as he stared down the skinny man.

Mitch interrupted again, "I have the vid if you would like to see it for yourself, Station Chief."

"No, I don't think that will be necessary, Captain. I'll discuss the matter with this man in my office after we come to an agreement."

"Chief, I've stated my purpose very clearly. There isn't anything else to discuss," Mitch repeated.

"Captain, you need to understand that we must inspect your vessel for contraband. You are a visitor to our system and this is how we do things. If you don't allow this, then your ship will be seized, and it will become the property of the Madeus Empire. Now, if you will comply and let us do our jobs, then we can get the cargo delivered and you can leave whenever you're ready. That is as simple as I can make it."

Mitch recalled the warning that General Harris had given him. Don't let them on your ship, don't start a fight and don't leave your own ship. How was he supposed to do all of that?

Mitch tried to smile warmly and said, "Chief Hargrove, your people are dying of a Centaurian Flu epidemic and on this ship I have enough vaccine to cure all of those who are currently infected, in addition to everyone else in your system. That is the only cargo I have onboard. You are welcome to inspect it as soon as it lands on your dock. Hell, I'll even wait until you have inspected it before I leave, but I will not allow your people on my ship and that's final. Either accept delivery of my freight or let me leave this place."

"You're from Alderon aren't you, Captain?" Hargrove asked.

"That's correct, but what does that have to do with this?"

"I just want to make sure where I need to send the remains when we seize your ship and execute your crew. I'm sure the families would want their people returned for proper burial."

Athena took a step forward toward Chief Hargrove and Mitch put his hand in front to stop her. The Chief placed a hand into his pocket as if he had something important there. Mitch's anger had reached the boiling point and he tried to reel in his temper. Now was not the time to lose his cool. Athena asked him telepathically if he wanted her to eliminate them. He replied that this was not the time.

Mitch returned to his game face and smiled again saying, "Station Chief, my ship and crew are very capable of defending themselves from you *and* your defenses. This talk is a waste of your time and mine. We can stand here and brag about what we can or can't do until we are blue in the face, and we'll accomplish nothing. Let's be civil and understand that we each have a job to do. You need this vaccine and I have a business to run. I can have your head removed from your body and thrown from the outer hatch before you have time to press the button on the device that you hold in your hand right now. Mr. Breen has seen examples of our capabilities, haven't you, Mr. Breen?" Breen nodded his head. "My ship isn't without its defenses and I wish no harm to you or to your station or its people. I'm just a simple freighter captain with a job to do and I'd like to get on with it, with your permission, Chief."

The Station Chief removed his hand from his pocket and said, "You're obviously a very astute man, Captain. I'll tell you what I'll do. If you will accompany me to the loading dock, then we'll allow you to offload your vaccine and you can observe us while we inspect the delivery. If everything checks out, then you can return to your ship and be on your way."

Immediately Mitch received a telepathic message from Athena saying that she detected deceit in his emotion and speech. Mitch quickly formulated a plan and told her what to do. He also sent a message to ALICE and asked that she relay his orders to Chief Tanner as soon as he departed the ship.

"Very well, Chief Hargrove. As you can see, I am unarmed and I'm going to hold you to your word as to our agreement. The Mercon Corporation loaded and inspected the cargo. You are on record in my ship's log that you have given your word that if the cargo is safe and as ordered, that I may return to my ship and leave your space unharmed and without pursuit. Correct?" Mitch smiled as he repeated the words for the record.

The Chief knew that he had been put on the spot, but saw no reason not to agree, so he replied, "Certainly, Captain, just as you said."

Mitch pointed ahead and said, "If you will kindly turn around then we will get this delivery underway."

Mitch's congenial tone caught them off guard so both men turned toward the opening hatch. The Station Chief glanced behind to see that Mitch was following, but he didn't see Athena. He discounted the importance of this because the Captain was the prize, so he continued walking out of the hatch with Mitch following. Athena also followed, unseen, thanks to her cloaked armor. Mitch also wore his stealth armor with the hood neatly concealed inside the neck of the uniform collar. By this time the cargo-bots had begun unloading the cargo of vaccine and placed it inside the grid of the loading bay dockside receiving area for inspection. Chief Tanner would have received his orders via ALICE by this time, and would be making preparations for their departure. Nothing else was said between the Station Chief, Breen and Mitch as the cargo was unloaded. Several men with hand scanners approached to begin the inspection. Unseen by Mitch, one of the inspectors placed an object inside the packing material as he inspected the cargo. Athena, alerted him to this deception, removed the object and discreetly placed it in Breen's pocket. Another inspector repeated the trick and she again placed the object in Breen's pocket. They passed their scanners time and again over the cargo, but couldn't get the scanners to respond to their satisfaction. Finally, the Station Chief grew frustrated at their obvious inability to get the scan results that he expected.

"What seems to be the problem with you people? Bring that scanner over here" he barked.

The inspector closest to Chief Hargrove walked meekly over and handed him his scanner. The Chief activated the machine, which promptly emitted a sharp tone, startling him when it did.

"It seems to be picking up something close by, Chief Hargrove," Mitch offered.

The Chief then smiled at the alert but the smile went away and he grew annoyed at the readings on the unit. He turned toward Breen and the closer the unit got to Breen, the louder the alert sounded.

"I don't think the machine likes Mr. Breen, Chief. But since all the cargo has passed inspection, I will be on my way, and you and Breen can figure out what's going on with your scanner."

Mitch turned, only to be surrounded at once by the eight armed men that still waited on the dock. The Chief said nothing. Mitch looked at him calmly and said, "We had an agreement, Station Chief. The cargo has been inspected and nothing was found. I'd like to be on my way, *now*."

Breen reached into his pocket as the scanner continued to scream the alert, and pulled out the objects that Athena had placed in his pocket. Chief Hargrove immediately gave Breen a disgusted look.

"I don't know where those came from, Chief Hargrove!" Breen announced loudly.

"Ah, I see you have the evidence that you were looking for. I'd hate to be in your boots, Second Class Moderator. Chief, call off your dogs over here so I can be on my way," Mitch said as he pointed a finger at the armed men.

The Station Chief snapped his head toward Mitch and sharply spat out, "They are *not* going anywhere and neither are you, *Captain* Saber. I don't know how you avoided my deception but it's of little consequence. You're out here and away from your crew, so you and your freighter are all mine now. I've heard the stories about how you defeated Asher and his people. All of the weapons capabilities of your ship are now mine. Consider yourself a permanent guest for the rest of your life!"

"Chief Hargrove, here I was thinking that we were getting along so well, and now I see your true intentions. I must admit that I'm not surprised. I actually suspected your deception and I'm quite prepared to defeat you if you don't let me go back to my ship right now." Mitch stated this so casually that it caused Chief Hargrove to laugh out loud.

"Damn, Captain, you are one confident son of a bitch. I've got eight armed men surrounding you. Breen and I are also armed. All I have to do is press the little button that you so innocently presumed that I have, and of course I do, and I'll have fifty armed soldiers on this dock in less than two minutes. If it makes you feel good to make such wild ass statements, then you just go right ahead and amuse yourself." He continued to laugh and Breen smiled broadly, assuming that everything was going according to plan.

The Station Chief had not noticed that when they exited the Phoenix, the hatch remained open on both sides. Mitch's security team should be in place by now. Mitch used his implant to access ALICE and checked on their status. ALICE, utilizing the ships external sensors, confirmed that his team was in place.

"Chief Hargrove, I want to give you one last opportunity to hold up your end of the bargain before I take action," Mitch said, looking into the eyes of the still laughing Station Chief.

"Captain Saber," the Chief replied, "If I didn't know better I'd think you were serious," he replied with a sly grin.

Mitch didn't return the smile this time and stated simply, "I'm as serious as an Atlantian shark, Chief, and I won't make this request again."

"You're a fool, Captain if you think for even a moment that your people can do anything for you."

"Very well, Mr. Hargrove." Mitch raised his empty hand and snapped his fingers.

To the astonishment of Breen and Hargrove two of their armed men were instantly thrown against the bulkhead and knocked unconscious, followed by two more. The squad was stunned by the action because no other persons were visible on the dock. The inspection crew was suddenly knocked out by the impact of silenced ultrasonic pistols, as were the last of the armed squad. Hargrove started to reach into his pocket when he felt something touch his temple. He froze as the invisible pressure increased and his eyes revealed his mounting fear of that unseen threat. Breen started to say something when he also felt something pressing against his temple. He reached for the unknown object and his arm was wrenched behind his back causing him to cry out in pain.

"Now, what you are feeling is an ultrasonic pistol set to kill, pressing against your temples. When the triggers are pulled, the impact will turn the grey matter inside your skull into a gooey mass of painful death."

"How...how are you doing this?" the Station Chief asked, fearing for his life, and afraid of what he could not see.

"Oh Chief, I wouldn't want you to worry over something as simple as this maneuver. Now, if you will follow me back into the Phoenix, you can become my guest, but only after you inform your people that we are cleared to leave the station. Okay?"

The Chief nodded and Breen was knocked unconscious. The Chief quickly walked to the station's bulkhead where a comm unit was mounted, and informed his staff that the delivery was complete and the Phoenix was cleared to leave. As the Chief was escorted into the ship, Mitch's security team used hypo's, supplied by the med staff, to keep everyone on the dock sleeping for several hours while Athena placed hidden charges inside the vaccine cargo containers. Another security team waited inside for the Captain and his hostage. After the crew was all confirmed to be inside, Security Chief Hargrove was also rendered into a peaceful sleep that would last for a short time.

"Excellent work, Athena, Chief and Mr. Richter. You've earned your pay today. Is everyone accounted for, Rock?"

"Aye, Captain," he replied as Athena reappeared upon deactivating her stealth armor. "What are we going to do with our hostage?"

"Bring a rescue pod down here and place our friend inside with a short burst radio transmitter. We'll revive him when we are ready to exit their space," Mitch directed. "I'm going to see the Doc and then return to the bridge. Athena, guard our guest until I return." She nodded.

Back on the bridge, Mitch ordered his crew to depart just as if everything was normal and make speed for the system's outer perimeter. Much to his surprise, no one called or came in pursuit of them. He called ahead to the Mercon cruisers, telling them of his plan to send a rescue pod back to the station, then returned to the cargo bay where Station Chief Hargrove slept peacefully inside the open rescue pod.

"Wake him up," Mitch ordered.

The antidote was administered and Hargrove slowly regained his senses. As his vision cleared he looked around worriedly.

"Where am I?"

"You're still my guest, Chief Hargrove. In fact, we've arranged a nice little bed for your return home," Mitch said as Hargrove looked around and realized that he was inside a rescue pod.

"What are you going to do with me?" he asked nervously.

"Well for one thing, Chief, I'm going to treat you much nicer than you probably would have treated me and my crew. Here," Mitch handed Hargrove a small tubular shaped object with a button on the top, "now press that little button there." Mitch pointed to the small button. "Go ahead, nothing will happen to you, I promise."

Hargrove slowly pressed the small innocent looking button.

"Now hold that button down and don't release it!"

Hargrove looked at Mitch anxiously. "What is going to happen, Captain?" he exclaimed.

"Not much, Chief Hargrove. You see, if you release that button it will detonate the charges that we placed inside the cargo containers where the vaccine is located. If your staff tries to remove them, then motion sensors will detonate the charges. Now, to your right there is a transmitter that will just reach your outer patrols. We've given you six hours' worth of air so that you'll have enough time to contact your people to let you back into your station. Once you're within ten feet of the vaccine, then you can release the button and the charges will reset for one hour giving you enough time to get them safely off the station and into space before they explode. Don't try to cheat the system because the reset switch is a proximity fuse and it will only work when you're within the range that I specified."

"I don't believe you!" Hargrove barked.

"That's certainly your choice, Mr. Hargrove but if you think about it, I've been honest and upfront with you from the very start. I'm sorry to say that I can't say the same about you. If you follow my directions to the letter, then you will be rescued and upon your return to your station, you will have the vaccine that your people desperately need."

"I guess I don't have a choice," Hargrove replied.

"Sure you do, Hargrove, if you want to blow up the vaccine. But you should know that I've taken the liberty to infect you with the Centaurian Flu virus, so that vaccine should be very important to you. Don't you think?"

Hargrove's eyes grew large and beads of sweat broke out on his forehead. "You wouldn't dare do such a thing!" he hoarsely blurted out.

"When it comes to the safety of my ship and her crew, Mr. Hargrove, there are few limits to the actions which I will take. I suggest that you remember this should we ever meet again. I am curious about something that you said. You mentioned Asher by name. What do you know about him?"

Hargrove didn't answer. "Come on now, Hargrove, the virus clock is ticking," Mitch said calmly.

"We've done business with him before," he replied in a hurried tone. "He came through some months ago and needed supplies to get to his destination. He told us about his encounter with you."

"Well that was certainly nice of Asher to share that with you, Hargrove. You could have learned from his experience. If you see him again be sure to tell him that I still intend to kill him. Now, let's get you on your way. I have a fee to collect, and no offense, Hargrove, but I hope I never see your puny little arrogant ass again as long as I live." Mitch turned and, as he walked away, the crew closed the lid on the rescue pod, placed in the ejection tube and launched into space as the Phoenix left the Madeus system.

Entering Sector 725, the Phoenix made contact with the two waiting missile cruisers from the Mercon Corporation, gave them a brief report on the incident, and asked them to advise General Harris that a full report would be presented to them in due course. The cruisers turned and entered FTL flight. The Phoenix was about to do the same when Yurie interrupted, "Captain, I'm showing a gateway approximately thirty-five thousand miles off our starboard side. Would you care to investigate since we're here?"

Mitch thought for a moment and replied, "Sure, Yurie, why not. After all the drama back there, let's do something interesting before we make our way back to Gunners Redoubt. Set course for that gateway and engage when you're ready."

"Engaging now, Captain," Yurie replied.

They entered the gateway and an hour or so later when they exited, an excited Yurie called out to the Captain.

"Captain Saber! I can't believe this! We're back in our home system, Alderis!"

"What? Where?" the Captain asked in total surprise.

"We're on the far side of our own system, where there are no regularly traveled space lanes. This is exactly the opposite side of entry for normal space travel routes to bring us in. This is amazing!" Yurie said excitedly.

"Amazing indeed, Yurie. This could potentially be very valuable information, strategically speaking," Mitch acknowledged. He recalled the attacks that their system had suffered for many years, when their attackers would appear without any advance warning. He had often wondered how the raiders had escaped timely detection, but how could they have navigated the anomaly? It was only recently that this knowledge became available, showing how to travel through the anomalies, thanks to Yurie's late father, Dr. Nagamo.

"Shall I set course for the Prime station, Captain?" Yurie asked.

"Negative, Yurie," Mitch said. "Set an FTL course for Gunners Redoubt and let's get that mission completed first. I have some concerns that I need to address to General Harris before we close the books on this one. Engage when you're ready."

Yurie's fingers raced across her console and within seconds she replied, "Course plotted and laid in, Captain. Engaging in five seconds...four...three... two...one, engaged."

The gravity compensators made the jump into FTL flight barely noticeable and within four days they would arrive at Gunners Redoubt.

They were ahead of their expected arrival time at Gunners Redoubt by more than two weeks. They even got there before the two Mercon escort Cruisers, much to the surprise of the Mercon fleet commander. Mitch asked for, and was granted, an immediate meeting with General Harris. Athena and the Captain departed the Phoenix in the Minnow and headed for the General's Flagship Carrier, Rachael's Gift.

They were met in the landing bay and taken directly to the General's private office. Athena's presence caused many heads to turn in blatant curiosity as people admired her attractive appearance.

The General arose from his chair when they entered his office and came around his desk wearing a wide smile as he greeted Mitch.

"Mitch! It's so good to see you! You too, Athena, it is good to see you again," the General acknowledged. "She brings quite a presence to the room doesn't she, Captain?" the General noted.

"Activate your personal security measures, General, and give me your promise of secrecy. I'll tell you what I can about our completed mission"

The General looked intrigued as he returned to his desk and entered a code into his command console. The doors closed and the walls, ceiling, and floors shimmered briefly, as the electronic countermeasures were activated. Mitch told him the full story of how Athena came to be in his service and the specifics about his implant upgrades. The General listened with great interest and asked very few questions. Athena stood by the door and made no sound or motion as Mitch spoke.

"So you and Athena have a psychic connection?" the General asked.

"Yes. They made modifications to her implant that allows us to communicate telepathically. I don't understand it, but I know it works," Mitch answered.

"What did Samantha think about all this?" the General asked.

"Actually, she took to the concept quicker than I did. She and Athena had a long discussion and I believe that Sam considers her presence to be a superior safety factor for me and the Phoenix. Sam was right too, Athena has already saved my ass on more than one occasion."

The General smiled and said softly as he leaned forward, "I think that woman has great affection for you, Mitch."

Mitch tilted his head slightly and raised an eyebrow brow in surprise. "I don't see that all, General. Where did that observation come from?"

Still speaking softly the General replied, "I know women, Mitch, and I'm telling you that she has a thing for you. She may never admit it, but I'd bet my ship on it."

Mitch sat back in his seat and mentally asked Athena, "Is that true?" She neither looked toward him nor did she reply. "Athena, answer me please. We are friends and there shouldn't be any secrets between us."

She turned her head just enough to make eye contact with him and replied telepathically, "I am your guardian and protector, Captain," then looked forward again, without any change in her expression.

"I'm sorry, General, but you're wrong," Mitch said. Unseen by Mitch and the General, a small tear formed in Athena's eye. "Anyway, General, that isn't the reason I came to see you personally. I have a concern that I need to share with you. First let me say that I do not doubt your honesty or integrity in the slightest, but what I'm about to tell you may be hard to accept."

The General's forehead developed deep furrows of concern and his eyes narrowed as he leaned forward to listen intently.

"When I was with Hargrove in the Madeus Empire, he let slip things that made me question this entire mission's purpose."

"Explain," the General replied harshly.

"Easy, General, wait until I finish. Hargrove acted as though he was expecting me and my ship."

"Well of course he did, we told him you were coming!" the General shot back and smacked his hand on his desk.

"You misunderstand, General. He knew that I was coming before you informed him. He told me that the capture of my ship would be a boon for his military and he was going to execute my crew and send them back to Alderon in a crate. He even stated that Simon Asher told him about me and the Phoenix. Asher probably told him some ridiculous story about my ship, hoping that they would capture and kill us for him. General, I sincerely believe that we were lured into a trap. I believe the need for the vaccine was sincere, but I think that you and I were both played somehow."

"Incredible! How is that possible?"

"Let's think about it. When you were first approached about delivery of the vaccine, what happened?"

"Well, we received the message and I called a meeting of my command staff to come up with a plan. I was going to have a remote controlled cargo pod jettisoned into their space and send them the command codes."

"What changed your mind?"

The General thought for a moment, "One of my junior officers suggested another plan, involving you specifically, now that I recall. In fact, he convinced all of us that you were the perfect option, considering all the things that could go wrong. Since I knew you and trusted your judgment, I agreed."

"Was he insistent on this course of action?"

"He was very convincing actually, now that I think about it," the General said as he slowly realized that what had happened was a ploy.

"Who was this officer?"

"He's one of my junior officers, Ensign Ikard."

"I think we should pay Ensign Ikard a visit, General, don't you?" Mitch asked.

"Damn right I do!" the General huffed as he deactivated the privacy screening. Pressing another key on his console, he called out, "Lieutenant Ortiz to my office immediately!" He looked up at Mitch and said, "Ortiz is my Chief of Security here and he's a good man. You can trust him."

Mitch nodded as he stood up with the General, the door chimed and a burly but muscular man entered the office.

"Reporting as ordered, General Harris," Ortiz replied.

"Lieutenant, this is Captain Saber and his Chief of Security, Commander Athena," the General said as he introduced them.

Ortiz smiled as he reached out to shake Mitch's hand. It was a firm, confident shake that gave Mitch the impression that the man was self-assured and capable. He turned and extended his hand to Athena, who also accepted it and shook it with the same authority, which seemed to impress the Lieutenant who smiled even more broadly at Athena. She remained stone faced and showed no expression, only bowing slightly in her normal manner of greeting. Ortiz seemed slightly puzzled but let it pass without question.

"Lieutenant, where is Ensign Ikard quartered?" The General asked sharply, his tone almost biting.

The Lieutenant touched several keys on his wrist comm device and replied, "L3A6, General...oh sorry, Captain, that's Level 3, Corridor A, Cabin 6."

"Take us there immediately, Lieutenant," the General commanded.

Without question, the Lieutenant turned, saying, "Follow me, gentlemen and Commander Athena."

They moved quickly, up a lift and down several corridors before Mitch noted a directional sign that read, "Officer's Quarters Level 3" with an arrow pointing to the right. They turned right and noted the "Corridor A" designator at the top of the bulkhead door. They were just coming into view of the cabins when a young officer exited his cabin and turned toward them, stopping briefly to adjust his uniform.

"That's Ensign Ikard," the Lieutenant said softly.

The three continued towards him as he began to walk in their direction. He looked up and saw them coming his way and instantly stopped and stared as they approached. Athena sent a mental message to Mitch that she sensed he was about to run.

Mitch quietly said to the General and the Lieutenant who were in front of them, "Watch out, he's about to run."

Before they could reply, the Ensign turned on his heels and ran in the opposite direction.

"Get him!" the General ordered.

Ortiz started to run when Mitch called out, "Wait! We need to secure his quarters first! Athena, go after him."

Athena raced forward so fast that she was almost a blur, and as she went she activated her stealth armor, vanishing from sight. The General and Ortiz watched in stunned amazement.

"What the hell just happened?" Ortiz blurted out.

"I'll explain later, Lieutenant. Don't worry, she'll catch him. We need to secure his quarters first," Mitch reiterated.

"I agree, Mitch," the General said. "See to it, Lieutenant."

Ortiz jogged over to the door controls for the Ensign's cabin and entered a code. The door closed and a red light glowed surrounding the door, indicating that a security lockdown had been placed on the cabin. They ran down the corridor, stopping at a "T" intersection, not certain which way to go, when they heard a commotion coming from the right. They ran in that direction and found a dozen crewmen watching Athena, who had the Ensign pinned against the bulkhead with his arms behind his back, his face against the wall, and his toes several inches off the deck plate.

"Commander on deck!" the Lieutenant shouted. The crew at once turned to face them and stood at attention.

The General frowned and the Lieutenant glared at Ikard as Mitch said, "Bring the Ensign over here, Athena."

She wrenched his arm upwards and the Ensign howled in pain.

"What's this all about?" the Ensign demanded.

"Why did you run when you saw us, Ensign?" the General asked.

"I didn't know it was you, General. I thought it was the other officers coming to haze me again," he replied.

"He's lying," Athena said.

"No I'm not! I haven't done anything wrong, General. I thought they were going to haze me!"

"He's still lying," Athena said again. "He was deliberately trying to lead us away from his cabin."

"That's a lie!" the Ensign shouted. "Who is this *woman*, to call me a liar?"

"I believe she is telling the truth," the General said. "Fact is, you looked directly at us and ran. Lieutenant, take this man into custody and summon a security detail to his cabin. Let's see if he has anything to hide before I decide on his punishment."

The Lieutenant took the man from Athena, but not before calling for a security team to meet them at the Ensign's quarters. They proceeded back toward the Ensign's cabin and as they neared the door, four security men ran towards them, weapons drawn.

"I want two of you stationed by this door, and then I want this corridor sealed off. No one in or out without my permission," the Lieutenant ordered. He released the seal on the cabin and pulled the Ensign through the door. The General, Mitch and Athena followed.

The cabin was slightly smaller than the officers' cabins on the Phoenix, but it was still roomy and well organized. The Ensign kept his room neat and tidy, as if ready for inspection. The Lieutenant pushed him towards his bunk and made him sit as they searched the room, discovering nothing of value.

"I haven't done anything wrong, General. This is a mistake. You've got to believe me!" the Ensign said nervously.

The General slowly sat down at the computer console. "If you're innocent, Ensign, then you have nothing to worry about. By the way, do you know who these two people are?" the General pointed toward Mitch and Athena.

"No, sir. But I'd like a little payback for the way the bitch slammed me against the wall," the Ensign replied.

"If you weren't an officer, I'd break your nose for insulting a guest on this ship and a fellow officer," the Lieutenant said as he glared at the Ensign.

"This is Captain Saber and his Chief of Security, Commander Athena," the General advised him, watching for his reaction. The Ensign's face paled. "Your lack of courtesy towards a fellow officer, and especially guests on my ship, will cost you your rank, SEAMAN!" the General barked. "Now, let's see what messages our new Seaman has here in his computer."

Mitch was impressed with how quickly the General's fingers raced across the keypad. He hadn't realized that the General was so skilled, but then he berated himself for the thought, as he wouldn't be a General if he wasn't capable.

"Well, it appears as if there have been messages sent and received, but the body of each message has been encrypted, and some have been deleted. What have you got to say for yourself, Seaman?"

The demoted man sprang from his bed and spat on the floor at Athena's feet. "I haven't done anything wrong and I don't deserve the treatment I'm getting. You can't prove anything against me and I demand an apology from this bitch that attacked me!"

In a flash of movement, Athena reached out and grabbed the young man by the neck, and with one arm, lifted him so far off the floor that his hair touched the ceiling. The Lieutenant leaned forward and whispered into Mitch's ear, "Is she a cyborg?"

Mitch shook his head.

The Lieutenant smiled and whispered again, "Can I marry her?"

Mitch turned his head a half turn, raised an eyebrow, and before he could reply, Athena said calmly, "I belong to Captain Saber and no one else."

Mitch, Ortiz and the General all looked at her with surprise. The other two looked at Mitch for an explanation. He just shrugged his shoulders with a straight face. The General gave Mitch an 'I told you so' look and returned to his work.

"Let's see if the back-up logs are here. Well, well, it looks like our little Seaman has erased the back-up logs as well." The General looked up and caught a brief glimpse of the smirk on the Seaman's face. Athena lifted him a little higher.

"You think you've covered your ass, do you?" the General said as he smiled and returned his attention to the keypad. "I've got a few surprises for you, Ikard. Do you understand the word redundant? Probably not, I'm guessing. You see, in this business you don't take chances. I have multiple redundancy systems, so that I have back-ups in various secure places just to handle emergencies, or in your case... arrogant stupidity." His face grimaced as he snarled the words in a hate filled tone. "Ah, here we are. The file is asking for an encryption key. Where's the encryption key, Ikard?"

"I don't know what you're talking about," Ikard shot back.

"He lying again," Athena said

"Screw you bit..." Ikard couldn't finish his tirade as Athena tightened her grip around his neck.

"Where is it, Ikard?" The General asked again.

Through gritted teeth Ikard mumbled, "I don't know."

Athena squeezed a little more and his face turned dark red from the restricted blood flow. She glared at him intently for a moment, and then said, "Pillow, it's in the pillow."

Ortiz snatched the pillow off the bed and ripped it apart. A small data crystal dropped onto the floor. Athena tossed Ikard back onto his bed, where he collapsed and gasped for breath. Ortiz handed the crystal to the General, who placed it into the data port. General Harris looked intently through the messages, and the longer he read, the angrier he became.

"So, you've been relaying our every movement and mission to the Madeus Empire for well over a year. You've even given them a complete list of all the officers in my employ, and a list of the systems that we are currently contracted to. So, they did instigate your recommendation to have Captain Saber deliver the vaccine. I should execute you myself. You're a traitor, Ikard." the General said with disgust.

Athena raised her arm towards Ikard and her weapon sprang up from beneath its concealed position in her armor. The end of the weapon glowed with energy, indicating that it was armed and ready to fire. The Lieutenant and the General were motionless in anticipation of her firing of the weapon.

"Athena," Mitch said calmly, "what are you doing?"

"This man is a traitor. Traitors are to be executed immediately. The General is an honorable man and he should not have a traitor in the midst of his officers. I will execute this traitor because the General is your friend."

Mitch smiled and placed his hand on her shoulder. "Athena, I think that it is a very honorable of you to offer, and I know that the General appreciates your sentiments. However, we are guests on his ship. Do you remember what I told you about the laws of a ship? The Captain is the law that governs his ship and crew, and his word is always respected. You should ask the General what *his* wishes are since this is his ship, or else we will be disrespecting his authority."

Ikard sat still in horror, his face showing his fear as he stared into the glowing end of the weapon that was pointed at his head.

"I understand, Captain. What is the General's command?" Athena asked.

Mitch looked to General Harris, who stood up and said, "Athena, do not execute this man. He must be interrogated prior to his execution." He watched Ikard as Athena retracted her weapon, and almost wished that he had let her execute the traitor. "Lieutenant, take this traitor to the interrogation room and keep him sedated until I'm ready, so he can't commit suicide. I expect he has more information that we need."

Ortiz snatched the man from the bed and practically threw him out of the cabin. The General looked at Mitch with disappointment in his eyes. "I never thought that something like this would happen here. I've gotten too comfortable and this is the price I've paid."

"I'm glad we know who it was, General," Mitch said as he patted his friend on the shoulder. "It may be a good idea to use his message key to see if you can ferret out anyone else that they may have planted in your service."

"I intend to do just that. In fact, I'll put my people on it before I begin that little bastard's interrogation. Athena...thanks for your help."

She nodded and bowed slightly, and the General bowed in acknowledgement.

CHAPTER TEN

Fourteen Years Ago – Planet: Destiny's Cross

THE YOUNG GIRL HAD INK BLACK HAIR AND A DARK TAN FROM spending long days working with her family outdoors. She sat on a large boulder under a ragged shade tree, overlooking a small pond as she finished her pencil sketch. She had an eye for detail and it showed in her artwork, although no one but her family ever looked at her sketchbook. Her favorite time to sketch was in the early morning hours, when the dew laid heavily on the grasses and the insects and birds ventured out from their night's rest. Off in the distance, she could see her family's herd of cattle grazing in the early morning sun. She smiled as she watched a young calf, only three days, old gallop towards its mother for an early morning suckle of milk. Making a couple of minor detail adjustments to her drawing, she smiled with satisfaction as she held it up for inspection in the light.

"Inna! Come in and help me finish breakfast before your father and brothers come back from the fields," her mother called from inside the house.

"Coming, Mama," she shouted in reply.

She ran back to the house and upon entering she opened up her sketchbook to show her Mama her latest creation. Smiling brightly she said, "Look Mama! See what I did this morning!"

The weathered woman turned and looked briefly at her daughter's art before returning her attention to her work replying, "Another beautiful piece of art, my daughter. Now put away your book and help me get the table ready to feed your father and brothers."

"Yes, Mama."

She ran to her room and placed the book under her pillow, then returned to help ready the table for breakfast. It wasn't long before they all came in for the morning meal, to ready themselves for another long day of working on their small farm. They raised cattle for meat and cows for dairy products that they sold in the local market. Destiny's Cross was inhabited by a peaceful people who desired a simple way of life. They had a space port and an orbital station for trading with the other systems, but their chosen way to live wasn't as dependent on technology as most other systems. Their cities were smaller, and the people were more devoutly religious than others. Energy weapons were not permitted on the planet and strict rules and guidelines were enforced on outside visitors. Trade was only allowed via the orbital platform and visitors to the planet were only allowed a limited stay. Many of earth's original cattle and farm animals had been brought as embryos, which had been raised into the generations of cattle now found here. The grasses and crop seeds had been brought with them when the planet was first settled. The people's morals and values extended to include several separate religious sects with all respecting their individuality and enjoying a peaceful coexistence. There was a small, but formidable, military presence that they maintained to protect the planet. Lately, they had been coming under increasingly stronger and more frequent attack by raiders and slavers.

Inna and her three brothers sat down for breakfast and eagerly waited for their father, Pavel Dubnikov, to bless the food before they began eating.

"Oh Lord in Heaven," Pavel began, "we thank you for this rich bounty that you have provided for us this day. Bless the hands that prepared this food and protect us as we go about your work and ours. Amen."

Pavel received his food first, followed by the three brothers and then Inna and her mother served themselves last. No one else ate until Pavel had taken the first bite. He quickly began and his family followed all of them hungry for the first meal of the day.

"I heard that there was another attack on the Capitol City last night," Pavel said between bites of food.

"What happened, Papa?" Inna asked curiously.

Pavel answered, "Young girls like my little Inna shouldn't worry about such things. You are safe here with us."

"Papa," Inna replied, "I'm nearly fifteen now. Don't treat me like I'm a child."

Her brothers laughed, as did her father. Inna's face turned red with anger.

"My darling child, this news is not for you to worry about. But if you must know, there were a dozen or so people killed as the raiders made strafing runs through the city. The authorities said that they are testing our defenses to see where they can land and take people, to sell for slave workers in the outer reaches. These raiders are not concerned with farmers like us," Pavel said dismissively.

"We should fight against these people who wish to capture us Papa! How else are we going to protect our homes?" Inna said firmly. Her father and brothers laughed again as her anger was increasing. "Don't laugh at me! I care about our planet and the people who live here. What's so funny about that?"

Pavel looked up at his family, smiled and said, "My little Inna wants to go and fight the bad men!" He chuckled as he made his observation.

Inna's brother Viktor, laughed with his father as he spoke, "Can't you see Inna now with her sketch book and pencil, waving them at her enemies? I'm sure that would scare them off!" They all laughed again and watched her, joking about her wanting to fight.

Another brother, David, jumped into the fray. "Maybe she could cook for them and they would all die from the smell of burnt food!"

Inna slammed her fork onto her plate with disgust and stood. "I'll show you! One day you will wish for someone like me to protect you men! You men who are afraid to even hold a real gun!" She ran out of the house and out of sight.

"Inna!" her mother shouted. "Come back here this instant!"

Her words were not heard by the young girl who felt the pain of ridicule and insult. She ran as fast and as far as her breath would allow until she finally stopped and fell to her knees crying. Tears streamed down her cheeks as she felt a soft touch on her shoulder. Her brother, Yuri, had followed her. He was only two years older than she and he felt sorry for his younger sister.

"Inna," Yuri said softly, "don't let them get under your skin. They still recall the old ways where women only stay at home and have babies."

"We are just as good at fighting as men are," Inna sobbed.

"I know that, and our brothers know that too. They are just being protective of their little sister, that's all," Yuri said trying to comfort his sister. "You have to admit that you are too young to go off to war, don't you?"

"I've been reading about the other systems and some of them put their children into the academies at early ages, some younger than I am. They know that we can fight and defend our people, just as well as the adults," she replied, wiping the tears from her cheeks.

"Don't let Papa know that you've been reading about those things or he will get very angry with you. Remember, he lost both of his grandfathers in the space service, trying to prevent the capture of our orbital station."

"But I don't want to stay here all my life. I want to see space and travel to other planets to explore and meet new people. Life here is boring. I feel like something is calling me to go out there."

"You might as well get used to staying here, Inna. Papa's never going to allow you to leave. One day you'll meet someone who you will want to marry and then you will feel differently."

"Now you sound like Papa. Stay here and marry and have many babies so Mama and I will have lots of grandchildren to carry on our work. Bleh, how boring can you be! Just think about all the new sights and smells and things you can do in space! Nothing here ever changes; it will always be the same today, tomorrow or next year. I don't want to be like the tiny fish that lives in a bowl. I want to be the bird that flies in the air and can go anywhere she wants!" She said as she pointed to the sky, her eyes glistening with excitement.

"I love you, little Inna, and I don't want you to go off to some strange place to be killed trying to defend people who you don't know. I want you to stay here with your family so that we can love you forever."

"I love you too, Yuri. I love all of my family but I don't understand why they get to make the decision about where I spend my life. It isn't fair!"

Yuri held his sister tightly in his arms and wished he could give her the answer that she wanted, but he knew that his father would never allow Inna to leave their small ranch, especially to depart from the planet.

"We're taking a load of cattle to market in the Capitol City tomorrow. I'll try to look around to see if I can get you some information about the other systems and their academies. My friend, Timor, told me that he knew someone who enrolled in the space academy in the Alderis system and he loves it there. I don't know where that system is, but I'll see if I can find out for you."

"Oh thank you Yuri! You're such a good brother to me."

"If Papa catches me, being a good brother won't keep me from being punished." He held his sister away at arm's length and looked into her teary eyes. "Inna, if anything ever happens to me, go to my bedroom and lift off the bed post closest to the window and take what's inside."

"What do you mean if something happens to you? Don't say such things, Yuri, you're scaring me!"

"I don't mean to scare you, little sister, but these attacks on the Capitol City have been coming every other day, and tomorrow will be the odd day again. I mentioned this to Papa and he laughed at me. He said that I was crazy to believe everything I heard, but it still worries me. I've been saving my allowance to buy my own personal transport and I almost have enough. I want you to have my savings if something happens to me, so that maybe you can have the life you want." Tears formed in Yuri's eyes as he spoke and Inna cried again, hugging him closely.

"Nothing can ever happen to you, Yuri! I need you and I love you. Please don't do anything foolish, just come home tomorrow. I don't want your money, I want you!"

"I'm sure I'll come home, Inna, don't you worry. My brothers will look after me and Papa will be with us too. Just remember what I said."

Inna stepped back and punched Yuri in the arm, "Don't you ever scare me like that again, Yuri Dubnikov, or next time I'll punch you in the nose!"

Yuri held up his arms in mock surrender and replied, "Okay sister! I promise!"

They walked back to the house together. After a verbal scolding from her father and mother, she went up to her room and sat gazing out her window into the sky.

The next day her brothers and father left for the Capitol City with a full cargo of cattle for the market sale. When evening came and they hadn't arrived back home at their usual time, Inna and her mother became concerned and paced nervously about the house. It was nearly dark when they heard the rumble of their vehicle coming down the road. They rushed outside to welcome their family home, but as they looked at the approaching truck, Inna was first to notice that the cattle hauler wasn't there.

"Where's the cattle hauler, Mama?" Inna asked.

"Maybe it broke down on the way back, Inna. The mag lifter has been giving your father problems lately," her mother replied.

The truck slowed as it approached the house and stopped. When Pavel and two sons got out of the vehicle, Inna and her mother could see that their clothing was ripped and torn and they were battered and bruised. Inna, looking for Yuri, didn't see him and she felt a knot of dread form in her stomach.

"Where's Yuri?" she called out. Her father simply lowered his head and shook it. "Yuri!" she shouted as she ran towards the truck in a panic. Her father reached out for her and held her in his arms as she tried to look into the truck.

"Don't look, child," her father said softly.

"What happened to Yuri, Papa?" Inna asked through her tears.

"The city was attacked again just when we were about to leave. Yuri ran back to close the ramp on the cattle hauler as they strafed the road. Yuri was killed and the hauler was destroyed. We were all outside when the attack came and didn't have time to run for cover," her father answered.

Yuri and her mother cried as Pavel held his wife and daughter close. Tears streamed down the faces of the brothers as they lifted Yuri's body from the truck and carefully carried him to the small family cemetery, not far from the main house. The ceremony was brief as they laid him to rest, and Inna remembered her brother's last words to her from the previous day. Later, fighting to control her tears, she went to his room and removed the bed post. Concealed inside was a small pouch with her brother's savings inside, just where he said she would find it. She quickly stuck it in her pocket and as the rest of the house slept that night, she made up her mind that she was leaving the next day for the Alderis system that he told her about.

It was early morning, prior to the rising of the sun, when Inna left a note for her parents that she was leaving for the Alderis Space Academy and that she would contact them when she could. With a single bag in hand and her brother's money in her pocket, she left hurriedly for the Capitol City Space Port. She had the necessary documentation for passage to the station, and from there onto a passenger ship, so she was prepared for her new adventure. At least she thought she was.

Arriving at the Capitol City Space Port, she wasted no time securing passage to the orbital station and was waiting in the passenger line, when suddenly she was yanked out of line. Her father looked down at her angrily demanding, "What do you think you're doing, Inna?"

"I'm going somewhere to can learn how to protect people and not be the person who just sits by and watches while others die like my brother," Inna replied in a shaky voice.

"You're not going anywhere! We're going back home and you'll stay there until you come of age and maybe then you'll see the idiocy of your plan." Her father grabbed her by the arm and pulled her further away from the line.

Inna jerked her arm away from his grip and retorted, "My brother's last words to me were of his fear of coming to the city yesterday. He told me that you laughed at him when he tried to tell you how he felt. Now he's dead and it's your fault, because you wouldn't listen to him!" She said angrily as tears ran down her cheeks. "If you want to ignore me too, then that's fine, but I'm leaving to make my own way, Papa."

"Inna, if you leave this planet, don't ever bother coming back because you won't have a home any more. You will not be welcome in our house ever again, daughter."

Tears streamed down Inna's face as she looked at her father and realized that he meant every word. She placed her hand on his heart saying, "I love you and Mama and my brothers. I'm sorry that we have to part like this, Papa, but this is what I want and it's what Yuri wanted for me too. I'm fulfilling his last wish for me and I pray that someday you and Mama will understand."

She turned and went back to the line that was now boarding the shuttle to the station, without looking back. She heard her father's last words as she entered the shuttle. "I meant what I said, Inna!" The door closed behind her and she sat down, sobbing quietly as the tears continued to roll down her cheeks. A man came and sat in the seat next to her but she didn't pay him any attention. She felt a slight nudge on her arm and looked over to see him handing her a small towel with which to wipe her eyes. She refused, but the man gently pushed it into her hands.

"Young ladies shouldn't cry like this. Is there anything I can do to help you?" he asked quietly.

She shook her head and blotted at her eyes. He looked at her single bag and noticed that she didn't have a connecting ticket for the station.

"Where are you heading, if you don't mind my asking?" he asked politely.

Inna finally looked up at the man and saw that he was wearing a uniform. He had a caring look in his eyes and although his voice was soothing and calm, he had an air of authority about him.

"I want to get to the Alderis system, but I don't know where it is," she said trying to regain her composure.

"Why would you want to go there and leave a beautiful planet like Destiny's Cross?" he asked sincerely.

"I want to enter their Space Academy. It was my brother's last wish for me to do this before he was killed yesterday in an attack in our Capitol City. My Papa said that if I left the planet, then I would never be welcomed back home again, but this is what I've always dreamed of doing. It's all I have left now, for me *and* for the memory of my brother."

"I see. So that's what was going on back there on the gangway. Now I understand," The man said as he nodded his head.

"You heard my Papa?"

"Yes...uh Inna, I think he called you. Is that your name?"

"Yes, my name is Inna Dubnikov. That was my father, Pavel Dubnikov. He meant what he said. He will never allow me to come home again, so I have to get to the Alderis System. Do you know how I can get there?" Inna asked as she sniffed the last of her tears away.

"Yes I do, Inna. Actually, I'm going there myself."

"Really? Can you help me get there? I have my own money, so I won't cost you anything. Please?" Her eyes reflected renewed hope as she pleaded for his help.

"Keep your money, Inna. You might find that you need it elsewhere. I have my own ship waiting for me at the station. If you like, you can come with me back to Alderon, that's the home planet in the Alderis System, and that's where you'll find the Space Academy."

"Oh thank you, Sir! Praise the Maker for the blessings of your help on my journey! Wait a minute; you have your own ship? You must be really important if you have your own space ship! What is your name?" she asked, regaining control of her emotions.

"Oh, I'm not anyone special, Inna, but I think I can help you get into the Academy if you want my help," he replied sincerely.

Her smile widened as she answered, "That would be so kind of you to help me, but I don't know how I can repay your kindness."

"If you study hard and do your best, Inna that is all that anyone will ever ask. Can you promise me that?"

"I will, I promise I will. You have my word."

"That's all I need to hear. I'll make the arrangements for you after we board my ship, then all you have to do is work hard to fulfill your promise." He smiled and extended his hand towards her. She accepted it and tried to shake his hand even though it was much larger than her own. He chuckled at her effort and she smiled.

"I still don't know your name," Inna said.

The man smiled as he sat back in his seat, and said, "My name is Rich Jonas. Commandant Rich Jonas."

"Commandant? That's an important title. What are you the commandant of, Rich Jonas?" she asked quizzically.

"I'm the Commandant of the Alderon Space Academy, and your future commander, young lady."

Inna's eyes nearly popped out of their sockets when she heard who he was. She remained silent until after she boarded his ship and they departed for Alderon.

CHAPTER ELEVEN

Present Day

THE PHOENIX DOCKED AT THE ALDERON STATION TO REPLEN-ish their water and food supplies, and Mitch's Executive Officer, or XO, Lt. Cmdr. Yurie Nagamo posted the list of crew names for those eligible for three day furloughs. Mitch was on the bridge when Communications Officer Lt. JG Inna Dubnikov alerted him to an incoming message.

"Captain," she called out, "I've got Fleet Admiral Jonas on the comm for you. Do you want privacy screening?"

Mitch answered, "No, put him on the open channel on my screen, Inna."

The holographic vid screen materialized at his station and he answered, "Hello, Admiral Jonas! It's good to see you again."

"Hello, Captain. I saw that you were docking and we haven't spoken in a while. How have you and your crew been doing?"

"Everything is good, Admiral. Say, I'm heading for our corporate offices on the station to catch up on some paperwork for Laurel. How about you meet me there and I'll have Miranda bring in lunch? We can all catch up and share a meal at the same time."

"And here I was thinking that I was the only man in town with an appe-tite! It's worth the trip to the station just to see Laurel and Miranda, so count me in. I need an update on your activities too, so we can get every-thing done at once and that makes my job easier."

"Great, then I'll see you later in our offices, Admiral. Saber out."

The screen de-materialized and Mitch smiled at the notion of seeing his Uncle Rich again. They were very close and it had been too many months since they last visited.

"Captain?" Inna inquired. "I don't mean to intrude on your work, but I haven't seen the Admiral in a really long time and I'd like to say hello to him again. He helped me out when I first came to the academy and I've always thought very highly of him. I can leave after I say hello to him so that I won't intrude on your visit."

"It's no intrusion at all, Inna. I'm sure my Uncle would love to say hello to you. In fact, why don't you plan on having lunch with us? It will be mostly small talk and you can meet my sister and Miranda, our executive secretary. She's quite a character and we can all socialize a little. Afterwards, you will have time to visit or shop on the station before we get ready for departure."

"Thank you, Captain, I appreciate that." Inna smiled as she returned to her console, pleased to have a chance to see the Admiral once more.

Arriving later in their corporate offices, Mitch, Athena and Inna walked into the conference room to find Laurel, Miranda and Uncle Rich chatting away like they hadn't seen one another in years.

Mitch grinned at the spectacle and turning to his companions said, "Aren't they like a bunch of old hens that have nothing better to do than gossip?"

Inna and Mitch laughed, but Athena just stared at them, not getting the inference. Mitch patted Athena on the shoulder and suggested, "We really need to spend some time on your humor skills, Athena."

Athena smiled back at his comment, understanding that Mitch was actually paying her a compliment in a polite way. Miranda turned when she heard his voice and bounded across the room towards Mitch and hugged and kissed him generously. Inna took a step back, afraid that she might get the same treatment, but Miranda just gave her a wide toothy grin and said, "Don't sweat it honey, Mitch and I are like long lost lovers every time we meet. I'm Miranda and I'm very pleased to meet you, Lt. JG Inna Dubnikov, Communications Officer for the Phoenix."

Inna smiled back at Miranda, making a mental note of her extraordinarily tight dress and very high heels. "Thanks for welcoming me, Miranda. I've heard so much about you from Captain Saber." They hugged like girlfriends hug, even though they were strangers.

Miranda paused as she eyed Athena. "Wow, I thought I was a presence in a room, but you've got me beat by a solar system, girl!" She reached out to shake Athena's hand, but was caught off guard when Athena hugged her in the same fashion that Miranda had just hugged Inna. Miranda tilted her head to one side and said, "My you are just full of surprises!",

Mitch laughed. "I'm sure that Laurel gave you a report on Athena, but it has been a while since we have been here, so her social skills have improved a great deal."

"Well Mitch, I have to tell you that she makes one hell of an impression on me! I'm definitely glad to call her friend and *not* enemy!"

Miranda stepped back as Laurel and the Admiral approached to greet everyone. The Admiral was obviously quite taken upon first meeting Athena. Laurel was pleased to see her once more and welcomed her like she did all her friends. Athena had worked hard learning how to greet others, when to smile and when a smile made the best impression, but overcoming her lifetime of training was difficult. She could never let her guard down, as she only had one responsibility in her life, and that was the protection of Mitch Saber. Even though she was as quiet and friendly as she could be among others, she was always on guard, and it was apparent to everyone. That didn't bother the Admiral, but it was obvious that Miranda and Laurel would take some time to adjust to Athena's nature.

The Admiral, after greeting Athena, stopped and looked Inna up and down approvingly, and then smiled a broad smile and held his arms wide. Inna immediately returned his smile with one of her own and darted into the Admiral arms, hugging him like he was her lost family.

"Inna, my little lost girl, look how grown up you've become! You're a beautiful young woman now. How many years has it been since I saw you last?" the Admiral asked.

"It's been seven years, Admiral. When I heard that the Captain would be seeing you today, I asked if I could come along and say hello. I hope you didn't mind," Inna said, feeling somewhat embarrassed.

"Why should I mind seeing one of my favorite students? You know Mitch, this young woman couldn't even find the Alderis system on the star charts when I first met her. She promised me then that she would study hard and always try her best not to let me down, and she has fulfilled that promise faithfully."

"I didn't know that you recruited her, Uncle Rich. She's an excellent bridge officer and only just recently earned her grade increase to Lt. JG," Mitch responded.

The Admiral stood back and looked at her from top to bottom once more. "She was a little puny when we first met, but she really fills out that uniform nicely now!"

Inna blushed and everyone except Athena laughed. Mitch patted her on the back and said, "It seems that you've come a long way since my Uncle first met you. Perhaps you will tell me that story someday."

"I think that's one that will stay between the Admiral and me," she said shyly.

The Admiral laughed and put his arm around her shoulders as he escorted her to the table, where a small buffet was waiting. After lunch and time spent talking, discussing upcoming duties and deliveries, Inna and the Admiral left. Mitch, accompanied by Laurel and Miranda went to his office while Athena stood guard outside his office door.

"Doesn't she ever relax?" Miranda asked, pointing toward the door where Athena stood.

"No. She takes her duties very seriously. It took me a while to accept her just the way she is. I was expecting her to behave like everyone else, you know, so I tried to change her behavior. Then I realized that I was doing more harm than good. I had to take a step back and spend a great deal of time with her one-on-one, so that I could better understand what her training compels her to do. I didn't understand the depths of the intense indoctrination that she was subjected to from such an early age, and here I was trying to undo a lifetime of training to make her fit my expectations. Now that I understand her, our relationship has changed greatly. She really is a very unique and strong willed person. She has only one purpose in life and that is to be my bodyguard. I honestly was offended at the notion for a while, but the more I accepted her for who she was, the more I appreciated her duty and devotion," Mitch said as he looked in her direction. He hadn't admitted that aloud to anyone and it felt good to say what he felt.

Athena said to him telepathically, "Thank you, my Captain, for your understanding and devotion to my purpose in life. My life belongs to you alone."

Mitch broke into a boyish smile as Laurel and Miranda watched, not understanding why.

"What's with the odd smile, Mitch?" Laurel asked.

"It's nothing important, just something that came to my mind," he replied. He noticed a slight grin appear on Athena's face. She got the joke this time. He was glad that he had not told them of his mental connection with Athena, and decided that for now it was best to keep it that way.

Miranda and Laurel exchanged suspicious looks, wondering if that was really the truth. They let it go and got down to work. Much had happened since Mitch was in the office last, so they spent the afternoon and late into the evening catching up.

Arriving back on the ship the following morning, Mitch and Athena sat in his office reviewing crew directives when Athena said, "Captain, I felt an unusual bond between you and Miranda. It wasn't like the one with Laurel. I understood the sister bond. Can you explain your bond with Miranda?"

Mitch took a deep breath and sat back in his chair.

"I'm sorry, Captain. I feel this is a subject that you don't wish to discuss."

"It's just complicated, Athena. The reason it's complicated is because I did something wrong."

"There is no need to speak the reasons, Captain. Relax in your chair, close your eyes and let your memories tell me the story so that I can understand." Mitch hesitated a moment, not wanting to rethink the experience, but finally decided that it would make no difference. Athena was smart enough and her empathic abilities strong enough that she probably already knew, so he did as she said and closed his eyes. It was like a movie being replayed in his head down to the last detail. All the confused emotions came raging back to him and his guilt hurt the most.

When he opened his eyes only a few moments had elapsed and Athena stood beside him with one hand on his, kneeling at his side. She placed her other hand on his shoulder and said, "I too experience pain and joy at the same time, my Captain. I can push the pain into the deeper recesses of your mind if you wish, so that you won't have to experience it any longer."

Mitch looked into her eyes and saw a deep emotion and caring that he had not seen in her before. This was something that she had never shown him previously.

He smiled and answered, "No, that won't be necessary. I acknowledge my faults and mistakes and I accept the responsibilities that go with them.

I didn't know you could do that and I consider it a sincere offer from your heart. Thank you, my friend."

She picked up his hand, placed it on her cheek and flashed him the memory of the little girl chasing butterflies near the stream once more, laughing as she looked up into his eyes. Mitch smiled and instinctively reached around and hugged her. She was hesitant for a second and then returned his hug with a generous one of her own. She stood and walked towards the door and without turning around she said, "If we're finished here, Captain, I need to go to my quarters."

Mitch didn't think anything of it and replied, "Of course. I'll see you in the galley at lunch."

"Affirmative, Captain," she replied as she exited his office. Athena was glad that Mitch didn't see the shine of tears in her eyes because she didn't understand them herself. She needed time to push those emotions into the deeper recesses of *her* mind.

It was 0900 Standard Time the following morning when the Phoenix departed the station docks for their next freight run.

"Yurie," Mitch called out, "Set course for the Chinese Federation, best speed. We've got a full load of farm implements and machinery headed for Destiny's Cross," Mitch directed. "Inna, I understand that's your home world. Is there anyone there who you would like to visit while we unload our cargo?"

Inna spun around in her chair and Mitch saw an overload of emotion in her eyes as she tried to respond, but the words just wouldn't come out.

Sensing that there was a deep personal issue preventing her from speaking, he said, "We'll be there for a couple of days since we will have to cargo bot this equipment down to the planet. Let me know when you make up your mind."

She gave him a little smile of appreciation then quickly returned her attention to her console. Yurie also noted her reaction and decided to speak to her good friend after their shift was over.

Late in the evening, after speaking to Inna in her quarters, Yurie went to the Captain's office to share her concern for her friend with him. Mitch listened patiently and said that he shouldn't interfere with family problems, but Yurie was convinced that Inna needed his advice and that she would respect anything that he said. After Yurie left his office, he placed a call to his Uncle Jonas to inquire about how he had met Inna. Hers was a story that broke his heart after hearing the details from his uncle. When he sought his uncle's advice about getting involved, the Admiral quickly cautioned him about the visitor policies on Destiny's Cross. He offered to make a call to their Minister of Planetary Relations to see if he could get permission for Mitch to visit her family. Mitch agreed to accept his offer to help, only as long as it didn't interfere with his uncle's job or the relationship that his uncle had with the Minister on Destiny's Cross.

The next day Mitch received a message from his uncle, telling him that Inna was still a citizen of Destiny's Cross and therefore she was free to travel to the planet anytime she wished. As a citizen with a military rank that they recognized from Alderon, she could bring up to five people with her, but six days was the maximum length of time that any non-citizen would be allowed to stay on the planet. His uncle observed that the minister seemed to be very proud that one of their citizens had obtained such a distinguished rank in the service of an allied planet. He explained that very few of their citizens were in military service or ships service to other systems, and that their weapons policies were very restrictive on Destiny's Cross. Fortunately, Athena's weapons package wouldn't show up on a weapons scan and Mitch knew there was no way that he could go to the planet without her accompanying him. He decided to wait until they entered the system to offer Inna the option to visit her family again. He hoped that she could make peace with her family. However, it still concerned him that he was placing himself in the middle of someone else's personal business.

Cronus System – Planet Aurora

"Charlie 3! Break left, break left! You've got two raiders on your six!"

The interceptor craft broke left, pitched up and rolled, trying to dodge the pursuer's fire.

"Charlie 3, roll left, they're coming around again! Hang on! I'm trying to catch you!"

"Roger, Charlie Leader, rolling left...I think I can shake..."

The transmission ended in static as the Charlie Squadron Leader listened and watched the ship's designator on his screen vanish.

"This is Charlie leader to Charlie Alpha Wing, do you copy?"

Static was the only reply.

"Charlie leader, this is Charlie 6, I've got at least twenty raiders on my screen heading our way. My power cells are weak and I've got damage to my port stabilizer thrusters. Captain, we need to warn the station and get the hell out of here while we can."

"Roger, Charlie 6. Charlie leader to Delta Leader."

"This is Delta leader, go ahead Charlie 1."

"We've sustained significant damage and lost ten of our twelve interceptors. We've got a force of at least twenty raiders on the scope headed your way. We're heading planet-side for refueling and repairs. Good luck, Delta leader."

"Thanks, Charlie 1, we'll do our best."

The Charlie squadron interceptor craft were fast and highly maneuverable but not as well armored as the Delta squadron's fast attack fighters (FAF). The fast attack fighters sacrificed speed and some agility for better armor, plus front and rear rapid-fire laser pulse cannons. Their forward-swept wing design gave them a menacing appearance, even in space. The FAF Delta Squadron was made up of twelve FAF fighters divided into four wings of three fighters each. They were all experienced pilots and they trained often to hone their skills, however, this was the first time that they had experienced the loss of a fighter wing. Delta wing leader Commander Garrus MacNeil was anxious for battle, but feared for his squadron's safety.

"Charlie 1, did you locate a base ship on your scans?"

"Negative, Commander, if it's out there we didn't find it."

"Delta leader, we have numerous raiders on our screen approaching at high speed. You are clear for intercept."

"Roger that, Station Master. Delta Squadron, we are cleared for launch. Launch!"

The FAF fighters launched from the station and immediately activated their boosters to achieve maximum speed to intercept the invaders. Commander MacNeil and his two wingmen lagged behind to coordinate his other three wings.

"This is Delta 4, we're engaging now."

"Delta 3, engaging now."

"Delta 6 engaging now."

Delta 3 shouted, "Damn these guys are fast! Watch out, they're coming in groups of four!"

Delta 6 sang out, "Watch out, the fourth guy is breaking off. He's trying to maneuver down under for a belly shot! Watch out...his ship has an extra booster! He's gaining on you fast, Delta 3! Pull Up! Pull up! Damn! They got Delta 3. Delta leader! I've got..." Only static continued as his ship evaporated into space.

"This is Delta 4, we've taken out three raiders but they are coming in fast! I've got a pair on my six and another at my two o'clock! Firing rear pulse cannons! Bam! Take that you assholes! Two more down!"

"Delta 5, I've got the other two! Roll left, hit your boosters and take her down!... Perfect! Got him! Delta leader, we can't take them all. There's at least ten raiders headed your way!"

"This is Delta leader, all remaining Delta wing fighters' return to form a defensive position at once!"

The commander watched as the remaining four ships boosted toward his position. He noted that the raiders backed off and reformed their units. They were apparently well trained and MacNeil observed that there were still at least thirteen raider ships headed his way, nearly twice the number of his seven remaining fighters.

"This is Delta wing leader, form up on me. We're going to punch our way through their line before they have a chance to break up again. Once we're past them we'll reverse and come back through them before they realize what we're doing. Return to this position after our run. Be sure to put your rear pulse cannons on auto-fire. Go!"

It was a good plan and he was sure that they wouldn't expect such a maneuver. They lost only one ship on the first punch through their line and took out four of the raider ships. As the raiders turned to pursue them, the Delta group had already reversed and boosted nearly into their lines again. The raider ships were fast and well-armed but slow to turn, and that was his advantage. They managed to take out three more raider ships on the return pass but one of their own ships suffered major damage and would have to return to the station while he still had power. Now the Delta Leader had five and the raiders were down to six. Those were odds that he liked, but he didn't fool himself into thinking that they would fall for that last maneuver a second time.

"This is Delta leader, good job, people, but they won't go for that one again. This time we're going to lineup in a single line and head straight for them. When I say "GO" everyone is going to peel off and hit their boosters, targeting the closest raider ship that you see. Keep your boosters on 'til they redline and don't let off the laser fire! With any luck, we'll confuse the shit out of them again and we'll have a moment's advantage."

They lined up as ordered and flew directly toward the center of the group. "GO!" MacNeil shouted and each one peeled off in a different direction opening fire at full boost. Two of his ships received minor damage but were still in service. Their power cells were nearly depleted, but the excitement of the battle had pumped their adrenaline up high.

"This is Delta Leader, good work, people; you've earned your pay today. I think that did the job. Return to base."

"Delta Leader! This is Delta 2! Look at your long range scanner! I count... twenty, no thirty raiders headed this way! What are we going to do now?"

MacNeil answered, "Where in the hell are they coming from? Delta leader to Station Master."

"Station Master here, go ahead."

"Do your long range scanners show another approaching group of raiders?"

"Affirmative, Delta leader. We count thirty raiders on our scan."

"I'm down to five fighters and two of those with dirty wings. Our power cells are nearly depleted and we don't have enough fuel to start a new chase. Awaiting orders."

"Return to base, Delta squadron, and refuel immediately."

The station commander, Colonel Ian Palmers, looked at the long range scanner and shook his head. The station had a decent array of automated laser defense cannons, but he had serious doubts about whether they could hold off thirty raider ships. The station held more than one thousand personnel and many lives would be lost if they had to defend themselves.

"What do we do now, Colonel?" The wiry man asked as he looked over the Colonel's shoulder.

"Back to your comm station, Mr. Smith! First, warn the planet of an imminent attack, then activate all defensive weapons systems and sound the emergency alert."

"Yes, Colonel!"

Their only remaining fighters were on the planet and they would be needed to defend the populace, so he knew he that would not receive any help. He watched the screen as the enemy came closer, then he spotted a much larger ship coming into range.

"There you are, asshole," he said softly. "So you finally decided to show yourself... Damn, you are big!"

The comm officer looked over his shoulder at the screen. "What the hell is that thing, Colonel?"

"I'd say she's a battle cruiser, judging by her mass," he replied.

"Can cruisers carry that many fighters?"

"Battle Cruisers can. Only a carrier can support more than that and she isn't that big, for certain. No matter anyway, we can't defend against something that size. We don't have anything that can out-range her batteries."

"Are we going to abandon the station?"

The Colonel looked at the man and saw raw fear in his face. "And go where, Mr. Smith? We're safer here than in a transport heading down to the planet." He reached over to his console and pressed the intercom. "Attention all hands, this is Colonel Palmers, all non-essential personnel, to the escape pods until further notice. All others, to your emergency stations. Prepare for attack and possible boarding!"

He continued to watch the screen as the raider ships got closer. Suddenly they began to split apart into two smaller groups and they appeared to be positioning themselves to bypass the station altogether, until they began to slow their approach.

Comm officer Smith alerted the Colonel, "Sir! I'm receiving a communication from one of their ships. I think it's the cruiser, audio only."

"Send it to my station, Smith." He paused and his comm rang-out, "This is Colonel Ian Palmers of the Aurora Station. What is your business here?"

"This is the Captain of the Cruiser Dragon's Breath. I commend your fighters for their destruction of our vessels. It is rare that I see such sacrifice. But that isn't a concern. I have many more raider ships than you have fighters, so I have lost nothing."

"What is your name, Captain?" Palmers spat.

"My name doesn't matter, Colonel. Power down your weapons now, or I will destroy your station."

"Their weapons are targeting the station, Colonel," Smith whispered. The Colonel held up his hand for silence.

"And why should I do that, Captain? At least I can take out a few more of your fighters before you kill us."

"Captain," his voice remained noticeably calm, "are you really willing to sacrifice over a thousand personnel on your station to take out maybe a dozen fighters before I blast your station to pieces? Consider your answer carefully, Colonel. I will spare your station and its personnel if you power down your weapons now, and let my ships pass unmolested. Perhaps you need a demonstration."

The Colonel watched as an energy pulse erupted from the cruiser and impacted one of his laser defense turrets with an explosion that buffeted the entire station. Alarm claxons rang out and the crew scrambled to extinguish the resulting fires.

"I think I have made my point, Colonel. What is your decision?" the cruiser Captain asked sharply.

The Colonel considered his options, and then paused for a moment.

"I need your reply now, Colonel."

"Power down the weapons, Mr. Smith," the Colonel ordered.

"Are you crazy?" Smith blurted out. "At least we can go down fighting!"

"Either do as you are ordered, Smith, or you're relieved of duty!"

Smith spit on the floor in disgust and reached for the controls to power down the weapons.

"A very wise decision, Colonel. Today you have managed to spare a thousand of your people. Now remain a good Colonel, while we complete our mission."

The ships resumed their previous speed, avoiding the station and began their attack on the planet. The Colonel watched his scanner helplessly, as they attacked. Then his attention returned to the Cruiser as he saw three large transports emerge from behind its position. Each one was flanked by at least two smaller shuttles, probably filled with soldiers.

"What are those ships, Colonel?" Smith asked.

"They look like transport ships," he replied cautiously, as he examined the scanner's sensor readings. "Shit!" he said in disgust as he keyed his comm back to the cruiser. "You're slavers! Is that why you're here?"

"Very good, Colonel. Did you figure that out on your own or did you have some help?"

"What kind of man are you that you can sell people as slave workers?"

"I'm just a businessman, Colonel. I have customers that need employees and I can provide them. If they work, they eat, and if they eat, they live. Today we need highly skilled workers, so you won't mind if we're a little picky on whom we take. No children or elderly, you can keep them," he chuckled.

Palmers felt his blood begin to boil. If only he had a missile launcher or two, or maybe one remaining fighter, he would show this arrogant Captain what he could do.

The transports cruised past the station and down to the planet. The scanner didn't show any remaining defensive fighters and the raiders were strafing the streets causing mayhem. He noted that the transports were landing in the more upscale districts, closer to manufacturing facilities. He guessed that the transport ships could carry close to a hundred people each. Tears swelled in his eyes as he read the reports coming over the comm links. Anyone who refused to come with them was being killed where they stood. The gruesome scene played out for several hours before the first of the transports took off, soon followed by the others. The raiders strafed the streets once more for good measure before they left the atmosphere and followed the transports back to their base ship.

"I'll be taking my leave now, Colonel. It was nice doing business with you. I'm sure that we will return soon, now that we have destroyed your defenses. Until next time...Colonel."

"I hope I get to meet you in person one day, Captain. Just so that I get the chance to slit your throat!" The Colonel replied.

The Captain laughed wickedly over the link before it went dead. The invaders departed and the Colonel could only sit in his chair, sobbing over the loss of people on Aurora. He had saved the lives of a thousand people on the station, but that had cost the lives of hundreds of people who might never be seen again. What were their leaders going to do? It could take months and months to build more fighters and train new pilots, and they still wouldn't be able to defend against a battle cruiser. He recalled a memo regarding a military outfit that was up for hire, but they were on the other side of the galaxy. He didn't even know if the planet could afford what mercenaries might charge for protection.

"What do we do now, Colonel?" Smith asked somberly.

"We rebuild, Smith, and try to be better prepared next time. Right now, our friends on the planet need our help. Get everyone organized and make preparations to send whatever assistance we can. I've got a call to make."

"So, what do you have to say for yourself, Chief Hargrove?"

"I'm sorry Master Warden, Viktor. I guess I underestimated them," Hargrove replied as he stood at attention and looked forward blankly.

"I would say that underestimated is an UNDERSTATEMENT! You had a squad of men at your disposal AND two squads awaiting your signal if you needed backup and you say you UNDERESTIMATED THEM?"

"Yes, sir."

"Then I guess that I have underestimated your abilities also, Sub-Commander!" the Master Warden shouted as he approached Hargrove, reached up and ripped his rank insignia off his uniform. I'm moving you to the maintenance division to see if you can estimate abilities there better than you did at your previous position!" Master Warden Viktor walked back around to his desk and tossed Hargrove's insignia into the waste recycler. Hargrove remained motionless knowing that one wrong move or word could get him a far worse punishment.

Viktor sat down in his seat, leaned back and stared at Hargrove to observe his reaction. When none was forthcoming he leaned forward and sneered as he spoke. "I viewed the observation cams to see what occurred and they apparently have an invisibility cloak. But what I find most insulting is that you were captured by a woman!" He pointed to the image on his desk of a woman dressed in a gold colored uniform. "They swatted your people around like bugs. I should show this at our next council meeting. Maybe then the governing caste will give us more credits to fund our expansion and maybe they will train our lesser qualified people, like you, to perform their duties as they are assigned!" He slammed his fist onto the top of the desk. Hargrove flinched slightly but remained still.

"We did get the vaccine, Chief Warden."

"Yes, we did get the vaccine. Fortunately you didn't release the button on that device and blow it into space. That's the only thing that kept me from having you executed! You were given a simple task. You only had to capture the ship, undamaged, and the crew, unharmed, so we could learn their secrets. Apparently they had some very valuable secrets, judging from what I've seen on the observation screen."

"How many secrets can a freighter ship have? That was probably the only thing they had that was of any value."

"If that's what you think, Sub Commander, then I made a serious error in promoting you to the Station Chief position in the first place. That freighter Captain Mitch Saber was able to defeat Simon Asher's entire operation and we still have no idea how he did it. Now Asher has gone back to Antares to try and rebuild. We need more workers and so do our neighboring systems. The slave traders will have to expand their operations to fill our orders and that means the price will go up. If we don't take control over this end of the galaxy, then someone else will, and then we will have nowhere left to expand! The Warrior Caste has been designated to fulfill the plans of the Governing Caste, and in order to do that, we need technology, equipment and workers to get us there. Manufacturing needs workers, mining needs workers, development needs workers, everyone needs workers and we need warriors! Women are needed for egg production so that we can grow our numbers. There is still so much to do while here I am dealing with issues like you! Get out of my office before I change my mind and have you executed!" he bellowed.

Hargrove saluted sharply, turned and left the Chief Warden's office without another word. The Chief Warden's intercom rang out for his attention.

"Yes, what is it?" he growled.

"I've got Moderator Breen out here to see you, Chief Warden," the voice over the comm announced.

"Take him out and have him executed!" he shot back.

"Sir?"

"You heard me! Take him out and execute him!"

"But, Sir..."

"Carry out my orders or you can go with him!"

"Yes, Sir, yes, Sir. Your orders will be carried out immediately," the frightened voice replied and the comm channel went silent.

Viktor looked out his fourth story window onto the courtyard and watched as Breen was escorted out. He flailed his arms wildly as the guards raised their weapons and fired. His limp body, minus most of his head, fell silently onto the ground.

Viktor returned to his seat and leaned back with a satisfied grin. "I feel better already," he said to himself.

The Phoenix slowed to a stop several thousand miles from the orbital station at Destiny's Cross. Earlier the previous day Mitch had received a communication from Destiny's Cross that the Minister of Planetary Relations had requested the presence of Inna and himself in his office upon their arrival. Although their culture frowned on weapons and war, they understood that there were times when both were necessary to keep peaceful societies, like their own, safe. They allowed some of their citizens to leave and serve in the military of other systems now, but they limited the number of people who could leave each year, and women were rarely permitted to go. It had only been in the past few years that they had started to allow women to leave for space service. This was a small but significant cultural change that had been made since Inna had left, so they was still considered her to be a citizen of Destiny's Cross. Her service to the Alderon Defense Force, and subsequently to Captain Saber, had earned her substantial merit in the eyes of their government, and she was therefore held in high regard. The Minister wanted to thank her personally for making his people proud of one of their own citizens, and he wanted to present her with the Distinguished Citizen Award, which was rarely given. Mitch had not informed Inna of this honor and he hoped that she would take the opportunity to visit her family as a result.

"Inna, the Minister of Planetary Relations has requested our presence. They want to give you an award for your service to Alderon. It's quite an honor that they're giving you," Mitch said as he grinned.

Rion and Yurie turned and applauded Inna which caused her to blush.

"But I haven't done anything, Captain," Inna responded.

"Apparently they think your actions in service to the Alderon Defense Force deserve acknowledgment. You know how politicians are. Just be gracious and accept it, then we can be on our way." Mitch smiled and shrugged like it wasn't a big deal, but he knew better.

"Mr. Stevens, see to the unloading of our cargo. Yuri, you and Inna meet me in the Minnow in ten minutes."

The four of them boarded the Minnow, counting Athena, and they left for the Capitol City Space Port. They were met as they landed by representatives of the Minister's office and escorted to his chambers. After a brief meet and greet session, they were conducted into a meeting room where the award was to be given to Inna in a live broadcast to the public. Mitch, Athena and Yurie stood off to one side as the Minister took to the podium.

"Citizens of Destiny's Cross, it is a rare occasion when we get to recognize one of our own for meritorious service on behalf of our people. Today we are honoring a citizen who left at an early age to seek a military service position, so that she could help protect our home world and the worlds of many others. She has performed her duties with loyalty, honor, and distinction. She has represented our planet, her people, and our values with dignity and respect. I'd like to introduce you to Lieutenant JG Inna Dubnikov who is attached to the Alderon Defense Force and now serves the Saber Mining & Manufacturing Corporation under the command of Captain Mitch Saber, the same Captain who single handedly destroyed over one hundred and fifty pirate raiders who attacked his home world of Alderon. With respect for her service, it is our pleasure to present her with the Destiny's Cross Distinguished Citizen Award."

Everyone in the room applauded as the Minister signaled Inna to his side, and he placed the Medal of Honor on her tunic. She saluted sharply then shook the Minister's hand. Mitch and his party were proud of how Inna played her part and they offered their congratulations too. The Minister pointed her toward the podium, requesting that she say a few words. She blushed a little and glanced back to her fellow crew, who all smiled. Mitch mouthed the words, "Go ahead".

With a little hesitation she approached the podium and, after the Minister adjusted the height to match her small frame, she spoke with confidence.

"Thank you, Minister, for this gracious award. It is my honor to serve in the defense of my friends and family, both here and elsewhere. I will continue to serve in the reserve forces of the Alderon Space Defense and also, under the leadership of Captain Saber, his company and crew. I will endeavor to always be worthy of this honorable distinction that you have conferred on me today. I would also like to say hello to my family, the Dubnikov's of Zone 9 in the agricultural district. I hope that I have made you proud. Thank you."

The applause began again in earnest. Mitch went up to congratulate her with a salute, a handshake and a polite hug, as did the rest of his party.

"I'm very proud of you, Lieutenant. You certainly know how to make a Captain proud. I could not have done that with the grace and poise that you did. You're a fine officer and I'm proud to have you as one of my crew," Mitch said with sincerity.

Inna's eyes swelled with tears as she thanked him and the Minister. After the usual parade of handshakes and meeting the other officials who were present, they returned to the Minister's office.

"Inna, since we're here, would you like to go visit your family?" Mitch asked.

Inna's face paled as she replied, "My Papa said I would never be welcomed back home again and he meant that."

The Minister walked in as she said those words. "Lieutenant Dubnikov, I would be surprised if your Papa still felt that way after all these years. I'm sure that he meant well when he said that, but why don't you give him the benefit of his years of missing you and go see your family. I have checked and they are still operating the farm. Both your brothers are now married with their own families. They have purchased adjacent property and they all farm it as a family unit. Captain, I have the authority to offer you an official escort or you have my permission to take your personal craft to their farm if you wish."

Mitch looked back to Inna, raised an eyebrow and smiled as he nodded for her approval. After some hesitation, she finally agreed.

"Minister, let me thank you for the hospitality that you have shown us. With your permission, I'll accept your escort. If you'll allow my XO Lt. Cmdr. Nagamo to meet us there with our own ship, then we won't have to hold up your people while we visit."

"Of course, Captain. If that is your preferred course of action, then you certainly have my permission. I understand that your ship is now delivering our cargo which will take at least three days. Please remember that you are only allowed a six day stay on the surface, after which time you must return to your ship." The Minister said politely. "Of course, Lt. Dubnikov may stay as long as she likes."

"Thank you, Minister but I still have a business to run so the six day window is more than satisfactory," Mitch answered.

Yurie returned to retrieve the Minnow and was given directions to the Dubnikov ranch. Mitch, Athena and Inna boarded the transport and followed their escort vehicles. The trip wasn't long and as the parade of vehicles slowed to a stop in front her old home, Inna was noticeably nervous. They remained inside for a moment until the door to the house opened. Inna's mother walked out first, closely followed by her father. The years showed on their faces and their hair had grayed considerably. Tears began to form in Inna's eyes as she watched hesitantly. Mitch opened the door and stepped out, followed by Athena and finally Inna. Their dress uniforms were impressive in the bright mid-day sun and Inna's father held his hand to his forehead to see who was there. The Minister got out of his vehicle and went to speak to her father. They shook hands briefly and as the Minister spoke she saw her mother lean aside to look her way. Time seemed to move in slow motion as she watched the Minister stand to one side and her parents looked at her, seemingly without emotion. Then a big smile came over her mother's face. Her father just looked at her expressionlessly.

Mitch decided that action was needed at this point, so he placed his hand gently on the center of Inna's back and gave her a subtle nudge.

"Come along, Inna, let's meet your parents," Mitch said softly.

Approaching to within a few feet, Mitch spoke in his typical Captain's commanding tone, "Mr. and Mrs. Dubnikov, I am Captain Mitch Saber. It is a pleasure to meet you." He reached out his hand and after a moment's hesitation Pavel extended his hand to the Captain. Lorna Dubnikov, Inna's mother, didn't take Mitch's hand but instead opted to a give Mitch a big motherly hug. Mitch beamed a wide smile and could tell that she was proud and happy to see her daughter, but she was waiting to see what Pavel's reaction was going to be.

"Your daughter is one of my best officers and I'm proud to have her as a member of my crew. She has served the Alderon Defense Force with dedication, working her way up through the ranks. She has often spoken of you both, and I know that she has missed you greatly. The Minister was gracious enough to escort us here after she was presented…"

Pavel interrupted, "I watched the ceremony, Captain. Your words are not necessary. I told my daughter that she would never be welcomed back here again if she left, and she made her choice."

Inna pushed Mitch aside. "Papa, you would have never allowed me to leave this planet. I left so that I could learn to help and serve others and to fulfill my brother's last wish for my life. I thought that you might be happy to see me, but I guess I was wrong."

"Well, your Mama is proud of you, Inna, and I'm happy to see my little girl again," Her mother said forcefully as she stepped in front of Pavel and hugged her daughter tightly and kissed her forehead. He remained motionless, his eyes full of anger. Mother and daughter hugged for a long time before separating.

Her mother turned to Pavel and gave him a serious, angry look. "You think that I haven't seen you cry at night worrying about our daughter? Wondering where she was and if she was alive? I offered to read you her letters, but you refused to listen. You're too afraid to admit that you were wrong to treat her the way that you did. Now you're just an angry old man who refuses to tell his only daughter that he loves her and misses her."

Pavel's anger rose, and Mitch sensed that Athena's empathic read on him was about to cause her to react. He silently cautioned her to maintain her position; they needed to see what would happen between the family members without interference. Inna's mother had control of the situation for the moment, and he wanted her to have her say. This was apparently something that had been building for a long time. The Minister also was silent and didn't intervene.

Pavel's fists tightened and his teeth clenched, readying himself for a reaction. Mitch and Athena each suspected that he may reach out and strike either Inna or her Mother, at which point they would definitely have to get involved. Lorna also observed his reaction and she reached around Inna's shoulders, holding her tightly in a protective hug. Her face and mouth drew tight as she looked at him.

"You've never struck me, Pavel, but I promise you that if you do now, one of the men, or women, present here will beat the color right off your stubborn hide. Look at your daughter." She pushed Inna directly in front of Pavel and held her there by her shoulders, as tears streamed down Inna's cheeks. "Are you the kind of father who can look his daughter in her eyes and say that he doesn't love her anymore? *Can you*? Your daughter has become a fine young woman all on her own. The Captain said that she *worked* her way up through the ranks. She wasn't given anything that she didn't earn. She has made the Dubnikov name proud. Tell her that you don't love her. Tell her *NOW*, in front of everyone here Pavel!" She shouted as she shook her finger towards him.

All the color left Pavel's face as he fell to his knees and cried. He held out his arms to Inna who leaped forward into them and hugged him with all her strength.

"Oh child, I am so sorry. Can you ever find it in your heart to forgive a stubborn old man? I *do* love you, daughter, I love you so *very* much and I've missed you all these years," Pavel said through his sobs and tears.

"There's nothing to forgive, Papa."

"Yes, there is. You must forgive me or the Maker will hold it against me when I die."

"Then I forgive you, Papa. I just wanted you to be proud of me. I never wanted to hurt you or Mama."

"I'm the one who has caused the hurt, child." He stood and looked at the bystanders. "Please, everyone, I have made a fool of myself and I ask your forgiveness. Let's go inside and talk. Please allow me to make amends."

Yurie landed the Minnow near the house and a few hours later the Minster and his party left to return to the Capitol City. Inna's brothers and their families came to rejoice at Inna's return and everyone enjoyed a huge celebration that evening and the following day. On the third day, Mitch received confirmation that the cargo had been safely delivered and they had a new destination on the log. Goodbyes were said and they returned to the Phoenix. Inna was immensely relieved that her relationship with her family had been restored so she could finally put the unhappy part of her life to rest.

CHAPTER TWELVE

THE COMM ALERT RANG OUT SEVERAL TIMES BEFORE THE snoozing Captain Saber realized that he wasn't dreaming. He rubbed the sleep from his eyes and said, "Answer, audio only."

"Mitch? Are you there?" Said the familiar female voice of his wife, Samantha.

Mitch sat up in bed, surprised and thrilled to hear her voice. "Sam! Hang on a sec, let me get to my console." He rolled out of bed and quickly activated his console. The holographic display came into view and for the first time in months he looked at the beautiful face of his wife.

"Damn, you're so beautiful. I've missed you Sam! Where have you been?"

"I've missed you too, lover. We've been out exploring and mapping and letting you do all the dirty work. We just arrived back in friendly space and I wanted to call you first. Where are you?"

"We're two FTL days flight out of Destiny's Cross headed for Atlantis to get cargo for Outlanders Run. What's up?" Mitch detected some concern in her voice.

"I need to stop by Alderon to resupply. Our stores are nearly empty, so I'll meet you at Outlanders Run."

"What's up Sam? Is something wrong?"

"Nothing is wrong, Mitch, but I need to discuss something with you in person as soon as I can."

"Tell me now, Sam, I can change my route if I need to reach you sooner."

"I can't talk about it over an open channel, Mitch. Besides, you need to see what I'm talking about in person to fully understand. There is no rush and meeting you at Outlanders Run will give me enough time to resupply while you make your freight run. The company still has bills to pay you know." She smiled and winked.

"As long as you're sure, Sam."

"I'm sure this will work out just fine."

They spoke for a while longer as Mitch filled her in on his latest happenings. The call ended but the concern was still present in Mitch's mind. He sensed a real concern in Sam's voice and he wasn't sure what it meant. Nonetheless, he knew his wife well enough to know that if there was truly an urgent situation, then she would have told him right up front. Just to be certain, he sent a message ahead that his ship needed to resupply while he was at Atlantis. He could have waited longer, but he wanted to be prepared, just in the event that he might have an unexpected change in plans.

Two weeks later, the Phoenix arrived at Outlanders Run. Samantha and her ship, the Rivers Run, were already there waiting for his arrival. She had stopped on the way to Alderon and picked up some small cargo at the Chinese Federation that was scheduled to go to Alderon, so the trip would still be profitable. Mitch signaled for the cargo bots to begin delivering the cargo containers to the drop-off location, and then he contacted Sam.

"Inna, contact Samantha please, and bring up my privacy screens."

"Aye, Captain," Inna replied.

The electronic privacy screens shimmered into place as Sam appeared on his display.

"Hi, Mitch, is your station secure?" Sam asked.

"All screens are up, Sam. It won't take long for us to drop this load. Why don't we just hook up via the external space tube?"

"That's a good idea, Mitch," Sam replied. "Bring Athena along with you."

Mitch was immediately curious. "Certainly. Do I need to give you two some private time?" He smirked.

"I was going to invite you to stay in my cabin tonight, but you just blew the invite, Saber!" She winked.

Mitch smiled and shook his head. "Should have seen that one coming," he said in mock disappointment.

"See you when we get hooked up," Sam said as she ended the call.

Mitch motioned to Inna to end the screening. "Inna, notify the Master Chief that we will be connecting the tube with the Rivers Run when we're finished here."

"Aye, Captain," she confirmed.

The cargo bots worked quietly and efficiently placing each cargo pod into the correct position so that the freight crew could activate the pods' automated reentry boosters. The delivery was quickly made and the Phoenix moved slowly into position next to the Rivers Run. Each ship extended a flexible tube made from spun carbon and titanium fibers interwoven with Kevlar and four layers of flexible polymer material. When a small electrical charge was sent through the material, it turned into a solid surface providing a stable platform on which to walk. Flexible lighting panels were also incorporated into the material that unfolded as the tube was extended to illuminate the tube's interior. Not taking any chances, although the tube was considered safe to pressurize, they chose to wear pressure suits with an independent air supply when passing through the tubes. Athena, when offered a suit declined, stating that her armor didn't require a pressure suit as it was a part of the design. She activated the suit's armored mask and proceeded, unhindered, through the tube. Mitch shrugged his shoulders and followed after the Master Chief gave him the thumbs up.

Once through the tube and past the pressurized seals, Mitch removed his suit and opened the interior door. Sam was standing there waiting with a huge smile. She wrapped her arms around him and kissed him, long and hard. Afterwards Sam greeted Athena like she was part of their family. Mitch saw the surprise on Athena's face and the warm smile that followed. It wasn't a forced smile either, it was a heartfelt smile, and that pleased Mitch. Athena's companionship had become more important to him than he had expected. He valued their deep friendship greatly. His ability to communicate with her mentally had reached a level that didn't require deep concentration to complete. It now came quite naturally, and he realized that sometimes they carried on conversations mentally as they performed separate duties. The crew had caught him occasionally laughing out loud and spontaneously smiling for no apparent reason, and he was embarrassed when forced to make excuses for his behavior. His favorite excuse was, "Sometimes you just do something dumb and all you can do is laugh at yourself and keep on going." The crew seemed to appreciate the sentiment and he overheard it often repeated among the crew.

"Well, Sam, you've worried me silly, so what's this all about?" Mitch asked seriously.

"Come to my quarters and I'll show you something that will take your breath away," She replied.

Mitch pursed his lips and wondered what was in store for them. Sam walked forward and motioned them to follow, so they did. They took the tram toward the front of the ship where the officer's quarters were located, exited and walked toward the Captain's cabin. As they approached, Samantha saw someone exiting her cabin, and she knew that it had been secured when she left.

"Stop where you are, mister!" she shouted down the corridor. The man stopped abruptly and turned around. "Ensign Iverson, what do you think you're doing?" Sam demanded in an angry tone of voice.

"Nothing, Captain. I just came to find you and you weren't in your office, that's all," Reese Iverson replied.

Athena whispered to Sam from behind, "He's lying, Captain."

"Are you sure Athena?" Sam asked quietly.

"Positive. I'm detecting elevated hormones, a rapid pulse and agitation. I'm getting a strong impression of the word escape. He is lying for certain."

"Mr. Iverson, return to your quarters and wait for me there," Sam sternly ordered the young Ensign.

"Yes, Captain," he replied hastily as he turned and almost fled down the corridor.

Samantha moved quickly to her quarters and opened the door. Right away she knew that some of her things had been moved and upset, as if they had been searched through. Mitch could see that her door key pad was loose. "Sam, I think he hacked your keypad to gain entry. Apparently we arrived when he was attempting to reattach it to the door frame. I'm surprised no one else saw him," Mitch observed.

Samantha pressed the comm pad on her console, "Captain to Chief Henley."

"Henley here, Captain," he promptly reply.

"I told Ensign Iverson to wait for me in his quarters. I want him detained there under guard until I arrive," she said sharply.

"Captain," he asked, somewhat unsure that he had heard her correctly.

"You heard me, Reggie. Do it now!"

"Aye, Captain! On my way!"

They left her quarters and had turned to go to Iverson's quarters when Reggie called back to Sam. "Captain, Iverson isn't in his quarters."

"Find him now, Chief!" Sam said angrily. She reached behind her ear and touched her implant. "ALICE."

"Yes, Captain, ALICE is available." The ships AI replied.

"Can you locate Ensign Iverson?"

"Ensign Iverson is located in cargo bay two," ALICE replied.

"Damn it! He's trying to get to my Praxanon samples! We need to catch him before he leaves in one of the fighters," Sam replied frantically.

"Athena, get to cargo bay two and stop him, but don't kill him. We need information from him," Mitch said to Athena. She sprinted away down the corridor.

"My God, that woman can run!" Sam said with surprise. "ALICE, seal all outside cargo doors."

"Doors sealed, Captain." ALICE confirmed.

"No one can outrun her, that's why I sent her ahead. She'll stop him cold," Mitch replied.

They ran down the primary corridor, turned right and immediately back left again where the corridor split in two different, but parallel, directions. They made it as far as the main cargo corridor when just ahead; they saw a man lying on the deck, in front of cargo bay two.

"That's the guard I had posted here," Sam yelled as she slowed down just enough to get inside the cargo bay.

Inside, Athena was standing about twenty feet away from Ensign Iverson. She commanded him to drop his weapon, but he continued pointing it at her.

"What are you doing, Iverson?" Sam demanded.

Iverson directed his attention to Sam and Mitch as they came through the door. Sam could see that he had been trying to break the seal on the container that held the pieces of the Praxanon hull.

His eyes were full of fear as he spoke. "This is too big for just one person to have control over, Captain. I've got to take it to people who will make better use of it than you will."

"That's not your decision to make, Iverson. Now drop your weapon, before Athena takes it from you," Sam ordered sternly.

"I don't know who this woman is, but she can't stop me," he said glaring arrogantly at Athena.

"That would be a *wrong* assumption, Ensign," Mitch said firmly. "She could kill you without so much as moving a finger, so drop your weapon now, Ensign."

"I can't do that! I have to take this out of here! Give me the code to open the crate, Captain!" Iverson said frantically.

"Not going to happen, Iverson. Now stop acting like a fool before you get into more trouble than you are already in, and drop that weapon!" Sam ordered.

Iverson pointed the gun at Sam. Mitch pushed her quickly out of the way, just as the crazed Ensign fired. The shot went past them as a sudden pulse of energy filled the room, quickly followed by the acrid odor of burned flesh. Mitch helped Sam up off the floor and they looked back at Iverson's position, his body now sprawled out against the bulkhead. One arm was lying by itself on the floor, at least what was left of it. From the elbow to the shoulder it had been completely vaporized. From the elbow to the fingers it remained in one piece, with his fingers still gripping the weapon. There was little bleeding as the energy pulse from Athena's weapon had cauterized the flesh. Iverson sat there in stunned disbelief and shock, looking at what was left of his arm. The color quickly drained from his face and his eyes rolled back into his head.

"Dr. Sands to cargo bay two for medical emergency!" Sam called out with urgency.

Athena deactivated her helmet armor as Sam went to check Iverson's vital signs. Dr. Sands arrived running, and slowed as she observed the remains of the arm on the deck and Iverson against the wall.

"I checked the man by the door and he's dead," Dr. Sands informed them. She quickly moved to Iverson and held up her diagnostic device, running it across his body. "He's in shock and it looks like that arm is a complete loss. I need to get him into a med pod."

She was calling for assistance when Chief Henley walked into the room. "Damn, what happened, Captain?"

"Iverson tried to shoot Samantha and Athena took him down. She could have killed him, but I ordered earlier her not to kill him, so she took the next best course of action, which was to disable him," Mitch answered.

"He killed one of my security personnel! What was he doing?" Reggie asked.

"He intended to take the Praxanon samples to give to someone who we have not yet identified," Sam said as she inspected the container containing the samples.

Iverson was removed from the area as was the dead security guard. Sam ordered the area to be re-secured, this time with two guards.

"So, Sam, what's this about a Praxanon and samples? What started all this?" Mitch asked as he looked at the container. "Iverson was willing to kill you in order to get his hands on whatever this is."

"That's what I needed to see you about, Mitch," Sam said as she pressed her hand on the control pad releasing the locking mechanism. A soft click announced the lock's release and she pulled open the lid.

Immediately upon the light reaching inside the sealed container, the hull pieces began to react with small arcs of electricity dancing over their surfaces. The container, which was one quarter the size of a Minnow, held several large pieces of a ships outer hull and a few smaller ones.

Not knowing what he was seeing, Mitch asked, "What the hell is that?"

Sam reached down and picked up one of the larger pieces, it measured about six square feet. With one hand and she tossed it toward Mitch. He instinctively reached out with both hands to catch it, expecting it to be heavy and was surprised by its lack of weight.

He held it with one hand, studying it cautiously. "Where did you find this?"

"On a derelict ship that we ran across, and that's the hull material."

"Is this all that's left of it?"

"No, that's actually wreckage from a shuttle that came from the larger ship. Several of them crashed landed on a nearby planet when they escaped the mother ship."

"Whoa, too much information here! Mother ship? What exactly did you find out there?"

Sam smiled. "I've got all the information secured in my quarters. That's probably what Iverson was looking for, but he didn't know where to look. The mother ship was called the Praxanon and she is nearly three miles long. She was an exploration vessel and more, much more, she was capable of traveling through time!"

"I didn't think that was possible. Obviously I have a lot more questions, so let's go to your quarters and see what you've got."

"We will, but first I want to ask Athena if she has ever seen anything like this." Sam directed Athena's attention to the material in Mitch's hand.

Athena took the material, turning it over and over, observing how it reacted to the light. Then she replied, "It's an organic material that is self-regenerating. It seems to draw its power from any available ambient light source. I would surmise that it's capable of storing and reflecting light energy for power and defensive purposes."

Sam's smiled widened and Mitch took this as affirmation that Athena's assessment was correct.

"All of which is exactly correct, Athena. I wish that you had been with us when we found her. You surmised in a few minutes what took us days to figure out. Do your people have material like this?" Sam asked, as she took the material from Athena and placed it back in its storage container.

"Not exactly, but we have materials that react in a similar manner. My armor is an example of that. It stores light energy and uses it in multiple ways. The primary difference between the two is that my armor is flexible and non-organic, rather than solid like the shuttle material, but the properties are very much the same," Athena answered.

"I kind was hoping that would be the answer I got. Let's go to my quarters so I can show you the rest." She motioned them to follow her and as she exited the door she turned to the two men now posted there to guard the cargo. "Absolutely no one is to enter this cargo bay except me, Mitch, or Athena. No one, do you understand?" They both nodded. "If anyone should insist that they are authorized to get in, or object in any way when you turn them away, then place them under house arrest immediately, or shoot them if necessary!"

Back in her quarters, Samantha shared the information regarding the Praxanon with Mitch and Athena. Mitch was astounded by the images and vids of the ship in action. He read her reports of their visit to the fifth planet and the details of how the Praxanon crew met their end.

"It's really sad in most ways. Those people had all of these capabilities and technical knowledge, but they had to return to the past to find a way to continue their existence. After all of that, it took just one mad man to end it. These people already had this level of technology, at the same that time our people were just beginning to venture into space and settle other worlds. That's really incredible. So what's our next move?" Mitch asked as he poured himself a drink from the bar in her office.

"That's what I wanted to talk to you about. We left her partially powered, but immobilized, until our return. My concern is, well...I don't think that we're ready for this." She paused and reclined back in her seat. "There are so many risks that I can't even name them all. However, I think the tech needs to be studied. I would like to try to reverse-engineer that hull material into something that we could use for our ships. For a peaceful operation, it would provide a level of security unlike anything in the galaxy. But that also works two ways. If we were an aggressor military organization, then we would be hard to stop with ships made of this stuff. The trick is to prevent it from being stolen. The attempt that we witnessed here today is only the first of what I fear would be many to follow. The whole issue of time travel is something that I don't want entrusted to any government. I've visited all of the discovered systems on this end of the galaxy, and the other end I don't know a lot about. There are rogue planets that are hostile to everyone and the Mercon Company suspects that they are probably the true home of the slavers who have raided our side of the galaxy. The only slave trading ship that we ever encountered was from the far side, so General Payton determined that it was in our best interest to build ourselves into a force with which to be reckoned. If they invade any of the planets that we contracted with, we would be a formidable force. That's one of the reasons that General Harris never spreads his forces too thin, because he wants to always be in a position to send aid if needed." Sam raised her hands in an upwards shrug, "So, what do you suggest? Where should we go from here?"

Mitch sipped his drink, first looking thoughtfully at Sam, and then at Athena, compiling his thoughts. There was a long silence as he took the last drink from his glass and returned to the bar for a refill.

While he poured another drink he said thoughtfully, "Athena, Your people have always strived to remain peaceful and non-threatening, haven't they?"

Athena looked up at Mitch and focused on the query. "Yes, Captain. We believe that the best offense is a strong defense. We don't believe that war is an end to anything except life itself. However, we will defend our people and our beliefs with all our might when necessary. With the same intensity that I will defend you, Captain, our people will defend each other."

Sam gazed at Mitch with understanding in her eyes. She knew where he was going with his question. She interjected, "So, if I'm reading you right, Mitch, you think that perhaps we should deliver this material to her home world for study?"

"You're half right, Sam. I think that we should deliver the ship to the Aegean's for study and safe keeping, assuming that they are even interested or want to get involved in this. I would hate to destroy such a find, but I would if I need to keep it out of an enemy's hands. This is just what an evil person like Simon Asher would use to fulfill his greediest dreams. Even if you were to take out the time travel and the organic hull, you would still have a powerhouse of a vessel that could be used for any number of things. It was designed as an exploration vessel and I think it should stay that way." Mitch returned to his seat and played the video sequence that demonstrated the ships defensive capabilities again. "That is incredible to watch."

"How do we approach the Aegean's?" Sam inquired.

"I'll have to handle that. I have a...method of communication that I have been provided, should that become necessary." He was reluctant to answer any further.

"Okay, if they accept, how in the hell do we get the ship to them without being seen? It kind of sticks out in a crowd, you know." She smiled.

Mitch thought about this for a moment, and then answered, "One of our ships will run interference. We'll update our charts to reflect all the new gateways and utilize them to make best time with the least chance of being observed. If we stay in the outermost reaches of inhabited systems, then they won't even see us pass through. The other issue will be getting enough trustworthy crew onboard to operate her systems. Systems about which we know nothing, I might add."

"Actually that won't be as hard as you might expect. Everything is laid out similarly to our own vessels. We've got all of the engineering specs and training documents, and the translator is up and running. I expect that a crew the size of the Phoenix's could probably handle her just fine." Sam smiled.

Mitch carefully phrased his suspicion, "I would have expected you to want that job with a ship her size. That's where you're more comfortable. What's your reasoning?"

"Easy there big boy, don't get your jets in a bind. I'm thinking that if we run into any trouble, then a ship the size of the Rivers Run would be more capable of getting everyone to safety or using for defensive purposes."

"Ah..." Mitch responded, "You're playing the strategist again, I should have known. If it works out that our friends accept, then we can set up a simulator for training. I assume that you have full vid records of all the controls?" He already knew what her answer would be, but he enjoyed toying with her.

"Keep it up, Saber and I'll have Athena spank you for me," she grinned innocently.

Mitch looked at her with a sly grin and glanced toward Athena, who replied telepathically, "I'd like that a lot!"

"I bet you would," he said aloud without thinking. Sam gave him a puzzled look and Athena actually shrugged her shoulders as though she didn't have a clue what he meant. This was the first outward expression of humor that he had seen from her.

He replied back telepathically, "Wow, I'm impressed!"

Athena replied silently, "There are a lot of things I can do that will surprise you, my Captain."

Mitch blushed and Sam's puzzled look became one of bewilderment.

Sam finally offered, "There's something going between you two that I haven't figured out yet." She said this while pointing her finger at them.

"It's an inside joke, Sam," Mitch said in reply.

"I hear you. Now, I'm down two people and need replacements, any suggestions?"

"Actually, yes. I would suggest that your new navigation officer come from Bion4. I think you can handle the other replacement with help from your Chief, Reggie."

"I never considered having a bi-mod on my bridge crew," Sam mused.

"I'm sure that Richter will help you find the best. He's been a great addition to my crew, and if you're welcomed back to Aegea, having a bi-mod in your crew could be a real asset."

"Alright, you're the owner of this company, so make it happen."

"Done. I'll make the appropriate contacts and we'll see what happens. In the meantime, I suggest that we go about business as usual. However, I think we should move those material samples over to my ship, where they will be out of sight, and no one will know what's in that container."

"Agreed, and a good suggestion. That will take the pressure off both me and the crew."

"What are you going to do with Iverson when he recovers?"

"I was going to sentence him to prison on Outlanders Run since we're already here, assuming that the Saber Corporation will pay the prison fee."

"I'll authorize it for you. However, the biggest problem we have is the stories that he will tell the other prisoners."

Athena interrupted, "I can handle that if you like. I am capable of removing those memories from his mind and replacing them with something else."

"Really!" Sam said, greatly surprised, "I didn't know that you could do that."

"I'll bet there are a lot of things that she can do that would surprise us," Mitch shot back as he smirked at Athena. He was startled when she kicked him under the desk.

"You two are acting like two school yard buddies. What's up with all that?" Sam asked with a curious look.

"It's just a game that we play to increase her comfort level when she is reacting to other people. We get a little silly sometimes, so just ignore us," Mitch said with a chuckle. Sam just shook her head.

"Okay, Athena, I'll let you erase his memory of everything pertaining to the Praxanon, and then I'll have him charged with attempted mutiny so that he'll never be able to serve on a ship again. He'll serve at least twenty years hard time for that," Sam decided.

"That's pretty lenient, Sam. You could have him executed for his actions. Attempted murder of a ship's Captain is a capital offense. I don't think that I would be that easy on him," Mitch said sincerely.

Sam reflected a moment, and then reasoned, "Up 'til now he's been a good officer. I think that he was overwhelmed with this discovery and that he wasn't mentally sound when he took this action. He's young enough that he can still lead a good life once he regains his balance, but I won't let him go unpunished. He'll need a replacement arm. That limb will take at least four years to grow in a cloning tank, so I think that he will have paid his dues, when it is all said and done."

"I'll pay for his incarceration, but not for the arm replacement. He'll have to earn that money on his own," Mitch said flatly.

"If he doesn't waste his bonus pay then he can afford it. That will be his choice to make."

Athena returned to the Phoenix while Mitch stayed the night with his beloved Samantha. The following day the organic hull material was transferred, without incident, to the Phoenix. Copies of all the information related to the discovery of the Praxanon were given to Mitch. He left for the Chinese Federation while Sam stayed to transfer Iverson to the prison officials on Outlanders Run. The only memory that Athena left with Iverson was his attempted murder of Samantha. This was done so that a formal court martial hearing could be held onboard the Rivers Run and his admission of guilt could be established. He couldn't remember the specific reason for his crime, but the memory of it was very real and that satisfied the judicial requirements.

Athena and Mitch sat in his quarters discussing the possibilities of utilizing the organic hull material. The hour was getting late so their conversation was getting less serious in nature.

"Athena," Mitch asked, "do you ever take your armor off? I mean that's all I ever see you in, so please forgive my curiosity."

She tilted her head slightly to one side reflecting on his question. "Are you asking if I wear anything other than this?" she asked pointing to her armor.

"Yes. I know that you brought a gold crate with you when you first arrived, so I naturally assumed that you had other clothing, but you always wear your armor."

"The crate, as you refer to it, contains several replacement units and some personal effects, but no other clothing. My armor is self-repairing, requiring no maintenance, and it provides temperature fluctuation for all of my needs. You've already seen many of the other functions it provides."

"So, you sleep in the buff?"

"Buff? I don't understand, buff."

"Sorry, you sleep without clothing."

"Yes, without...clothing, as you say."

"The armor material looks comfortable, but there aren't any obvious clasps, buttons or zippers, so how do you get it off?" he asked with a puzzled expression. His curiosity was about to get the best of him.

"How do I remove my uniform? Oh, that's very simple." She pressed a tiny spot just about where her belly button should be, and the material instantly withdrew itself to an area around her waist in the shape of a belt. The fluid motion looked just like water pouring off her body in the shower, leaving Mitch taken aback by the unexpected demonstration. Her full uniform was now only a belt around her waist and it took Mitch a moment to realize that she was completely naked, in his office. He sat there, shocked and a bit embarrassed, looking at her muscular body and her platinum colored skin. She was lean and muscular with no visible body fat, and very well developed in all the areas that mattered. She wore nothing other than the belt. He also saw that she had no body hair and he wondered if that was natural or intentional.

His thoughts gave him away and she replied telepathically, "The lack of hair is a result of the armor. I hope what you see pleases you, my Captain."

Mitch had to dial back his natural urges and concentrate on what he needed to say in order to hide his reactions. "You always please me, Athena. You are an extraordinary woman. You're beautiful on the outside and on the inside. I could never have anyone more perfect than you to protect me."

She gave him a warm smile and Mitch could literally feel her pride being reflected toward him. He had made her feel that she was very special, and that made her very happy. She leaned over his desk, still naked, and hugged him generously. This was the first time that he had actually felt her skin, and he recalled her comment, made many months ago, that the Aegean peoples' skin was leathery and thick. He now agreed with that description, but noticed that it was also soft. She started to let go, but he held her for a brief moment longer before he released her. She resumed her upright stature and had started to turn when Mitch said, "You might want to activate your clothing before you leave. I don't think the crew would understand why you're leaving my office without your clothes."

"Certainly, my Captain."

He smiled and her armor, like water in a clear stream, flowed back into place. She left his office and he sank back in his chair with a grunt. That was something he that never expected to see! On reflection, he decided that now was definitely a good time to take a cold shower and go to bed. Samantha was perfect in her beauty too, so after his cold shower he would let her know just how perfect she was.

Laurel sat at Mitch's favorite table near the waterfront in the small café and pub, Al's Nighthawk. She recalled the times that her father had taken her from their Saber Island retreat to meet Mitch for lunch at Al's place when he was in the ADF. It was lunch time now, and the place was full of officers and cadets who frequented Al's nearly every day. Although she was not often seen in the city, Laurel was a very recognizable figure, especially among the academy and defense force personnel. She smiled politely and greeted many of the officers who stopped by to briefly say hello and ask about her brother, Mitch. She had been working in the Saber offices on the surface for a couple of days, interviewing new hires and handling general duties that she typically assigned to Miranda, who was off for a couple of days. Laurel had decided that it was past time for her to get out of the office for a bite.

Laurel reflected on the thought that Miranda, who was also her best friend, would be proud of her current choice in attire. Typically a conservative dresser, today she wore a black one-piece dress with a gold belt. The hem of her sleeveless outfit fell just short of half way between her knees and her bottom, so it revealed much more of her long legs than her usual attire, and the neckline was just low enough to delight and tease. The last few days on the island had afforded her the time to acquire a nice tan. Her black high-heeled knee length boots accentuated her sleek look and the long locks of curly deep brunette hair drew looks of appreciation from the other café patrons. Laurel was very attractive, but she always played down her looks, unlike Miranda who flaunted everything that she had. Complimenting her attire, she wore a string of fourteen aqua and turquoise pearls around her neck that were known as the "Tears of Alderon". They came from the other side of the planet from the deepest of waters, so they were extremely rare. One single pearl could buy a dozen places like Al's. Today they looked particularly striking against her tanned skin. Platinum and gold hoops dangled from her ears and glistened when the light was reflected from them. Her hair was held back behind her ears by two barrettes made from crushed and laminated Tears of Alderon pearls. She also wore numerous gold and platinum bangle bracelets on each arm, one of which inconspicuously held an emergency alert that was monitored by her security staff and her uncle, Fleet Admiral Rich Jonas, whose office was only a few blocks away.

She sipped her drink as she finished lunch and enjoyed her view of the water. Her two security escorts sat just behind her at another table, keeping a discreet watch over her. She had balked at first over having to use body-guards, but after the attempted assassination of her family on the island, she had accepted their constant presence and had grown accustomed to them. She scrolled through several screens on her data pad and hardly noticed the three darkly dressed men who entered Al's place and sat at a table not far from hers. She sat sideways with her legs crossed in a particularly attractive fashion, not intentionally, but in order to get the best view of the waterfront. It wasn't long before she had the uncomfortable feeling that she was being watched. She adjusted her data pad's angle and saw, reflected on the screen, the three men, seated several tables away, watching her intently.

The server, a young man wearing a white shirt and khaki shorts, brought her a fresh glass of water, and as he sat it down on a fresh napkin, he pulled the napkin up slightly to reveal a message: "You're being watched." He smiled and she thanked him for the water. She glanced over to see Al watching her and he nodded from behind the counter. His eyes cut directly towards the three men that she had just observed. She glared at them, disapprovingly, and without looking toward her guards reached up and gently tugged three times on her left ear lobe. That was her signal to them to be on alert that trouble may be coming. They adjusted their positions slightly to allow a fast and direct response to help her if need be. She casually took another sip of her drink and returned her attention to the data pad.

Out of the corner of her eye, she saw the three men stand and walk in her direction. The man in the center took the lead, stopping within inches of her table.

"Would you be Laurel Saber by chance?" he asked.

"Perhaps, who's asking?" She looked at him with a cold expression. Something about him raised her guard and suspicions.

"The man who is about to become your new business partner, Ms. Saber. They call me Talonis." He extended his hand, which she ignored.

"I don't need a business partner, Talonis of Cerberus. Especially one like you."

"Ah, you know of me! Such rudeness from such a *lovely* young woman. I expected better from the sister of Mitch Saber."

"Don't play games with me, Talonis. What do you want? Why are you here on Alderon?"

"Like I said, I'm going to be your new business partner. Since you've endeavored to explore all these new planetary systems, you need my help to govern them. I have the expertise and personnel to do this...for a small fee of course."

"Neither you nor your services are required, Talonis. I believe that my brother made that perfectly clear when you last met."

"I don't think he that understood my position on the matter. Since you're fifty percent owner of the corporation, I'm bringing my case to you."

"You have no case. You're not welcome here and we sure as hell don't want your assistance. You and your boys might as well go home."

His eyes hardened as he tried to intimidate her with his gaze. Laurel wasn't easily intimidated and she was very capable of defending herself. Mitch had seen to that and she also held several black belts in various martial arts skills. She and Miranda had a trainer come to their offices once every week and train with them to sharpen their skills.

"This isn't an option for you, Miss Saber," he said gruffly and stepped to within arm's reach.

Laurel stood up and with the height of her boot heels, she looked directly into the eyes of Talonis. In a flash she slapped him across the left cheek, her long finger nails leaving neat lines down his face. She watched as a red welt rose on his cheek and his face flushed with anger. The restaurant became instantly quiet as everyone turned to see what had happened.

Laurel stepped around the small table, closer to Talonis, and her guards stood up ready to go into action. They didn't approach, waiting to let her make her play. They knew her well enough to let her make her own move first.

"Ladies and gentlemen," she announced loud enough for everyone to hear while adjusting her bracelets and, unknown to anyone, activating her alert signal, "this is Talonis of Cerberus. He operates gambling and prostitution houses and he is demanding that he become my business partner. Do we allow Cerberus Empire Citizens to do business here on Alderon?"

A loud "NO!" erupted from the officers and cadets who were closing in behind Talonis and his two men.

"As I said, Talonis of Cerberus, you're not welcome here."

"I have diplomatic papers that permit me to be here, Miss Saber, so I will do as I wish. I will not tolerate the likes of you to strike me again. I have..."

Laurel turned as if she was going to walk away from him, then she wheeled around with speed and precision, landing a spinning back-fist against his right jaw, snapping his head sideways. Another large red swelling began to rise on his other cheek. His two companions started to reach inside their tunics, when several ADF officers came up from behind and yanked their arms around and behind their backs. Talonis rubbed a hand against the side of his face where blood trickled down from the scratches left by one of the several rings she wore on her hand. He gritted his teeth in anger.

"How dare you! I will make you pay for this. No one insults Talonis this way. Especially a...a woman!"

Laurel stepped closer and jabbed her right hand between his legs and squeezed his jewels until he bellowed in pain. Talonis reached for her throat, so she twisted and continued to squeeze as she backed him up several steps. Several of the officers grinned and some grimaced at his pain. She released him and turned, as if to walk away. He dropped his hands to his groin in agony and spit in her direction. She spun again, this time sweeping his legs out from under him, and he fell hard onto his back. As Talonis landed, several vehicles swiftly pulled up to the curb. ADF guards and her uncle emerged. Talonis lay stunned on the floor as she walked over to him and placed the sharp heel of her boot onto the soft part of his throat. Carefully balancing herself, she pushed ever so gently until he gasped for air. She put her arms on her hips and smiled at him, in victory.

Al ran outside to meet the security team, giving them a brief report before they entered. They were followed by the Admiral and someone in the back shouted, "Admiral on deck!" Everyone snapped to attention.

The gathering crowd parted allowing the security force to push through and the Admiral quickly returned the salutes. He approached Talonis' two men who were being held in arm and head locks, and motioned to his team, saying, "Search these two and take them into custody." He spotted Laurel across the room and smiled when he saw how she held down her captor. As he drew near he said, "Niece, if you are trying to attract a man, I'd say that you have succeeded. I think half of our cadets and officers are here." Everyone laughed and some of the officers nodded their heads in agreement.

The Admiral took a closer look at the man on the floor and asked, "So, who do we have here, my dearest niece?"

Talonis looked up, surprised at the news that Laurel was his niece.

"Are those three inch heels, Laurel?" the Admiral asked as he observed her heel on his throat.

"Three and a *half*, uncle," she answered.

"Oh, forgive me, three and a *half*. And just who is this fellow?"

"This is Talonis of Cerberus," she replied with disdain, "from the House of Talonis, Uncle. He just informed me that he is going to be my *new* business partner."

"Informed, did he?" The Admiral clasped his hands behind his back and began to pace around Laurel and her captive.

Some of the officers snickered and one whispered, "Here it comes." When the Admiral would clasp his hand behinds his back and proceed to sarcastically analyze something, highlighting stupidity or lack of understanding they knew a lecture was impending.

"Ladies and gentleman, this is an *excellent* learning experience for you all. First question; According to Alderon law, are citizens of other worlds allowed to have ownership or partnership status in any business entity in the Alderis system?"

A collective "NO!" resounded from the group.

"Apparently, Talonis, you need to brush up on your Alderon policies."

Laurel glowered angrily at Talonis as she pressed a little more, and he gasped for a breath.

"Oh, Talonis, I should inform you that Laurel's heel is long enough that if she pushes much harder it may *accidently* pierce your air passage, and with any luck, go right through your neck, severing your spinal cord. It would be a most painful death. Have no fear though, as long as you don't move, I'm confident in her ability to hold her position," the Admiral said confidently.

One of the security team men approached and held out his hand, presenting two weapons that they had seized from the two henchmen. The Admiral tossed them to the officers who had held the two men until their arrival. "Trophies for your actions today, gentleman." They smiled as they placed the weapons in their tunics.

The Admiral returned his attention to Talonis when Laurel informed him, "He says he has diplomatic papers."

"Does he now?" He motioned for one of his team to approach. He took out a data pad and skillfully glided his fingers across the keypad. "Well, it appears that there isn't any record of your arrival here today, Talonis, and you know that anyone entering with diplomatic papers, must register with the authorities on the station prior to coming down to the planet. In fact, I don't even see you registered on any arriving passenger vessels. I guess that means that we have a rogue ship in our space." He handed the pad back to the security man and ordered, "Alert the ADF Space Force that we may have an unidentified ship, either at our station or in our space. Tell them to seize it, or if necessary destroy it."

Talonis attempted to speak but Laurel continued the pressure on his neck.

"As far as your diplomatic papers Talonis, consider them revoked, effective immediately," the Admiral said abruptly.

Talonis managed to speak out in a gruff tone, "You don't have the authority to do that!"

"Correction, Talonis, I do have that authority, and more." He looked around the room and asked, "Did this man threaten the safety of one of our citizens?"

A loud "YES!" sounded in the room.

"And did he try to force his will on this Alderon citizen?"

"YES!" They answered again in unison.

"Perhaps we should demonstrate just how delicate his position is at the moment. I believe that I saw Cadet Barnet as I entered. Cadet, approach the front." The Admiral had a knack for remembering names and faces. Once he met someone, he never forgot his or her name. This was a skill that continued to impress both officers and cadets, alike.

The petite form of a young cadet pushed through the crowd and the Admiral motioned her to his side. The Admiral studied her carefully. "My cadet, I am impressed. Your uniform is pressed perfectly and there isn't a smudge on you. Who is your group leader?

"Cadet First Class Rodriguez, sir," she answered.

"Cadet First Class Rodriguez, I saw you here when I entered, please come forward."

A young man made his way to the Admiral and saluted sharply.

"Cadet Rodriguez, she is one of your charges, is that correct?"

"Yes, Admiral," he replied assertively.

"My compliments, Mr. Rodriguez, on your mentoring of this young Cadet. I'll see that it is noted in your record."

The cadet smiled happily and saluted the Admiral saying, "Thank you, sir!"

"Now Cadet Barnet...I want you to stand on this man's midsection," He directed.

The Cadet looked at him with confusion, but when the Admiral held out his hand for her support, she took her position as ordered.

"Cadet, I would guess you weigh about, ohhhhh I'd say a hundred pounds?" he guessed.

She replied quickly, "Only ninety, sir!"

Laughter was heard around the room.

"I'm sorry, Cadet, I'll remember that next time! Cadet Varris, I believe you are also present, please come forward."

Another petite Cadet pushed her way through the group and approached the Admiral. He gave her a quick visual inspection.

"Cadet Rodriguez, is she also one of your group?"

"Yes Admiral," he replied.

The Admiral looked at her again, carefully and gently brushing aside a stray hair that lay on her shoulder, and smiled at her approvingly.

"Another excellent job, Cadet Rodriguez. I'm proud to have young future officers like you in the service."

"Well, Cadet Varris, I wouldn't want to embarrass myself with *another* wrong guess so tell us your weight please."

The young Cadet blushed as she replied, "One hundred and five, Admiral."

"Oh my, it must be that lovely long hair you have, Cadet. Will you join Cadet Barnet, please?" He held out his hand and helped her to stand carefully on the midsection of Talonis, who now pushed with all his might to keep the two cadets balanced without forcing his head to lean upwards as he spread his arms apart to help his balance.

"A round of applause for our two young Cadets, everyone," the Admiral said as he clapped his hands and was followed in unison by everyone present. He then held out his hands to help the two young cadet's move from their positions and return to the group.

"I am glad to see that you do indeed know how to control yourself, Talonis. Remember this the next time we meet. I have all the reasons that I need to revoke your diplomatic status. Laurel, I guess you will have to make the decision on what you're going to do with your captive." The Admiral walked back toward the center of the room, where he stopped and waited.

Laurel looked coldly at Talonis, slowly removing her heel from his throat, and backed away allowing him to stand. He slowly stood and rubbed the imprint of her heel on his throat. The four distinct scratches left down his cheek from her nails stood out noticeably. He glared at Laurel, his anger still evident.

Laurel stepped close to him again and he stiffened in expectation of another assault as her guards closed in behind her. She poked her finger forcefully into his chest. "I think I have made myself perfectly clear, Talonis of Cerberus. The next time that we meet I won't hesitate to push your smug face into the dirt. Don't ever threaten me, my company or my friends ever again. You will surely pay with your life. Do not doubt me, Talonis of Cerberus!"

Laurel turned to leave when suddenly Talonis reached up and grabbed her around the neck, pulling a weapon from inside his tunic. The Admiral and her guards had started to move forward when Laurel dropped her head to her chest and snapped it back, smashing his nose, forcing him to let go. She turned on her heels to see his nose bleeding profusely and he brought his gun up towards her. She stepped within his reach and quickly twisted the gun from his hand in a reverse motion. Intertwining her fingers in his, she bent his hand backwards and the sound of breaking bones could be heard from across the room. A collective groan could be heard from the crowd while Talonis shouted out in agony, grasping the broken hand with his other. For her finale, Laurel slammed the heel of her boot into the top of his left foot, breaking several more bones. Talonis tottered painfully on his feet then passed out from the pain, falling back onto the floor.

It was no secret that Laurel had a temper, just like her brother, but it was rarely seen, especially by so many. Her uncle looked on and shook his head at her display of anger and retribution. He strode over and placed his arm around Laurel, calmly saying, "I suspect that you have made a permanent enemy here today, my dear."

"No one tells me what to do, Uncle, especially when it comes to our business. He was lucky that Mitch wasn't here, he would have surely killed him. I *nearly* killed him but I didn't want to cause trouble for you," she said.

"He arrived here illegally so we have discretion to handle him as we wish. He's broken enough laws that I can have him expelled. But I'm really curious to know what he's actually doing here."

"He mentioned our explorations again, just like he mentioned them to Mitch the last time they met. Mitch said that he made a similar offer to him, but he was rebuked."

"Most interesting indeed. Well, you handled yourself very well, my dear." He hugged his niece and turned to his team. "Take this idiot out of here and back to HQ. Find out how he came here and take those other two in for interrogation. Everyone, return to your duties, it's all over. My gratitude to the officers who assisted my niece. I'll see that a commendation is entered into each of your records."

Some of the cadets and officers left and some returned to their tables. Laurel and her two bodyguards sat at a single table as a server brought them fresh drinks.

Al approached asking, "Are you okay, Miss Laurel?"

"I'm fine, Al, and thanks for the heads up. I appreciated that," she replied as she smiled at him warmly.

Al smiled, nodded and returned to his work. One of her guards spoke up, "You shouldn't take chances like that, Miss Saber."

"I appreciate your concern, Lonnie but I knew that you two guys had my back. Besides, I needed to take out some aggression and this was a good opportunity. Now *you guys* know what will happen to you if you piss me off!" she said with a laugh. The two guards laughed with her and toasted her with their drinks. Noon was past, it was time to return to work and they hoped that the rest of the day would not be so eventful.

Back at the ADF HQ, Talonis was sedated and his wounds attended to while his guards were interrogated. The Admiral learned that they had come to Alderon, using false identities, aboard a space liner. He was surprised that the surveillance systems hadn't registered their likenesses and created an alert. This was highly unusual and he would investigate the lapse in security. While Talonis was sedated, a small tracking device was placed into his bloodstream so that his location would be known if he ever attempted to return to Alderon. Under the premise of needing blood tests to be certain that they carried no illnesses, the two guards were also treated to trackers. He would have them held in the space liner's brig under guard, until they reached Cerberus Empire space. After that he would place a call to Mitch and Samantha to inform them of what happened. He knew that Laurel would tell them, but he wanted to let them know that there may be more to this story, and to stay alert.

Mitch was making his usual pre-shift rounds through the ship when he happened by the weapons locker, and upon looking inside he saw Richter working busily.

Stepping inside he said, "Hello, Richter, what are you doing in here?"

Richter turned partially around and seeing the Captain he smiled and answered, "Just doing some cleanup work, Captain. We had a new replicator installed during our last service and inspection, but I noticed that it hadn't been tested and brought online. I wanted to get that finished prior to our next inspection. Everything looks good so far, but I'm not finished yet."

"Good call, Petty Officer. By the way, Richter, I need your help."

"Certainly, Captain."

"Samantha's ship is in need of a navigator and I'd like to find a good bi-mod to fill that position. Can you make any recommendations? We'll be enroute to Bion4 after our next pickup. The Chinese Federation's cargo was small and can't justify a direct trip there, so we're stopping by Alderon for a load of crystals. I'd like to get that navigator position filled before the Rivers Run and the Phoenix get too far apart."

"Actually, I think I have a candidate for you, Captain. A friend of mine by the name of Donavan is a good navigation specialist. But you should know that he was kicked off another ship several years ago, and the Trader's Union blacklisted him from service on ships of any class."

"Why was that?"

"Well, Donavon has empathic abilities, but not as deep as Athena's. When he went to service on the ship that removed him, he hadn't completed all of his mod training. He wanted desperately to fit in so, he began to behave as he saw others behaving around him. He got by until their skipper took on this young yeoman to work in their galley. She was very attractive and their skipper, who was much older than her, had a real eye for this girl. So one day, Donavon was in the galley sitting at the same table with this yeoman when the skipper came in. He sat down clear across the room and began giving her the eye. Well, Donavon thought that he could do the skipper a favor, so he told the yeoman what the skipper wanted to do to her. Needless to say, it was more than just wine and moonlight. In fact, Donovan was very graphic in his description. The yeoman understandably flew into a rage and quit at their next port, and filed a report on the skipper causing him to be demoted to a lessor rank. Donavon was fired and dropped off at that port and was blacklisted as a result."

"I'm not sure that I blame them."

"I agree. Donavon was clearly at fault, plus he hadn't completed his mod training either. Unlike Athena, he can only sense emotions at close range and he hadn't learned how to 'turn off the switch' as we say. He didn't understand that there are things, and times, when you have to ignore some perceptions and keep them to yourself. This happened several years ago, and like I said, he has since completed his training, having learned a very costly lesson. His knowledge, skills and personality have all matured since that incident, and I know that he would make a good crewman if someone would give him a chance. He's very talented and well trained when it comes to his navigation abilities."

"That's quite the sales pitch, Richter. He must be a good friend."

"We are friends, Captain. I believe that he wasn't ready when he went into service. Now I believe that he is ready."

"Very well, Richter, we'll see what the people at Bion4 have to say, and go from there. But it will be on your head if he becomes a problem. I'll have Inna send a message ahead to Ambassador Tesslena to meet us when we arrive."

"Why, Captain? You can do that yourself"

"That's why I have a comm officer, Richter," Mitch replied a little frostily.

"No, you misunderstand, Captain. You can mentally tell her that you're coming. Remember?"

"Ah, yes I forgot. I haven't tried that yet from a distance. I'm not sure if I can."

"Sure you can. It's just like speaking to Athena. You think about the Ambassador and see her in your mind, and she will be there. Why not give it a try?"

Mitch closed his eyes and recalled the image of Ambassador Tesslena in his mind, concentrating on her as he thought, "Ambassador Tesslena, I need your attention."

He tried it several times before he very clearly 'heard' her voice in his head.

"Hello, Captain Saber, how good it is to hear from you. What do you require?"

He thought the words, "I need to speak to you regarding a matter of importance. We will be at your station in nine days. Will you meet me there?"

"Certainly, Captain. I'll inform the station master to notify me when you arrive in our space, and I'll await you at dockside."

"Thank you, Ambassador. Thank you."

Mitch opened his eyes and smiled broadly. "That was easier than I thought."

"Remember, you can reach out to Madera on Aegea in the same way."

"I'm not ready for that just yet, but I won't forget the time arrives."

Mitch left the weapons locker and Richter to complete his work. Several days later the Phoenix arrived on time and docked at the Bion4 station.

"Inna, tell Richter to meet me at Cargo Hatch 3."

"Aye, Captain, Cargo Hatch 3."

As they opened the outer hatch, they saw Ambassador Tesslena waiting for them as promised. After greeting one another, the Ambassador said, "I have a small private office just off the main concourse; perhaps it will be best to discuss our business there."

Mitch agreed and the Ambassador led the way. She still wore the same style dress and it flowed elegantly as she walked down the corridors. Mitch was impressed with her poise and the gracefulness with which she moved. Her long stride didn't hide her lovely legs and, as much as Mitch tried not to look at them, his eyes were constantly drawn in their direction as they were fully exposed, from her feet to her waist. Mitch could only guess at her true age, but he was impressed that she held so much beauty so late in life. They traveled down several corridors before she stopped at a blue accented door, opened it and motioned them inside.

The room wasn't too small and contained a desk, a couch, three side chairs, and a buffet set with an assortment of drinks and fruit.

"So, Captain, what can I do for you and Mr. Richter?" she asked politely.

"Richter tells me that you have a navigator by the name of Donavan who could potentially be qualified to fill a position that I have on my wife's ship, the Rivers Run. She is in need of a trained navigation officer and I would like a bi-mod to fill that position. I think he could be an asset to her crew."

"I see," she replied as she glanced at each of them. I assume that Richter has informed you that he is currently blacklisted from space service?"

"He explained the circumstances of the dismissal, yes. However, I'm of the opinion that everyone deserves a second chance. It appears that he has completed training and he understands the nature of his error. If he is a qualified navigator and can pass our proficiency examination, then I'm willing to give him a second chance."

"Even though your own Trader's Union has black listed him?" she asked with surprise.

"Everyone makes mistakes, Ambassador. I would rather make my own judgment and give him a chance to get it right. If he makes a similar error, then I was wrong, and I'll bring him back here where he will live out his life in service to his people."

"Once again, Captain, you have proven to be a very unusual man." She turned and walked over to a communications console and spoke quietly to someone, then returned her attention to her guests. "I have informed his superiors that he will need to ready himself to depart with your ship. Richter, since this is someone who you know, will you help him gather his things and escort him to your ship?"

"And, Richter, remember that he will require his implant prior to boarding the ship," Added Mitch.

"Aye, Captain, I will do as you ask," Richter replied as he bowed politely to the Ambassador and left the room.

"Captain," the Ambassador said, "I detected that you wanted to discuss something in private, so now we are alone."

"Yes, Ambassador. I need to contact the people at Aegea and request permission to return to seek their aid."

"Aid for what, Captain?" she asked, her curiosity aroused.

"One of our ships has found something that I will need their expertise to examine."

"Perhaps we can help you here, Captain."

"Thank you, but no. I've seen an example of a similar technology on Aegea and I think they would be my best resource. There is more to this discovery than I am at liberty to discuss."

"Do you not trust us, Captain?"

He detected some annoyance in her tone. "This isn't a trust issue Ambassador, it's more of a security issue at this point. If I thought that you could provide the answers I seek, then I would ask. The fewer people who know of what we found the better, for now. It nearly cost one man his life already and I want no one else involved."

"I see. Perhaps I do understand, Captain. I can feel the concern that you harbor for your crew. Come, hold my hands and we will make the contact now."

Mitch stepped closer and placed his hands in hers. They were soft and warm and she held his gently.

"Close your eyes, Captain and think of Madera."

He did as she asked and a moment later Mitch felt a tingle at his neck as he clearly heard Madera's voice in his head. "Hello, Captain and hello, mother. I am so happy to hear from you! Why have you waited so long?"

"Madera," Mitch thought, "I need permission to come to Aegea again for something of great importance."

"I will give your request to the Chief Prefect myself, Captain. You will hear from us soon."

"Thank you, Madera. It will be good to see you again."

"You are so kind, Captain. Mother? Will you be coming this time?"

"No, dearest Madera. My work here must continue." Tesslena replied.

"Very well. I miss you, mother. Talk to me again soon." Madera's voice faded away.

The Ambassador released Mitch's hands and smiled. "Next time, Captain, you should try it on your own. You are quite capable of reaching my daughter by yourself."

"I know, Ambassador, I just felt like this was the appropriate way to do it this time."

"I appreciate your respectfulness, Captain, but you don't have to worry about it. All is well. Now, how about sharing a drink with me before your departure? It will take some time for Richter to get his friend prepared for the trip."

"Certainly, Ambassador."

She walked over to the buffet where several beverages were already in glasses. One had a yellow liquid in it, another was clear, another was a brownish color, another red and yet another was as green as grass with had a thick disgusting looking foam on the top. There were small dark things floating in it and Mitch thought of a chemistry experiment. Hoping that wasn't what she expected him to drink. He watched her pick up the green goo and the glass of red liquid and return to him.

She handed him the greenish concoction and he could not help but turn his face away from the glass, expecting a foul smell to envelope his senses.

"Come now, Captain. It isn't what you are expecting." She smiled at the funny look on his face.

"No offense, Ambassador, but is that stuff even safe to drink?"

She pushed it towards his hand, "I give you my word, Captain that once you taste it you will be delightfully surprised."

"I'll be surprised if I can keep it down if you want my opinion. It looks like something you'd find...well, I won't say it aloud."

"Just take a sip, Captain, and if you don't like it I won't be offended."

Mitch held the glass and slowly brought it close to his nose and sniffed. It didn't have an odor, which surprised him, but looking at the contents he felt his stomach churn in objection. "Why do I do these things..." he asked himself as he closed his eyes and took a sip of the frothy liquid. The corners of his mouth turned down for an instant, waiting for a nasty taste to strike, when suddenly his mouth was filled with the taste of fresh fruit and berries. His mouth swelled with saliva and he swallowed as an aroma filled his senses.

He smiled brightly and said, "That's incredible! It tastes just like a fruit drink that my mother used to make when I was a kid. Wow, what memories it brings back to me." He took a large gulp.

"Careful, Captain. The drink is very potent, especially the first time you try it. I caution you not to drink it too quickly or the reaction will not be pleasant."

Disregarding her suggestion, he took three more large gulps and the beverage was finished. He smiled in delight as he sat the glass down. A sudden feeling of warmness and lightheadedness came over him. His sight became blurred and he staggered a little.

The Ambassador took him by the arm and gently scolded, "I warned you not to drink it too quickly, Captain. Let me help you to your seat."

He sat down heavily and looked up at the Ambassador. "I hope you won't mind me saying that you are a very attractive woman, Ambassador." The beverage was doing its work on his speech too. He slurred his words and shut his eyes.

The Ambassador kneeled beside him and placed her hand on his face. "Captain Saber, are you okay?"

Mitch opened his eyes and after a brief moment the fog cleared and he focused on her voice. The Ambassador was kneeling beside him calling his name. She appeared to be slightly flustered and Mitch figured that he had passed out.

"Yes, yes, Ambassador. I hear you. Wow, that stuff really has a kick."

"Here, Captain, drink this. It will rehydrate you and help you recover from the effects. I tried to warn you not to drink so fast but you didn't listen," she repeated.

"I'll listen next time, Ambassador, I promise." Mitch accepted the glass and was pleased to find that it was only water. "I must apologize, Ambassador. I've never had anything like that happen to me. It would be best that I return to my ship now. Please accept my apologies, Ambassador."

"No need to apologize, Captain. There is a first time for everything. Next time you will be more careful I'm sure." She spoke in a gentle understanding tone.

Mitch experienced the same feeling of peace and calm that he had felt when he first encountered the Ambassador, and he wasted little time making his way back to the Phoenix. Richter was waiting for him at the hatch.

"What took you so long, Captain?" Richter asked with concern.

"Long? Was I gone that long?" Mitch asked with concern.

"We've been here waiting for nearly an hour, Captain. I expected that you would already be back before we arrived. Is everything okay?"

"Fine, Richter. Let's get her buttoned up and see where Samantha's ship is, so that we can transfer her new navigator aboard."

The Ambassador returned to her office where a man awaited her presence inside.

"Were you able to retrieve the sample?" he asked.

"No, the mix wasn't strong enough and he awakened early," Tesslena replied.

"That's not good enough, Tesslena. Our males are being born sterile every day now. We must have an adequate supply of sperm to impregnate our women. We have thousands ready to conceive and we need that supply desperately. The Captain is an excellent example of the superior genetic material that we need to repopulate our planet," he replied.

"He woke too soon, the drug wasn't strong enough! I told you this was dangerous."

"We must get him in here again."

"Why don't we just ask him for a sample? I've read his thoughts, I know the kind of man he is, I know he would help if we just ask him," she pleaded.

"And if he refuses? Then what? The next time he comes, make up a reason to get him in here again. We'll double the dose next time."

"But Counselor, that could be dangerous. If he gets too relaxed he can't produce and then we've gained nothing. Let me tell him the problem that we face."

"NO! You get him back in here again and do whatever is necessary to get that sample!"

"We have to trust someone at some point. We can't continue on this way!" She said angrily.

"Out of the question, Tesslena. Our needs are too great. Follow your orders!" The counselor walked out of her office and closed the door behind him.

"You're wrong, Counselor," Tesslena muttered. "Captain Saber is not the kind of man that you think he is. He would help us, or find a way to help us. He should be told, I owe him at least that much for protecting my daughter."

CHAPTER THIRTEEN

"COLONEL PALMERS, I DON'T BELIEVE WE'VE MET," GENERAL Peyton Harris replied as he viewed his screen.

"We have not met before, General. I've heard your name mentioned in military circles and I've been told that you're someone we can trust," Palmers replied.

"You shouldn't always believe everything you hear, Colonel," the General replied with a smile and a nod.

The Colonel returned the gesture and said, "General Harris, most of our planetary defenses have been wiped out by a large group of raiders... slavers actually. They've taken hundreds of our people captive and they said it would only be a matter of time before they return to continue their so-called *harvest* of our citizens. We don't have the manufacturing capabilities to build enough defenses before they return, nor can we afford to hire protection. I need a solution General and I'm hoping...no, I'm praying that you can offer some direction."

"I'm not familiar with your system, Colonel, but I can see from your signal that you must be on the other side of our galaxy."

"That's correct, General. I implored some of our neighboring systems to allow me to bounce our signal off their satellites in order to reach you. I expect the raiders will return in three of our lunar cycles, more or less. That's about one hundred days in standard time units."

"Well, Colonel, I guess the matter will revolve around what you can afford. Let's hammer out a hard number and then we can figure something out for you."

The discussion went on for some time and finally the General said that he would make some contacts on their behalf and see if there was a solution. Colonel Palmers was grateful for the General's help but understood that he still had several hurdles to overcome.

Several days later the General contacted Colonel Palmers with the information that he had compiled.

"I hope you have something good to offer me, General," the Colonel said, his voice reflecting his worry and fears.

"Colonel, I don't know if this will help you or not, but it's about the only option that I can offer you. Answer one question for me. You said that most of your fighters were destroyed during your last altercation with the raiders. Do you have the resources to train and field more pilots?"

"Between our regular and reserve forces we still have a fair amount of trained pilots."

"How many would you estimate, Colonel?"

"I can probably field at least a hundred that are flight certified now, and perhaps another fifty or so within a few weeks. They will be simulator trained only, these additional fifty pilots, but that's the best we can do. We've converted our few remaining training ships into strike ready craft. At the most, we have ten flight ready ships. They destroyed our manufacturing facility and it will take us at least a year to rebuild it if they don't return and destroy it again. I don't mind admitting, General, I'm plenty fearful for our planet and our people."

"I'm sure you are, Colonel, and I'll help if I can, but the cost of getting my resources there to help you is far beyond your budget. I'm sorry. However, if you have the pilots then perhaps I may have a solution. I just don't know if it will be in time to do you any good. There is another system close by that has developed a new fighter craft called an Advanced Tactical StarFire, or ATS as they're calling it. It's the latest generation of formidable fighter in space and in atmosphere. It carries better speed and rate of fire and doesn't sacrifice armor. In fact, it includes electronic shielding in addition to hull plating. I've negotiated a deal on your behalf that will deliver one hundred and ten of these fighters to you. However, we don't have a ship large enough to deliver them to you and flying them there is impossible.

Even if I had a freighter large enough for delivery, I don't know what that expense would be, so we still have a dilemma to solve."

The Colonel sighed and replied, "I don't know what else we have to offer for payment, General. We are just a small system and a small planet. We mine some of the other planets in our system, but we're not really in the mining business."

"Would you be open to issuing mining rights to someone else maybe, in exchange for payment?"

"I don't know. We've never considered that before, but I don't see why there would be an objection, as long as our laws and citizens are respected. I would need confirmation of course. Do you have something specific in mind?"

"Perhaps, Colonel, it's a long shot. Actually it's a very, very long shot, but I will ask just the same. I'll contact you when I have more information."

The call disconnected and the General shouted to his aid, "Get Laurel Saber on the line for me!"

Mitch rubbed the bridge of his nose with his thumb and middle finger trying to relieve the strain of several days of intensive bouts in the ring with Athena. The calls that he had received, first from Laurel and then his Uncle Rich, detailing the altercation that she had with Talonis made him so angry that he had spent those days in the ring trying to work off his anger. He had nearly injured one of his crew with his aggression in the ring, so Athena took him to task as a sparring partner. She was much stronger and could defend herself with more agility against his kicks and punches. Several times, she swept his feet out from under him to bring him back to reality. He later apologized for his aggression, but she laughed and said that she enjoyed the exercise.

Now they waited in the small room for Ambassador Codas to enter. Mitch and Athena were the only ones present on Aegea because he didn't want anyone else to know the nature of his visit. The organic hull sample that he carried was only a small piece of the samples he had available, but he wanted to gauge their interest and reactions before bringing on the rest.

The door opened and a hooded figured entered and closed the door behind it. Stepping closer the hood was tossed back and a smiling Madera appeared. She reached up and hugged his neck and even hugged Athena, much to her surprise.

"I know this isn't protocol, Captain but I'm so happy to see you and Athena again, I just couldn't help myself. I hope you aren't offended." Madera said joyfully.

Mitch smiled broadly, his mouth turned up to one side as he replied, "Not at all, Madera. It's very good to see you too. I hope they have been treating you well since your arrival."

"Oh they've been very kind and there is so much to learn. I've been quite busy. Mother told me that you were coming. I got the oddest feeling from her when we spoke. I'm not sure what it meant. Was she okay when you saw her last?" Her eyes showed concern as she asked.

"She appeared to be fine as best I could tell, Madera. I think I was somewhat the worse for wear, not her."

Madera looked at him questioningly, her head angled to one side with a raised brow.

"Nothing worth mentioning, really. I can check with her when we return to our home space again if you're concerned."

She shook her head and glanced to Athena. "Well Athena, I can see that you've adapted to your new life very well. I can sense the pride and happiness in your heart. This makes me very happy for you."

Athena said nothing, but smiled warmly.

"Oh, Athena, you can speak around me. Just be careful around anyone else. It doesn't matter that your speech abilities were restored, they won't understand." Madera placed a hand on Athena.

"I am very happy to serve my Captain, Ambassador Madera," Athena said in a low tone. "He has taught me very much since I went into his service."

Madera's smile became even broader and she hugged Athena once more. She stepped back and started to speak when the door began to open. She stiffened and became more formal saying, "It's so good to see you both again. Please don't forget to say goodbye before you depart for home."

Ambassador Codas entered the room and greeted them while Madera politely bowed and left, leaving them alone with the Ambassador. They all bowed in the traditional greeting and the Ambassador apologized for not meeting them upon their arrival.

"I'm sorry again, Captain. I got involved in something that took far longer to resolve than I had expected. I hope all is well with you," she said sincerely.

Mitch replied, "No problems for us, Ambassador. I'm sorry if we have intruded on your time."

"Not at all. Your message was somewhat cryptic. How can we help you?"

"One of my ships has made a discovery that is of great concern to me. I needed to discuss this with someone who I know that I can trust."

"You don't trust your own people, Captain?" She seemed surprised at the statement.

"Please don't misunderstand, Ambassador. It isn't so much that I don't trust my own people, it's more about their lack of understanding of the potential ramifications of this discovery."

"I see, so it's the same old distrust among all peoples that has you concerned?"

"Like I said, it is very difficult to explain, but once I do... I think you will appreciate my concerns."

"As you wish, Captain Saber. What is it that you have brought with you?" she asked pointing to the large object wrapped up in dark cloth.

"This is something that we found. It's a part of a crashed shuttle and I was hoping that you could help us identify it and tell us how, or if, we can reproduce it." He motioned to Athena, and she unwrapped the hull fragment. Instantly upon receiving a light source the organic material began to arc and react as he expected. The Ambassador observed the fragment without any signs of recognition. A few seconds passed and she walked over and touched the material.

"It's organic, how very interesting," she observed. "Where did you find this?"

"In an unexplored system some two thousand light years from here."

"Our technicians would be very interested in analyzing it. What would you like us to do?"

"Honestly, Ambassador, I'm not certain yet. I'm in the process of growing my fleet of interstellar freighters in hopes of servicing the outer rims of our galaxy. We're slowly making roadmaps, you might say, of the gateways so that we can traverse these distances, bringing all our people closer together and hopefully bring an end to the slavers too."

"That's a rather complicated wish isn't it, Captain?"

"Perhaps, but I intend to try. I know there are many colonized planets that need help, but don't have a way to get it. I hope that we, and some of our friends, can change that for the good. I am hopeful that this material can be reproduced, manufactured if you will, so that I can incorporate it in my new freighters."

"I'm not a technician. Let's take it to one of our labs and let them do a quick analysis and we shall see what they have to say."

The people they took the sample to were very excited and got straight to work. Feeling as if they were in the way, Mitch asked that they be taken to an observation area and they watched from there. Minutes turned into hours and eventually Mitch nodded off into a fitful sleep, while Athena stood guard over her Captain. Mitch had been asleep for seven hours when he was awakened by the sound of applause. He rose quickly to see more than a dozen people in the room applauding and bowing to each other. For a society that didn't seem to show much emotion, it was a sight to behold. The tech to whom they had first given the sample motioned for them to come and they did as requested.

They entered the research area. The Ambassador wasn't there, but the tech rushed over to them and said in an excited voice, "I am Tomulous and I have some very interesting news for you. The material that you brought is very exciting. It is a melding of nanobots with organic matter. Each has been designed to actually feed off one another's waste byproducts. When the organic side absorbs light, the nanobots distribute the energy and store the excess. In return, they provide the means for the organic materials to reproduce and heal themselves. Their programming is actually quite simplistic. They have a symbiotic relationship; each component acts as the host parasite to the other, each servicing the needs of the other. The outer skin can actually be grown in the laboratory and then it's fused onto the substrate that contains all the connections necessary to provide the interaction with the other energy sources and computers. The simplest way I can describe the substrate material is to think of a huge computer circuit board that is bonded to the organic material and you simply provide the connector and a pathway to the controls. The organic material grows exponentially when exposed to UVA particles. We took a sample smaller than a human hair and by exposing it to UVA particles it grew to a thousand times the original size in less than an hour. We found encoding in the program that tells it how big to grow so that it can be adjusted as needed. The bonding polymers are easily duplicated with common materials."

"So you're saying that it can be grown, like in a green house?" Mitch asked, greatly surprised.

"In a sense, yes. It can be done on an industrial scale quiet easily. What was also surprising is that the substrate material is actually white crystals that have been ground into powder and, after adding a bonding agent, have been pressed and rolled out into sheets, by our guess. We need to run some more experiments but we are certain that we can duplicate the process."

"One more question, if you don't mind."

"Certainly, Captain."

"I saw a vid of a ship covered in this material. The ship was fired upon with energy weapons by several other ships and this material looked like it absorbed it, sustaining no damage. And then it took that same energy and redirected it back to the attacking vessels and destroyed them. Does that sound possible?"

"Oh yes, that would be very simple for this material. It is designed to absorb as much energy as possible and the parasite is going to store that energy for the host, to keep it regenerating and repairing itself. As far as redirecting the stored energy, that capability is stored in the nanobots' programming as a self-defense mechanism. Of course the computer's AI system will have full control, but it's no different than turning a switch on, or off. I imagine that a ship covered in this material could be attacked from all directions and the return energy could be reflected back in the same manner, thus striking as many attackers as necessary to preserve itself. It almost gives the host vessel a mind of its own. We've experimented with such things but we never found an organic matter that was suitable. I don't know where this original organic material came from, but as long as you have even a tiny piece of it, it can be grown into whatever size that you need. The bots are self-replicating so the challenge now is reverse engineering the substrate. For that we'll need a sizeable amount of white crystals. As far as breeching the material itself, if that happened, all you would have to do is provide pieces of the substrate materials and the organic part would essentially regrow itself back into place. Actually this would happen without the substrate, but you would lose the connectivity for ships systems and defenses."

"I have ten metric tons of white crystals aboard my ship right now. How much do you need?"

The tech's eyes nearly popped out of his head. "If you can provide one ton that will give us enough to run our experiments. But it may take several days or several weeks to perfect the method."

Athena alerted Mitch that the Ambassador was entering the room, so Mitch turned to greet her.

"Ambassador, your lead tech, Tomulous, tells me that he can grow the organic material, or give me instructions on how to do it. He also has indicated that if I can provide him with enough white crystals, then his group can begin to recreate the substrate material. Of course, I'm willing to contract with you to provide these services."

"Come with me first, Captain." She turned and Mitch was curious why she didn't address his questions first.

Re-entering the monitoring room she said, "Captain, while this material is of great potential it doesn't tell me what you are fearful of. I detect that there is something you haven't told me yet. Provide me the complete story about why you are here and then we will discuss matters further."

Mitch took a deep breath and motioned for the Ambassador to sit with him, and then he relayed the details to her of their discovery of the Praxanon and her time travel capability.

"Obviously, Ambassador, I don't feel that we are capable of having this kind of technology at this time in our history. While we have come a long way since the days of old Earth with never-ending wars, class warfare and social engineering experiments, I don't think that time travel will be received as a strictly scientific discovery. It may be by some, but there are those in the other worlds who still desire power and control. We can hide the ship for a period of time, but once we release the knowledge of how to travel through the gateways, it won't take long before it is discovered."

"A most fascinating discovery it is, Captain. I understand now why you are so concerned. What are your plans?"

"I don't have one yet, Ambassador Codas. I've considered destroying the ship to keep it out of the control of others. We've downloaded all of the computer files that it stored and it could take years to read through them all, so their knowledge won't be wasted, but there is still a real danger if it should fall into the wrong hands."

"I get the impression, Captain that you want to ask me something, but you're uncertain if it's the right decision."

Mitch bowed his head and thought for a long moment. Finally he answered, "Ambassador, you and your people have welcomed me and my crew and provided me with abilities that I didn't think I would ever want, or need. You've given me Athena, who has become a great source of friendship and protection. Some days I think that I am the student and she is the teacher. She has told me much of your society and its edicts. I suppose that in some ways I trust your people more than I do those on my home world."

"Don't be so generous, Captain. We've had our share of problems over the past few centuries too. We are not a perfect society by any means, but we all agree that living by our principles allows us to discuss our disagreements and settle them in a civil manner. No society will ever be perfect, Captain Saber. We are just fortunate to share a common set of core values and beliefs."

"I get it, Ambassador, I really do...I was considering asking if your people, or government, would consider letting me bring the Praxanon here, for safe keeping, until I can decide what to do with her."

The Ambassador didn't say anything for several long and uncomfortable minutes as if she were absorbing everything that had been said. Finally she replied, "That is a great responsibility you would be giving us, Captain. Are you certain that this is your only option other than destruction?"

"Yes, Ambassador. At this time I feel like I have only two alternatives."

"Very well. I will need to present this to the Prefect and I've no doubt that he will also want to speak to you. I notice that you didn't bring any of your other crew with you."

"No, Ambassador. None of my crew knows about the Praxanon. My wife Samantha...it was she..."

"It was her ship that made the discovery wasn't it?"

Mitch nodded.

"And it nearly cost one of her crew his life?"

Mitch was thinking that very thought when she repeated it aloud. "Yes," he replied.

"We'll arrange quarters for you and Athena since you'll be staying the night. Inform your ship that you will remain here until we can discuss this in greater detail with our Prefect. You and Athena will share the same quarters."

"But, Ambassador..."

"I'm aware of your concerns, Captain, but this is necessary. She will be there only as your guardian, as her position requires."

They were moved to their quarters, which were exceptionally comfortable, and provided with food and drink for the night. The next day there were long discussions with the Prefect, Ambassador Codas and Ambassador Madera along with several of the Aegean techs and engineers. They brought in additional scientists and other people who Athena explained were part of the Praetorian Guard. They discussed alternatives that Mitch had not considered. Finally they agreed that it was best to bring the ship into Aegean space for safe keeping. They would construct a special docking station to house the vessel so that they could study it in greater detail. They hoped to better understand the people who built it and what they had endeavored to accomplish with such a vessel. In return for this research, they would provide all information that they learned along with the organic materials and substrate, as long as Mitch provided the white crystals for the manufacturing processes. The techs and engineers indicated that the organic material, when produced, would be so flexible that it could be wound into enormous rolls for transportation. When a ship was skinned with the new materials, the sides would automatically grow together when butted against each other, so no welding or riveting was necessary. They would begin construction of the new docking station immediately and Mitch was to transport the Praxanon there as soon as he could. They also offered to provide additional personnel to aid in transporting the huge three mile long ship, but Mitch said that he didn't think it would be necessary, much to the disappointment of the techs.

Pleased with the outcome of their discussions, and with a plan in mind, Mitch and the crew of the Phoenix returned to their home space.

Samantha finished delivering Iverson to the prison officials at Outlanders Run and was preparing to depart for the Atlantis sector, when Lt. Roth Saperstein alerted her to a ship arriving in their sector.

"I've got Captain Chen of the Odyssey entering our sector, Captain. He just appeared in the area where the gateway to Helios is located."

"Thanks, Roth. Aaryn, contact Captain Chen and bring him up on my screen," Sam ordered.

Her holographic screen materialized at her station and shortly thereafter Captain Chen appeared.

"Captain Saber! I am so pleased to see you! We are on our way to Alderon for more supplies and personnel. The Dolphin transport should be coming in right behind us. We're escorting her back home." Chen said, smiling with every word.

"Captain Chen, it is good to see you again too. How are things going on Helios?" Sam asked.

"Very well, Captain Saber. The people there have paved roads now and we've built them new housing after getting the polycrete construction equipment up and running. It is such a beautiful planet that many of our crew and miners are thinking about relocating their families there."

"That sounds really nice, Captain. Have you provided enough security while you are away?"

"Yes, Captain. The Saber Corporation's Cruiser *Pegasus* arrived a couple of weeks ago with her crew of Mercon Military personnel. I understand that they will provide security in the sector until we can hire enough of our own people to fully crew the ship. We should be able to return there in a couple of weeks. The mining crew is nearly self-sufficient now. We built a number of greenhouses and food replicators and provided several dozen head of cattle. Some of my crew complains that our cargo bays still smell of...well, you know what I mean."

Laughing at the thought of the odors, Samantha said, "There are worse things they could smell like, Captain."

"I hope I don't find out what they are, Captain Saber. I found that I now have a greater appreciation of the independent air supply of our bridge."

"I've got the Dolphin entering the sector, Captain," Roth advised. Sam nodded.

"Your Dolphin just arrived, Captain. Do you require any assistance getting from here to Alderon?"

"No, Captain. I have twelve fighters aboard in case we need additional protection, plus they increased her shielding before we left to make her safer for travel through the gateways, so she is well protected."

"Very well Captain, Chen, we will continue on to Atlantis. Rivers Run out."

"Captain?" Ensign Wang queried,

"Yes Aaryn?" Sam replied.

"When will the other Captain Saber let us know what to do about the Praxanon?"

"He'll let us know, Aaryn, that isn't a concern at the moment. We have to pick-up and deliver some freight and make some credits or we won't be welcome back home anytime soon. Let's get this ship moving, people. We've got a schedule to keep and we're already a day behind!" Samantha barked, and everyone quickly went about their business, much to her amusement.

Planet Antares

"Well, Captain Dragos, you've made a good haul this time I see. Where did these come from?" the man asked as he watched the new arrivals move down the corridor.

"The Cronus system. It is small but they have good skilled labor. No children this time, only good workers and some engineers," Dragos answered.

"Keep the family members together, they will work harder that way. Madeus needs a better class of worker, so these will do nicely. Once the count is completed your credits will be brought to you."

"Thank you, my Lord Farkus. I will bring you more people and continue to look for other tech and weapons. Freighters are few on this side of the galaxy, my Lord, but we will bring you anything we find."

"Where are you heading now?"

"We're still raiding in the UKP outer rim, my Lord. They have many defense ships, so we must be careful. They are beginning to spread into the nearby systems, so we watch and take what we can. Right now I need new fighters. Those fools on Aurora destroyed a number of my fighters in the raid."

"We should be able to deliver more ships to you as soon as this new group gets to work. Where is your other cruiser?"

"They are raiding another system even as we speak. We expect to bring another three or four hundred back this time."

"Excellent. I'm told there is a new colony being built in the Madeus sector that will need many new prostitutes. Be sure to bring all the young women you can find on your next trip."

"Yes, Lord Farkus." Dragos bowed and left the room.

A side door opened and a huge hulk of a man entered.

"Why won't you go where I told you to go?" he demanded.

"Shut up, Asher, or I'll have your head mounted on my bathroom wall so I can laugh at you every time I piss."

"You can have the best people and ships if you go where I told you to go!" Asher said smugly.

"You don't get it do you? I leave them alone and they leave us alone! The last thing I need is to get the other systems in an uproar and start a major conflict. As long as they keep to themselves, we've got a good thing going here. Our former leader tried that and we lost most of our ships, so we killed him and *I* took control. Or have you forgotten about the rather large mercenary fleet that is over there? They've got two carriers and dozens of frigates and cruisers that we are *no* match for! Do you think for a moment that I want to bring those people here? It will take a *lot* of people *and* facilities to build the kind of fleet that we'll need before we dip our toes inside their space."

"What about me?" Asher spat.

"What about you? You *fool*! I set you up and you had it easy, but your arrogant fat ass got lazy and you lost the entire operation! Now Talonis has gone rogue, so I've lost my source of Intel. You had the perfect position to assist our expansion, but your *stupidity* ended that! You're damn fortunate I didn't remove your fat head from your even fatter body when you showed back up here, Asher! Now get out!"

CHAPTER FOURTEEN

SAMANTHA AND MITCH SAT AT THEIR FAVORITE CAFÉ, CALLED Neptune's Rest. It was situated along the waterfront on the planet of Atlantis. The ocean air was fresh and invigorating and was a welcomed change from the recycled air aboard their ships. Of course when they docked at the various stations, they refreshed their ships air supplies but it was not the same as being on the surface. They loved the small café because it reminded them of Al's back on Alderon and the food was actually a little better, but they would never tell Al that. The café had a short polycrete pier with a dozen or so tables and a bar that extended into the water and afforded a view of the local marina. It reminded Mitch of home and whenever he came down to the planet he always stopped here. Now he and his wife enjoyed the view, the food, and some time alone. Athena stood at the end of the pier watching the people and the water while giving her Captain all the privacy he wanted. Samantha tried to get Athena to sit and join them, but Athena was insistent that the two have some time alone.

"Athena really is a remarkable woman, Mitch," Sam said as she watched her at the end of the pier. "I'm not really sure how to refer to her. Is she friend, or employee, or family? I guess it doesn't really matter and maybe we're wrong to try and attach labels to people, but I guess it's just our nature to do that."

Mitch reached across the table and held Sam's hands. "I think she is all of the above, Sam. When I need a friend she's there, when I need someone to depend on she's there. We are very close as friends and she understands our needs as co-workers but also we communicate on a level that is mostly reserved for family. They told me when she was assigned to my service, that she would eventually become more than just a guardian, that she would be much, much more. I didn't understand that then, and I think I'm only beginning to understand it now. It makes me curious why everyone, humanity if you will, can't be the same way with one another."

"No one has ever been able to answer that question, Mitch, and probably doesn't want to. Anyway, the cargo bots are transferring our load over to your ship. Why did you have me go back to Alderon and bring you all the white crystals you can carry? You could have gone there yourself."

"I could have, but this saves me two weeks travel time, and I get to spend a day with you so I thought it was worth the detour." He smiled and winked.

"Oh I'm not complaining, Captain Saber, I'll do *your* bidding anytime." She winked back. "But seriously, what's up with this?"

"My visit to Aegea went better than expected. They've agreed to harbor the Praxanon in exchange for letting them research the vessel and her creators."

"That's great news then! I was really concerned that we would have to destroy her and that would have been a great loss."

"That's not all. They are going to manufacture the hull materials for us. The organic component can be easily grown in something similar to a greenhouse, but the substrate material requires crushed white crystals in large amounts to be combined with a bonding agent so that it can then be pressed and formed into flexible sheets. To keep it simple, they will give us the finished product and we can take it back to our shipyard and have it applied to our ships, new or old. Obviously new is easy, but replacing the old will require the removal of the ship's existing skin. Anyway, once it's in place it will actually grow together, making itself into a single surface without the need for welding or rivets. It will require some changes in electrical components so the ships systems will integrate, because the stuff actually has a program that operates its functions. Integration is necessary for the weapons systems and power storage and regeneration. The skin can store an amazing amount of power, but we may need to install something to bleed off the excess, or better yet, to store it for use in our drive systems. They are going to work on that for us."

"I like the sound of that because we won't have to contract with someone to manufacture it and risk losing the tech to someone else. Maybe we should claim rights to the product under Alderon law and reserve the technical aspects as intellectual property rights," she said thinking aloud.

"That didn't occur to me, but you're probably right, and that's an excellent point. I'll check with Uncle Rich to see what I need to do then get it registered. However, once we have a ship equipped with the new skin it will draw people's curiosity. You can't exactly hide the way it will look. The green and black surface and the way it shimmers and arcs will draw people's attention."

Sam grunted, "That's the truth. The electrical static dancing around the superstructure looks like fireworks." She looked back towards Athena, who had moved over a bit and appeared to be very interested in something. "Anyway, when are we going to move the ship to Aegea, and how do you plan on doing it?"

Mitch didn't reply. He had a blank look on his face as if he was somewhere else.

"Mitch?" Sam asked softly as she gently squeezed his hand.

He didn't blink. He remained motionless for a few more seconds and finally answered, "Someone is watching us. Apparently we've been followed since we arrived at the station."

"How do you know?"

"Athena told me, she's watching them now."

"Them...so that means there is more than one person. Wait, you said she told you? How?"

"Never mind that. Apparently they don't seem to think that Athena is in our party, so we will make that work in our favor. I'm looking at a map on my implant of this area. There is a causeway a couple of blocks away and it looks to be very private. Let's be romantic for a moment and then make our way there, and Athena will follow, cloaked. Let's find out who they are and what they want."

Sam smiled. "I like the romantic part..." she leaned over and kissed him long and deep.

They got up from their table and walked hand-in-hand down the street toward the causeway. Athena told Mitch that they were still being followed, as expected. With his arm around Sam, Mitch turned down the causeway. Once they were briefly out of visual range, they darted down the road and hid behind some convenient shrubs. The two men rounded the corner and were momentarily startled at their quarries disappearance. They ran past the shrubs where Sam and Mitch were hiding, then came to a sudden stop and argued about which way to go. Sam and Mitch stepped out of their concealed position.

"You fellas looking for someone?" Mitch asked in a friendly tone.

The two men, taken by surprise, turned around and were still for a moment. One of them began to reach inside his tunic. Mitch said, "I wouldn't do that if I were you, friend."

Ignoring Mitch's warning he continued reaching. When he nearly had his weapon out of his tunic his arm was wrenched upwards and his weapon was snatched from his hand. The other man tried to reach for his weapon as well, and a sudden impact to his mid-section caused him to jackknife downward and fall onto the pavement. The first man's arm was then wrenched behind his back and upwards causing him to shout in pain.

Mitch and Sam checked the man on the ground. He was out cold. Looking harshly at the other man, Mitch asked, "Who are you and why are you following us?"

"I don't know what you're talking about," He replied in a pain inflected tone of voice.

Sam drew back her arm and punched the man square in the face, breaking his nose. The sound of the cartilage breaking was audible and blood began to pour from it profusely. The man's head snapped backwards and forward again and he cussed them as he wiped his mouth clear of the salty froth with his free hand. Mitch was surprised, but proud of the outcome.

"Answer him, who are you!" Sam demanded, "Or the next sound you hear will be me breaking your fingers one at a time."

"Go screw yourself!" he said as he spit blood onto her uniform. Sam grabbed his free hand, bending the fingers backwards, and the sound of breaking bones made Mitch grimace.

The man screamed in agony. Mitch said in a humorous tone, "Better be careful, friend, it's that time of the month and she's a little testy today. You would be wise to answer her. Tell us who you are and why you're following us before she gets ahold of your other hand."

"Name's Marsh," he grunted. "Talonis hired us to follow you and if possible to bring the woman back to him."

Sam and Mitch looked at each other with raised eyebrows.

"He's already gotten his ass kicked by one woman, does he really think he will fare any better with this one?" Mitch remarked. Sam looked at him curiously, not aware of the altercation that had taken place between Laurel and Talonis.

"I don't know, I was hired to do a job and that's all I can tell you. Talonis didn't tell me anything other than to bring one of you to him, preferably the female captain if possible."

Mitch, using his implant, directed ALICE to alert the authorities to their position. "You know, the authorities here on Atlantis have severe punishments for acts like this." Mitch knocked the man out cold with an uppercut to his jaw and Athena released him, allowing him to fall to the pavement.

"Athena," he said, "I need you to keep us in visual range, but out of sight of the authorities who are on their way. Get going before anyone sees you."

Sam looked at the two men lying on the ground with a satisfied look on her face. "That *time* of the month, huh? Admit it, Saber, you just keep me around to take up your light work don't you?"

Mitch pulled her close, kissed her passionately, and said, "Wait 'til we get back to your ship and I'll show *you* some heavy lifting, *Captain*."

Later in the day after answering a multitude of questions for Colonel Turbone of Atlantis Defense, they returned to Samantha's ship. Ahead of their arrival they had made arrangements for a catered meal to be delivered for the crews of both ships. The fresh fruits and foods were a real treat for them and it was seldom that they were awarded a brief pause to unwind and enjoy such luxury. Sam, Mitch, and Athena had eaten with the crew and now sat in Sam's quarters, discussing their next assignments.

"I didn't know about Talonis making a move on Laurel. That really pisses me off!" Sam said angrily. "I think we need to pay him a little visit."

"That will be difficult on his home turf. There is more to this story than we know. I wish we could find out who all the players are."

"We can't let him get away with this crap, Mitch. That's twice he has tried to make a move on us," Sam said as she smacked her hand on the desk.

"He's trying to bully his way into the company to obtain the information on the gateways. He wanted that same information the last time that I spoke to him in person. He wants control over some, or most, or all of this new space. I think expansion is an understatement for this guy. Everything in Cerberus is owned by one of the Cerberus Houses, so we can't go against him there. We need to take something from him that he values greatly, but I don't know what that would be," Mitch mused.

"If he wants one of you as a hostage, then why don't we take him as a hostage instead?" Athena asked matter-of-factly.

"That's an interesting idea, Athena!" Mitch said with a smile.

Beaming a wide smile Sam replied, "Damn, why didn't I think of that! That's a great idea!"

"We've got a lot on our plate right now, but this deserves serious consideration and it will take some planning. We'll have to lure him away from Cerberus, somehow," Mitch said.

"We'll come up with something, Mitch. What I want to know is when you get this new hull material, what ship are we going to put it on?" Sam asked.

"I've been thinking about that, Sam and I've decided that our new Scorpion III Class ship the Colossus will be the first. I've checked with the shipyard and with a little planning, I think we can get Ernie and his crew over there about the same time that I have the first shipment available. Since she is too large for a cloaking field to work reliably, this will be a great addition to the Colossus. Not to mention that we won't have to deal with the problems that come with the cloaking devices. I had her well equipped to defend herself, but with this new skin and all the power it stores, we might be able to use that for the weapons systems, leaving more power for mobility and thrust for the FTL drives. The Aegean's are designing a new power storage unit that we can incorporate on the Colossus because the new hull needs vast new energy storage capabilities. There's just one hitch," Mitch said looking over to Athena.

Athena spoke up, "The Phoenix isn't large enough to carry all the materials necessary in one trip. However, your ship is."

"Okay, so I'll take my ship and make the pick-up. No problem, right?" Sam said shrugging her shoulders.

"There's a bug in that stew, Sam. So far I've not been able to get them to allow you to come. They simply don't trust anyone else."

"Then how in the hell are we supposed to deliver that ship to them? It will take your entire crew to get it over there, you know that, and you'll need an escort ship to help get you there."

"They will eventually agree, Samantha," Athena said slowly nodding her head. "Please understand that our people are slow to adopt change. Eventually they will understand and agree, but more than anything they want to insure their privacy and security. We will have to work around this obstacle temporarily, but perhaps it will offer us a chance to have your presence with us on one of our trips there and let them meet you…"

"And have them read my mind line they did his?" Sam said pointing a finger to Mitch. "No thanks."

"Samantha, that's not the way it happened. I don't think that's a fair assessment. Put yourself in their place and try to realize how the bi-mods have been treated here, then imagine how they would be treated if they came here now. Just helping us the way they are is a huge step for them," Mitch said sincerely as he patted her hand.

"I'm sorry, Athena, I shouldn't have said it that way. I meant no disrespect to you or your people. I guess it's easier to criticize than it is to try and understand."

Athena smiled and laid her hand on Sam's shoulder.

"I guess there are a lot of things I don't understand," Sam said as she glanced first to Mitch and then to Athena.

Telepathically, Athena told Mitch that Samantha wanted to know more about their unique connection. Mitch had successfully avoided that topic on several occasions now and eventually he would have to explain, but he wanted to wait until the timing was better. If there would ever be such a time.

"I know what you mean, Sam," Mitch said innocently, "perhaps together we'll figure them out."

Sam gave him a look through squinted eyes and he smirked back. Athena left them alone, closing the door behind her.

Early the following morning they sat together when Donavon entered Sam's office, as requested.

"Donavon reporting for duty, Captain," he said.

"Welcome aboard Mr. Donavon. My husband has provided me with your records and I've reviewed them carefully. He and I are willing to give you a chance to prove yourself, if you can give me your word that the previous issues you had serving on a ship have been addressed and corrected."

"I have completed my training, Captain, and I've learned from my mistakes. I never meant any harm. I thought I was helping. I know how to exercise discretion now. I can assure you that my empathic abilities are well harnessed and I will only utilize them per your orders. I am extremely grateful to you both for giving me a second chance. I give you my word that I won't let you down." Donavon extended his hand and Samantha and Mitch accepted it.

"Mr. Donavon," Mitch said, "Mr. Richter has been a valuable asset to my ship. He has given me his personal word that you will earn the same degree of respect aboard the Rivers Run. Don't let him down, Mr. Donavon or me either."

"Grab some breakfast, Mr. Donavon, and get ready, you've got a busy day ahead," Sam advised.

Fleet Admiral Rich Jonas poured a double bourbon on the rocks and handed it to Laurel as they returned to the comfortable loungers under the portico, overlooking the lagoon on Saber Island. The ocean winds moved the palm fronds in gentle motions as Laurel sighed with relaxation.

"Uncle Rich, did you find out how those men slipped through your security onto Alderon?"

"Not entirely. I found that the recognition software was conveniently down when they came in. The security people over that area claimed that they were unaware of the lapse, but when I looked through the logs, I saw that someone deliberately took the system offline during the time that the liner's passengers were disembarking."

"So someone knew that they were coming?"

"That would seem to be the logical conclusion. My people are still trying to determine who issued the command, but it was definitely someone on planet, not on the station. I thought I had weeded out all of Hendricks people, but perhaps I didn't."

"Uncle, I hate to ask this, but do you think he took orders from someone else?"

"I've asked myself that question too, but I haven't found any solid evidence of it. Not yet anyway. I do have another concern that maybe you can address, Laurel."

"What's that, Uncle?"

"I've noticed a significant reduction in the number of newly explored systems in your latest reports. Can you tell why, the numbers have dropped?"

"We have been very busy Uncle and Mitch delivered some cargo for Bion4 that took over a month to transport. With Captain Chen concentrating on capital improvements and moving people and equipment to Helios, it's left Samantha to do most of the freight runs. She did explore one new system and reported that it held no other gateways or mineral deposits. The only habitable planet had a large number of resident hostile creatures and the crew barely escaped without injury. Mitch and Samantha both are at Atlantis now, taking a couple of days leave. But as far as I know, everything is fine. You know that our freight business has to come first so we get our crystals and fuel to market."

"I understand. I know that the President will ask me that question the next time we meet. I haven't given him my report on Talonis yet. That will probably raise his temperature a bit. I also hear that you have a new ship under construction. Is that true?"

"We do, actually. It's a Whale, freighter. Mitch has modified the design, as usual. Between him and Ernie, I don't think that any of our ships are ever the same as they were originally designed. Mitch said this would be a Scorpion III Class Freighter and he has already named it the Colossus. It's three times the size of Samantha's ship and will carry a minimum of twelve of the latest fighters, the ATS, or Advanced Tactical StarFire. The Chinese Federation consulted with him on the design. He told me that he was very proud of it. The CF government paid him a handsome fee for his work on the design."

"If he and Ernie had a hand in designing the thing then I have no doubts it will be a top line fighter. The ATF must be the new fighters that Peyton Harris was asking me about a couple of weeks ago. Any idea how many of those your new ship could carry?"

Laurel thought for a moment. "If my math is correct, I'd say about one hundred and twenty-six. Her bays are double height and there are forty-two of them, all with retractable launch rails."

"Let me guess, he's got enough weapons in the plans to wipe out a small fleet?"

Laurel chuckled. "You know how Mitch is. What is it he is always telling me? Hope for the best and plan for the worst?"

Her uncle laughed with her and together they toasted Mitch. Laurel avoided the details that included sharing the knowledge of how to traverse the gateways with the Chinese Federation. She suspected that her uncle wouldn't care as long as they upheld the terms of their agreement with the President. Little did either of them know of the collusion that was taking place between the President and Talonis.

"So, what is your plan for this mammoth freighter?" her uncle asked.

"The idea is that we can deliver massive amounts of equipment and supplies all at one time when we locate a suitable planet for colonization and mining. Instead of tying up several ships and losing our contracts, we can make one trip with maybe two ships and get up to speed quickly."

"You've still got manpower needs to fill."

"Not anymore. We took the Dolphin transport out of mothballs and had her refitted. We've also purchased another Dolphin, one that never went into service, from the Atlantis shipyard and the CF is building a third. The only issue that has Mitch concerned is that when we begin putting people and equipment on these wayward systems, we don't have an adequate way to defend our people and property."

"Laurel, you realize that when you begin colonizing these systems, you are becoming independent unless you align yourselves with someone like Alderon or Atlantis, or...well, you get the idea. Obviously it stands to reason that Alderon would like to be part of those plans, but we can afford to expand only so far, so I guess I'm saying that there is, or there will be, a point when you're going to have to defend and govern these new colonies."

"That didn't occur to me, Uncle. I just assumed that Alderon law would follow us anywhere we went."

"When it comes to colonization, it depends on several factors. I've looked into the matter and you're establishing a presence on behalf of a corporation to mine for resources that you intend to make available to anyone, not just the Alderon government. Therefore, according to our charter, you're establishing an independent colony. Unless you specifically request it to be governed by Alderon, you're on your own. Alderon's resources can only be stretched so far, so you, Mitch and Samantha need to have a plan in place for this eventuality. I can promise you that it will come to a head earlier than you think. Or, some other system, like Madeus for instance, will come and lay claim to a planet giving you only the mining rights that you were originally granted, or they will simply kill everyone there and take it over. It probably won't matter to them in the end which way they do it. I think you know what would eventually happen if that were the case."

"Damn, I'm sure Mitch has not thought of that." Laurel chugged the last of her drink and handed it to her uncle for a refill. He smiled and complied.

As he poured her a fresh drink he said, "So, from what you said, you are going to need a planet based defense system. You'll probably need it to be coupled with a satellite based system too, similar to what we use here. You should probably consider an orbital station complex for the larger operations." He sat down and handed her the glass.

"Maybe you should retire, uncle, and handle some of those plans for us."

"Not yet, Laurel, I feel that there is still something afoot here and I want to weed out whatever it is before I even think about retiring."

Laurel chuckled and replied as she lifted her glass to take a drink, "I expected that would be your answer, Uncle, but that's okay. You know where to come when that day arrives." She lifted her glass in another toast and her uncle did the same. They reclined in their seats and watched as the evening sun began to cast the final shadows of the day. It felt good to be home.

"Prefect Rohm, what is your opinion on allowing this other ship of Captain Saber's into our system?" Ambassador Codas inquired.

"I have not decided, Ambassador. I like Captain Saber and your reports on him to indicate that he is exactly who he appears to be, a most honorable man of good morals and values. You queried his guardian, Athena, when she was here last, did you not?"

"Yes, she shared her memories of the past months. He actually exceeded my expectations, Prefect. Nothing has come to harm her and he has been diligently working to acquaint her with her new environment. She has come to care a great deal for this man."

"Are you telling me that she loves him?" he asked with surprise.

"I'm not sure, Prefect. Emotions such as love are something that she had not experienced, so she isn't sure if that word applies."

"Very interesting, Ambassador. This Captain Saber appears by all accounts to be a most unusual man of good character. Nevertheless, that doesn't mean the same for his crew or the crew of this other ship, does it?"

"No, Prefect, it does not. Perhaps we should suggest that he bring his wife to us so that we can evaluate her as well. That may give us additional insight."

"Yes, that is a wise move, Ambassador. Make that suggestion on my behalf. And what about this time travel ship?"

"I scanned his mind while he slept, Prefect. He made no deceptive statements to us about the vessel or his concerns. He sincerely believes that the capabilities of the ship should not fall into the hands of other systems. His fears are very real and I believe that we made the best decision to help him."

"I see, what about our scientists? Are they prepared for this task?"

"They are prepared to follow your directives explicitly, Prefect."

"Excellent. We will increase our knowledge vastly by carefully studying the ship and her records. Perhaps we can help our Captain Saber as he has helped us, but we must use extreme caution. We need to maintain our secrecy as much as possible. I don't want to expose our people unnecessarily to the excesses of other systems. We must keep our culture intact."

"The Captain understands that, Prefect, although he has not verbally acknowledged it, I read those thoughts in his mind. He trusts us and feels a bond between us that he greatly respects. Your idea of assigning Athena to watch over him, and protect him, has already paid off greatly. She is slowly sharing the aspects of our way of life and he feels a responsibility to protect that and her too. He also has a great affection for Ambassador Madera and Athena, which has solidified his bond to us."

"I admire this, Captain, Ambassador. So many women are in love with him and he finds a place in his heart for each of them and still honors his wife above them all. I think he has also earned our respect, wouldn't you agree?"

"I do, Prefect, but we must still use caution. We do not know the intentions of those who serve on his ships and we can't scan them all without drawing their attention and anger. I suggest that we take small steps and aid him as we can. I would like to eventually meet his wife and his sister. They are a great source of his strength, support and focus. He places an immense amount of importance on family. That is something we can learn from him. Perhaps that will aid in solidifying our relationships with our brethren on Bion4."

"Well-spoken, Ambassador. Then we shall proceed with the plan to assist Captain Saber. Have the engineers double their efforts to get this organic material process completed and into production."

The Ambassador had turned to leave the room when the Prefect said, "Oh, Ambassador." She turned and looked back, "Once the process is considered a success, I want that material added to all of our defense fighters as well as our planetary defense towers. In fact, see if it can be utilized on our orbital station too. We'll give the Captain all the materials he wants, but we shall also use this new technology to better defend our people too."

She nodded and proceeded out of his chambers. Ambassador Madera waited for her outside and Codas motioned her to follow. They entered a side room and closed the door behind them.

Madera asked quietly, "What did the prefect say?"

"We are going to help the Captain as we promised," Codas said.

Madera signed in relief. "I was worried that he would think that the Captain has asked too much of us."

"He has asked a lot, Madera, but he has also not given us any reason to doubt his sincerity. The Prefect likes and trusts him. I read the Captain's mind while he slept and there was no deception there."

"I could have told you that, Ambassador Codas. I spent weeks on his ship and read his thoughts and dreams and those of his crew."

"But you haven't done that on his other ship, and that is where the Prefect's concern lies. He suggested that Captain Saber bring his wife to visit us, so we can evaluate her. Your help will probably be needed then."

"I will do what I can if it helps Captain Saber. But why not let me go back with him to Bion4 for a short visit and then let his other ship pick me up to give me a few days aboard to observe her crew? Then she could take me back to his ship for the return trip here. Wouldn't that accomplish what the Prefect wants without exposing Aegea unnecessarily?"

"I have to admit that is an interesting idea, Madera. One which I had not considered. I will present it to the Prefect and see what he says. Obviously we would have to have a reason for your return, as that would be highly unusual. If you recall, we told the Captain that your assignment here was for your lifetime."

"I don't like the idea of deceiving the Captain. He is worthy of our trust. Perhaps if we explain why and how we need to do this, he will understand. I could place the idea in his mind and then he would not suspect us."

"It would still be a deception, my dear Madera. If we are to maintain relations between our people and the Captain we must not break his trust. The wind does not break for the mountain; instead it simply goes over or around it. If the wind were to cease because of the mountain, then we would never have need of the wind because it would not be free. Trust works the same way; if we were to break our trust because of a simple barrier, then we would not need to have any trust. Like the wind, we will not break our trust, but we may find a way around it to continue our journey. We will do what we must to protect our society, but we must also continue to deserve and earn the respect of the Captain...and his people. The Captain will render punishment to his crew if they do wrong, and we must trust him to do this. That will be difficult for our Prefect to accept, but accept it he will as time goes forward. Contact your mother; perhaps she will have an idea to bring you home briefly. Then if the Prefect allows this, we will have a plan with which to proceed."

"As you wish, Ambassador Codas." Madera bowed and left the room. She went to her quarters and considered contacting her mother first, but decided instead to reach out to the Captain's mind and advise him how things were progressing. During that contact she could suggest to him that his wife needed to come to build additional rapport with the Prefect.

Mitch relaxed on his bunk as they made their way back to Aegea with the load of crystals. He brought his knees up to his chest and entered a code into his wrist-comm. "Captain's personal log," he began, "Talonis has now tried on three occasions to either gain control of our gateway explorations or to accumulate information on our activities as they relate to the exploration of the gateways. I've determined that he isn't working alone and after considering my options, I've determined that I must either capture him and leave him somewhere permanently where he can't interfere, or... kill him. I have considered using the time travel vessel to travel backwards and save my family by preventing their deaths, but I can't overcome the fear that doing this will somehow be destructive. Father always taught me to make decisions based on facts, not emotions. Perhaps his advice was even wiser than I thought. I miss and love Samantha so much. I wish that we were aboard the same ship and could share each other every night. Athena has become such an important part of my days here too. Sometimes I spend more time thinking of her than I do Samantha, and that worries me. Many nights I go to sleep thinking of Sam and wake up thinking of Athena. What's wrong with me? Is it possible, or even right, for a man to love two women equally, yet somehow differently? I know that Yurie Nagamo has deep feelings for me too, but she hides them well. I see glimpses of her in my mind and I can sense how she feels. The dream that I had about making love to her remains clearly in my mind. It was so vivid...so real. When she touches me the memory of it comes alive. Then I have this connection to the young Ambassador Madera. She also cares for me deeply, but on a level that I don't quite understand. There is a bond there too that I do not understand. Perhaps I am putting too much thought into it. Male hormones gone stupid or some such. No man should have this many women in his life that care for him, should he? I love them all but I can only have one, and that is the woman I married and love so very deeply. Yet...I care for them all so much. Even Miranda, whose child is mine, still has great emotion for me. Perhaps it is my fault because of my protective nature. I love my ship, her crew, Laurel, my Uncle, the people that work for us...these are all the greatest loves of my life, but where and how do I draw the line? Is my desire to help and protect everyone my weakness or my strength? I will work to make it my strength because it gives my life purpose and meaning. I refuse to be deceived and I will do whatever it takes to protect those I care about. I was not there to prevent the deaths of my parents and I understand now that I can't do it all by myself. But that doesn't mean that Laurel and Sam and I can't build upon what we already have to help discover new places to live and grow. I am surrounded by good people and I owe it to them to be the best at what I do. I won't disappoint them. On another note, I have noticed that my senses and perceptions have sharpened significantly. I suspect it is a result of my new implants. I hope that this is an asset and will not become a hindrance. Personal log, ended."

Samantha was thinking about how much she missed Mitch as she closed the daily report logs. She opened up a file on her personal data crystal, entered the password and began, "Personal journal entry 21-7-3744. Mitch and I parted once more to go our separate ways. God I miss that man so much that it hurts to tell him good-bye. I am so lucky to have him and I know that many others are envious of me, but not in a hostile way. They love him too, but in different ways, I think. I can tell that Athena has a special love for him and I know that Miranda has loved him for years. I know and understand why she had his child. I wish that I could give him a child so much that I have sleepless nights. What kind of woman am I that can't even bear a child for the man I love? I know why others love him too, and I get it, because he is an easy man to love. He's protective, strong, purposeful and loyal as hell to his family, friends and employees. I wonder if he knows how many people really do love him and in so many ways. Laurel is such a blessing to me. She is the sister I never had and Miranda has become the friend I thought I never needed. But there is some kind of odd connection between Mitch and Athena. I've asked about it and been rebuffed each time by Mitch. I don't feel threatened but I do feel something else, which I can't describe. I don't understand why he won't tell me and that hurts a little, like it's a secret he can't trust me to know. Maybe he thinks he is protecting me, or maybe he is embarrassed. I do find that hard to believe. Mitch Saber...embarrassed? Ha! On Atlantis he said she 'told' him but I didn't hear anything. Maybe he has an ear implant, but why would that embarrass him? No, I think it's something else...some kind of mental link between the two, perhaps. How I would love to be able to just reach into his mind every night as I sleep, so I could tell him how much I love and miss him." Tears began to form in her eyes. "How I wish I could bear his children too. What greater show of love can there be than for a husband and wife to create a new life that will carry part of each of them into future generations? And that damned Talonis, who the hell does he think he is to threaten us! How easy it would be for me to get onto his planet and assassinate him. He thinks he is untouchable and that women are weaker and are of no threat to him. I've commanded over five thousand men and Talonis is a waste of flesh. Perhaps that is a better plan than Mitch thinks it is, and I *still* have resources at my disposal that he isn't aware of. Yes...this deserves more consideration Mr. Talonis. This is one woman who will prove to be more than a match for a man like you. Journal entry complete."

I hope you have enjoyed this volume of the Saber Chronicles II, The Golden Warrior. Look for The Saber Chronicles III coming soon.

~Donald Hill, Author

www.ingramcontent.com/pod-product-compliance
Lightning Source LLC
Chambersburg PA
CBHW050014180626
46810CB00002B/410